Praise for

holly hepburn

'The Star and Sixpence sparkles with fun, romance,
mystery and a hunky blacksmith. It's a real delight'
JULIE COHEN

'Like a ray of sunshine on a cloudy day, this sparkling story
will sweep you away and leave your heart full of love'
CATHY BRAMLEY

'Joyous – a treat of a tale that whisks your heart
away to the beautiful shores of Orkney.
Prepare to fall in love with this fantastic series!'
MIRANDA DICKINSON

'A fresh new voice brings wit and warmth to
this charming tale of two sisters'
ROWAN COLEMAN

'Like the dream pub landlady who always
knows exactly what you want, Holly Hepburn
has created the most delightful welcome to
what promises to be a brilliant series'
KATE HARRISON

'Warm, witty and utterly charming . . . It left me
with the most wonderful happy glow'
CALLY TAYLOR

'A super sparkling star of a story'
ALEXANDRA BROWN

Holly Hepburn is the much-loved author of commercial women's fiction. She lives near London with her grey tabby cat, Portia. They both have an unhealthy obsession with Marmite. Follow Holly on Twitter @HollyH_Author.

Also by Holly Hepburn

A Year at the Star and Sixpence
The Picture House by the Sea
A Year at Castle Court
Last Orders at the Star and Sixpence
Coming Home to Brightwater Bay

holly hepburn

The Little Shop of Hidden Treasures

SIMON &
SCHUSTER

London · New York · Sydney · Toronto · New Delhi

First published in Great Britain by Simon & Schuster UK Ltd, 2021

This paperback edition published 2021

1 3 5 7 9 10 8 6 4 2

Simon & Schuster UK Ltd
1st Floor
222 Gray's Inn Road
London WC1X 8HB

Simon & Schuster Australia, Sydney
Simon & Schuster India, New Delhi

www.simonandschuster.co.uk
www.simonandschuster.com.au
www.simonandschuster.co.in

A CIP catalogue record for this book
is available from the British Library

Paperback ISBN: 978-1-4711-7035-5
eBook ISBN: 978-1-4711-7036-2
Audio ISBN: 978-1-3985-1234-4

Typeset in Bembo by M Rules
Printed and bound by CPI Group (UK) Ltd, Croydon, CR0 4YY

*To Meena Kumari, whose kindness,
generosity and brilliance are legendary.*

PART ONE

Starting Over

Chapter One

It was the flamingo that first caught Hope Henderson's eye.

Tall and proud and gloriously pink, it stood in the middle of the shop window demanding her attention. And it wasn't alone, she saw as she slowed down to take a closer look – it had several feathery siblings, of varying heights and pinkness, and a grey and black heron loomed beside them, cleverly made from twisted metal. Above, a sign warned them to *Mind The Gap*. Another pointed cheerily to the circus, although as far as Hope could tell, the arrow was aimed directly at an ancient flowery chamber pot. And above that was a framed vintage poster advertising a balloon race to Paris.

Hope stopped walking, fascinated both by the variety of stock and the lack of any apparent design. The shop occupied a corner slot, with two wide, arched windows on each side of the glossy yellow, angled door. A magnificent grey rocking horse dominated the window next to the flamingos, its shiny black mane glistening in the late-morning sunlight.

One eye seemed to fix upon Hope as she stared and she was sure she could almost hear a whinny. She had always been drawn to the shop as a child, demanding a visit to peer into its windows whenever her family came into York. And as a student in London, she had spent too many Sunday afternoons wandering up and down Portobello Market, fantasizing about what she would buy if she had any money. This wasn't Portobello Road, though, and she was a long way from London; the gothic spires of York Minster peeking through a side street reminded her of that. She was home, after more than a decade away.

The shop's name, picked out in cherry red and adorned with gold leaf above the bright yellow woodwork, tugged at Hope's imagination the same way it always had: *The Ever After Emporium*. How could anyone fail to be enchanted by a name like that, she wondered. Underneath the name, in smaller letters, were the words *Purveyors of Treasure Great and Small*. And beneath that, *Est. 1902. Proprietor: James T. Young Esq.*

Hope spent a few minutes gazing at the windows, marvelling at the mindboggling mix of items and oblivious to the crowds of late-spring tourists jostling along the pavements behind her. Only the chimes of the Minster bells roused her, ringing out quarter to twelve and reminding her it was time to meet her sister for lunch. With a final nostalgic glance into the Emporium, she stepped back and hoisted her bag onto her shoulder, preparing to walk away. And then she saw the advert.

4

Part-time Staff Required.

No Experience Necessary.

Apply Within.

It was handwritten in a vibrant turquoise ink, and the extravagant loops and swirls of the cursive script suggested to Hope that the writer was the kind of person to imbue even the most practical things with a sense of style. For a moment, she was tempted to push open the door and go inside. She had never been allowed to go in when she was younger but there was nothing stopping her now. Besides, hadn't her family been suggesting for a while that she found a new job? It had been a few months since she'd taken redundancy, after all, and she'd been too busy with the sale of her home in London and the move north to think about what might come next. But they meant a proper job – in an office, with people she could get to know over chats about their weekend and the boxsets they'd binged. They didn't mean a part-time role in an antique shop, no matter how much she'd loved it as a child.

Reluctantly, Hope turned away from the Ever After Emporium and made her way through the cool and shaded Minster Gates alleyway towards the cathedral, where Charlotte would be waiting. Maybe she would pop back to the shop after lunch; there must be something inside she could buy to brighten her new apartment. And maybe she'd ask about the job too.

*

'So, how have you been?'

To a casual observer, Charlotte's attention seemed to be fixed on spooning apple puree into her daughter's mouth faster than the toddler could spit it out but Hope wasn't fooled by her sister. She'd seen the way Charlotte's gaze had sharpened as they'd greeted each other outside the Minster and that watchfulness hadn't dissipated as they'd strolled to Lucia in Swinegate Court and settled into their seats in the sun-dappled courtyard. Not even the cute waiter or the buzz of their fellow diners could distract her; she'd placed her order and resumed her barely concealed appraisal of Hope without missing a beat. It was the way Hope's entire family regarded her and she knew that the details of how she looked and behaved today would be shared. Not in a gossipy or unkind way, but with love and concern and born from a desire to help. And Hope loved them all the more for it, even as she wished they'd accept her assurances that she was fine.

'I'm all right,' she replied, pushing some haddock puttanesca onto her fork. 'Starting to settle in. I've unpacked most of the boxes, at least.'

Charlotte glanced across the table, briefly, then focused on her toddler, Amber, once more. 'You're still too thin. Are you eating?'

That was also a regular on the 'Is Hope Okay?' bingo card. She lifted the forkful of haddock into her mouth and chewed. 'Yes, I'm eating,' she said, once she'd swallowed. 'Getting my five a day and plenty of exercise. Staying off the drink and drugs.'

'Glad to hear it,' Charlotte said, and frowned. 'Although there's no shame in taking anti-depressants, if you need them.'

Trust Charlotte to turn a flippant remark into a nudge about her mental health, Hope reflected. But it wasn't a surprise; she'd known how it would be if she moved back to York and subtlety had never been Charlotte's strong point. 'I know,' she said softly and tried to catch her sister's eye. 'I'm fine, Charlotte. Honestly, don't worry.'

Whatever Charlotte had been about to say next was lost as Amber blew a full-lipped raspberry, spraying apple puree across the wooden tabletop. The hubbub of the busy court-yard seemed to quieten a little and there was a brief silence around the table, punctuated by the toddler's delighted gig-gles and a weary sigh from Charlotte. 'It's a good job I chose the pork belly,' she said, looking down at her plate. 'At least apple goes with it.'

Raising her napkin, she started to remove globules of apple from the coppery fuzz that covered Amber's head. Hope took the opportunity to change the subject. 'I can't believe how much she's grown. Last time I saw her she was barely crawling.'

Charlotte gave a wry nod. 'That's babies for you. I wish someone would invent clothes that grow with them.'

Hope grimaced in sympathy. Charlotte often grumbled that their older brother, Harry, had been inconsiderate enough to have two sons, with a third on the way, which meant very few hand-me-down outfits for Amber. 'I'm sure Mum is happy to help – you know she loves shopping for the kids.'

'She does,' Charlotte agreed. 'And I'm very grateful. It's just that Amber seems to grow overnight – what fits her one day is too small the next and I've got so many things she's only worn once. I'm keeping them all for—' She stopped and wiped her daughter's face, not looking at Hope. 'For whoever has the next baby.'

The unspoken words hung in the air. Harry and his wife had declared three boys was enough for any sensible parent and weren't planning any more children once the newest one arrived. Charlotte had been through a difficult pregnancy with Amber, which had culminated in an emergency caesarean, and had repeatedly said she never wanted to go through anything like it again. Logically, the baton to produce the next grandchild should be handed to Hope – it was certainly the way she'd expected things to go when she'd married Rob five years earlier. Then the diagnosis had come and everything had fallen apart. And now she wasn't sure she'd ever get close to kissing another man, let alone doing what needed to be done to make a baby.

'As long as it's not Joe,' Hope said, keeping her tone light.

Joe was their nineteen-year-old brother – a surprise arrival all those years ago – who was currently in his first year of university in Edinburgh and widely considered to be a responsibility-free zone. Charlotte shuddered. 'Can you imagine? He's still a baby himself.'

And that was the lot of many 'happy surprise' kids, Hope supposed; Joe would always be the baby of the family, even if he had children of his own. She pictured him, his russet curls so like her own, albeit much shorter, and smiled. 'He's a good lad. He'd cope.'

'And he'd have all of us to help.'

With a side order of meddling, Hope thought, hiding a grin. She'd counted her family among her blessings a thousand times over the last few years, but there was no denying their well-meaning ministrations could also be a bit overwhelming. 'Luckily, Joe is eminently sensible and knows all about the birds and the bees,' she said mildly. 'I don't think you'll be handing over Amber's baby clothes any time soon, unless there's someone in the village who needs them.'

Charlotte was quiet for a moment as she scraped the last of the puree from the container. 'Speaking of the village, I ran into Simon Wells last week. He asked after you.'

The sentence itself was innocuous enough and it was said in a tone that dripped innocence. But Hope was used to this game too. Simon Wells was an old schoolmate who lived in Upper Poppleton, where she'd grown up. The same village her parents and Charlotte still lived in, where everyone kept a friendly eye on their neighbours and asked after family members who might have moved away. It was perfectly possible that Simon had politely enquired how Hope was doing, especially since she was sure the whole population knew she'd moved back to York. But that wasn't what her sister meant. 'Charlotte—'

'I'm just saying,' her sister said, wide-eyed. 'He's a nice guy – single and not too difficult to look at. You could meet him for a drink, chat about old times.'

'I'm not interested in going on a date with him,' Hope said flatly.

'Okay,' Charlotte said, unperturbed. 'I get that. How about online dating – didn't you download Bumble?'

Hope swallowed a sigh. She had and the app had sat there on her phone, unopened and faintly accusing, until she'd deleted it. 'I'm not ready.'

Charlotte took a mouthful of cannellini beans and chewed with a meditative air, her gaze fixed on Hope. 'But you went on a few dates in London, didn't you?' she said once she'd swallowed. 'I know these dating apps are a bit hit-and-miss but was it so awful that they put you off meeting anyone entirely?'

Hope fought the urge to shake her head and instead watched the late-spring sun play on the amber sandstone walls of the courtyard. She'd been up for dating at first – not exactly enthusiastic but willing to accept that after eighteen months it might be time to start living her life again and knowing she had to start somewhere. And one or two of the dates had gone well, leading to second and third dates. She'd allowed one of them to kiss her, a guy called Matt, and it hadn't felt awful. Just odd, as though it was happening to someone else. On their next date she'd opened up about her relationship history and the ground had suddenly shifted. He'd listened in horrified sympathy, had rallied for the remainder of the date, and then simply stopped replying to her messages. Next had been Adam, who'd puffed out a long breath on their second date and said he wasn't sure he was ready to be the man who followed Rob. She'd begun to gloss over the subject after that, giving vague answers that hinted at a failed marriage, and then cried into her pillow when she got home because it felt wrong to pretend. And, eventually, she decided her heart had been bruised enough. She hadn't dated since.

'I'm just not ready,' she told Charlotte again and then sought something to soften the words. 'I want to get myself settled here first, find my feet and spend some time rediscovering the city. Maybe look for a job.'

Charlotte's face lit up. 'That's a great idea. I saw something the other day that would be perfect for you – good money with a decent company—' she said animatedly, then seemed to notice Hope's expression. 'But I'm sure you know what you're looking for.'

That was half the trouble, Hope thought. She had no idea what she was looking for. Except for an unspoken desire to get away from who she had been before, to try something new. Her mind strayed back to the looping turquoise ink on the advert in the Ever After Emporium's window and she felt something flutter deep inside her, a tiny ripple of something that might have been excitement.

She smiled at Charlotte. 'Haven't a clue,' she said, as a burst of optimism warmed her heart. 'But I'm hoping I'll know when I see it.'

A bell rang as Hope pushed open the door of the antique shop. It didn't tinkle, as shop bells usually did; this sound was deeper, almost too loud, and she wasn't sure if she imagined the hum of vibration as the ringing died away. Glancing up, she saw a large, perfectly polished brass bell coiled inside an ornate framework over the door.

'Sorry about that.' A rich, broad Yorkshire accent cut through the dust motes dancing in the disturbed air and caused Hope to look around to see who was speaking. 'Our bell once adorned the door of Figgis and Blacks in Mayfair. I'm afraid it has delusions of grandeur.'

A man rose from behind an old-fashioned dark oak counter, a cardboard box in his hands. He had an abundance of neatly combed white hair, with a pair of golden wire-rimmed spectacles perched on his nose, and wore a tweed jacket that was certainly vintage, if not quite antique. His appearance was somehow familiar and strange at the same time and Hope knew that if she'd been challenged to come up with someone who looked like they might own an antique shop, she would probably have described the man before her now, gazing at her with an enquiring expression.

'Is there something in particular I can help you with?' he asked, placing the box on the counter. 'Something you're looking for? Or would you prefer to browse?'

Now that it came down to explaining that she was interested in the job, Hope felt a little of her confidence drain away. Was she crazy to be even thinking about working there?

'I suppose I'm looking for Mr Young,' she said slowly, fighting the urge to seize the ready-made excuse and spend a happy twenty minutes wandering around the shop.

'Then you're in luck.' He smiled and held out a hand. 'I'm James Young, owner of the Ever After Emporium. Welcome!'

Too late to back out now, Hope thought as she walked forwards to shake his outstretched hand. 'Hope Henderson. It's about the advert in the window. For the part-time assistant.'

If he was surprised, he didn't show it. 'Of course. Would you like to hear more about the role?'

She nodded and felt her apprehension ease. He hadn't laughed, that was a good start. Although that might follow when she revealed her total lack of relevant experience. 'Yes, please.'

'Why don't we start with a quick tour? I can fill you in on the way round.'

He raised a solid-looking flap in the counter and pulled back a carved door panel beneath to make his way out to stand beside her. She noticed an understated forest green waistcoat beneath the tweed jacket and caught the gleam of gold at waist height. Of course, Hope thought, almost nodding to herself. Of course he has a pocket watch.

'It sounds grand, describing it as a tour, but the Emporium is bigger than it looks from the outside,' Mr Young went on, waving a hand that took in the full length and breadth of the shop, spanning the two sets of windows on either side of the door. 'There's another room through the back where the books are kept, and a small kitchen, plus the storerooms upstairs. Over the years I've experimented with trying to organize the stock into eras but people seem to prefer a more higgledy-piggledy approach.'

Which explained the gloriously mismatched window displays, Hope mused. 'I suppose they don't always know what they're looking for – browsing and discovering a hidden treasure is half the fun.'

Mr Young's eyes gleamed. 'Exactly so. Besides, I'm not totally sure the shop doesn't rearrange itself overnight. It would certainly solve one or two mysteries.'

His voice was so matter of fact that Hope wasn't sure he was joking. But he didn't elaborate. Instead, he pointed to an aisle that ran parallel to the window with the flamingos. 'We'll start this way.'

Hope followed, hardly believing she was inside the Ever After Emporium. The shop was blessedly cool, a welcome relief on a warm April afternoon, and she realized she'd expected it to be gloomy, like something from a Dickensian novel. But it wasn't like that at all; the natural light from the windows was perfectly complemented by discreet modern spotlights in the ceiling, bathing everything on display in a clean silvery light. Her attention was instantly caught by an exquisite bone china tea set laid out on an occasional table to their right. Delicate yellow and pink roses wound their way around the teapot and cups, spilling across the saucers and plates and climbing around the milk jug and sugar bowl. She let out a delighted puff of appreciation as she stopped to stare.

Mr Young glanced over his shoulder. 'Beautiful, isn't it? It's Wedgwood, you can tell from the quality but the three-letter code on each piece removes any doubt. This particular set dates back to 1934.'

She had been about to reach out to lift one of the teacups but withdrew her hand hurriedly. If she dropped it, the interview would be over before it had even begun and she'd have to buy the set, broken cup and all. This must be why she hadn't been allowed inside the shop as a child; she was less likely to break something now but decided it was best not to take any chances and thrust her hands into her pockets.

'Over here, we have a pair of chairs by Charles Rennie Mackintosh,' Mr Young continued. 'Beside them, you'll see a working gramophone but that's not for sale. There are a few items like that – marked with a red dot and just for display. Production companies sometimes get in touch to enquire about hiring things and the gramophone is popular.'

Again, Hope made sure she stayed in the centre of the aisle as she followed him, but her gaze flicked left and right as they walked. A glossy grandfather clock ticked to one side, its walnut case burnished to a mirror-like gleam, and she was tempted to stop and study the sunlit ship sailing sedately through a wedge-shaped panel in the ivory clock face. It reminded Hope of the one Rob's grandmother had kept; she had always insisted it would come to him, when she died, never dreaming for a moment that she'd outlive her grandson. Hope pushed the memory aside and forced herself to focus on the here and now. The shop was everything she'd imagined it would be, a treasure trove of delights, and she longed to linger over some of the things Mr Young led her past. If she didn't get the job, she'd certainly be back to browse. Possibly every day.

'The position is for twenty hours a week, Monday to Friday, with the occasional weekend to cover the other staff,' Mr Young said. 'I'm fairly flexible and happy to work around family commitments, if you have them.'

He waited and Hope thought of her too quiet apartment. 'No commitments,' she said with what she hoped was a brisk smile.

'The work is mostly customer-facing on the shop floor but there'll be a bit of inventory and record-keeping when things are quiet. We offer generous annual leave, on-the-job training and a competitive salary, plus there's a staff discount scheme.' He led her through a crooked wooden doorway into a softly lit square room. 'This is where we keep the books.'

The breath caught in Hope's throat as she stepped inside. It was the kind of room every book lover dreamed of; the walls were lined from ceiling to floor with shelves, and every shelf was filled by spines of all colours and sizes. The walls on her left had glass doors on the top half of the shelves – some of the books inside were wrapped in clear covers and she assumed they were valuable first editions. To her right, she saw a mahogany ladder that rolled parallel to the stacks, giving access to the upper shelves. The air was heavy and still, filled with the unmistakeable scent of old paper, old print, old words. She inhaled deeply, drinking it in, and allowed herself a contented sigh. The Emporium held more treasure than she'd ever imagined.

'Are you a reader?' Mr Young asked, and Hope realized he'd been watching her reaction closely.

'Absolutely,' she replied and her eyes wandered to the shelves again. 'Anything and everything.'

He nodded. 'We've a number of excellent first editions here, including a wonderful *Pride and Prejudice* and a mint copy of Bram Stoker's *Dracula*.' His eyes twinkled. 'As well as some lesser-known classics – are you familiar with *A History of British Carpets* by C.E.C. Tattersall?'

She hesitated, once more unsure whether he was joking. 'Er . . . not really.'

Mr Young laughed. 'Consider yourself lucky. But you never know, one day a historical carpet enthusiast might walk into the shop and we'll have exactly what they're looking for.'

Hope looked more closely at the nearest shelf, imagining herself opening a worn leather cover, turning the age-tinted pages and breathing in their distinctive smell. If she hadn't been in love with the Ever After Emporium before, she was now. Although she was beginning to suspect that if she worked there, she'd have very little of her wages left at the end of the month, in spite of the staff discount Mr Young had mentioned.

'The first floor is home to the store rooms and the office and the second floor is home to me,' he said as they left the book room and continued to the last corner of the shop, where he paused beside an ornate dark wood staircase marked *Staff Only*. 'But I'm sure you must have questions. Is there anything you want to know?'

Hope cast her mind back to her last job application, some seven years earlier. It had been a well-paid, responsible position and had therefore involved a lengthy and stressful process. She was sure there'd be no psychometric testing for this role but it would be useful to know what she could expect. 'Do you know when the interviews might be?' she asked.

He shook his head, causing Hope to immediately assume he hadn't been planning to interview her at all. But he surprised her. 'We're not big on formality here. I find it often works better to have a nice chat. A bit like the one we're having now.'

'Oh,' Hope exclaimed, wrong-footed again. 'I'm sorry, I didn't realize.'

Mr Young waved a hand apologetically. 'My fault – I should have explained. But now that you've had a look round and got a rough idea of what the job entails, are you still interested?'

The Emporium was everything she'd anticipated and more, Hope thought, remembering the delicate floral tea set, the arching chairs and, most of all, the room full of books. And then she recalled how little she knew about any of them. 'Yes, I'm interested, but . . .' She trailed off, filled with certainty that she was wasting both their time. 'Look, I'll be honest – I used to pass this shop when I was growing up and always loved looking in the windows. And seeing the advert today reminded me of that. But I have to admit I don't know anything about antiques.'

Mr Young studied her for a moment. 'I'm not necessarily looking for someone who knows the business. I like to think I'm pretty good in that department.'

Hope puffed out a breath. 'I don't really have any shop experience, either.' She offered him a self-conscious grimace. 'Sorry, I shouldn't have troubled you.'

'It's no trouble,' he replied easily. 'Truth be told, I've never been one for judging people solely by their CV and qualifications and it sounds like the shop has been calling you for a long time – you just didn't know it. So how about a different approach? Why don't you choose an object – anything you like – and tell me about it.'

Confusion swirled in Hope's brain. Hadn't she just explained she knew nothing about antiques? 'But—'

He gave her an encouraging smile. 'I don't mean the manufacturer or provenance or anything like that. Just have a look round, find something that speaks to you, and tell me its story. Whatever you think that might be.'

Immediately, Hope's thoughts flew to the book room, where hundreds of stories were patiently waiting to be told. But she knew it would be cheating to choose one of those; Mr Young wanted something that came from her, from her own imagination. The trouble was, now that she needed it her mind had gone completely blank. Mr Young waited – it felt to Hope as though the whole shop was waiting – and the steady tick-tock of the grandfather clock seemed impossibly loud in the silence, although she worried her thudding heart might give it some competition. Taking a deep breath, Hope forced herself to remember the items that had caught her eye. The Wedgwood tea set had been first – she could imagine that being used to serve afternoon tea in the parlour of a well-to-do 1930s house ... Hope frowned. No, not a wealthy family, perhaps one that didn't have much money but saved what they could and used the tea set on special occasions. And then there was the gramophone – she could almost hear it playing at a wartime tea dance, with that distinctive faint crackle as the needle travelled along the groove. But although she could picture both items being used, neither gave her anything more – a story she could tell. She felt the hot rush of failure burn her cheeks and was about to shake her head when her gaze fell on the clock again. Rob had once told her that, as a child, he'd believed his grandmother's clock hid a secret door leading to another world.

'Like the wardrobe that goes to Narnia,' he'd said with a self-deprecating head shake. 'I must have been reading the books.'

'Did you ever find it?' Hope had asked, and he'd smiled.

'Would you believe me if I said yes?'

That had been the moment she'd known she loved him – really loved him – and his refusal to elaborate, because he'd sworn an oath never to reveal the secret, only delighted her more. And now, listening to the tick of the clock in this quirky, magical shop, she could half-believe that all grandfather clocks hid doors to other worlds. Here was a story she could tell, although she doubted she'd do it justice.

Taking a moment to calm her racing heart, she gathered her thoughts. 'I'd like to tell you about the clock,' she began, clearing her throat. 'It was made centuries ago for a duke and duchess and stood in the hallway of a grand house for many years, although they never really noticed it until it was gone. Even then, it was the absence of the tick they noticed, which was a great shame, because the clock had a secret that might have changed their lives.'

Hope paused and risked a glance at Mr Young but he gave no indication whether this was what he'd been expecting. Instead, he tipped his head to indicate she should continue.

'The clock was given to a boarding school, where it stood for many years, watching children hurry past on their way to and from classes. Until one day, a child didn't hurry past. This child stopped and studied the clock. That evening, at midnight, he crept downstairs when everyone else was asleep and lifted the hook at the side of the door.'

Now when Hope looked at Mr Young, she thought she detected a spark of interest in his expression. 'Inside the clock, the child found another doorway – one that led him to a world of adventure and enchantment.' She hesitated and swallowed the lump that had suddenly appeared in her throat. 'And when he ran out of time in this life, far sooner than anyone expected, he breathed his last breath without sadness or complaint, knowing he'd lived a thousand lives in the world through the clock.'

The words seemed to hang in the air for an age as Mr Young regarded Hope steadily. 'Wonderful,' he said at last, with the gentlest of smiles. 'Just wonderful. When can you start?'

Chapter Two

One month later

It had been raining for three days. Hope watched rivulets of water cascade from the awning over the florist's shop opposite the Ever After Emporium and sighed. The River Ouse was fuller than normal for the time of year and the Foss seemed higher too. If it didn't stop raining soon, Hope thought she might actually need the faded orange and white lifebuoy that was propped against a battered ship's chest opposite the counter. In fact, it was just possible they might need to drag the Noah's ark from the window display.

High Petergate was uncharacteristically empty of its usual horde of May tourists, although Hope knew they were rarely deterred for long. The occasional car splashed through the puddles and any pedestrians who had braved the deluge hurried along with their heads hidden by umbrellas or tucked inside hoods. No one was stopping to gaze into the windows of the Ever After Emporium, let alone come inside. It was the quietest Thursday morning Hope had experienced since she'd started work there three weeks earlier and she was starting to wonder whether she'd see a single customer before lunch. Of course, it meant she had plenty of time to study the book Mr Young had given her on Victorian furniture but although she was keen to learn, it wasn't the most engrossing read she'd ever picked up.

The Minster chimed outside, accompanied by the faint call of the cuckoo clock that hung on a wall deeper inside the shop, and Hope saw the time was 11.15. Stretching her arms over her head, she bookmarked the page and considered making a cup of tea. Mr Young was in the store rooms upstairs, undertaking some restoration work with a local craftsman, but she didn't want to disturb him. Surely it would be fine to leave the till unattended for a few minutes while she nipped into the tiny kitchen tucked away beneath the curving staircase at the rear of the shop . . .

No sooner had she clicked the kettle on than the bell above the door jangled. Swallowing a huff of disbelief, Hope dropped the teabag she held into a cup and hurried back to the shop floor. A man stood in front of the door, his umbrella dripping onto the mat. Beside him was a blonde-haired little girl of around four or five, dressed in a bright yellow raincoat, with matching wellington boots.

'Good morning,' she said, smiling. 'There's an umbrella stand by the door if you'd like to use it.'

The man looked up as she approached but the child's eyes

stayed firmly downcast. 'Thanks,' he replied. 'Although I'm bound to forget it on the way out.'

She watched as he slotted the folded umbrella into the stand. 'Don't worry, I'll remind you. Is there anything in particular you're interested in or would you prefer to browse?'

His gaze flickered to the little girl as he wiped the rain from his fingers. 'Brodie was very taken with the rocking horse in your window. And the flamingos next door.'

Hope's smile deepened. 'Ah, the flamingos are my favourites too,' she said, trying to catch the girl's eye. 'Would you like a closer look?'

But Brodie didn't look up or respond. Instead, one yellow-booted foot turned inwards to rub against the other.

'I think she'd like that very much,' the man said, moving away from the doorway and into the aisle that led deeper into the shop. 'Thank you.'

Hope lifted the counter and slipped through the gap to join them. 'I hope they're going to behave themselves,' she said gravely. 'Last time I took someone to meet them they caused a dreadful hullaballoo.'

This time she did get a reaction but it wasn't the one she'd anticipated. Rather than laugh, Brodie moved closer to her father's leg and hid her face. He threw Hope an apologetic look. 'She takes things a bit literally, I'm afraid.' He dropped down to the child's level and spoke in a soothing voice. 'It's okay, the lady was only joking. The flamingos aren't going to hurt you.'

Hope shook her head in dismay. 'No, they absolutely won't. I was being silly – I'm sorry.'

This met with silence, although a tell-tale wobble of the shoulders suggested it wouldn't last long, and Hope felt a scarlet flush of consternation start to creep across her cheeks. Any minute now the child was going to burst into tears and it would be all her fault.

'I'm really sorry—' she began, as the man straightened up and looked around.

His gaze came to rest on a small North African puzzle box that sat on the counter beside the till. 'Look, Brodie, it's a secret keeper,' he said. 'Like the one Grandma has.'

He glanced at Hope, as if asking permission to pick it up, and she hesitated. The polished cedarwood puzzle box was one of the items that wasn't for sale – Mr Young had given her a list and reminded her that a red dot meant 'Do Not Sell'. But it wouldn't hurt to let Brodie look at it, would it? Especially since the box didn't open. Little fingerprints could be polished away and no one would be any the wiser. 'Go ahead,' she said.

Brodie's focus changed the moment her father held out the box. She let go of his leg and took it, stretching her small hands around the ornate cube and tilting it this way and that. A faint rattle from inside seemed to catch her attention and she raised the box to her ear, shaking it gently. A moment later, she sat cross-legged on the floor and began to probe the carved cedarwood surface with deft fingers.

Disaster apparently averted, the man relaxed and studied Hope with fresh curiosity. 'You're new here, aren't you?'

She nodded. 'Yes, I started a few weeks ago. Look, I'm really sorry for upsetting your daughter. I was just trying to be friendly.'

An odd look crossed his face and Hope cringed inside, wondering if she'd made another faux pas. But then he glanced down at the girl, engrossed in the puzzle box, and he offered Hope a wry smile. 'No harm done. Brodie is – well, I suppose you might say she's sensitive.' He held out his hand. 'I'm Will Silverwood. I own Silverwood's jewellery shop, over in the Shambles.'

Something in the way he spoke suggested there was more to Brodie's reaction than simple sensitivity. For a split second, Hope was tempted to ask what he meant but it wasn't really any of her business. She shook his hand instead. 'Hope Henderson. Pleased to meet you.'

His fingers were still cool from the rain and the skin felt the tiniest bit rough against hers. But it was his smile that really caught her attention – the kind that was so warm it was like coming in from the cold on a frosty day. She liked the way it made his eyes crinkle at the edges, as though she was an old friend he hadn't seen for ages. His eyes were nice too, she decided – hazel, framed with generous lashes – and he had good hair, golden brown with a hint of curl, although it was touching the collar of his coat and looked in need of a trim.

Will cleared his throat, a gentle, barely there sound that

brought Hope back with a jolt. With an icy rush of horror, she realized she'd been staring dreamily at him for an embarrassingly long time. And worse – so much worse – she was still holding his hand. 'Sorry,' she said, letting go as though his fingers had burned her. 'I didn't mean to – I'm so sorry!'

'Don't apologize,' he said, and the crinkles at the corners of his eyes deepened. 'I've been known to daydream mid-conversation too. I like to think it's the sign of a creative mind.'

His generosity made Hope cringe even more, because she hadn't been daydreaming, she'd been – what, exactly? Not perving, she thought with an inward shudder, but definitely ... admiring. And that wasn't something she wanted to admit to a total stranger – to a customer, no less. 'Ha ha,' she said weakly. 'I'll have to remember that for the next time I – er – drift off.'

'It's a useful explanation,' he agreed. 'So what brings you to the Emporium? Have you always worked in antiques?'

Praying she didn't look as flustered as she felt, Hope wondered how to reply; admitting she'd applied for the job on a whim would make her seem even flakier than she already appeared and it was hardly a professional response. 'I've always had an interest in old things,' she answered, choosing her words with care. 'And who could resist the opportunity to spend every day somewhere like this?'

'Not me,' Will said. 'Or Brodie, for that matter.'

They both glanced down at the girl, who was still absorbed in her task. 'I'm afraid the box isn't for sale,' Hope said. 'It's a bit of an enigma – no one's been able to work out how to open it.'

He nodded. 'My mother has one. I remember spending hours trying to get into it and was ready to take a hammer to it until my brother revealed the secret.'

'Which was?'

'A few impossible-to-detect sliding panels and cleverly hidden compartments,' he replied. 'But each box is individually crafted – what opens one won't work on another. They wouldn't be much good for keeping secrets if they all worked in the same way.'

Hope smiled and felt the last vestiges of embarrassment fade away. 'Well, this one seems set to keep its secrets forever. I don't think Mr Young would appreciate us taking a hammer to it.'

Will laughed and Hope decided she liked that too. They stood for a moment, smiling at each other, until the bell over the door jangled again and a tall woman with a hood over her eyes hurried inside. 'Hells bells, Hope, is it ever going to stop raining?'

She paused in the doorway, shaking down her hood to reveal a mane of lustrous dark hair as she took in the scene. 'Oops, I didn't realize you had a customer.' And then her expression lit up. 'Oh, but it's only Will. I don't have to mind my manners after all.'

Hope had to swallow a grin; she'd met Iris on her second day at the Ever After Emporium, when the florist had hurried across the road and begged to borrow an Art Deco vase for the Blooming Dales window display. From that first whirl-wind encounter, Hope had formed the distinct impression that Iris wasn't really one for observing the social rules that governed most people's behaviour. She was forthright and bold, wore scarlet lipstick and winged eyeliner as though she woke up that way every day, and had the kind of irrepressible smile that hinted she might bubble up into laughter at any moment. Hope had warmed to her immediately and thought she might be on her way to making her first new friend in York. It wasn't surprising that Iris would know Will – Hope got the impression that there was a real sense of community within the ancient walls that surrounded the city's heart. There was probably a traders' association, where the glamor-ous florist must turn heads and steal hearts in equal measure.

'Not just me,' Will said, shifting slightly so Iris could see the child at his feet.

'Oh,' she breathed, walking towards them. 'This must be Brodie.'

'It is,' he replied. 'So, minding of manners is definitely still required.'

Not that Brodie was paying any of them the least bit of attention. She was still poking and prodding at the box, turning it over and over in her small hands, and Hope could almost feel the girl's determination to solve the riddle. But the secret had eluded all the adults of the Ever After Emporium – was it possible that a child would succeed where they had failed? Hope pictured her nephews and their bois-terous, exuberant approach to play; the box would have been discarded in favour of a football within seconds. But Brodie was entirely different – all her concentration was focused on the job and she seemed to be enclosed in her own little world. It was remarkable.

'How is she coping?' Iris asked, lowering her voice. 'More to the point, how are *you* coping?'

Will smiled but this time it didn't reach his eyes. 'Oh, you know. Taking it one day at a time.'

Wary of being caught staring again, Hope let her own gaze drift around the shop as she wondered about the exchange. There'd been sympathy in Iris's tone and sadness in Will's. Hope recognized the vagueness of his reply too, using the sort of words she had when she'd needed to politely fend off well-meaning enquiries after Rob's death. A failed marriage, perhaps, and all the heartache and adjustments that brought. It would certainly explain the way Iris was watching Will, as though he might break at any moment. Hope was familiar with that look as well, although thankfully not from Iris or anyone else in York, apart from her family. She'd told Iris she was single, when the florist had asked what her partner did, and then deflected the conversation onto safer ground. Another coping mechanism.

'How's business?' Will asked, glancing at Blooming Dales through the rain-speckled window. 'I suppose the flowers don't mind the wet weather.'

'They might not but I do,' Iris said, wrinkling her nose. 'Walk-in trade is down this week – it's a good thing we've got plenty of wedding orders to keep us busy.'

His eyes drifted to Brodie once more. 'Your windows always look so amazing. Maybe we'll pop in and pick up a bouquet for home, to remind us it's almost summer.'

Iris dipped her head. 'I could deliver it, if you like, save you having to carry it in this rain. Do you have a favourite flower, Brodie?'

That got the little girl's attention. She raised her blonde head to study Iris, then flicked her gaze towards the window.

Hope thought she understood. 'Pink, like the flamingos?'

Brodie gave a shy nod.

'Flamingo pink,' Iris repeated approvingly. 'Very nice. I'm thinking gerbera, roses and maybe some alstroemeria. Tall and graceful, just like the birds.'

Will gave her a helpless look. 'They won't look graceful if I have to arrange them. Do they come in a vase?'

Iris winked at Brodie. 'I'll take care of everything. All you'll have to do is put the bouquet into water.'

'I can probably manage that,' Will said. 'With Brodie's help, obviously.'

'Then how does a Saturday morning delivery sound?' Iris asked. 'You can drop me a message later with the address for delivery.'

'Sounds like the perfect way to start the weekend,' Will said. 'Thanks, Iris. This is very kind of you.'

The florist waved away his thanks. 'It's no trouble. I deliver all over the city – have bike, will travel.'

Hope blinked as she tried to build a mental picture. 'You deliver flowers by bike? How?'

'Of course,' Iris said, grinning. 'We're very eco-conscious. I attach a lightweight trailer to the back, load it up and off I go.'

'In all weathers?' Hope said, with a dubious glance at the rainy street outside.

'Us Yorkshire women are made of stern stuff,' Iris replied. 'But we're practical too – I also have a cosy little Volkswagen van for when the weather is really grim.'

Hope was about to say that she was a Yorkshire woman too, although her years in London had worn her accent away, but Brodie stood up abruptly and handed the puzzle box to Will. He checked his watch. 'You're right – we should probably think about lunch.' He gave the box to Hope. 'Thanks for letting her handle it.'

'It's a shame she didn't crack the mystery,' Hope said. 'Mr Young would have been delighted.'

His eyes creased at the edges as he smiled. 'I'm sure we'll be back.'

'Maybe next time, then,' Hope said. 'I'll have a word with the flamingos too.'

It was only after Will and Brodie had made their way back out into the rain, with the umbrella safely in hand, that Hope realized what had been troubling her. In the whole time they'd been in the shop, she'd hadn't heard the little girl make a single sound.

Iris puffed out her cheeks when Hope mentioned Brodie's silence. 'No, she doesn't speak. Not since the accident.'

Cold dread settled in Hope's chest. Maybe Will wasn't

newly separated. Maybe it was more awful than that. 'The accident,' she repeated slowly.

'The car crash,' Iris said. 'Back in February, on the A64. You might remember – the road was closed for the best part of a day.'

Hope swallowed, her mouth suddenly dry. 'I wasn't living here then.'

The florist sighed. 'It was terrible, one of those freak accidents that doesn't seem to be anyone's fault. You only needed to glimpse the car to know no one could have survived.'

One hand flew to Hope's mouth as Iris confirmed her worst fears. 'Oh no.'

'Brodie was devastated, as you'd expect. Will's doing his best but it takes time, doesn't it? I know kids are resilient but that's an impossible hole to fill.'

Especially when he'd be struggling with the loss of a partner himself, Hope thought as sympathy and pity welled up inside her. It was a miracle he was coping as well as he was; she certainly hadn't after Rob's death.

'Poor Brodie,' Iris went on, with a sorrowful shake of her head.

'Poor Will too,' Hope said. 'He must be grieving as well.'

A frown creased Iris's forehead. 'Of course. Losing a brother is awful. But Brodie lost both her parents – I'm not surprised she's retreated into herself."

The words crashed over Hope like a wave. Had Iris said Brodie had lost *both* parents? 'But I thought . . . isn't he—'

Iris stared at her for a moment, then slapped her own forehead. 'Oh, I'm an idiot! Of course you assumed Will was Brodie's dad – why wouldn't you?'

Bewildered, Hope pieced together the evidence. 'So he's her . . . uncle?'

'And her closest living relative,' Iris replied. 'Or at least, the only one capable of looking after a four-year-old. His mother has dementia, I think, and lives in a care home. And Will is Brodie's godfather – there was no question of her going anywhere else.'

Anywhere else being foster care, Hope guessed, or a distant relative or family friend who were virtual strangers. Another wave of pity swept over her. 'That poor girl.'

'Yeah,' Iris agreed. 'Obviously, it's been tough for Will too. It's not as though he's got anyone to help him. Imagine going from being a single bloke to a surrogate parent overnight.'

While dealing with his own loss too, Hope thought. Although she could imagine having someone else to care for might help with the grief; plenty of people had suggested she get a puppy or a kitten in the months after she'd lost Rob but it hadn't seemed fair when she'd be out at work every day. A child was another ballgame entirely. The sense of responsibility must be overwhelming.

'He took a shine to you, though,' Iris went on, a smile playing at the corners of her scarlet lips. 'And you're single too. New in town.'

Hope's face bloomed with sudden heat. 'What? That's not

34

true. I mean, yes I am single and new here but he definitely wasn't . . . he didn't—'

She broke off as Iris threw her a disbelieving look. 'Hope. You could have cut the tension between you with that silver letter-opener over there.'

'But –' Hope flailed in mortified bewilderment, thinking back to the moment Iris had burst into the shop. 'But there was no tension – we were chatting about the puzzle box.'

'It looked like more than that to me. You were both smiling for a start.' Iris waggled her eyebrows. '*Really* smiling.'

She couldn't deny that, Hope thought, resisting an urge to fan her overheated cheeks. 'Maybe we were,' she said. 'But it was on a strictly professional basis.'

The other woman nodded. 'I'm sure it was. But even so, I know chemistry when I see it.' She paused to smirk at Hope. 'Sexual chemistry.'

Hope wanted to crawl under the nearby Edwardian occasional table. Iris was sharp – of course she'd noticed her admiring Will. She might as well have been projecting an enormous cartoon love heart over her head. 'I'm sure he has enough on his plate at the moment,' she said, hating the stiffness in her voice. 'And I'm not looking for a relationship either.'

Instantly, Iris looked contrite. 'Ah, I'm getting carried away – making assumptions. It's a weakness of mine – sorry.'

Hope took a deep breath and willed her flaming skin to cool down. 'It's okay. No harm done.'

'Good,' Iris said and paused, looking at Hope with a

speculative gaze. 'If you're not looking for a relationship, are you at least in the market for making new friends?'

'Yes,' Hope said cautiously.

The florist beamed at her. 'Great! How do you feel about dancing?'

Chapter Three

Hope tugged self-consciously at the borrowed belt around her waist. The attached coins jingled musically, which only made her feel more awkward, even though the sound was barely audible among the chatter from her fellow dancers. When Iris had suggested Hope came along to her dance class on Monday evening, she'd been vague about the details and Hope had assumed it would be something like Zumba. She wasn't sure she'd have agreed if she had known it was a belly dance class.

'I don't think I can do this,' she told Iris, glancing nervously around at the other dancers. 'I'm not very . . . bendy.'

Iris gave her a sunny smile. 'You don't have to be. The beauty of belly dancing is that it's gentle and progressive, so you can be led by your own body. And Fleur is a wonderful teacher – you're going to be fine.'

Their teacher certainly looked wonderful, Hope thought with an envious glance towards the front of the studio.

Dressed in a neon-yellow yoga top and sky-blue leggings, Fleur was every inch a dancer. Her exposed belly was an expanse of smooth golden skin and her long dark hair almost brushed the band of the sequined belt that sat on her hips. Hope sighed and undid the knot that held her own belt in place, moving it down so that it settled in the same place as that of the teacher. The word *lithe* might have been invented to describe Fleur. And Hope was sure it wasn't a word anyone would use to describe *her*.

'I'm too tall to be any good,' she warned Iris. 'I tried dance lessons before my wedding and the teacher said she'd never seen anyone so ungraceful.'

Iris gasped and let out a short huff of indignation. 'I hope you told her where to shove it.'

She hadn't, Hope remembered, but Rob had, with the icy politeness that always came out when he was furious. He'd wanted to try again, with a better teacher, but Hope's confidence had been too badly bruised. Consequently, their first dance had been a self-conscious swaying shuffle around the floor, until their guests had given in to her cajoling and joined them. It hadn't really mattered at the time; all Hope had cared about was the look in Rob's eyes and his arms around her. But in the long days after his diagnosis, when he'd lost the ability to walk . . . then she couldn't help wishing they'd whirled like Fred and Ginger while they still could.

She knew what Rob would say to her now, just as she knew he'd be right. Straightening her shoulders, she summoned up a smile for Iris. 'I'm being silly. Sorry.'

'Not silly,' Iris replied, squeezing her arm. 'But look around – no one here has a perfect body, apart from Fleur and dancing is her job. Belly dancing isn't about that, anyway – it's more inclusive.'

Now that Hope looked more closely, she could see what Iris meant. There were around a dozen other women in the studio and they were a mix of ages and sizes. Some wore leggings and t-shirts, some had skirts with splits that travelled the length of their thigh and skimpy tops, but no matter how much skin they had on show, every single woman seemed comfortable and relaxed. It was a total contrast with Hope's own body language, reflected in the floor to ceiling mirror opposite: dipped head, folded arms, tension radiating as though she was waiting for a hammer blow rather than a dance class. Taking a deep breath, she unfolded her arms and shook them out, shifting her weight from one foot to the other as she did so. 'Okay. I'll give it a go.'

'Excellent,' Iris said, smiling. 'I think a bit of shimmying is going to do you the world of good.'

There was no time for Hope to ask what she meant – Fleur was looking around expectantly and the buzz of conversation dimmed. 'Welcome!' she called with a dazzling smile. 'If you'd like to find yourselves some space, we'll start with some gentle stretches.'

Hope automatically gravitated to the back of the studio, allowing the rest of the dancers to fill the space in front of the mirrors; the last thing she wanted to see was her own flustered face as she failed to follow Fleur. Iris took her place beside Hope without comment.

'Listen to your body,' Fleur said as the first few slow chords of a delicate Arabian melody drifted across the room. 'Only stretch as far as you need to and if this is your first class, be kind to yourself.'

Iris waggled her perfectly groomed eyebrows at Hope. 'See? Be kind.'

'I'll try,' Hope replied.

The stretching was as gentle as Fleur had promised. By the end of the song, Hope's heart had stopped thudding and she felt a little encouraged that she hadn't fallen over while copying the teacher's movements, not even when she'd balanced on one leg and raised the other to make circles with her foot. There'd been some furious wobbling but Hope hadn't actually hit the floor, which was a definite win.

'So far, so good,' she whispered to Iris, who smiled.

'Keep going. You're doing great.'

That was the last time Hope had time to talk, as Fleur led the class through a whirlwind of hip lifts, shimmies, snake arms and belly pops. Each movement was clearly explained and demonstrated but Hope was acutely aware that she was at least half a beat behind everyone else, in spite of her fierce concentration. Fleur seemed to notice that Hope was struggling, however; the teacher made frequent eye contact in the mirror as she broke down the techniques, with encouraging nods and smiles. And every once in a while, something seemed to click within Hope and her body moved in a way that was similar to everyone else. She found the shimmy particularly fun, even though it made parts of her wobble in a most alarming way, but she was still relieved when Fleur announced it was time to warm down. Hope winced as she eased into the stretches and she realized her muscles were going to be complaining more over the days to come.

'I thought you said it was low-impact,' she said to Iris, as the class disbanded. 'I'm sweating!'

'That just means you worked hard,' Iris replied. 'Did you enjoy it?'

The word 'no' started to form on Hope's lips but she caught herself. She'd missed some of the moves, had been shaky on the turns and her goddess pose had been more *oh god* than anything else but, in spite of all that, a strange sense of wellbeing was bubbling up inside her. And she had focused so hard on keeping up that all the frustrations of the day had flown out of her head, leaving her mind clear and her spirits cheered. She smiled at Iris. 'Yes, I did.'

'Good,' the florist said, with obvious satisfaction. 'Now come and meet Fleur.'

She introduced Hope to the dance teacher and they chatted for several minutes, as the other dancers called out their goodbyes. Hope wasn't surprised to discover Fleur was every bit as kind and encouraging as she'd appeared during the class.

'But it was your first time,' she said, when Hope apologized for not keeping up. 'You did very well, especially considering it was a mixed ability session.'

'Oh, I don't know about that,' Hope said, embarrassed. 'But at least I didn't hit anyone with my flailing arms.'

'Not even close,' Iris responded. 'And next time it will be easier. Right, Fleur?'

The other woman nodded. 'Absolutely. Today you planted seeds that will grow each time you dance.'

'Which basically means you have to come back,' Iris said, with an exaggerated wink. 'Or the flowers will die.'

Hope laughed. 'Well, since you put it like that . . .'

'We're here every week,' Fleur said warmly. 'It would be lovely to dance with you again.'

It wasn't as though she had anything else to do with her Monday evenings, Hope thought. And it would be nice to master some of the moves she'd tried, or at least learn how to do them in time with the music. 'Okay,' she said. 'Thank you.'

It had been a hot day and the summer heat was lingering in the narrow courtyard outside the studio. Hope felt the contrast to the cool of the air-conditioned studio immediately; sweat bloomed on her forehead and she stopped to remove the cardigan she'd pulled on at the end of the dance class. Just ahead, Iris was checking her phone. She let out a loud groan that bounced off the buildings and echoed around the yard.

'Everything all right?' Hope asked in concern.

Iris stared at her screen for a few more seconds, then stuffed the phone into her pocket with a sigh. 'What would you do if you'd been on a first date with a guy and he was keen for a second but you knew it wasn't going anywhere?'

The ghost of a smile pulled at Hope's lips. She hadn't found herself in that situation during her brief foray into dating but she'd certainly watched her messages go unread and it hadn't been a pleasant experience. 'I'd tell him,' she said, starting to walk towards the alley that led onto Newgate. 'No point in wasting everyone's time if you're not into him.'

'That makes sense,' Iris said as they made their way along Newgate. 'It's like ripping off a plaster, isn't it? Best done fast and decisively.'

'Something like that,' Hope agreed. 'It's kinder than leaving him hanging for days and then disappearing altogether.'

Iris gave her a sidelong look. 'That sounds like the voice of experience. Did you have a tough time getting back into dating after the divorce?'

Hope hesitated. She should have expected this, especially after mentioning her wedding earlier in the evening. But she wasn't sure she'd ever get used to the flutter of panic that hit her every time she had to explain about Rob's death; people looked at her differently once they knew. For a moment, she considered going along with Iris's assumption that she was simply divorced, but she liked the florist and didn't want to lie.

She kept her gaze fixed on the cobbles and strove to keep her voice light. 'I'm a widow, actually. Almost two years ago now.'

Iris stopped walking, her face a mask of consternation. 'Oh my god. I'm so sorry – I'm an idiot.'

Hope shook her head. 'Don't apologize, you couldn't have known.'

'But I could have been a bit more sensitive.' Iris bit her lip. 'Is that why you moved to York? To get away from the memories?'

'Partly,' Hope admitted as they picked their way through the sporadic clusters of window shoppers and diners. 'I've got family nearby so it seemed like as good a place as any to start over.'

There was a silence, which was something else Hope was familiar with after she'd used the W word, then Iris cleared her throat. 'Have you dated anyone since . . . since you lost your husband?' She cast a mortified look at Hope. 'Sorry if that's too personal. It's just that you're so young to be a widow.'

Tell me about it, Hope thought but didn't say. 'I went on a few dates,' she answered. 'But they backed off when we got to relationship history.'

'Idiots,' Iris said, scowling. 'And I bet they didn't even have the courtesy to be honest with you. I bet they just stopped messaging.'

'Pretty much,' Hope said. 'Which is why you should tell your super keen guy that there's no chance of a second date. It'll sting but it's much better than being left hanging.'

'You're right,' she said, opening her phone and tapping at the screen with a purposeful air. 'One plaster, coming right off.'

Dusk was falling and the streetlights were beginning to glow as they walked. The narrow, twisting streets that made up the heart of York – the ginnels and snickelways, as they'd been known for centuries – were one of Hope's favourite things about the city, although not when they were thronged with tourists. But now, when the shops were closed and fewer people were out, that was the best time to wander round and gaze into the backlit shop windows. She was enjoying getting to know the hidden alleys and secret snickelways again. It was like meeting up with an old friend.

'There's Will's shop,' Iris said, pointing past the Shambles main street to a black and white timbered shop with ornate bars across the window. 'He's a really talented jeweller – an artist, to be honest. You should go in and take a look sometime.'

Hope never needed an excuse to visit the Shambles; the ancient street that ran alongside the marketplace was made up of crooked, higgledy-piggledy buildings that grew nearer to each other with every storey. It had such an otherworldly air that just to walk along it felt almost like stepping back in time. But Iris's observation reminded Hope of the incredible floral displays on show in the window of Blooming Dales. 'Speaking of artistry, did Brodie like her flamingo flowers?'

'I think so,' Iris replied. 'She especially liked the feathers I wove in among the roses. And it was my last delivery of the day on Saturday, so she got a little ride in the empty bike trailer.'

'I bet she enjoyed that,' Hope said, picturing the solemn-faced little girl laughing as Iris pulled her along.

Iris tipped her head. 'She did. I told Will he should get her a bike of her own and teach her how to ride it. He didn't look entirely thrilled.'

Hope grinned. 'Ha. My brother has two boys and he claims his back has never recovered from teaching them to ride.'

They reached Fossgate, where their paths diverged. Iris was going back towards her flat above Blooming Dales, and Hope was heading for her own apartment, one of many in a converted mill beside the looping River Foss.

'Thanks for inviting me this evening,' Hope said as they prepared to go in opposite directions. 'I really enjoyed it.'

'Thanks for coming, I'm glad you had fun,' Iris said. 'And you're working tomorrow, right?'

Hope nodded. 'I'm on the shop floor in the morning and helping to do a stock check in the book room in the afternoon.'

'I'll wave at you from across the street, then,' Iris answered. 'See you tomorrow.'

'Yes, see you tomorrow,' Hope echoed with a smile and gave a little wave.

The glow from the ornate streetlight sparkled on the water as she crossed the gentle curve of the tiny Foss bridge and made her way to the wharf. Being near the river had been top of her list when she'd been looking for somewhere new to live; the flat she'd owned with Rob in Greenwich had over-looked the Thames and she had wanted to be near the water in York too. And Rob had made sure that money at least wasn't something she had to worry about – their mortgage had been settled upon his death and she'd discovered another insurance policy he'd never even mentioned that gave her a cushion against the aching loss that permeated every other aspect of her life. But although she'd fallen in love with the top floor flat in York almost the moment she'd seen it, she didn't feel settled there yet. It felt strangely empty, as though something vital was missing despite having all her furniture and possessions filling the space, and she often felt a dip in spirits when she came back after a day at work or time spent with her family.

Something was different tonight, however. She was glad to hang her coat on the hook in the hall, grateful to kick off her trainers and pad out onto the still-warm balcony that over-looked the river, with a glass of cold white wine in her hand.

She sat for a few moments, stretching her tight calf muscles and gazing across the rooftops to the peeping spires of the Minster, twinkling against the darkening sky in the distance. Perhaps this little shoot of contentment was a sign that York was beginning to feel like home, she thought as she sipped her wine. Perhaps she could carve out a fresh start, one where she actually lived instead of simply getting through each day. And perhaps Iris might turn out to be part of what Hope was missing – a friend to make new memories with.

On impulse, she raised her glass towards the Minster. 'Here's to starting over,' she said softly, picturing the Ever After Emporium and Blooming Dales nestling in its shadow. Then she remembered something both Fleur and Iris had said. 'And here's to being kind.'

Chapter Four

The Emporium already had its first visitors when Hope arrived the next morning. Mr Young was leaning against the counter, chatting to Will, and Hope wasn't at all surprised to see the puzzle box in Brodie's hands as she perched on a rose velvet armchair nearby.

Mr Young glanced across the shop with twinkling eyes. 'Ah, and here's Hope. Good morning.'

'Hello,' she replied. 'How are you today?'

'We're grand,' Mr Young said. 'Will was just telling me about the puzzle box his mother owns. They were popular in the Victorian era and around the turn of the century, so the older ones do pop up as family heirlooms.'

Will smiled. 'I'm not sure I'd call ours an heirloom. My brother and I weren't exactly delicate in our efforts to open it.'

Hope eyed the little girl, who was methodically testing every inch of the cedarwood box. 'Luckily for us, Brodie is more careful.'

'She is,' Mr Young said approvingly. 'I'm afraid I don't know much about the provenance of the box, other than to say it's probably from Morocco rather than Japan or Switzerland. It came in from a house clearance some years ago and we've all spent hours trying to work out its secret.'

'I think Brodie has similar plans,' Will admitted dryly. 'She practically dragged me in here today.'

'She's very welcome to spend as long as she likes – I'd love someone to work out its secret,' Mr Young said. 'But you'll have to excuse me now, I'm afraid. The dreaded paperwork beckons.'

He nodded at Will and Hope, then bent to catch Brodie's eye. 'Do you know, I've got a feeling you're going to solve the mystery. Keep going!'

The little girl's hands stopped moving for a moment as she glanced briefly up at him and Hope thought her mouth curved into the faintest of smiles before she bowed her head again.

'Thank you for letting her try,' Will said.

Mr Young shrugged as he straightened up. 'No need to thank me. Puzzles are made to be solved, after all.'

With a final amiable nod, he made his way along the aisle and out of sight, leaving Hope and Will standing together in a slightly awkward silence. She was just wondering whether to offer him a cup of tea when Will spoke. 'Iris told me you're new to the city as well as the Emporium. How are you settling in?'

'I'm not exactly new,' Hope replied, uneasily wondering

how her name had come up in conversation between Will and Iris. 'I grew up on the outskirts of York so I know it pretty well. But a lot has changed – I'm still getting reacquainted with some things.'

He tipped his head. 'It's a lot busier, I expect. Especially in the high season.'

'I don't remember quite as many visitors,' Hope conceded, thinking of the packed public gardens that lined the River Ouse and the crowds spilling out around the Minster. 'But I'm used to London, which is always full of tourists. High Petergate hasn't reached the terrifying heights of Oxford Circus in the sales yet.'

A pained look crossed Will's face. 'Let's hope it never does. I know tourism is a huge part of the local economy but it brings plenty of challenges too.' He paused and seemed to mentally change tack. 'Look, I know you're not a stranger to York but if you ever need someone to show you round, I'd be happy to help. There are a few new places you might enjoy that the tourists haven't discovered yet.'

The offer caused a pleasing fizzle of excitement in Hope's stomach even as her brain reared up in panic. Was he asking her out? Or just being friendly? Had Iris put him up to this? What had been said? And how should she respond? 'Thank you,' she managed, after a momentary tussle with her suddenly jumbled thoughts. 'I don't know many people here now so that's a very kind offer.'

Will opened his mouth to reply but whatever he'd been about to say was interrupted by the merest of clicks and a sharp intake of breath from Brodie. Hope looked down to see her holding the puzzle box out in front of her. Its lid was open.

'You did it!' Hope gasped. 'That's amazing!'

Will crouched down beside her, tilting the wood so he could see inside. 'There's something in here.'

Carefully, he tipped the box sideways until a small package wrapped in yellowed tissue paper tumbled into his palm. He glanced up at Hope. 'Over to you, I think.'

He placed the package in her hand. It was heavier than she expected and the temptation to peel back the aged paper was strong. Reluctantly, Hope forced the urge down. 'Over to Mr Young, I think,' she corrected. 'I'll call him down from the office.'

Moments later, the antique shop owner was standing beside them. He beamed at Brodie. 'Didn't I say you'd crack the mystery? Let's see what treasure the box was hiding.'

Hope held her breath as he gently pulled the paper apart. Something sparkled in the light and she craned her neck to see what it was. Mr Young became very still. 'A treasure indeed,' he said, his voice soft. 'Look.'

He held up a silver and gold ring with the biggest emerald Hope had ever seen. The gold had dulled with age but the oval jewel shone brightly under the shop lights, amplified by a cluster of diamonds set in delicate silvery filigree on each side. Will let out a low, appreciative whistle. 'That's a beauty.'

'It certainly is,' Mr Young said. 'I wonder how long it's been in the box.'

'May I?' Will asked.

'Of course,' Mr Young said, placing the ring in his hands. 'You're the expert where jewellery is concerned.'

Will held the ring up to the light and Hope felt the breath catch in her throat at its beauty. Now that she looked closely, she saw that the diamond clusters were wider at the top, thinning and curving into the side of the emerald as they neared the base, like folded wings. Two tiny silver triangles peeped over the top, adding height to the jewel. The effect was breath-taking; she'd never seen anything quite like it.

Will ran a finger across the domed emerald and smiled. 'It's a scarab beetle,' he said, tilting the ring so that it was angled in the light. 'Look, you can see the shape of the carapace has been carved into the surface of the jewel. The diamonds on either side have been set in platinum to form the legs, neatly tucked into the body.'

Legs, not wings, Hope noted as the gemstones sparkled. And platinum, not silver. Just how valuable a treasure had Brodie discovered?

Will was now squinting at the inside of the golden band of the ring. 'Unfortunately, there's no hallmark but the Art Deco style and scarab detail suggest that it was made sometime in the 1920s. Ancient Egypt was a huge influence back then, particularly on jewellery.'

'Almost a hundred years old,' Hope murmured and then remembered she was surrounded by a myriad of objects that were considerably older. But none of them were as breath-taking as this.

Mr Young seemed to understand. 'Everything in the Ever After Emporium has a story but every now and then, we discover something special. I strongly suspect this is one of those times.'

Still holding the now empty puzzle box, Brodie tugged at Will's trousers. 'Not now, sweetheart,' he said absently, studying the ring. 'It feels like 18 carat gold, and the emerald is probably 10 carats alone.' He looked at Mr Young. 'I could clean the whole thing up, verify the quality if you'd like?'

'That would be wonderful,' Mr Young said. 'If you're sure it's not too much trouble.'

'It would be an absolute pleasure, believe me,' Will said, as Brodie began to pull on his arm. He frowned. 'Wait a minute, please, Brodie. I'm talking.'

Hope caught the look of frustration on the girl's face; it was the kind of expression she'd seen before on the faces of her nephews and it usually meant an explosion was imminent. While Will and Mr Young continued to discuss the find, Hope bent to Brodie's level. 'Is everything okay?'

Brodie glanced upwards, clearly wanting Will's attention, but since that didn't seem to be forthcoming, she fixed her blue eyes on Hope and pointed inside the puzzle box. Obediently, Hope peeked inside. And there, folded into a tiny square and flattened against the bottom of the secret compartment, was a flimsy piece of paper.

She straightened up without touching it. 'There's something else in the box.'

Both Will and Mr Young stopped their conversation to stare at her.

'That's what Brodie is trying to tell you,' Hope went on. 'There's something in the box – it might be some kind of paperwork, a receipt or something.'

'Well, now. Do you mind if I take a look, Brodie?' Mr Young asked.

The little girl hesitated for a moment, then nodded and held the puzzle box up for him to take. Using a pair of tweezers, Mr Young slowly teased the paper out.

'Sadly, it's not a helpful receipt that tells us everything we want to know,' he said once he'd unfolded the yellowed and almost translucent sheet. 'In fact, it's a letter, date marked nineteen twenty three.'

'Who is it from?' Hope asked, wondering if it held a clue to who the ring might have belonged to.

He scanned the letter, his forehead furrowing as he read. 'Fascinating,' he said, beckoning Hope forwards so that she could see the letter laid out on the counter. 'Why don't you take a look?'

With tentative fingers, Hope turned the paper towards herself and stared at the faded, old-fashioned handwriting.

10th April 1923, York

My dearest K,
I trust that you are well, and that the excavations
continue apace. How I envy you for being there! It is hard to

believe it has been over a month since I left Egypt – the days have passed so slowly but somehow it is already April.

I have not the faintest idea how I shall write these next words – I know they will break your heart as surely as they break my own. And yet they must be written, for as much as it feels impossible for us to be apart, it is now equally impossible for us to be together. It grieves me sorely but I must therefore end our engagement and return this precious ring to you.

I know you will refuse to accept this but I implore you not to argue. I do not believe I shall ever return to Egypt and you cannot come to England so we must, from this moment on, be as though separated by death. Please know that I will hold you in my heart always and pray that we may meet again in the next life.

Ever yours,
B

Hope's heart began to thump as she reached the final paragraph. 'Oh,' she said softly, gazing at Mr Young. 'It's a *Dear John.*'

He nodded. 'That certainly explains the ring.'

'The writer is breaking off her engagement and returning it to her fiancé,' she explained to Will. 'But it doesn't give any names – just their initials. And it's dated April nineteen twenty three.'

Will appeared satisfied. 'Which fits with what I thought.' He glanced down at the letter. 'I wonder who they were.'

'There's mention of an excavation in Egypt,' Hope mused. 'You said there'd been a revival of interest in the Egyptian style during the twenties – isn't nineteen twenty three around the time Tutankhamun was discovered?'

'Nineteen twenty two, in an expedition led by Howard Carter,' Mr Young replied. 'There were a number of women involved with the excavations so there could be a connection. I'll have to look up the paperwork regarding the house clearance, find out who the customer was.'

Hope blinked. 'How long ago was it?'

Mr Young pursed his lips as he thought. 'Six or seven years, I believe. But I'll do my best to track them down. It would certainly be interesting to see if we can find out more about the provenance of the ring.'

'And the woman who broke off her engagement,' Hope added, with a curious glance at Will who was reading the letter. 'What do you think – family pressure?'

'It certainly sounds that way,' he replied. 'That line about breaking both their hearts makes it fairly clear that ending the relationship isn't what she wants to do.'

Hope nodded. 'And the part about hoping to meet again in the next life. I think it broke her heart to write the letter. I wonder what made her do it.'

Mr Young was eyeing her shrewdly. 'Would you like to try and find out?'

'Could I?' Hope asked. 'I mean, wouldn't you rather do it?'

'Why don't we consider it part of your training? You can go over the paperwork and liaise with Will in case he uncovers who made the ring.' He shrugged. 'There's only a small chance you'll get anywhere but I think it would be good for you to try.'

Hope glanced at the puzzle box, still resting in Brodie's hands. 'A mystery within a mystery,' she said, smiling. 'I'd love to try and unravel it.'

Mr Young beamed. 'Then it's settled – Hope Henderson investigates. I think it's got a bit of a ring to it, don't you?'

It took Hope a moment to register the joke but she couldn't help laughing when she did. 'It's got a lot of a ring to it,' she answered, and smiled at the little girl beside Will. 'Well done for opening the box, Brodie. I can't wait to find out more.'

Chapter Five

'How's the job going, love?'

It was Wednesday evening and Hope was at her parents' house in Upper Poppleton. What had begun as a one-off invitation when she'd first moved from London – dinner with her father while her mother was at choir practice – had developed into a weekly tradition, almost without her realizing it. But she enjoyed spending time with him, just the two of them. Sunday lunches in Upper Poppleton usually involved the whole family and were always chaotic and noisy. Wednesday night dinner was much less hectic and Hope found it a real comfort to relax amid the quiet familiarity of her childhood home.

She finished her mouthful of cottage pie and smiled at her dad across the battered oak dining table that had been at the heart of the kitchen for as long as she could recall. 'Really well, thanks. Everyone is so friendly and I enjoy the work.'

'You always did love that shop,' he said fondly. 'Do you remember the time you gave us the slip at the Minster? One minute you were behind us, squabbling with Harry and Charlotte, the next you'd vanished. We eventually found you with your nose pressed up against the windows of the Emporium, the way other kids stared into sweetshops.'

'Really?' Hope asked as a bubble of incredulity rose up inside her. 'I don't remember that at all.'

He raised his salt-and-pepper eyebrows. 'You'd have been around seven or eight, I think. And you had no idea what the fuss was about – you seemed to think we'd know where you'd gone.'

Hope shook her head. 'Wow. Sorry, Dad, you must have been frantic.'

'Your mother was,' he said. 'Once the initial panic died down, I had an inkling where to find you. And it's no real surprise you've ended up there as an adult but I'm glad it's going well. You need something solid to lean against.'

It was an odd way of putting it but Hope thought she knew what he meant; to anyone looking in, working at the Emporium might seem like just a job, and a part-time job at that, but already it felt like more than just a workplace. Perhaps it had something to do with feeling useful again – she'd drifted along for months, just getting through each day. Now she had a purpose and it felt good to be connected to something again, to be part of a team. Meeting Iris had helped too; making a friend who hadn't known Rob some-how helped cement the idea that Hope was starting again. But it was possible her dad was right – maybe it was the Emporium itself that was the steadying presence. She felt a sense of rightness when she was wandering along the aisles, admiring the everyday treasures that surrounded her, as though she was somehow exactly where she was meant to be.

'There's something very soothing about being around things that have lasted a lifetime or more,' she said with a wistful smile, then paused. 'I guess you don't have to be Freud to unravel that one.'

'No,' her father conceded. 'But I wouldn't worry too much about unravelling things. Has Mr Young got you working on anything interesting?'

Hope leaned forward. 'Funny you should ask that. The most amazing thing happened yesterday.'

She described how Brodie had solved the secret of the puzzle box and revealed the scarab ring, with its mysterious letter.

'I spent most of yesterday evening trying to find out if there were any society scandals involving the Tutankhamun excavations in nineteen twenty two or twenty three, but no real luck so far,' Hope finished, shaking her head. 'The only gossip I could find was about Lord Carnarvon's daughter, Evelyn, and Howard Carter, the famous archaeologist, but that was all strenuously denied and certainly never reached the point of an engagement.'

Her dad shrugged. 'It might have been a clandestine affair. Maybe no one knew they were engaged.'

Hope considered the suggestion. 'It would definitely have been a scandal – he was quite a bit older than her and didn't move in the same social circles. But Evelyn was still in Cairo in April nineteen twenty three. Her father died there and she came back to England afterwards, plus the letter was signed *B*, so it can't be her.'

'Sounds like opening the box was just the start of the puzzle,' he said. 'I agree that your mystery writer was probably a member of the aristocracy, though. Archaeology held a real fascination for a lot of them so she might even have been work-ing on the excavations, if she had the right family connections.'

It was a possibility that had occurred to Hope too but details about the women who'd been part of the incredible discoveries in Luxor were almost non-existent, at least as far as Hope had been able to discover. There had been plenty about the men, of course. 'Maybe,' she said, sighing. 'But I don't know where to start looking. The only facts I have are a date, an initial and a location.'

'And the ring,' her father pointed out. 'That sounds quite distinctive.'

She brightened. 'That's true. Will was going to see whether he could find out who manufactured it, which might lead us somewhere.'

'It might,' he agreed. 'You could also try the university. They have a pretty distinguished Department of Archaeology and I'm sure they'd be interested in looking at the ring. And if your heartbreaker was a local archaeologist, they might know who she was.'

It was a great idea, Hope thought as she sat back in her seat. 'Why didn't I think of that?'

Her dad tapped the side of his head gravely. 'See? Not just a hat rack.'

'Definitely not,' she said, grinning. 'Thanks, Dad, I'll look up who to contact on the university website.'

'Just make sure you keep me in the loop,' he said. 'I'm hooked now.'

'I will,' Hope said, and reached for her phone. The sooner she emailed the university, the sooner she'd get a response.

It took two days for a reply to come through. Hope had sent it to a general address, with a request that it might be forwarded on to the most appropriate person, and the response came from a Professor McCormack.

Hi Hope,

Thanks for contacting the university with your enquiry. I'm a specialist in Egyptology so your email has found its way to me and I confess I am intrigued by both the letter and the ring you describe. You mention that the ring is being restored by a local jeweller but it would be a good idea to put the letter in an acid-free document sleeve, to ensure it is protected from damage.

I'd be very interested in seeing your artefacts and shedding any light I can on their origins – might it be possible for you to bring them to the university? The Department's administrative manager is Judy Medrington and she has access to my diary – for ease, I've copied her into this email.

I look forward to being of help.

Kind regards,
Ciaran McCormack

She forwarded the email to Mr Young, who suggested they discussed its contents further on Tuesday morning, when Hope was working next. But the mystery scratched at Hope's subconscious and she found herself falling down online rabbit holes, searching for clues that might help her identify the letter writer. By Saturday afternoon, she gave in to her restlessness and braved the hazy heat that hung over the city's crowded streets to visit her favourite bakery for a much-needed treat. And since she was already out, it seemed silly not to wander a little further north to High Petergate and the Emporium.

Predictably, the shop was busier than during the week and the aisles seemed to be bursting with treasure seekers. Mr Young was behind the counter, manning the till, but he caught her eye and smiled as she walked in.

'Five minutes,' he mouthed over the head of the woman he was serving and Hope nodded in reply. She made her way to the book room, where the browsing customers seemed to sense a respectful silence was required, and immediately lost herself among the shelves.

She wasn't surprised to see half an hour had passed when Mr Young finally came to find her. He apologized for keeping her waiting but she waved it away. 'It's my own fault for coming in at the weekend,' she said ruefully. 'I should have known you'd be busy.'

'Never too busy to turn detective,' he replied. 'At least, I assume that's why you're here.'

Hope nodded. 'Tuesday seemed such a long way away,' she admitted. 'Have you got a few minutes to talk now?'

Mr Young smiled. 'Of course. Shall we escape upstairs?'

Once they were seated in the small but impeccably organized first floor office, Hope pulled up the email on her phone.

'Obviously, the ring isn't an actual Ancient Egyptian artefact but I thought I'd mention it to encourage a speedier reply,' she explained. 'Who can resist the whiff of romantic scandal?'

Mr Young inclined his head gravely. 'Who indeed? I hope you reassured Professor McCormack that we have taken professional care of the letter.'

Hope felt her cheeks grow warm. 'Of course. I didn't say that I worked here in my initial email, but I mentioned it in my follow-up message.' She hesitated. 'I hope you don't mind but the Professor had a window in his diary on Monday afternoon so I snatched it up.'

'I don't mind at all,' her employer said. 'Enthusiasm is always to be encouraged. But you'll need to collect the ring from Will. I understand he's finished his analysis so that shouldn't be a problem.'

She allowed herself an inward sigh of relief. The ring was clearly a very valuable object and she hadn't worked at the Emporium for very long – there'd been a faint worry in her mind that Mr Young might not trust her to take it away from the safety of the shop. 'Thank you. Maybe I could pick it up on Monday, on my way to the university.'

Mr Young frowned. 'I believe Will doesn't open on Mondays. Let me call him now, see if you can collect it today.'

A few moments later, he replaced the office phone on its

stand and nodded. 'He says they close at five o'clock but you can pop in any time before then. Perhaps you'd like to choose a little gift for Brodie from the stock, since she's the one who set us on the trail of this mystery.'

'That's a lovely idea,' Hope replied. 'I'll see what I can find.'

The Emporium was a little quieter when they made their way back downstairs, which allowed Hope to browse the aisles in comfort. The obvious choice was one of the flamingos but she wasn't sure how Will might feel about welcoming a large, feathery bird into either his shop or his home, and Brodie's response was equally uncertain. Eventually, Hope settled on a set of exquisitely painted Russian nesting dolls.

'Ah, the Matryoshka dolls,' Mr Young said. 'I think Brodie will like these very much.'

The May sun seemed to have brought everyone outdoors and the Shambles was thronging with tourists and shoppers. Hope eased her way through the crowd, edging around the outside of the glass-covered marketplace to Will's shop, and she was glad to push open the door and step into an oasis of air-conditioned tranquillity. A smartly dressed, middle-aged woman behind the counter looked up as she entered.

'Good afternoon,' she said, smiling. 'How can I help?'

Hope explained she was there to see Will and the woman nodded. 'Ah, you must be Hope,' she said. 'Will mentioned you'd be stopping by. One moment, I'll let him know you're here.'

She disappeared through a doorway behind her, leaving

Hope alone. Glancing around, she took in the floor to ceiling display cases filled with glittering jewellery and watches. Everywhere she looked, something sparkled; it was a real Aladdin's cave. Had Will made all of this, she wondered, remembering Iris describing him as an artist. She took a step towards one of the displays and the first thing her gaze settled on was a tray of wedding rings. Some were traditional in design, thick bands in gold and white gold, but others were more intricate, studded with diamonds or interwoven with a combination of different metals. A few had clearly been designed as matching pairs – his and hers. Almost subconsciously, Hope touched the ring finger of her left hand, where the skin still felt smooth and naked without her own wedding ring. Rob had insisted she shouldn't continue to wear it after he was gone.

'I don't want you to feel bound to me forever,' he'd said, when they'd finally faced the devastating truth that he wasn't going to get better. 'I want you to meet someone else and be happy again. Promise me, Hope.'

At the time, she'd shaken her head and tearfully declared she would never take it off but his gentle insistence had worn her down. Now she wore it on a chain around her neck, still there but hidden. She didn't think Rob would object to that.

'Hello, Hope.'

She turned to see Will in the doorway behind the counter, with Brodie peeking out around his legs. 'Hi. I hope I'm not disturbing you.'

A smile wreathed his face. 'Not at all. Brodie and I were just about to have a biscuit and some tea. Will you join us?'

Once again, Hope felt herself drawn in by the warm sincerity of his expression. 'That sounds lovely.' She raised a hand in a tiny wave. 'Hi Brodie.'

The little girl studied her for a moment, then turned around and vanished. 'I think that means come on through,' Will said, in a half-apologetic tone.

Behind the glamorous façade of the shop's glittering displays was a white-walled workshop. A heavy wooden workbench sat in the centre of the room, its scratched and grooved surface littered with tools. Above it, a bright over-head light hung from the ceiling but there were also several angled lamps on the table, alongside an impressive silver and black microscope mounted on a stand and a couple of long-handled magnifying glasses. A door to one side seemed to lead into a kitchen and there was a battered velvet sofa set against another wall, with a thick rug in front of it that was scattered with Lego, books and toys.

'Welcome to the workshop,' Will said, waving a hand around the room. 'Don't worry, I've switched the security lasers off.'

Hope nodded. 'That's good to know. Obviously, I'm only here to case the joint.'

'Ah,' he said gravely. 'I'd better not mention the invisible guard dog, then.'

Brodie glanced back and forth between them, her fore-head creased in a bemused frown. 'Oh, that's right,' Will said, slapping a hand to his forehead. 'I forgot, it's a goose, not a dog.'

'Sounds like a genius idea to me,' Hope replied. 'Have you seen the geese down by the river? They're fiercer than any rottweiler.'

He grinned. 'Aren't they? There are signs up in the Museum Gardens, warning tourists not to even make eye contact.' Pausing, he fixed her with an enquiring look. 'Anyway, what can I get you? I've got tea, coffee or banana Nesquik.'

'Hmmmm,' she said, pretending to consider the options. 'I think I'll have tea please – milk, no sugar.'

With a cheerful nod, Will slipped into the kitchen. Hope smiled at Brodie. 'I guess the Nesquik belongs to you?'

The girl nodded but her eyes were fixed on the open kitchen door, where the sound of a kettle being filled could be heard.

'And are these your toys?' Hope went on, pointing to the rug. 'What are you building with your Lego?'

Brodie hesitated, as though she was trying to decide whether to make a bolt for the safety of her uncle. But the opportunity to show off her toys was too great to resist and instead, she reached for a multi-coloured rectangle of blocks.

'Are you building a house?' Hope asked and had to hide a grin when Brodie flashed her a look that clearly suggested she was insane. 'A castle? A rocket?'

Sitting down on the rug, Brodie reached for another

brick and added it to her construction. She stared at Hope expectantly.

'A car?' Hope hazarded, scouting around for further clues. Her gaze landed on a plastic silver dressing-up ring, complete with a flashing emerald in the middle, and the penny dropped. 'Oh, it's a puzzle box!'

Brodie beamed at her. She picked up the ring and dropped it inside, placing one hand over the top as though she'd just completed a magic trick.

'It's just like the one at the Emporium,' Hope said, clapping. 'But I can't help noticing it doesn't have a lid. Would you like somewhere safer to hide your treasure?'

Eyes wide, the girl nodded. Hope knelt on the rug, reaching into her bag to take out the gift she'd brought. She placed the tissue-paper wrapped package on the rug in front of Brodie. 'This is a thank you present from Mr Young for opening the puzzle box.'

Will appeared, with a steaming mug of tea in one hand and a glass of creamy yellow milk in the other. 'That's very kind of him. Go ahead and open it, Brodie.'

At first, the little girl picked carefully at the edge of the tissue, peeling back one thin layer after another. But then impatience got the better of her and she seized the parcel to tear rest of the paper away. When the bright red and gold decoration of the rounded doll peeped through, Brodie slowed down and slid the last of the wrapping away. Then she looked up at Hope, her gaze questioning.

'She has a secret too,' Hope said, getting to her feet and

taking the mug of tea from Will. 'If you play with her, she might tell you what it is.'

Immediately, Brodie lifted the doll to her ear and gave it a gentle shake. Her eyes lit up when she heard the rattle and she ran her fingers across the smooth painted wood, searching for the way in.

'This is enormously kind of you too,' Will said, leaning against the workbench with his hands cupped around his own mug. 'Thank you.'

'As I said, it was Mr Young's idea,' Hope said as she turned towards him. 'But I chose the dolls. I thought she'd find them interesting.'

Will tipped his head. 'You chose very well. She's going to be engrossed by them all afternoon.'

The praise sent a ripple of satisfaction through Hope and she wasn't able to prevent herself from smiling. 'I'm glad.' She glanced down at Brodie's bowed head and her smile faded. 'Iris told me a little about what happened. I'm very sorry for your loss.'

He was silent for a moment, eyes fixed on his hands, but then he looked up. 'Thank you. It's been a very difficult time.' He paused, as though trying to find the right words. 'Some days are easier than others. But life goes on – the sun comes up and goes down and sometimes I think she forgets for a few minutes. Like right now.'

Hope followed his gaze to the rug, where Brodie was employing the same methodical diligence she'd brought to opening the puzzle box. 'It takes time. I'm sure you're doing a great job.'

Will sighed. 'It helps to see her smile. Gives me optimism that she might start talking again one day.'

'I'm sure she will,' Hope offered. 'Grief affects us all differently – sometimes we think we're coming through it only to find another layer hiding underneath.'

'A bit like the dolls,' Will said, with a glimmer of understanding.

'Yes,' Hope said, her own lips twisting in acknowledgement. 'Maybe one day, we finish opening all the layers and find a new version of ourselves waiting – smaller than we were, sadder, but ready to face life again.'

He gave a thoughtful nod. 'And then we put ourselves back together, hiding the joins from the rest of the world.'

'But we always feel them there,' Hope said quietly. 'We're never quite whole again.'

She wasn't sure if it was what she said or the way she said it that made him study her. For a moment, she thought he might ask how she knew. But instead, he took a long sip of tea and when he spoke again his tone was determined and bright. 'Anyway, the present is perfect, as you can see. Thanks.'

She couldn't blame him for backing away from the deeper waters; hadn't she done the same more times than she could count? Mindful of the unspoken boundary, she took refuge in professionalism. 'You're very welcome.'

Silence hung in the air, long enough to cause a stirring of social anxiety in Hope. She opened her mouth to say something – anything – to fill the gap in conversation but Will beat her to it. 'So, Mr Young said you're taking the ring to someone at the university.'

'Yes, there's a professor who has asked to see it,' she said. 'Although it's the letter I really want him to take a look at.'

'If this was a movie, the letter would have been written by his great-grandmother, he'd tell you everything about her and the mystery would be solved.'

Hope snorted. 'If this was a movie, we'd all have been sucked into a parallel dimension the moment Brodie opened the puzzle box.'

'True,' Will conceded with a grin. 'Well, I hope your professor is more help more than I've been. I was able to confirm the physical qualities of the ring but got nowhere with finding out who made it. I'm beginning to wonder if it might have been manufactured abroad.'

'Maybe even in Egypt,' Hope offered. 'In which case there's no hope of a paper trail, right?'

'Probably not,' Will said. 'I mean, the emerald is a beauty – that originated in Colombia – but they were popular throughout the nineteen twenties and thirties so that doesn't tell us much. I'm surprised there aren't any markings inside the band but that happens sometimes.'

'You've been really helpful,' Hope replied. 'I'll let you know what the professor says – he sounded intrigued in his emails.'

Will grimaced. 'Just don't let him hang on to it. It's hard to know for sure but the unusual design probably means it's worth at least ten thousand pounds.'

Hope almost swallowed her last mouthful of tea too fast. 'Really?'

'Something like that,' he said, then threw her an amused look. 'You look like the people on the *Antiques Roadshow* who find out the painting they've kept in the garage is worth millions.'

The ring might not be worth millions but it did make Hope worry about putting it in her handbag to walk through the crowded market. 'Wow. I'm not sure I'd have agreed to take it if I'd known.'

Will eyed her with concern. 'I can walk you home if you're worried.' Then he seemed to replay the offer in his head and his cheeks grew pink. 'With Brodie, I mean. Although I've just realized I have no idea where you live – it could be miles . . .'

He trailed off, looking even more embarrassed and Hope took pity on him. 'I live on the wharf, down by Foss Bridge. But honestly, you don't need to walk me anywhere. I'll be fine.'

'Are you sure?' he said, frowning. 'It's no trouble and we could probably use some fresh air.'

Hope looked at Brodie, who had discovered the secret of the dolls and had them all laid out in front of her. 'No, don't worry. But I should probably get going. I'm meeting Iris for dinner this evening.'

'Of course,' Will replied, and stood up straight. 'The ring is locked away in the safe, I'll just grab it.'

While he was gone, Hope watched Brodie playing for a

moment or two. On impulse, she crouched beside her on the rug. 'Do you like them?'

The answering nod was immediate.

Hope smiled. 'I think they like you too. And the nice thing about these dolls is that they love to listen. So, if you ever want to tell them anything – anything at all – they'd love to hear it.'

Brodie's blue eyes were wide as they met Hope's. She brushed a strand of blonde hair from the little girl's forehead. 'Do you believe that?'

Again, the nod was instant.

Hope smiled. 'Good. And the best thing is, they'll never tell anyone else. So, you can trust them no matter what is worrying you.'

Will came back into the room. He held out a dark green, velvet-covered ring box. Hope rose and took it. 'Thanks.'

He glanced down at Brodie, who was once more happily engrossed in the dolls. 'No problem. But I think it's me who should be thanking you.'

'You did,' Hope reminded him. 'I've thanked you and you've thanked me, so I think we're all sorted for thanks.'

Will laughed. 'I think we are. We'll pop into the Emporium next week for a catch up – I'm already curious about what this professor is going to say.'

'Me too. I hope it's going to be worth the trip.' She gave a little wave towards the rug. 'Bye, Brodie.'

The girl raised her own hand to wave back and her face split into a shy smile.

'I think she likes you,' Will said as he showed Hope to the door that led to the market square. 'She doesn't smile for just anyone, you know.'

Warmth washed over Hope and she was glad all over again that she'd chosen the Matryoshka dolls. 'That's good,' she answered, more than a little touched. 'Because I like her too.'

Chapter Six

Hope wasn't entirely sure what she'd been expecting a Professor of Egyptology to look like but a tousle-haired, chiselled-cheeked rock god had definitely not been on the list. Embarrassingly, she'd gaped when Ciaran McCormack had crossed the parquet floored entrance hall of the grand King's Manor campus building to greet her and she felt she'd been on the back foot ever since. Were university professors supposed to wear leather jackets and skinny jeans and look like they'd just come off the Pyramid stage at Glastonbury, she wondered faintly as she sat in his wood-panelled office and watched him study the letter. Did they all have the kind of glorious Irish lilt that made everything they said sound like poetry? Attendance at his lectures had to be through the roof. In fact, he didn't belong in a classroom at all – she could picture him battling bad guys and saving the world without even breaking a sweat. All he needed was a hat.

'I can see why this letter caught your imagination,' he said, without looking up. 'There's so much that isn't being said.'

Hope dragged her gaze from the way his dark hair fell perfectly across his forehead and forced herself to focus on what he'd said. 'That's what fascinates me the most. It must have been pressure from her family that made her break off the engagement but she doesn't actually give a reason. She's too intent on making sure he knows how much she loves him, which is at odds with the message overall.'

Professor McCormack looked across the desk at her, his grey eyes interested. 'So, what's your theory?'

She blinked. 'My theory?' she repeated, not sure if she understood the question. 'About who she was?'

'No, I already have a good idea who might have written the letter,' he said, and leaned back in his chair. 'But put yourself in her shoes for a moment. What would bring you to end a relationship with a man you knew it would be impossible to live without?'

Once again, Hope found herself floundering. Of course, she'd wondered what had made the writer cut off all communication with the man she loved, but she hadn't expected to be sharing that wildly romantic speculation with the expert she'd gone to in search of clues to unravel the mystery. Yet here he was, waiting for her answer with all the patience of a teacher who was used to students being slow to reply, and she knew she was going to have to give him something before he'd share the identity of the letter writer.

'Okay, I do have a theory as it happens,' she began, and

took a deep breath. 'Whoever B was, she came from a wealthy family – she might possibly have been a member of the aristocracy – and was working on the excavations in the Valley of the Kings. While in Egypt, she fell in love with K, who was outside her social circle and not English, but that didn't matter to B and they embarked on a secret engagement. She fell ill and returned to England for treatment, where the engagement was discovered by her family, who forced her to break it off.'

'Not bad,' he said and smiled in a way that simultaneously made Hope feel like a teenager again and caused her stomach to somersault. 'A few leaps of faith not directly supported by the source material but I can see why you went with them. Now, let's have a look at the ring.'

He opened the velvet box Will had given Hope a few days earlier and whistled when he saw the emerald. 'Now that's what I call an engagement ring. I'm not surprised it never found its way back to Egypt.'

Hope sat up a little straighter. 'So, it is Egyptian? The jeweller who assessed it suspected it might have been made abroad but he couldn't say where.'

Professor McCormack held the ring up to the light, admiring it. 'I can't be totally sure of the provenance just from looking but the carving is exquisite. And, of course, the scarab beetle is very symbolic – it represented rebirth or regeneration to the Ancient Egyptians. So perhaps this ring was meant to herald the beginning of a new life.'

'I suppose marriage was often seen in that way,' Hope

replied. 'At least for the woman, who basically left everything she knew behind her.'

'Good point,' he said and placed the ring back in the box. 'And, in this particular case, I suspect you're right to suggest there was a mismatch in status so the marriage would definitely have changed everything.'

Hope forced herself to ignore her growing sense of impatience. 'Who do you think wrote the letter?'

He held up a hand. 'Let's not jump the gun. Tell me how you found it.'

She explained what had happened – that the Emporium had undertaken a house clearance in York that had included the puzzle box, how it had remained unopened for years until Brodie had solved the puzzle and why that had led Hope to the University in her quest for more information.

Professor McCormack considered her for a long moment. 'Have you ever heard of Elenor Lovelace?'

Hope racked her brains. 'I've heard of Ada Lovelace,' she said doubtfully.

'Everyone has,' he said without rancour. 'Lovelace was a reasonably common surname for centuries – it means lawless or outlaw – and Elenor's family was distantly related to Ada. But that's all beside the point. The Right Honourable Elenor Lovelace was one of the most promising female archaeologists of her day. Howard Carter allegedly claimed he might never have found Tutankhamun's tomb without her and the list of her previous archaeological achievements is impressive.'

Hope couldn't help herself. 'But the letter is signed B.'

His forehead furrowed into a frown. 'A nickname, maybe? Term of endearment?'

Abruptly he stood up and strode to a bookshelf to Hope's right. 'I'm sure it's here somewhere,' he murmured, trailing one hand along the spines of the titles that lined the top shelf. '*Five Years at Thebes* ... *The Tombs of Tutankhamun* ... Ah, here it is!'

He pulled a slim volume from the bookshelf and held it out so Hope could see the title. '*Uncovering the Valley of the Kings*, by E.E. Brunton,' she read. 'I suppose the B could stand for Brunton.'

But Professor McCormack wasn't listening. His attention was focused on flipping the pages of the book, scanning each one until he found what he was looking for. 'This is our girl,' he said, raising the open book and tapping one finger on a fuzzy black and white photograph of what was clearly a group in front of a sizeable archaeological dig. 'Elenor *Beatrice* Lovelace, who was born in York in before the turn of the century and vanished without trace in 1923.'

'Vanished?' Hope echoed, staring at the photo in consternation. 'What do you mean *vanished*?'

'I mean she disappeared without trace,' Professor McCormack said as he sat down and slid the book across the desk for Hope to take a closer look. 'There were rumours of a relationship that had come to an unhappy end and she was seen walking the cliffs around Whitby the day before she disappeared, but her body was never found.'

Hope studied the picture, picking out the young woman identified in the tiny print beneath as Elenor. Her spirits plummeted as she recalled the quiet desperation of the letter. 'Suicide, then?'

'That was the accepted explanation,' he agreed and tapped a finger in the middle of the triangle formed by the book, the letter and the ring. 'Until now.'

The meaning of that sank in. 'You don't think she killed herself?'

'I'm not saying that,' he said evenly. 'But there are a number of things that don't add up. If Elenor posted the letter ending her engagement and returned the ring to her fiancé, how did both items remain in York?'

It was a good question, especially since the letter had suggested the fiancé couldn't come to England. 'Do you know who she might have been planning to marry?'

He shook his head. 'No. But there were a lot of people involved in those excavations, locals as well as visitors from other countries, and very few detailed records have survived. Short of discovering *Elenor's Secret Diary, aged 26 and ¾*, you might never find out who her betrothed was.'

Of course it made sense, Hope thought; the odds of finding a name when they had so little to go on must be miniscule. 'Mr Young was going to go through the paperwork, to see if he could find out who authorized the Emporium to clear the house,' she said slowly. 'Maybe that will lead us to a relative who can fill in some of the gaps.'

'It might,' Professor McCormack said. 'I'll put some feelers out among my colleagues at other universities, see if any of them can shed any light on who the mystery man might have been. As I said earlier, Elenor was a very well-regarded archaeologist. And she became something of a legend when she disappeared.'

Hope's eyes came to rest once more on the photograph and she realized she was more intrigued than ever. 'I'll let you know what Mr Young finds out.' She looked up gratefully. 'Thanks for your time today, Professor. You've been very helpful.'

He smiled, reminding her all over again how distinctly out-of-place he looked in the rather dusty academic office. 'Call me Ciaran, please. The only people who call me professor are my students.'

I bet that's not all they call you, Hope thought, and had to catch herself before she blushed. 'Thank you, Ciaran,' she said, collecting up the letter and the ring. 'I really appreciate your help.'

He picked up the book and gave it to her. 'You can borrow this, if you like. A bit of background reading.'

'Thanks,' she said, slipping it into her bag. 'I'll get it back to you when I've finished it.'

He held the office door open for her and shook his head as they made their way down the stairs to the entrance hall. 'You know, you're not at all what I expected from your email. I thought you'd be older.' He glanced sideways. 'Less like the kind of model who inspired Titian himself.'

Hope felt her face start to glow; no one had ever compared

her to an artist's muse before. 'I expected you to be older too,' she said, as much to cover her blush as anything. 'My university lecturers certainly were.'

Ciaran tipped his head as they walked into the sandstone courtyard that lay outside the ornate entrance to King's Manor. His grey eyes held hers as they faced each other. 'Good point. Do you think it's fair to say we were both pleasantly surprised?'

She couldn't ignore it any longer – he was definitely flirting with her. But even more unexpectedly, she was tempted to flirt back. 'I think that is fair.'

He grinned, as though pleased she was playing the game. 'We've got each other's contact details. Let's see what we can dig up between us.'

'Thanks again for your time,' she said, and stepped back before he could offer to shake hands – the last thing her suddenly overactive imagination needed was the touch of his long lean fingers on hers. And as she walked across the gravel to the gates that led off campus, she had to fight hard not to glance over her shoulder for a final glimpse of him, outlined against the carved doorway of the old building, but she couldn't prevent a smile from tugging at the corners of her mouth. The afternoon had turned out to be even more interesting than she'd anticipated. The tragedy surrounding Elenor Lovelace had her intrigued, regardless of whether she turned out to be the author of the letter. And, if Hope was honest, Ciaran McCormack had exceeded her expectations too. Charming, smart, knowledgeable and far more attractive than a professor had any right to be, she couldn't help hoping their paths would cross again.

Iris guessed something was up before Hope could confide a single word. Throughout their belly dance class, she kept darting curious looks Hope's way and the final track had barely finished before the florist was standing in front of her.

'Okay, what's going on?' she demanded, hands on hips. 'There's a dreamy look in your eyes and I'm pretty sure it's not from the spins we've just done.'

'Sssshhh!' Hope hissed, glancing around to make sure no one had overheard. 'It's nothing, honestly.'

Iris raised a disbelieving eyebrow. 'Nothing. Right.'

Hope bit her lip. The truth was she was bursting to talk to someone about her afternoon. She had good friends in London, of course, but couldn't quite bring herself to tap out a jaunty *Guess what?!* message. Part of the problem was that they'd all known and loved Rob, and although they had been encouraging when she'd dipped her toe back into dating, Hope still felt oddly uncomfortable about discussing her unexpected attraction to Ciaran. Her sister was off-limits for a different reason: Charlotte would be only too delighted to hear a man had caught Hope's eye and wouldn't let it go until she had done something about it. All of which meant she was tempted by the opportunity to confide in Iris. 'Okay, I do have something to tell you,' she admitted. 'But not here.'

'Come on,' Iris said, untying her coin belt and stuffing it into her rucksack. 'I know just the place.'

It wasn't until they were tucked away in a booth of a nearby basement cocktail bar, with a half-drunk Cosmopolitan in front of each of them, that Hope felt relaxed enough to spill the beans. Iris listened, wide-eyed, as she described both Ciaran and the information he'd given her. And although the florist was interested in the revelations about Elenor Lovelace and her mysterious disappearance, she was definitely more fascinated by Hope's description of Ciaran.

'But this is great,' she said, when Hope had finished. 'He sounds perfect. Does he have a whip? More importantly, does he have friend? We could double date!'

Hope shook her head. 'I'm not going to date him. He's very good-looking and I'm flattered he flirted but that's the end of it.'

Iris quirked her eyebrows. 'Give me one good reason why not.'

Hope hesitated. 'It's unprofessional.'

'Rubbish,' her friend replied without missing a beat. 'It might – *might* – be considered borderline unprofessional if you actually worked together but that isn't the case. Next.'

'I'm not ready.'

Iris gave her a look that was more sympathetic but no less implacable. 'I get why it might feel that way. But look – it's been a while since you dated the numnuts who couldn't handle your past – you're stronger now. How can you know if you're ready to swim if you don't get into the water?'

What if the water was cold, Hope was tempted to ask, but she didn't doubt her friend would somehow find a way to make it sound rude. 'I might be imagining the whole thing,' she said instead. 'Maybe he was just being polite.'

'He called you a muse,' Iris replied and downed the remainder of her cocktail. 'Guys don't do that unless they're trying to get into your knickers.'

'Iris!' Hope spluttered but the other woman simply nodded in affirmation then stood up to go to the bar. By the time she came back, bearing two Porn Star Martinis, she'd clearly marshalled her arguments.

'Okay, let's recap. A hot guy fancies you. Correct?'

Hope opened her mouth to disagree but Iris carried on talking. 'Don't argue – he does. And you fancy the hot guy. Yes, you do – it's written all over your face.'

'But—'

'Don't even think about using that unprofessional line again,' Iris warned, raising a hand. 'It's not like you work together. So, what's stopping you from going for a drink and getting to know him a bit better?'

She made it sound so easy, Hope thought wistfully. 'When you put it like that, nothing, I suppose.'

'Exactly,' Iris replied. 'Although you should try and be a bit more enthusiastic when he actually asks you out.'

Instinctively, Hope looked down at the bare finger on her left hand. 'Fine. What if I say yes and he's amazing and I fall in love and it all goes wrong? Or worse, what if it goes right and I start to forget Rob?'

Iris reached across to squeeze her hand. 'You're never going to forget Rob. But I can't promise you won't ever get hurt again because that's the risk we all take when we let someone into our hearts.'

Hope picked at the skin around her thumbnail. 'I'm just scared.'

'I know you are,' Iris replied softly. 'But it doesn't have to be for ever, or even for a night. Just think of it as a drink in a bar, or a coffee in the park, or whatever it is you decide to do. One step at a time.'

Hope took a gulp of her drink and willed herself to be less of a wimp. 'Okay. You're right.'

'I am,' Iris said with some satisfaction. 'And obviously if you decide to tear his clothes off at the end of the date, that's fine too. Meaningless sex with a hot guy is never a bad idea. Unless you're still in the park.'

A snort of laughter escaped Hope. 'You're terrible.'

'Damn right,' Iris said, grinning. 'And don't forget to find out if he has any single friends.'

Chapter Seven

Hope exchanged several emails with Ciaran in the weeks that followed. At the Emporium, Mr Young had been through the paperwork that related to the house clearance and tried to contact the number listed in his records but hadn't had much luck. The house itself had been sold and the trail had dried up. There wasn't much more the Emporium could do.

'We'll keep the ring safe and try again to trace its owner,' Mr Young explained to Hope, 'but eventually we might have to accept that we've hit a dead end.'

Hope had passed the bad news along but although Ciaran had expressed disappointment that the paperwork hadn't thrown up any helpful information, he hadn't seemed particularly concerned at the impasse. He'd simply replied that he was following up a few leads at his end and he'd keep her posted. The messages were so business-like that Hope found herself wondering whether she really had imagined his flirtatious manner. And now that she'd allowed herself to visualize going on a date with him, she had also started to consider introducing a little flirtation of her own. Iris would definitely approve of that.

It was early on Thursday evening when an email marked URGENT! popped into her inbox. Hope sat up on the sofa and dropped the magazine she'd been reading.

To: Hope Henderson
From: Ciaran McCormack

I've got NEWS. Can you meet me somewhere? What's
your number?

Intrigued, she typed in her number and sent it. What news could he have that merited an urgent meeting?

Less than a minute later, her phone buzzed again. This time it was a text message and it contained the address of a bar on Walmgate, with the words See you at 7pm?

The sudden certainty that she was going to see him again caused Hope to dither over her reply for almost five minutes. But, eventually, curiosity overcame her fluttering nerves and she reminded herself of Iris's observation that it was just a drink in a bar. OK, see you there.

And then she spent the next thirty minutes in the shower, washing her hair and shaving her legs, and repeating in her head that this wasn't date preparation – she'd do the same regardless of whoever she was meeting. And it wouldn't hurt to look her best, she reasoned as she applied some make-up and tugged on a dress. How long had it been since she'd made this much effort, she wondered as she surveyed her glammed-up reflection. And then decided she preferred not to think about that.

The venue Ciaran had chosen was only a few minutes' walk from her apartment and she arrived just before seven o'clock. The decor had an understated, upmarket feel and several tables were occupied by couples and groups, giving it a busy but not overly crowded feel. She ordered a gin and tonic and took one of the tall seats beside the polished wooden bar, trying to ignore the butterflies in her stomach.

When the door opened again, it was Ciaran. 'Sorry to keep you waiting,' he said, and surprised her by swooping in to plant a kiss on either cheek. 'An undergraduate emergency that turned out to be nothing of the kind.'

Hope nodded distractedly as she breathed in the lingering scent of his aftershave. Had her other dates smelled so appealing? And then she remembered this wasn't a date, which made it all the more inappropriate that she was practically drooling over the way Ciaran smelled.

Seemingly oblivious to the effect he was having, Ciaran ordered a pint of Thirsty Bishop before turning to appraise Hope properly. 'You look lovely. Thanks for agreeing to meet me.'

'How could I refuse?' Hope asked, trying to ignore the insistent little voice in her head that was pointing out how attractive he was. 'You know I'm a sucker for a mystery.'

He laughed. 'The enigmatic approach works every time.

Do you mind if we move to a table? I can never relax perched on these fancy bar stools.'

Hope looked around. Most of the empty tables seemed to be u-shaped booths towards the rear of the bar. Blue velvet seats curved around beneath dim golden lights. They looked dangerously romantic to Hope but the only alternative was to stay where they were and she had to admit she was already starting to regret her choice of dress; the silky material was riding up her legs no matter how still she sat. 'Sure, no problem,' she said.

She slid along the velvet seat of the booth, relieved when Ciaran sat opposite her rather than next to her.

'Cheers,' he said, raising his pint glass to touch hers. 'Happy Thursday.'

Hope took a sip of her drink, picturing the URGENT! subject header on his email. But whatever the news was, he seemed in no hurry to share it. 'How are you?' he asked. 'How's life in the antique business?'

She described her day at the Emporium and he made her laugh with some colourful observations about the students he'd encountered that week. 'They're mostly good kids but sometimes I wonder if they have any brains at all,' he said dryly. 'That's another reason I was glad you said yes – you rescued me from an evening of marking hastily-written assignments on "Funerary Beliefs in the Pre-Dynastic Period".'

'Happy to help,' Hope said, grinning at his pretence of a shudder. 'And I only live a couple of minutes away so it was easy to get here. How about you – do you live in York?'

'On campus during the week, for my sins,' he replied and grimaced. 'Which is why it's even more important to escape every now and then.'

The conversation began to flow and before Hope knew it, she'd finished her drink. 'Let me get you another,' Ciaran said. 'It's the least I can do for dragging you out this evening.'

He returned with a gin and tonic and a second pint for himself. 'So, I suppose you're wondering what news I could have discovered that was so urgent, right?'

'A little,' Hope said, smiling, but the truth was she was enjoying his company. It was exactly as Iris had said: they were having a drink in a bar and it was nice. And then she became suddenly aware that her leg was resting against his beneath the table. For a millisecond, she considered moving it away and then forced herself to relax. It was just the way they were sitting. It didn't mean a thing.

'After you left my office, I contacted some other Egyptologists to show them your letter and ask what they knew about Elenor's private life,' Ciaran explained. 'I didn't expect much – it's not exactly hot gossip, after all – but figured you never know. And today, I got a bite.'

Hope felt a stirring of anticipation. 'Oh?'

'Quite a big bite,' he said, and grinned. 'From someone who had information about Elenor's only surviving relative. A great-great niece, no less.'

If he hadn't had Hope's attention before, he certainly had it now. 'And?'

He leaned back against the blue velvet, his grey eyes

sparkling, and Hope realized he was enjoying himself immensely. Clearly, he was a born storyteller. 'Have a guess where she lives.'

Hope shook her head. 'No idea. London. Cairo.'

'Nope.' His eyes sparkled as he looked as her. 'Closer to home.'

Hope stared at him. 'Here? In York?'

'Here in York,' he confirmed. 'And she's willing to meet us, if you're interested.'

If she was interested, Hope thought faintly and almost laughed. 'Yes,' she told Ciaran. 'I'm definitely up for meeting her. Did you mention the letter and the ring?'

He nodded. 'I think that's what swung it, to be honest. I mean, she gave me her address and it's within spitting distance of the Minster so she's clearly not short of cash, but she seemed to recognize the ring when I described it. Would you be able to bring it along to show her, do you think?'

The ring was securely back in Will's safe but Hope was sure Mr Young would approve of another outing if it helped them to gather more information about its origins. 'I think so,' she said. 'And we wouldn't be going far – just around the corner from the Emporium. When did you have in mind?'

He pulled a face. 'She suggested this weekend but I'll be at my place in Scarborough. I'll be back on Monday, if you're free in the evening?'

And now it was Hope's turn to pull a face. 'I have a dance class on Monday evening. Sorry.'

'A dance class,' he repeated, and she thought there was a spark of something more than polite interest in his expression. 'What kind of dancing?'

Belatedly, it occurred to Hope that she should have kept things vague, because now she had to reveal exactly what type of class it was. Either Ciaran was going to laugh at the notion of a 5'10" redhead attempting to belly dance or he'd find it fascinating and she wasn't sure which she'd prefer. 'Belly dancing,' she said, forcing herself to sound confident. 'But I'm just a beginner.'

'Sounds great,' he said with an approving nod. 'I bet it's harder than it looks.'

'It is,' Hope agreed fervently. 'Anyway, that's where I'll be on Monday night. But I'm free every other evening.'

The words sounded ridiculously sad to Hope and she wished she'd made it sound like she had some kind of social life but Ciaran didn't seem to notice. 'Let's pencil something in for Tuesday and I'll confirm tomorrow.'

'Great,' Hope said and felt a quiver of anticipation at the thought of potentially discovering more about Elenor and her unfortunate fiancé.

Ciaran leaned forward expectantly. 'And now that we've got the business out of the way, let's get to the interesting bit. Tell me about you.'

She began with growing up in Upper Poppleton and it turned out Ciaran knew the village well. He had been part of a large family too, back in Cork, and they shared some hysterical stories of the awful things their siblings had done over the years. When Hope stopped laughing long enough to discover her glass was somehow empty again, Ciaran raised an enquiring eyebrow. 'One for the road?'

She hesitated. 'Didn't you say you've got assignments to mark?'

He shook his head. 'They'll keep. So I can join you in another drink if you feel like being daring.'

Hope could already feel the effect of the alcohol fizzing through her veins but it wasn't an unpleasant sensation. Why shouldn't she have another? It wasn't as though she had anything to get up for in the morning.

'Sure,' she said, smiling at Ciaran. 'I like the sound of daring. But it's my round.'

He flatly refused to allow her to go to the bar and in the end, Hope gave in. The drink he brought back wasn't another G&T but a Tom Collins. 'You said we should be daring,' he said, placing it in front of her. 'So I took a risk on what you'd fancy.'

His eyes met hers as he delivered the last sentence and a sudden fizzle of heat buzzed through her that had nothing to do with the alcohol she'd drunk. He was talking about which cocktail she might enjoy, of course, but it was still fun to entertain the fleeting possibility that he'd meant something else entirely ...

'You chose wisely,' she responded with a smile. 'It's perfect.'

This time when he sat down, his leg pressed against hers immediately and she knew it wasn't an accident. Relax, she told herself, nothing is going to happen. We are just two people enjoying each other's company.

The next time she checked the time, she was amazed to see it was 10.30pm.

'Time flies, doesn't it?' Ciaran observed. 'I should probably think about making a move, sadly – I've got a two-hour lecture to deliver tomorrow morning on the preservation of anaerobic environments.'

'Oof,' Hope said sympathetically. 'Rather you than me.'

The night was still warm but Hope couldn't hide a shiver as they stepped outside and the cooler air hit her bare arms.

'Do you want my jacket?' Ciaran asked instantly but Hope shook her head.

'I don't have far to go,' she said and pointed to the old wharf buildings just visible over the rooftops along Walmgate. 'See?'

'In the converted flour mills – very nice,' he said. 'But I'm afraid I'm an old-fashioned gentleman so I'll have to insist on seeing you home safely.'

'Honestly, there's no—' she began.

Ciaran held up a hand to interrupt her. 'Ah, but there is. My ma would never let me hear the end of it if she knew I'd let a lady walk home alone.' He slipped his leather jacket around her shoulders. 'And you might as well wear this and be warm instead of shivering the whole way.'

Hope pulled the jacket around herself and conceded defeat once more. 'Thank you. I haven't quite got used to York's slightly lower temperature yet. In London, the summer evenings feel much warmer.'

He nodded. 'Plus there's the sweat fest that is the Underground. Is that where you lived before – London?'

'Yes. But it's nice to be back in York, near my family again.'

'Of course. Except for when they leave dead frogs in your bed,' he said, grinning as he referenced one of the stories they'd swapped earlier in the evening.

She laughed. 'I think Harry's grown out of that now. Probably.'

They crossed the river and made their way slowly towards Hope's apartment block, chatting comfortably as though they'd known each other for years. It wasn't until they'd almost reached the door that it occurred to Hope that Ciaran might try to kiss her. She'd been aware of his hand pressed against the small of her back as they'd crossed the road but the pressure had vanished as soon as they were safely on the other side. What should she do if he did try, she wondered? How would it feel to kiss him back?

But it appeared she'd been worrying for no reason. He kept a respectable distance from her when she slowed to a halt a metre or so from the doorway. 'Thanks for seeing me home, and for a nice evening.'

'It was my pleasure,' he said, his expression warm and sincere. 'Although I will take my jacket back now. I'm not so much of a gentleman that I'm prepared to catch my death on the walk back to the campus.'

Hope laughed at his dramatic tone and gave him the coat. 'I hope your lecture goes well tomorrow.'

'Ah, they'll all be asleep within minutes anyway,' he

said, with a self-deprecating smile. 'I'll let you know about Tuesday. Have a good weekend.'

He raised a hand in a friendly wave and turned to walk briskly back the way they'd just come. Hope stood watching him for a moment, then pressed her fob against the keypad and made her way to the top floor. The apartment was silent as she let herself in but for once, she didn't mind – she was too busy mentally spooling back through the evening. There'd been a lot of laughter, she recalled as she removed her make-up, plenty of lively conversation and a flattering amount of flirting. She'd had a great time, only enhanced by the delicious pressure of his leg against hers beneath the table. And if she was totally honest with herself, she'd enjoyed being escorted gallantly home, with Ciaran's jacket around her shoulders to make her feel just that tiny bit more cosseted. He'd been the perfect gentleman. Hope could have no complaints at all.

And yet she had a niggling sense of frustration as she lay in bed staring at the ceiling, waiting for sleep to claim her. She'd panicked slightly when they'd reached her door but now that she'd had time to reflect on the moment, she felt irrationally disappointed. The only sensible explanation was that part of her had wanted Ciaran to be a little *less* of a gentleman, that she'd subconsciously hoped he would try to kiss her. And now that she had admitted it herself, she had no idea how to feel about the realization.

No idea at all.

Chapter Eight

The apartment belonging to Elenor Lovelace's great-great niece was even more grand than Hope had imagined. Part of the renovated Purey Cust hospital buildings, with the Minster looming large nearby, the red brick building shone in the evening sunshine as she and Ciaran approached and rang the bell.

'She's in the penthouse,' Ciaran murmured as they waited to be buzzed in. 'Like I said, not short of a bob or two.'

Hope half-expected the apartment door to be opened by a maid in traditional black and white but the woman who answered did not have the bearing of an employee. She was elderly, with a lined face that suggested she was in her eighties and an elegant twist of white hair pinned to the top of her head. She wore expensive-looking, tailored trousers and an immaculate silk shirt. Definitely not a maid, Hope decided.

'We're here to see Isobel Lovelace,' Ciaran said politely.

'I know,' the woman said, with more than a trace of irritability. 'Well, don't just stand there – come in.'

There was just time for Hope to exchange a look with Ciaran before going inside. The woman led them down a short hallway and into an ivory living room. Tall windows were swathed with gold edged curtains and billowing translucent cotton, vases of perfect white lilies graced the side tables and the floor was covered by pale carpets that Hope thought wouldn't have stayed clean for more than a minute in Harry's house. Belatedly, she thought about removing her shoes but the woman waved them towards the sofa. 'Don't worry about the carpet,' she said. 'My housekeeper will take care of it tomorrow.'

Smiling weakly, Hope perched on the edge of an elegant cream sofa. Ciaran sat beside her.

Isobel fixed them with an imperious stare. 'So, what is it you've come to show me?'

Her tone wasn't rude exactly but she definitely had the air of someone who didn't suffer fools gladly. Hurriedly, Hope reached into her bag for the letter and the ring, while Ciaran did the introductions.

'I'm Professor McCormack, from the university, and this is Hope Henderson from the Ever After Emporium. As I said when we spoke on the phone, we'd like to show you some artefacts that might relate to Elenor Lovelace and perhaps see if you can answer some of our questions.'

Isobel pursed her lips. 'It was all a very long time ago. She's been dead for decades.'

Hope summoned up her most professional smile. 'I'm not sure whether you know the Ever After Emporium – it's just around the corner from here, on the corner of High Petergate and Minster Gates.' Isobel grunted in recognition and Hope went on. 'A few weeks ago, we discovered a letter we believe was written by your great-great aunt hidden in a cedarwood puzzle box. With it was a ring – quite a special ring – and we've been trying to find its rightful owner ever since.'

The old woman's voice crackled with suspicion. 'What kind of letter?'

Hope glanced at Ciaran, who took up the tale. 'It's a letter breaking off an engagement. We thought perhaps—'

There was the merest hint of indrawn breath as Isobel became oddly still. 'What does it say?'

'We brought it with us – I can show you if you'd like?'

The old woman shook her head. 'No need for that. Just read it aloud, if you please.'

Hope didn't dare look at Ciaran as she passed him the letter. That elicited another ill-tempered sigh from Isobel. 'Not him – you. I'm sure you don't have the breeding, but I want to imagine it's my aunt reading it.'

Beside her, Ciaran seemed to be trying not to laugh. Hope took a deep calming breath. They seemed to have got off on the wrong foot with Isobel and she wasn't sure why, other than the fact that Isobel was clearly determined to be as disagreeable as possible. But Hope decided she might as well do as she'd been asked; she dug deep for her business voice and read the letter aloud, doing her best to imbue the words with all the emotion she thought Elenor might have felt as she wrote. When she'd finished reading, Isobel didn't move.

'Did you say there was a ring?' she said at length, when Ciaran had discreetly cleared his throat.

'I did,' Hope replied nervously. 'Would you like to hold it?'

Isobel gave an imperious nod. Hope got to her feet and crossed the living room to place the scarab ring in Isobel's wrinkled hands. At first, she wasn't sure whether she'd imagined the faint sigh as the old woman ran her fingers across the rounded emerald and diamond encrusted sides. Then Isobel smiled in a way that seemed to light up the whole room and Hope was stunned to see two tears appear on her cheeks. 'It's so good to hold this again,' she said in a voice that was warm with emotion. 'I thought it was lost forever.'

On the other side of the room, Ciaran leaned forwards. 'It did belong to Elenor then?'

Isobel stayed silent for a moment, still caressing the ring. 'I suppose there's no harm in telling you now. Everyone involved is long dead. Yes, it belonged to her. It was the ring Khalid gave to her when she agreed to become his wife.'

Hope glanced at Ciaran, who nodded imperceptibly in recognition of the matching initial but said nothing.

'This was back in nineteen twenty two, when Elenor was out in Egypt, working in the Valley of the Kings,' Isobel went on. 'That fool Carter hadn't been able to find anything of note and was about to give up, but Elenor knew they were close. She'd been working with the local archaeologists, you see, gaining their trust and encouraging them to confide in her. There was one in particular who seemed cleverer than all the rest – a doctor of Archaeology from the University of Cairo called Khalid Al Nazari. I suppose you can guess the rest.'

'They fell in love,' Hope said softly. 'But her family didn't approve.'

Isobel let out a long sigh. 'It didn't matter how well-respected he was in the archaeological community, or how well-educated. All Elenor's parents saw was the colour of his skin. How could they welcome such a man into their society, they asked? How could they be expected to accept any grandchildren?'

She lapsed into brooding silence for several long seconds. Neither Hope not Ciaran dared speak in case they broke the spell. Instead, they waited.

'When Elenor was taken ill and had to return to England, they took their chance,' Isobel continued, with a shake of her head. 'They ensured she was locked away in a sanitorium, supposedly for her own good. And they hired a group of Cairo street thieves to ensure Khalid got the message too.'

Hope couldn't help it; she gasped. Even Ciaran looked pale. 'Did they – did he . . .'

Isobel sniffed. 'They didn't kill him, if that's what you're asking. As bad as my forebears were, they did at least draw the line at murder. But he was badly injured. His recovery took many months. And in the meantime, they persuaded Elenor to write the letter you read to me, breaking off the engagement. But as you might suspect, it was never sent.'

'So, what happened?' Hope asked, wondering how the letter and ring had come to be included in a house clearance some ninety years after the events Isobel described. 'Did Khalid recover?'

'I don't know,' Isobel replied. 'As you probably know, Elenor took the broken engagement very badly. I don't know what they threatened her with, to make her write those terrible words, but she was almost mad with grief. She disappeared in the storms over Whitby one night in April.'

'It's an awfully tragic story,' Ciaran said, his tone heavy with respect. 'I wonder why they never sent the letter. It seems they went to a lot of bother to get her to write it – why not send it to Khalid and make sure he knew the engagement had been broken by Elenor herself?'

Isobel hesitated. 'I expect he went to ground after the attack. They probably didn't have an address for him.'

Ciaran frowned. 'But they could have sent it care of the University.'

The old woman sighed again, and this time Hope sensed she was running out of patience. 'I don't know why,' she said. 'Maybe they thought it had been sent. Or maybe they thought they'd done enough.'

Hope saw Ciaran open his mouth to frame another question and caught his eye. If they handled this the right way, Isobel might talk to them again. But if they pushed her now in a direction she didn't want to follow . . .

'Would you like to claim ownership of the ring, Miss

Lovelace?' she asked, remembering her instructions from Mr Young.

Isobel looked thoughtful for a moment and her fingers brushed the emerald once again. 'No,' she said, after a moment's reflection. 'I don't want it here. Elenor came to think it was cursed in the end. You keep it – put it on display somewhere or hide it away for another hundred years. I don't care.'

'Are you sure?' Hope said, frowning at the hint of something unspoken behind the older woman's words. 'It's worth a lot of money.'

The old woman tipped her head. 'Quite sure. Take it away, please.'

She turned her head to stare out of the window. Hope and Ciaran took that as their cue to leave and got to their feet. 'Thank you for sharing your family's story,' Hope said as Isobel showed them to the door. 'We really appreciate it.'

'It's all ancient history,' Isobel replied, and Hope wasn't sure if she was speaking to herself or to them. 'They're just ghosts now.'

Ciaran didn't speak until they were outside once more, being warmed by the evening sunlight. 'I'll tell you what, they say Irish parents are terrifying but they've got nothing on the English aristocracy.'

Hope shuddered. 'I know. What an awful way to behave.'

He shook his head and sighed. 'Yeah. Look, I don't know about you, but I need a drink. Want to join me?'

This time, Hope didn't need to think twice. 'Absolutely. As long as the first round is on me.'

Unsurprisingly, one drink led to another. At some point, Hope had realized she was hungry and they'd gone to a beautiful old Italian restaurant Ciaran knew on Gillygate, where they'd eaten pasta and drunk mellow red wine and laughed until the evening was almost gone. And now they were weaving slightly unsteadily along Fossgate, towards Hope's apartment.

'You really don't have to do this,' Hope said for the third time as they walked. 'I'm perfectly capable of getting home, you know.'

Ciaran smiled. 'I know. But indulge me, okay? I want to be sure you get back in one piece.'

'But who's going to make sure you get back in one piece?' she teased.

He laughed. 'I'll be fine. No one's going to pick a fight with a strapping Irish fella like me.'

Hope sniffed. 'I bet that's what Khalid thought.' She replayed the words in her head and made a mental adjustment. 'Probably not the Irish bit. But the rest of it.'

Ciaran was quiet for a moment. 'Did any of Isobel's story seem a bit strange to you?'

'Apart from all of it, you mean?'

'Well, yes,' he agreed. 'I can't shake the feeling it doesn't quite hang together. There's something about it that doesn't make sense.'

Frowning, Hope recalled the way Isobel had described the ring as cursed. 'I know what you mean. But maybe she doesn't remember it all. It happened a long time ago, and she could only have heard the details second-hand.'

'Or third-hand, if they didn't talk about it much,' Ciaran observed. 'I don't know, it was just a feeling. I'm probably over-thinking it.'

They had reached Foss Bridge and Hope stopped to watch the river flow beneath the modest stone parapets. Old-fashioned lamp posts stood like sentinels on the middle of the bridge and someone had woven lights in a tree that stood along one of the riverbanks. The reflection danced on the lapping water, reminding Hope a little of London. 'It's like a miniature South Bank,' she said, smiling. 'So pretty.'

'Beautiful,' Ciaran murmured, and it took Hope a heart-beat to realize he wasn't looking at the lights. She half turned and discovered he was much closer than she'd thought. 'Hope,' he murmured. 'How would you feel if I kissed you right now?'

Her heart thudded in her chest as she gazed up at him and tried to nudge her startled brain into answering. But her lack of reply didn't seem to matter; Ciaran evidently decided her eyes told him everything he needed to know. Slowly, he placed one finger under her chin and tilted it up. A moment later, his lips were on hers, the lightest of feathery touches that hardly felt like a kiss at all and yet somehow managed to set all Hope's senses alight. His face hovered above hers, waiting for a sign that he should go on, and suddenly Hope realized there was nothing she wanted more. Reaching up, she cupped his face with her hands and drew him towards her.

At first, it wasn't a passionate kiss. Neither of them seemed to be in a hurry to reach a particular destination. He tasted of Limoncello, the last drink they'd had at the restaurant, and Hope was dimly aware that they were standing on the bridge, leaning against the parapet and kissing like a pair of teenagers, but she didn't care. And as the kiss grew in intensity, she lost all sense of where they were. All she could think about was how wonderful it felt to be in Ciaran's arms, her heart thudding and her skin tingling; how she suddenly felt more alive than she had in years, and how she never wanted this kiss to end.

When they finally broke apart, she had to hold onto him for balance. 'Wow,' he said, gazing at her with a gentle grin. 'I'm better than I thought.'

She smiled and nestled against his chest, steadying herself both inside and out. 'I've thought of a solution to the problem of you getting home safely.'

'Oh?' he said, against her hair. 'And what's that?'

Taking a deep lungful of air, she exhaled all the way, silently testing the words before she let them escape. 'You could not go home at all.'

She felt the breath catch in Ciaran's chest. He pulled back a little to look quizzically into her eyes. 'You're sure?'

The question reverberated fuzzily in Hope's head: was she sure? Spending the night with someone was a big step, one she hadn't been tempted to take since Rob's death. But he'd been adamant that she learn to love again, in time, and if losing him had taught her anything it was that life should be lived in the moment, without regrets. And then her booze-fuddled synapses arced to Elenor Lovelace, whose mysterious letter had brought Hope and Ciaran together. She had a feeling his hunch was right – that there was more of the story for them to uncover – but that could wait for another day. Right here and now, the only thing Hope was interested in was the way Ciaran made her feel.

Aware that he was awaiting her answer, Hope did her best to focus. When it came down to it, all that mattered was whether she would regret letting him walk away from her again. And she knew beyond all doubt that she would.

Lifting her head, Hope smiled at Ciaran. 'I've never been surer of anything.'

And she stood on tiptoe to kiss him again.

PART TWO

Secret Loves

Chapter Nine

'Okay, Hope, spill the beans.'

It was Sunday afternoon and Hope's sister, Charlotte, was looking at her with the kind of determined curiosity the entire Henderson family knew well.

'What do you mean?' Hope asked, frowning uneasily. 'What beans?'

Charlotte reached for the roasting tin on the draining board and wrapped the tea-towel around it. 'The ones that have put roses in your cheeks and a dreamy look in your eyes. Something has made you happy.' She paused to fire another razor-sharp look Hope's way. 'Or is it some*one*?'

Hope fixed her suddenly panicked gaze on the sink full of post-lunch washing up. Charlotte couldn't know what she'd done the night before – she couldn't. Casting a hurried look over one shoulder, Hope checked none of their family was within earshot. Thankfully, everyone seemed to have gravitated into the garden to soak up the June sunshine – she and Charlotte were alone in the kitchen. 'I don't know what you're talking about,' she said, as robustly as she could.

'I think you do,' Charlotte replied. 'You've gone all red.'

Hope didn't need a mirror to know that was true – she could feel her face glowing like a furnace. Was there any point in trying to deflect her sister's laser-like focus when her own skin was betraying her? 'Must be the hot water,' she said, with an unconvincing nod at the soap suds covering her hands. 'And it is hot in here. Aren't you hot?'

Charlotte nodded peaceably. 'It is and I am. But there's no point in trying to distract me. I'm not the only one who's noticed.'

Not for the first time, Hope wondered what it was like to be part of a family that didn't regard privacy as optional. She was fairly sure their father wouldn't have observed anything different about her demeanour, and even if he had, he was far more likely to raise it with her discreetly – working up to it through a seemingly innocuous text message or phone call. But their mother held the same view as Charlotte and their oldest brother, Harry, which was that no part of Hope's life was off-limits. In their defence, they had only been this bad since she'd been widowed two years earlier and she knew they meant well. Now that she'd moved back to York, it was easier for them to keep an eye on her and take a more direct interest. Which was why she was blushing to the tips of her ears and desperately wondering how to deflect her sister's attention.

'I've been getting more exercise,' she said. 'I suppose

walking to and from the Emporium is making me healthier. Maybe that's it.'

And now Charlotte laughed. 'Nice try. I've heard exercise can work miracles but I can honestly say it's never put a twinkle in my eye.' When Hope didn't reply, she paused and placed a hand on her arm. 'Look, I know it's none of my business. It's just nice to see you happy, that's all.'

Hope swirled fluffy bubbles around a saucepan and sighed. The trouble was, it kind of *was* her sister's business – her whole family's business, in fact – because they'd been there for Hope when everything had fallen apart and whenever she'd needed them since. They'd held her tight in the bad times – wasn't it only fair that they shared in her good times too? Although perhaps not in too much detail, she thought, as a memory of the night before caused a delicious rush of heat to radiate up from her core. There were some things her mother never needed to know.

'If I tell you, do you promise not to get carried away?' she said, after a few more seconds of silence.

Charlotte gave her a wide-eyed look. 'When have I ever done that?'

That caused Hope to smile, because Charlotte was famous for picking up the ball and running with it. 'It's early days, we've only been on a couple of dates. Don't go planning a hen do.'

'I promise,' Charlotte said solemnly, then leaned closer. 'Now, who is he?'

Hope summoned up an image of Ciaran McCormack,

the tall, dark professor in whose arms she'd spent the night. With laughing grey eyes and a lyrical Irish lilt that could charm the Pharaohs from their pyramids, he'd reminded her what it was like to while away the darkness kissing and whispering and exploring. She ought to feel exhausted; instead, she felt alive.

'Someone I met through work,' she said carefully. 'He's helping me research the ring and the letter we found at the Emporium last month – the one inside the puzzle box.'

The story of the mysterious woman who'd apparently broken both her engagement and her fiancé's heart in 1923 had been the subject of much interest among Hope's family, as had the way it had been discovered, by a four-year-old girl named Brodie with a talent for impenetrable Moroccan puzzle boxes. Charlotte raised both eyebrows as she added two and two. 'Not the guy who's adopting his niece?'

'No!' Hope's hands flapped in consternation, sending soap suds flying through the air as she pictured Will Silverwood, who'd brought Brodie into the antique shop to escape the rain one Thursday morning in May and discovered more than any of them had bargained for. 'No, that's Will – he's a jeweller, owns the big shop beside the Shambles. Definitely not him.'

Charlotte reached out and caught an iridescent floating bubble in the palm of her hand. 'Okay, not Will. But does he have a name, this research assistant of yours?'

It couldn't do any harm to answer the question, Hope decided. It might only be two weeks since she and Ciaran had fallen tipsily into each other's arms but they'd spent three blissful nights together since then and she had no reason to think there wouldn't be more in the near future. Besides, there was no way Charlotte would give up until she had his name. 'Ciaran McCormack,' Hope replied, trying not to grin. 'And I think I'm his research assistant, to be honest. He's a Professor of Egyptology at the university.'

'An archaeologist,' Charlotte said slowly, as though testing the idea out. 'I don't think I've ever seen one, other than on TV. How old is he? Does he have a terrible beard?'

'No! He's in his forties, dark-haired, and has that stubble that looks really sexy on some men.' Hope paused to consider the best way to describe Ciaran's roguish appeal. 'He definitely doesn't look like a professor. At least, not any of the ones at my uni.'

'A *sexy* archaeologist,' Charlotte repeated, then bit her lip. 'Oh my god, Hope, you're shagging Indiana Jones!'

'Charlotte!' Hope spluttered. 'I am not!'

'Sounds like it to me,' her sister said, eyes dancing. 'Has he got a big whip?'

Hope felt her face start to flame again. 'Stop it!'

But it seemed Charlotte was having way too much fun to spare her blushes. 'Did he offer to show you his ancient artefacts? Is that how he got you into bed?'

'I'm not going to dignify that with an answer,' Hope said, as her sister tried to stop giggling. 'Are you sure you're older than me?'

'Sorry,' Charlotte said, regaining her composure after a

moment had passed. 'He sounds great and he's obviously good for you. That's all that matters.'

'Thank you,' Hope said, unable to prevent a small smile from curving her lips. 'He is pretty great, actually.'

'So, when do we get to meet him?' Charlotte's eyes widened as a thought obviously occurred to her. 'Hey, you could bring him to Mum and Dad's party!'

Hope rinsed the last pan clean and pulled the plug from the sink. 'Of course. A surprise ruby wedding anniversary bash is the perfect *en masse* introduction to the family.'

Charlotte shrugged. 'At least he'd meet us all in one go.'

'No,' Hope said firmly. 'The party is just over a month away and, like I said, it's still early days with Ciaran. It's way too soon to be thinking about meeting each other's families.'

'Spoilsport.'

'Realist,' Hope responded and attempted to change the subject. 'How's the planning coming along, anyway? Need me to do anything more?'

Thankfully, Charlotte seemed prepared to let the subject of her sister's love life rest. For now, at least. 'Everything is in hand, I think. Most of Mum and Dad's friends have confirmed now and they're all sworn to secrecy. Did you check with the caterer that they can supply the vegan options?'

Hope nodded. 'Yes, they've said there's no problem. They're increasing the champagne order too – another ten bottles.'

'That's Uncle Phil sorted, then,' Charlotte said wryly. 'Okay, so all we need to work out now is—'

A rustling noise outside the kitchen door caused her to stop talking abruptly. Both she and Hope looked up just in time to see their mother appear in the doorframe.

'You two look guilty,' she said, glancing back and forth between them. 'What were you whispering about?'

'Hope's new man,' Charlotte said, without missing a beat.

Their mother gave Hope an inquisitive look. 'So, there *is* someone – I look forward to hearing more. But don't skulk in here all afternoon – it's a lovely day and Harry has suggested a stroll around the village.'

'We're just coming,' Hope said, making a mental note to thank Charlotte for throwing her under the maternal bus. 'A walk sounds like a lovely idea.'

Charlotte appeared unrepentant as they followed their mother out into the garden. 'I'll call you later to discuss the party,' she murmured, 'But there's something I need to know as a matter of urgency before then.'

'Okay,' Hope replied. 'What is it?'

Her sister winked. 'Your professor. Did he keep his hat on?'

Monday was usually Hope's day off but she'd agreed to go into work to help Mr Young undertake a stock inventory. As the Minster bells struck nine o'clock, she found herself hurrying along High Petergate to the yellow-painted door of the Ever After Emporium, dodging the early bird tourists already filling the narrow, sun-dappled city streets.

'Morning!' a cheery voice called and Hope looked up from balancing cardboard coffee cups and a bag of almond croissants to see Iris, the owner of Blooming Dales, straightening up from the gloriously flower-filled buckets in front of the shop. 'What are you doing here today?'

'Stocktaking,' Hope replied. 'How are you? Good weekend?'

'Busy,' Iris said, pulling a face. 'All work and no play makes Iris wonder if running her own business is all it's cracked up to be.'

Hope grinned, knowing perfectly well that her friend loved being her own boss, although she didn't love the crack of dawn trips to the flower markets.

'But we can have a proper catch up later,' Iris went on, her expression brightening. 'Before class.'

'Of course,' Hope said warmly. Upon learning she was new to York, the florist had insisted Hope joined her weekly dance class. It was only when they'd arrived that Hope had discovered it was a belly dance class and by then it was far too late to turn tail and run. And now she wouldn't be without her weekly fix of shimmies and snake arms.

'Great,' Iris said. 'Meet you outside the studio just before eight?'

'Definitely.' Hope squinted up at the cloudless blue sky. 'Let's hope the air conditioning is working this week.'

Once inside the Emporium, she found Mr Young chatting with the other assistant, Frances. He broke off to beam at her from behind the dark wooden counter. 'Hello, Hope. Ready to do battle with the Spreadsheet of Doom?'

She laughed as she approached. 'As ready as I ever am. Are you expecting problems?'

Her employer shook his head. 'With the Emporium, any-thing is possible. But it's not a full moon so we should be fine.'

His matter-of-fact delivery gave Hope a moment's pause; she had worked at the Emporium for three months now and she still couldn't always tell when he was joking. But this time, she decided he was. 'I brought coffee and croissants. If the caffeine fix doesn't help us, the sugar rush will.'

'Impeccable logic, as usual,' Mr Young replied. 'We'll be done in no time. Wish us luck, Frances.'

'Good luck,' she said, grinning as she took the cardboard cup Hope was offering. 'Rather you than me.'

They began in the upstairs stockrooms, leaving Frances to handle customers on the shop floor. It wasn't the first time Hope had worked on the spreadsheet that helped to manage the Emporium's eclectic stock and she knew her way around it pretty well by now. Even so, it took them the best part of two hours to check off everything stored in the first-floor rooms and, as always, Hope was amazed by the wealth of treasure Mr Young deemed unworthy of display downstairs. Some items were too large for the current space available – a beautifully inlaid walnut tallboy with a matching chest of drawers that would take up far too much room on the shop floor. Others were variations of stock that was already out on display – there were seven delicate china tea services, any number of gilt-framed paintings, attributed by Mr Young to local artists, and a few old-fashioned typewriters. Hope eyed a smart Tiffany Blue machine, complete with elegant, rounded keys, and imagined how it would look in one of the Emporium's wide window displays, perhaps in front of the exquisite Japanese silk room-divider dotted with cherry blossom, and accompanied by one or two of the life size flamingos that passers-by seemed to love. Window dressing wasn't part of Hope's job but she'd whiled away several quiet afternoons in the shop mentally deciding what she'd put on display if it was up to her. Half the trouble was remembering everything the Emporium had to offer so she was enjoying the opportunity to remind herself of its hidden treasures. And it was especially nice to do so in the company of Mr Young, who had a story for almost every piece. He didn't share them all – the stocktake would have taken days if he had – but he broke up the monotony of data entry with a snippet of history here and there. And Hope found it wasn't always the obvious things that had the best tales; the ornate pewter bowl she'd initially mistaken for a soup tureen turned out to be a chamber pot that was rumoured to have belonged to Henry VIII.

'It's described in the diaries of Sir Anthony Denny, who was the King's Groom of the Stool,' Mr Young said, while Hope searched the spreadsheet for the correct record. 'If you look underneath, it's stamped with the royal symbol.'

Hope frowned. 'Groom of the Stool? Wasn't that something to do with the stables?'

Mr Young's gaze sparkled with amusement. 'Not at all. It was actually a highly prestigious job – those who held the role were among the King's most trusted advisors and could enjoy his undivided attention.' He paused for a moment. 'His *almost* undivided attention, at least.'

'But why would that include a chamber pot?' Hope wondered. And then she realized exactly why and wrinkled her nose in disgust. 'Oh! That kind of stool.'

'Not quite,' he corrected with a laugh. 'Although there's a pleasing double meaning to it, I'll grant you. No, the title refers to the close stool, which was a padded, velvet-covered seat above a boxed-in chamber pot where the King sat to follow Nature's call. The Groom's job was to keep him company while he did what needed to be done.'

Urgh. King or not, Hope couldn't imagine anything she'd like to do less. 'And that was considered a privilege, was it?'

'One of the highest,' Mr Young replied solemnly. 'The Groom could talk to the King about anything – could seek his advice or ask for favours. And listen too – I imagine he had plenty to say. But the role eventually fell out of use and evolved into general dressing duties.'

Hope shook her head. 'Thank goodness for that. Royalty or not, some experiences definitely shouldn't be shared.'

The entire stocktake was completed by mid-afternoon but Mr Young had a surprise for her. 'A consignment of Edwardian glassware came in on Saturday. I wondered whether you might like to help unbox and catalogue it.'

'Of course,' she said, without a moment's hesitation. There was a steady demand for glass of all kinds among the Emporium's customers, everything from Georgian vases to Victorian trinket boxes, and Hope was used to admiring them as she wrapped them up for their delighted new owners. To get a sneak preview of the latest stock before it went onto the shop floor was an unexpected treat.

Her employer nodded. 'There are some nice pieces, if memory serves. I think you'll enjoy them.'

His comments had been quite an understatement, Hope reflected an hour or so later as she sat among the glistening Aladdin's cave of treasure they'd created in the storeroom. There had been four large boxes from an auction Mr Young had attended in Harrogate and each box was filled with bubble-wrapped delights. She'd thought the set of etched, hollow-stemmed champagne glasses would be her favourites, until the silver-topped, blue scent bottle had caused her to gasp with delight. And then she'd discovered the amber and gilt sugar bowl and creamer, complete with matching tongs; all three items were in perfect condition, as though they had been made the week before instead of more than a century earlier.

'Imagine combining these with that yellow Wedgwood tea set we have downstairs,' she said breathlessly, holding the little jug carefully so that it caught the light. 'You could create an afternoon tea window display – no, a *champagne* afternoon tea – and showcase everything.'

Mr Young looked thoughtful. 'We could use that silver bucket and stand we catalogued earlier.' He smiled. 'It's a wonderful idea. How soon can you start it?'

'Me?' Hope said, startled. 'Frances usually does the windows, doesn't she?'

'She does,' he said. 'But this is your idea and I'm sure the two of you can work together. You're both here on Thursday, aren't you?'

Hope nodded.

'Why don't you see if you can carve out a bit of time and make some plans?' Mr Young suggested. 'Let me know which pieces you'd like to use and which window you think will work best.'

'The middle one, perhaps,' Hope said. 'Although the rocking horse might not be too happy.'

'He'll be gracious about it, I'm sure,' Mr Young said. 'In fact, he might even enjoy being out of the spotlight for a while – his coat could use a little TLC and this is the perfect opportunity to freshen him up.'

Hope couldn't deny that the project was appealing, despite the fact that she had no real idea where to begin. But that was the beauty of a team effort; her colleague could show her the ropes. 'Okay,' she said, taking a deep breath. 'I'll talk to Frances on Thursday.'

He beamed at her. 'Excellent. I can't wait to see what you come up with.'

Although she was as careful as ever, only half of Hope's attention was focussed on unwrapping the rest of the glassware – she was mentally working through the Emporium's stock, deciding what to put in the window. Even the turquoise trinket box that Mr Young identified as Victorian couldn't distract her. And then she peeled back the wrapping on the most beautifully etched decanter; semi-circles of red overlapped around the rounded bottom half like rose petals, before giving way to more delicate fronds that curled towards the slender neck. It was topped by a ruby red stopper. Six fragile cocktail glasses lay hidden by its side – Hope took them out one by one and the breath caught in her throat.

'Ah, the celebrated Edwardian overlay technique,' Mr Young said, peering over her shoulder and pointing to the red semi-circles. 'The colour is known as cranberry – very fashionable in the early part of the twentieth century. This set is by Webb, dated around 1905. A superb example, don't you think?'

'Absolutely,' Hope said, admiring the intricate pattern. 'Do I dare ask how expensive it is?'

Mr Young pursed his lips. 'Not as much as you might think – somewhere around the two hundred mark, I reckon.' He studied her. 'Without your staff discount, that is.'

She reached out a hand to touch the red stopper. 'It's my parents' ruby wedding anniversary,' she said. 'I've been looking out for something special, something completely impractical but equally irresistible. Is it okay for me to buy it?'

'Of course. It's certainly the right colour,' he said. 'You must pass on my congratulations – forty years of marriage is quite an achievement.'

Hope smiled. 'I will, thank you. And you're right, it is an achievement but the truth is they'd be lost without each other. In fact, I think they're more in love now than they've ever been – he still brings her a cup of tea in bed every morning and she still looks at him as though he's the most handsome man she's ever seen.'

'That's when you know it's true love,' he said, and she saw his fingers move to touch the chain of the fob watch that was folded away in the pocket of his neat grey waistcoat. 'When the years together feel like mere months.'

There was a gently wistful tone to his voice and, for the first time, Hope found herself wondering about her employer's personal life. She knew he lived alone, in a flat tucked away in the eaves of the building, but she'd never stopped to consider whether he'd always been alone. There had probably been a Mrs Young, she thought now, who'd given him the watch as a gift. And however long they'd had together, he wished it had been longer. As she did when she thought about the life she might have had with Rob.

'They're lucky,' Hope said. 'But I think they appreciate that.'

His pale blue eyes rested on hers and a flash of understanding passed between them. A brief silence grew, then Mr Young smiled. 'Lucky indeed to have a daughter to give them such a magnificent memento. Make sure you wrap it up well, and mark it with a sold sticker if you're not taking it home today.'

Hope reached for the bubble wrap and tried to sound casual. 'Do you believe in true love? The idea of a soulmate for each of us?'

'I certainly believe in true love,' Mr Young answered, after a pause. 'But perhaps not that we should spend all our time searching for that one perfect soulmate. Life isn't neat like that – sometimes we meet the right person at the wrong time, or even the wrong person at the right time.' He sighed. 'Love isn't neat, either – it might burn with the kind of slow flame that lasts a lifetime but more often it fades or something happens to smother the fire entirely.'

Again, Hope thought of Rob; people tended to assume they'd had the perfect marriage but she'd sometimes wondered, in the two years since he'd died, whether they would have lasted the distance. Now she'd never know.

Mr Young went on. 'And sometimes it burns hot and fast and consumes you both.' He gave a wry shake of his head. 'That's the kind of passion that gets all the songs and poems written about it, even though it's often the most destructive. Unfortunately, it's tricky to predict which love you're going to get. But they all feel true at the time.'

His hand touched his waistcoat again and Hope almost asked which love had given him the watch. But her nerve failed; he was her boss, after all. 'Thank you,' she said instead. 'My parents are going to be thrilled.'

A smiled creased his face. 'Then my work here is done.'

Chapter Ten

The balcony of Hope's riverside apartment glowed in the last of the evening sunlight. She gazed across the rounded bistro table at Ciaran and tried to sound casual. 'How is it?'

He finished his mouthful of sea bass and sat back in his chair, dark hair glistening and looking for all the world like a rock star who'd escaped his entourage. 'Like the food of the gods. Delicious.'

More relieved than she cared to admit, Hope scooped up a forkful from her own plate. She and Rob had loved to entertain but it had been a long time now since she'd cooked for someone else – kind friends had made meals for her in the weeks and months following Rob's death, or else they'd gone out to eat. As time went by, if she had invited anyone round to her apartment, they'd ordered a takeaway. She cooked for herself, of course, but that wasn't the same as making something for another person to eat. Cooking for others was more stressful than she remembered, especially when it was someone she wanted to impress.

'It's hard to go wrong with a Gabe Santiago recipe,' she said modestly, waving a hand at the lemon-drizzled fish with roasted cherry tomatoes and Jersey Royal potatoes. 'My mum got me his book for Christmas and this was so easy to make even I couldn't mess it up.'

Ciaran reached for his wine glass and raised it towards her. 'It's not the recipe, Hope. It's what you do with it that counts.'

The accompanying smile was so full of charm that it felt churlish of her to argue. Instead, Hope chinked her glass against his. 'Cheers,' she said, taking a long sip of crisp, cool Pinot Grigio. 'And thank you.'

'It should be me thanking you,' Ciaran went on. 'Between the end of year meetings, final assignments and stressed-out students, I've been living on Big Macs and Pot Noodles for weeks. It's grand to eat something home-cooked.'

'You have not,' Hope replied, eyeing the flat stomach beneath his shirt.

'It's true,' he said sorrowfully. 'I'm just a sad, lonely academic who needs the love of a good woman to save him from malnutrition.'

She laughed. 'I guess you won't be returning the invitation, then.'

He gave a mock shudder. 'Trust me, you don't want to visit my university digs. They don't have views like this, for a start,' he said, nodding at the pink-tinged sunset and the light dancing across the water of the wharf. 'And I'm no one's idea of a chef – it's better all-round if I take you out for dinner when it's my turn.'

She didn't believe Ciaran McCormack was inadequate at anything but his mention of final assignments did remind Hope of something she'd been meaning to ask. 'What happens when you get to the end of the year? Do you spend much time in York over the summer break?'

'Not much, no,' he said, taking another sip of wine. 'I've nothing against the city's tourists but you can hardly move for them most days. Although Scarborough's not much better.'

Hope's mouth twisted in wry agreement; the seaside town was a famously popular British holiday resort and tourists flocked to enjoy the golden beaches. 'I haven't been there for years,' she said. 'But I don't suppose it's changed much.'

'Not much,' he conceded. 'But I live just outside the town so the visitors don't really trouble me. And I like being near the sea – it reminds me there's plenty of world I've yet to explore.'

All of which tied in to Hope's growing suspicion that it was going to be hard for them to see much of each other over the summer. Unless they made a major breakthrough with their research into the tragedy of Elenor Lovelace and Hope could tempt him back to York. It wasn't the end of the world – she had plenty to keep her busy – but she had to admit she was enjoying his company more and more. She was going to miss their dates.

'So, what's the big news you mentioned?' she asked, deciding to change the subject.

His grey eyes brightened as he leaned forward. 'You know we'd hit that brick wall when it came to uncovering what had happened to Elenor's fiancé in Egypt?'

They had, Hope recalled, after a visit to Elenor's last surviving relative hadn't gone quite as well as they'd anticipated. Isobel Lovelace had revealed that her great-great aunt had fallen in love with an Egyptian archaeologist named Khalid Al Nazari, and that the relationship had scandalized her family back in England, but she'd been reluctant to give away much in the way of details. Hope knew Ciaran had spoken to a number of colleagues at other universities to see if they could shed any light on Khalid's professional accomplishments, or what had become of him after Elenor had ended their relationship. So far, information had been sketchy and Hope had begun to wonder whether there was anything more to uncover. 'Yes,' she said. 'Have you found something new?'

'Well, Isobel was right when she said he worked at the University of Cairo,' Ciaran said. 'I found him referenced in a number of archaeological reports between the late nineteen tens to early nineteen twenties – fairly standard stuff for the most part but he had some interesting theories about the Valley of the Kings.'

Hope thought back to their meeting with Isobel a few weeks earlier. 'She did say he'd worked on the excavations – that was how he met Elenor.'

'Exactly,' Ciaran said. 'So, I'd expected him to be named on some of the papers and reports that came out after Tutankhamun's tomb was discovered by Howard Carter. Plenty of other local archaeologists and academics were – Carter gets all the glory but it was a collaborative effort. I couldn't find anything naming a Dr Al Nazari, though.'

She winced as she recalled another part of the tale they'd heard from Elenor's great-great niece. 'Not a massive surprise, given that the Lovelace family had him beaten almost to death.'

Ciaran gave her a significant look. 'That's according to Isobel and she's telling the story second-hand – she didn't witness things personally. I wanted to see if there was anything that proves Khalid was involved with the excavations.'

For a moment, Hope felt like one of his students but his observation made sense; hadn't her school teachers always gone on about the reliability of historical sources? 'Let me guess – you drew a blank.'

But she could tell from the triumphant sparkle in his eyes that she was wrong. 'Nope,' he said. 'I mean, I wouldn't say it's an embarrassment of riches but it was in the most obvious place possible.'

He was really enjoying himself, Hope realized, and she supposed she couldn't blame him – this was his specialist subject, after all. 'Which was?'

'Howard Carter's excavation diaries!' Ciaran crowed. 'They're not what you'd call a riveting read – there's a lot of really dull detail about the comings and goings of various officials and visitors to the site, and he has a weird obsession with donkeys. But in amongst all of that, there was one reference to a Dr Al Nazari – a few mentions of Dr A–N and occasionally the name Khalid, which could be someone else with the same name, of course.' He paused and raised an eyebrow. 'And once or twice, I saw the initials EL. On the same dates as Dr A–N.'

Hope clapped her hands in delight. 'It must be them! What did it say?'

Ciaran sighed. 'Nothing much of any use, unfortunately. Carter was a brilliant archaeologist but his diary entries are eminently practical. I've only looked at the early journals so far but I'm going to keep reading to see if Khalid features after nineteen twenty three.'

'That's so exciting,' she said, and smiled. 'Well done for finding them.'

He tipped his head, acknowledging her praise. 'We may not be able to unravel what really happened,' he warned. 'But at least what we've learned so far ties in with Isobel's story and we've got a better idea where to start digging for more. And you don't have to leave it all to me – Carter's diaries are available online. You can have a look for yourself.'

The conversation she'd had with Charlotte about being Ciaran's research assistant popped into Hope's mind; that was exactly where this was heading. But his enthusiasm was contagious and, if she was honest, Elenor Lovelace had hooked her with the letter.

'Sounds like a plan,' she said, piling the empty dinner

plates of top of each other and getting to her feet. 'I'll just get rid of these and then maybe you can show me where to find the diaries.'

'Did I thank you properly for cooking?' he asked, once they'd cleared the table and Hope was rinsing the plates to load into the dishwasher.

'I'm sure you did,' she said over one shoulder as she ran the hot tap. 'But I wouldn't mind if you thanked me again. I'm a praise junkie.'

'Thank you,' he said, and she realized he was right behind her. His lips brushed the nape of her neck with feathery touches. 'Whoever said the way to a man's heart was through his stomach knew what they were talking about.'

Hope closed her eyes and swallowed a gasp as her skin tingled. 'You're welcome,' she managed.

'And at the risk of getting distracted from our very important research, I've realized there's another advantage to having a night in,' he murmured, his breath warm against her ear.

Hope gripped the sink, thoughts of Carter's dusty diaries melting away. 'Oh? What's that?'

Ciaran's hands rested on her waist as he turned her round to face him. 'It's no distance at all to the bedroom,' he said, and kissed her.

The glorious June heatwave stretched through to Thursday. The city's streets seemed busier than ever as visitors and residents alike took refuge in the shady snickelways or seized the opportunity to bask in the sun with some al fresco dining. The Emporium was busy, too; Hope wasn't sure whether it was the appeal of the cool interior or the glittering treasures inside but it felt as though she hadn't stopped all morning, much less found the time to start making plans for the new window display with Frances. By the time her lunch break rolled around, Hope was sorely in need of some peace and quiet. She cut through Minster Gates to Dean's Park and found her favourite bench, tucked away in a secluded corner beneath the shadow of the Minster. It was blessedly cool and she soon felt the stresses of the morning fade as she scanned through Howard Carter's diaries on her phone. Ciaran had been right: while the brief daily entries gave a fascinating insight into one of the most momentous archaeological discoveries of the twentieth century, they weren't big on detail. Names were often abbreviated into shortened forms or sometimes just the initials of the people who'd visited the tombs, which made it difficult to keep track of the key players. Mentions of Elenor and Khalid were sparse and neither appeared at all after April 1923, which was the date of the letter breaking off their engagement. That Elenor vanished wasn't a surprise; she'd been back in England and had tragically taken her own life just a few months later. But the fact that a noted local expert like Khalid Al Nazari was absent too made Hope uneasily wonder just how badly he'd been injured in the beating he'd endured. Isobel had been convinced he'd survived but, as Ciaran pointed out, she only knew what she'd been told. What if Elenor's death hadn't been the only tragedy?

Hope was so engrossed in her thoughts that she almost thought she was dreaming when she saw Isobel Lovelace walking purposefully along the path that led past the Minster. She was dressed in much the same way as she'd been when Hope and Ciaran had visited her at home, in wide-legged trousers and a classic linen shirt, although her white hair was hidden beneath a sun hat. Even so, Hope was sure it was her; there was something unmistakable about the way she carried herself. Should she wave, Hope wondered, or say hello? And then she remembered the elderly woman's lack of patience towards the end of their last conversation, and the definite suggestion that she didn't suffer fools. No, Hope decided, she wouldn't disturb her. Isobel Lovelace didn't seem the type to wave.

She was therefore surprised when the other woman slowed down as she passed. Isobel didn't immediately stop; as Hope watched, she took several more steps and glanced over her shoulder, as though trying to place Hope's face. Then she stopped and backtracked, frowning imperiously. 'It is you, isn't it? You're the one who found Elenor's ring.'

Hope nodded. 'Hello, Miss Lovelace. Yes, I'm Hope Henderson. How are you?'

The older woman didn't smile. 'I'm on my way to a meeting with the Archbishop. I just wanted to make sure it was really you.' There was a fractional hesitation. 'That I wasn't misremembering.'

'You're not,' Hope assured her. 'I'm sure you don't misremember much.'

Isobel sniffed. 'Well, that's true. Anyway, I'll bid you good day.'

She began to walk away. Hope almost called out after her, wanting to share the news of Ciaran's find but, really, what was there to say? A few initials in Carter's journal entries didn't amount to much and she could imagine Isobel's scathing response. But it felt rude to say nothing. 'Bye,' she called. 'I hope your meeting goes well.'

If Isobel heard, she gave no sign. Hope sighed and went back to her phone. So much for the idea that she and Ciaran might call on Isobel Lovelace again in the future if they had more questions. It looked very much like she wasn't interested in talking, at least not to Hope.

Hope stood in the middle of High Petergate, her head tilted to one side as she gazed critically at the centre window of the Ever After Emporium. It was Friday afternoon, the weather showed no sign of breaking and Hope's t-shirt was sticking to her back. But she didn't mind that sweat was mingling with dust to create a grimy sheen on her skin, nor was she bothered that almost all of her nails were broken, because the Afternoon Tea at the Emporium window display was complete. And it looked even better in reality than it had in her head.

'Wow!' Iris said, crossing the road to stand next to Hope. 'Are you sure you haven't done this before? It's amazing!'

'You can thank Frances for that,' Hope said, grimacing. 'She's the brains of the operation. I just shifted things around and made the tea.'

Iris snorted. 'I've been staring at the windows of the Emporium for years and they've never looked this good. And isn't it supposed to be your day off?'

Hope fanned her overheated cheeks. 'It was the only day we could do it – Frances is away on holiday tomorrow.'

'Hmmm. I'm just saying that you can't get away with pretending you don't deserve any credit,' Iris said. 'And I must say that collection of vases looks stunning. I'm half-tempted to buy them for my windows.'

Hope smiled. The vases were a mismatched selection from the stockroom that she'd clustered together at various heights to create a tumbling display of artificial blooms, supplied and arranged by Iris. A crystal chandelier dangled above the white-clothed table, which was set for a sumptuous afternoon tea with an eclectic assortment of fine china and glassware. Two Rennie Macintosh chairs stood angled on either side of the table, as though the diners had temporarily left their feast and would be back at any moment. Hope had to admit she was pleased; the mixture of styles and eras shouldn't have worked and yet somehow the result was magical. It was certainly catching the eyes of people walking along High Petergate; a small crowd was gathering on the pavement.

Iris gave her a sideways glance. 'Looks like you might have found your artistic calling,' she said. 'Welcome to the Dark Side.'

'I don't know about that,' Hope said, ruefully massaging her lower back. 'I might not be able to move tomorrow.

But if it helps some of the Emporium's treasures to find new homes, then it will all have been worth it.'

'Judging from this crowd, it definitely will,' Iris agreed, then checked her watch. 'Right, I've got deliveries to make. I'm going to see your Miss Lovelace, actually. She's one of my regular customers, takes two bouquets of lilies and roses every Friday without fail.'

Hope blinked in surprise. Of course – she'd noticed the scent of flowers in the air when she'd been to Isobel's penthouse apartment and had admired the bouquet in the living room as they'd talked. Why hadn't she guessed that the blooms came from Iris? And then an idea popped into her head – a way to soften Isobel's attitude towards Hope and perhaps pave the way for another meeting.

She turned to her friend with an optimistic smile. 'It's just possible you can do me a favour . . .'

Chapter Eleven

True to her prediction, Hope spent most of the weekend wincing as her aching muscles complained about the workout she'd put them through on Friday. She was almost glad when Ciaran called off their Saturday night date at the last minute. The soreness wasn't enough to stop her from cycling over to her parents' house for Sunday lunch but her pained expression was immediately picked up on by the rest of her family and it became a running joke for the rest of the afternoon. She'd even began to question the wisdom of going to her Monday evening belly dancing session with Iris but she knew her friend would be disappointed if she didn't go. And really, could there be anything better than shimmying to relieve the tightness in her muscles?

The studio was wonderfully cool after the heat of summer outside and was already filled with the usual diverse assortment of dancers when Hope and Iris arrived just before eight. The class was popular, aimed at a mixed range of abilities and it never ceased to amaze Hope so many no-nonsense Yorkshire women were happy to dress in gauzy, jingling outfits and twirl along to music that called to mind images of palm-shaded Arabian courtyards rather than the higgledy-piggledy streets of York. Perhaps that was half the appeal, Hope thought, as she let the chatter and laughter wash over her – perhaps it was a chance to escape real life and pretend to be someone else for an hour every week. Or maybe it was the almost palpable sense of camaraderie in the room; there was no judgement here, no sideways glance at a less-than-washboard stomach. In this dance class, the belly was queen and the shape of your body mattered less than the way you moved it. Which was why most of Hope's fellow dancers had more skin on show than they normally would, even in summer. It had taken Hope a while to summon up the confidence to wear her own yoga top to dance but now she barely gave it a thought.

Iris nudged her. 'Your window display has been getting a lot of love over the weekend. I had six corporate customers ask if I could recreate that flower arrangement for their premises, including Bells of York.'

Hope gaped. Bells of York was probably the most upmarket hotel within the city walls. 'Really?'

'Really,' Iris confirmed. 'On a bigger scale, for their Palm Court. They said they loved the "faded decadence" aesthetic of the window display. You'd better set up an Instagram account, sharpish – you're an influencer now.'

'Wow,' Hope said, with a small laugh at the suggestion

she was in any way influential. 'I had no idea it would make such a splash.'

'I imagine Mr Young is over the moon,' Iris went on. 'The shop seemed busier than ever on Saturday.'

'I guess I'll find out tomorrow,' Hope said. 'But I'm glad it's boosted your business too.'

The florist nodded in satisfaction. 'Oh, and I took the flowers you asked for to Isobel Lovelace. She seemed pleased.'

Her words gave Hope the quiet pleasure of ticking off something that had been niggling at her for weeks; now she felt as though she had thanked Isobel properly for sharing some fairly unflattering aspects of her family's behaviour to shine a light on the story of Elenor and the scarab beetle ring.

'I'm really glad,' Hope said. 'Thanks for delivering them.'

'My pleasure,' Iris replied. 'She's a strange one. I've been delivering her flowers for over a year now and I've never seen anyone there, other than the cleaner or someone else doing some kind of job. No family or friends.'

Hope thought back to her visit to Isobel's apartment. Had there been photographs on display? She didn't think there had. 'I'm not sure she has any family left. Nobody close, anyway.'

Iris sighed. 'That's sad. I know she's stinking rich and probably has connections all over the city but she seems pretty alone.' She paused thoughtfully. 'Maybe that's how she likes it.'

It was certainly true that Isobel had been prickly towards Hope and Ciaran, even unfriendly, but Hope had put it down to a touch of arrogance and the fact that they'd been intruding on her to discuss a subject that was clearly uncomfortable, even though Elenor Lovelace had been dead for almost a century. And yet now that Hope came to think about it, there had been a sense of solitude about Isobel. Whether it was something the elderly woman cultivated was anyone's guess but Hope was glad all over again that she'd sent the flowers via Iris.

A movement from the front of the studio caught her eye; Fleur had finished her conversation with Linda and was standing in front of the floor-to-ceiling mirrors that lined the wall, smiling at everyone in a way that signified she was ready to begin. 'Good evening, everyone,' she called, her smile as dazzling as ever. 'I hope you've all had a wonderful weekend. I'm looking forward to dancing with you tonight.'

As always, her warmth and enthusiasm rippled over the assembled women. They broke off whatever conversations they'd been having and started to move into their usual places. For Hope, that meant a spot at the back of the studio, where no one could see her mistakes. She'd come to appreciate that learning to belly dance was a gradual process, one where lengthening and strengthening the muscles and learning the right technique were just as important as remembering the steps – although it helped to avoid twirling left when everyone else was turning right, as Hope had discovered on several occasions.

The teacher guided them through the usual stretching routine and reminded them to soften their knees as they began some gentle shimmies and hip lifts. Hope watched her own reflection dance; she was definitely getting better. Most of the other women were long-term students and it showed – their movements were smooth and controlled and graceful. Iris was one of the best, Hope thought, her gaze flicking towards her friend's image in the mirror. Maybe with a few years of practice, she might aspire to be half as good. But none of them could hold a candle to Fleur, whose every move flowed effortlessly into the next. Hope could practice for a thousand years and she'd never come close to that level of skill. But, somehow, it didn't matter – the joy of trying was enough.

As always, the hour flew by and, before Hope knew it, Fleur was leading them through a nourishing warm down routine and thanking them for joining her.

'And a quick reminder for those of you who've recently joined our class, we do encourage you to work towards showing off your belly dance skills to others. Our next show-case will be in the autumn and you are all invited to perform, whether solo or as part of a group dance.'

Hope felt her smile freeze. Dancing in a studio among women she knew was one thing – getting up on a stage to perform in front of strangers was another entirely. Her gaze slid sideways to Iris. 'Is it compulsory?'

'Of course not,' she replied evenly. 'Fleur would never make you perform if you really didn't want to.'

'Great,' Hope said with relief, her smile relaxing a little.

'Although I have heard a genie dies every time someone refuses,' Iris went on. 'But it's entirely up to you.'

Hope couldn't prevent a snort of laughter from escaping. 'I think I can live with that.'

Iris sighed. 'Can you, though? What if a downtrodden, fairy-tale street thief rubs a magic lamp and nothing happens? All their hopes and dreams of untold riches and beautiful princesses could be ruined.'

'Or a scheming Grand Vizier's evil plan might be thwarted,' Hope countered. 'I could be saving the world. I'd certainly be saving myself a lot of embarrassment.'

Her friend shook her head. 'The showcase isn't for ages yet. You might feel differently in a few months.'

'Believe me, I won't.'

'That's what I said,' Iris replied. 'And then I tried on one of the costumes and suddenly wild horses couldn't keep me from dancing in public.'

Hope gazed at her. Iris was curvy and bold, in both the way she dressed and the way she carried herself. Her dark hair, wide smile and dancing eyes demanded attention no matter what she was doing; Hope had no doubt that she would look sensational in the bright chiffon and glittering jewels of a traditional belly dancing outfit. Just as Hope, with her coppery curls and pale, freckled skin, would look utterly wrong – like a child caught dressing up in her mother's finery. 'But you can dance,' she pointed out.

'So can you,' Iris said and raised her hand to forestall Hope's objection. 'Yes, you can. And you're only going to get better.'

But now something else was troubling Hope – something

she hadn't considered until Iris had mentioned it. 'I can't wear the costume.' She gestured at her reflection in the mirror. 'I don't have the boobs, for a start.'

At this, Iris pretended to roll her eyes. 'Oh yes, it must be a terrible curse having the figure of a model,' she said, with more than a hint of good-natured sarcasm. 'Look around, Hope. None of us have perfect bodies, except Fleur who is basically a goddess. But I can tell you that none of these ladies let that stop them from dancing in the last showcase.'

Hope didn't need to look; the women around her ranged in age from mid-twenties to late fifties, of all shapes and sizes, but she could easily believe they were unfazed, were fearless and fabulous, in fact. Of course they wouldn't shy away from showing off their dance skills, along with a considerable amount of skin. But it didn't necessarily follow that Hope could do the same.

'Just think about it,' Iris said, before Hope could express her reservations. 'Give it a month and see how you feel then.'

She sounded so reasonable that Hope didn't feel she could say no. 'Okay. I'll think about it.'

Iris grinned and patted her arm. 'Good lass. Now let's go and get a drink – I need an update on Professor Sex God.'

'Iris!' Hope said, half-laughing and half-embarrassed.

'Don't *Iris* me,' her friend said, reaching for her shoes. 'My dating app action is deader than Tutankhamun. Your love life is the only thing keeping me going.'

Charlotte had claimed much the same thing, Hope recalled, although she'd cited being mum to a toddler as the reason for her nosiness. She sighed and gave Iris a level look. 'Have I ever mentioned you'd get on well with my sister?'

'No, but I'm looking forward to meeting her,' Iris replied. 'Your parents' party is going to be all kinds of fun.'

For a moment, Hope almost regretted asking Iris to take care of the flowers for the table displays; the thought of her friend and her sister joining forces to discuss her romantic encounters was terrifying. But it was far too late to back out now. She'd just have to hope their interest had died down by the time the party came round.

'Come on, then,' she said to Iris as the studio emptied out around them. 'I'll give you the latest Elenor news too.'

'I can't wait to hear it,' Iris said, and winked. 'Right after you dish the dirt on the professor.'

Chapter Twelve

There was a parcel awaiting Hope when she arrived at the Emporium on Wednesday morning.

It was neatly wrapped in brown paper and tied with string, and the handwritten label was addressed to *Hope Henderson, C/O The Ever After Emporium*.

'Don't ask who delivered it because I haven't the faintest idea,' Mr Young told her as he placed the package on the wooden counter. 'It was on the doormat when I opened up this morning – they must have popped it through the letter-box overnight.'

Hope frowned. Who on earth would send her a parcel at work? The only person she could think of was Will and he was more likely to visit when the shop was open and hand over whatever it was in person. But she wasn't expecting anything from him. She wasn't expecting anything from anyone.

She lifted the package up and carefully turned it over.

There was a faint thud as something shifted inside the wrapping: a box, perhaps. But there was really only one way to find out. Dropping her bag to the shop floor, Hope pulled at the string.

The bow came apart easily, allowing her to slide the paper open to reveal a sturdy brown lidded box, a little larger than a paperback. No clue there, she surmised, rotating the box once more to look for labels. There were none. Pushing the discarded wrapping to one side, she placed the box back on the counter and glanced up at Mr Young, who raised a questioning eyebrow but said nothing. So she lifted the lid to reveal a silica gel sachet resting on folds of soft white tissue paper.

'Someone's gone to a bit of trouble to preserve whatever this is,' Mr Young remarked. 'That looks like unbuffered tissue paper – acid free and not the kind of stuff you find in the supermarket.'

Her curiosity now well and truly piqued, Hope gingerly pulled the leaves of tissue apart. She found a battered tan leather book inside, held together by a thick band of what looked like elastic. Yellowed bits of paper protruded from each end, as though it contained loose pages or additional notes, and she could just make out faint lines that looked a lot like handwriting. She hesitated for a moment, then dipped her hand into the box and lifted the book out.

Hope knew immediately it was old. The leather was worn and cracked in places and she suspected it had lost some of its suppleness. 'Maybe I should wear gloves,' she said and glanced up to see Mr Young had produced a white cotton pair from underneath the counter. She put them on, picked the book up once more and stretched the band of elastic over the cover to open the pages within.

It appeared to be a journal. Cautiously, she leafed through the loose sheets of paper, each one covered with tiny but immaculate handwriting. And then she reached the first page of the journal itself and the breath caught in her throat. Eyes wide, she stared at the words in disbelief. *Elenor Lovelace – Egypt 1922.*

Her gloved finger traced the name even as her brain struggled to accept what she was seeing. And then she was turning the pages, squinting at the writing, praying it was what she thought it was.

'It's a diary,' she breathed, transferring her wondering gaze to Mr Young. 'Elenor's diary from Egypt.'

Her employer looked as flabbergasted as Hope felt. 'Well, well, well. I fancy there's only one person in York who could have given you something so precious. Is there a note?'

Hope combed through the tissue paper. At the bottom of the box, she discovered a thick cream envelope bearing her name. Reluctant to relinquish the diary, she almost ignored it but Mr Young was watching her expectantly, so she put the journal aside and opened the envelope. A single sheet of matching writing paper was folded inside.

Flat 9
1 Purey Cust
York

Tuesday 8th June

Dear Ms Henderson,

I trust this note finds you well.

Firstly, I must thank you for the flowers you sent last week. It was an unexpected kindness and I appreciate the gesture very much.

I have thought about your visit often over the past few weeks and have come to realize I was perhaps less helpful than I might have been. You must forgive my reluctance to divulge the details of my scandalous family history – I have been guarding these secrets for most of my life and it was something of a shock to hear of Elenor's letter and to see that unhappy ring again. The way she and Khalid were treated has always been a matter of deep shame to me and that has encouraged me to stay silent, but your visit has forced me to accept that while I cannot change the past, nor should I pretend it did not happen. I am therefore entrusting you with Elenor's journal, which I hope will shed some light on both her remarkable life and the tragedy that befell her.

I know I do not need to ask you to take very great care of the diary – the photograph in particular is one of very few that remain and I would appreciate your utmost caution

152

*when handling it. Perhaps you could contact me once you are
ready to return them both.*

Yours sincerely,
Isobel Lovelace

Wordlessly, Hope handed the letter to Mr Young and began
to turn the journal's pages, searching for the photograph
Isobel had mentioned. She found it tucked inside a tattered
pocket in the back cover of the journal, a feather-edged,
grainy black-and-white image of two men and a woman
standing beside a set of stone steps leading down into a
shadowy square doorway. One of the men was Howard
Carter; Hope recognized the stern expression and bristling
moustache beneath his cream Panama hat from the pictures
she'd found online. In contrast, the man next to him was
smiling. His skin was darker underneath his traditional Fez
and he boasted an even more luxurious moustache than
Carter. Both men wore white shirts beneath heavy-looking
suits that Hope knew must have been unbearably hot in the
sweltering Egyptian temperatures. She had no doubt that the
picture had been taken at the Valley of the Kings – she'd seen
those steps before too: they marked the entrance to the tomb
of Tutankhamun and featured in a hundred photographs of
the famous excavations. But all of that was inconsequential
detail because Hope only really had eyes for one thing: the
woman in the photograph.

Elenor was also overdressed for the heat but Hope knew
she wouldn't have had much choice. She wore a white,

long-sleeved blouse with a wide tie and a high-waisted skirt that covered all the way down to just above her ankles. The wide brim of her hat couldn't mask the mane of blonde hair underneath, just as its shadow couldn't hide the spark in her eye or the hint of a smile that played around her mouth. Hope couldn't help wondering how much that secret joy had to do with the man in the Fez. Could he be the one she'd fallen in love with?

'This is quite extraordinary,' Mr Young said, lowering the letter to look at Hope. 'It should certainly help you to unravel the mystery behind Elenor's letter.'

'It really will,' Hope replied, as another rush of gratitude flowed through her. 'What a wonderful gift from Isobel.'

Her employed nodded. 'We don't always get to know the story behind the Emporium's treasures. This is a rare treat. And I'm sure Professor McCormack would be interested in reading it too, although I imagine his interest will be in the field notes, rather than the personal aspect.'

Hope kept her face as blank as possible as she nodded; no one at the Emporium had any idea that her relationship with Ciaran was anything other than professional and she wasn't sure she was ready for it to become common knowledge yet. But Mr Young was spot on – a first-hand account of Howard Carter's excavations was exactly the kind of thing Ciaran would drool over. 'I'll send him an email once I've read it,' she said neutrally. 'That way I'll know how much detail there is.'

'Excellent idea. Depending on what the diary contains,

there may be strong interest from the University and Isobel may not be keen for her aunt's writing to be widely shared.'

It was another good point. Wishing she could start reading immediately, Hope closed the journal and wrapped it back up in the protective tissue. 'I was going to catch up with a boxset this evening but I think that's going to have to wait,' she said, replacing the cardboard lid. 'I'm going to travel back in time instead.'

Hope couldn't get home fast enough that evening. She ate a hurried dinner, thrust the dirty plate into the dishwasher and poured a glass of wine. An hour later, it was still untouched on the coffee table and Hope was happily lost in the dusty streets of Cairo, where Elenor had travelled with Howard Carter. The plan was to meet an eminent academic from the university, who had reported some interesting artefacts being touted in the markets; if the items were genuine, Elenor hoped they might offer some invaluable clues in the search for Tutankhamun's tomb.

There is little doubt that time is running out; HC fears that Lord Carnarvon is losing patience and this may be the last season he supports our endeavours. We must find something soon and these artefacts, while almost certainly stolen by local tomb robbers and orphaned from their original context, may at least prove we are digging in the right area.

The descriptions of Cairo were so vivid that Hope felt she was there with Elenor and Carter as they made their way to the rendezvous. It was early evening and the sandstone streets were bustling with traders, musicians and locals. Elenor was fascinated by everything she saw and seemed particularly taken by the snake charmers, although she was sure the cobras must have had their fangs removed. But it was the academic from the university who impressed her the most – she compared his face to those she had seen carved in marble at the British Museum and declared him to be 'more beautiful than any Pharaoh', with eyes like liquid cocoa.

His intelligence had made an impact too – she found him 'extremely well-educated and knowledgeable', with a quick, dry wit that delighted her. In fact, she was so clearly smitten that her notes on the artefacts they had discovered and bought on the market were almost sparse by comparison.

The bracelets were particularly fine, made from gold and carnelian and together with the amulet, appear to be of the type that I suspect might have adorned a King's mummy. Dr Al Nazari kindly agreed, and said similar pieces might be found throughout the city, if one knew where to look. HC was much encouraged and asked if Dr A-N might advise him further. I think we may be seeing much more of him in the future, which I confess pleases me greatly.

Hope grinned when she read the last line. 'I bet it did,' she murmured, stretching her neck and reaching for her wine. There was no doubt that Elenor had fallen for Khalid from the first moment she'd seen him but her diary did not mention him for several more days. Even then, she seemed determined to keep things business-like, and merely mentioned that he had visited the Valley of the Kings to meet with Carter. Hope cross-referenced with Carter's journal online and saw that he referred to 'Meeting with K A-N'. It all tied up, she thought to herself with a quiet surge of satisfaction. She'd become so caught up in the doomed relationship that it felt like a huge privilege to be observing Elenor and Khalid's very first meeting. She wanted to binge on the whole journal but forced herself to slow down and appreciate the incredible sense of history unfolding; Ciaran would be interested in the build up to the discovery of Tutankhamun's tomb but for Hope, it was just background. She was 100 per cent invested in Elenor and Khalid, even though she knew how it would end.

Mr Young gave her a knowing smile when he saw the next morning. 'Late night?'

'Very,' she said, stifling a yawn. 'I fell asleep reading and dreamt I was being chased through Cairo by angry crocodile men.'

He laughed. 'And they say a book at bedtime is supposed to be relaxing. I assume the diary is as fascinating as you hoped?'

'Absolutely,' she said, nodding. 'Elenor has just returned to England after the close of the winter digging season in

Egypt and is trying to persuade her parents to allow her to go back in the autumn.'

Mr Young raised his eyebrows. 'I don't suppose she's told them why.'

Hope pulled a face. 'She's said they're on the brink of an astonishing discovery, that it's imperative she returns to Egypt. But, as we know, that's only half the story.'

Elenor had only grown more enamoured of Khalid as the weeks went by. She'd laid everything bare in her diary – the quiet desperation of wanting to see him, the longing looks when he did appear, the wondering whether he'd noticed her too and the cold, hard understanding that even if he had, nothing could ever come of it. But the attraction had proved impossible to fight and, little by little, the walls between Elenor and Khalid had been chipped away until she had admitted, if only to herself within the pages of her journal, that she loved him.

'It's like a novel,' Mr Young said. 'The kind that gets turned into a Hollywood blockbuster starring that young man who seems to be in everything at the moment.'

'Nick Borrowdale,' Hope supplied, because Iris had been swooning over him on Monday evening. She thought back to the photograph tucked away in the back of the journal. 'He'd make a great Howard Carter. But you're right, it has all the ingredients of an epic romance. Except it really happened.'

He smiled. 'Every romance feels epic to the couple at its heart. That's why we keep going back for more, even when our hearts get broken.'

A heavy weight settled over Hope at the mention of broken hearts. 'I wish this one had a happier ending. But I'm trying not to think about that.'

'We can't change the past, unfortunately,' Mr Young replied sympathetically. 'But we can at least learn its lessons. Now, do you think you're up to packaging up some of the online orders? Or do you need an infusion of coffee first?'

Smothering another yawn, she flashed him a grateful look. 'Definitely coffee first. Sorry.'

He waved her apology away. 'I could do with a cup myself and I didn't spend half the night in Egypt. And besides, you were working, after a fashion.'

'Hardly,' Hope said with a rueful smile. 'But thank you.'

The look he gave her was a mixture of satisfaction and pride. 'Don't thank me. The Emporium is full of stories, just waiting to be uncovered. I think you simply found one that was meant for you.'

Chapter Thirteen

It came as something of a surprise to Hope when she realized it was over two weeks since she'd seen Ciaran. Final preparations for her parents' anniversary party were taking up more and more of her time and, when she wasn't wrangling caterers or her sister's heightened stress levels, she was engrossed in Elenor's journal. And as much as she enjoyed Ciaran's company, she also had to admit she was enjoying the time on her own. In the weeks and months after Rob's death, she often found it difficult being alone but this felt different; this was her choice. Besides, seeing Ciaran would inevitably mean she'd have to share the diary and she wasn't ready to do that. Not yet.

Elenor had returned to Egypt ahead of Carter to help smooth the way for investigations into the possible location of Tutankhamun's fabled tomb. There was no guarantee that excavations would continue; rumour had it that Lord Carnarvon was ready to pull the plug on the quest and Elenor was desperate for that not to happen. She had, by then, fallen madly in love with Khalid; the two of them had spent the summer corresponding via letter and their reunion in Cairo had led them both to admit their feelings. Hope had practically punched the air as Elenor described the moment Khalid had first kissed her, after an evening trip to the theatre in downtown Ezbekiyya.

His lips were sweeter than I could ever have dreamed. Planets may have collided, stars burned until they were cold, and I would not have noticed, for all I knew was him.

They were careful and discreet, aware that their relationship would undoubtedly raise eyebrows, but the truth was that Cairo was in the grip of the Roaring Twenties – attitudes and taboos had relaxed. And then Carter had arrived, at the end of October, with the news that he had persuaded Lord Carnarvon to fund one last season. Elenor wrote that it was a gift in more ways than one and began to dream that she and Khalid might find a way to make things work. But the discovery of Tutankhamun's tomb, just a few days later, turned everything upside down. Suddenly, the eyes of the world were upon the excavations and Elenor was reminded that attitudes in England towards a mixed-race relationship were not as liberal as those in Cairo. Even so, she hoped her family would be swayed by Khalid's impeccable education and social standing and might see him through her eyes.

It was reaching the uncovering of the tomb that made

Hope think of Ciaran. She ought to contact him, tell him what Isobel had given her, but she told herself it made sense to read the whole thing first so that she knew exactly what she was sharing. She had a niggling suspicion that he might play the academic card and demand that she hand the diary over. If that happened, she would have to decline, or at the very least ask Isobel's permission first. But then he'd messaged out of the blue on Tuesday, asking if she wanted to meet for a drink after work, and she'd been filled with a sudden desire to see his smile. Dithering, she had forwarded the text to Iris, who was in favour of Hope meeting him and had walked across the street from Blooming Dales to reiterate her point.

'You don't have to mention the journal,' she said, leaning against the Emporium door frame. 'You can't tell me the two of you only talk about Elenor.'

Hope pressed her lips together thoughtfully as she considered the last few times she and Ciaran had been together. 'She's bound to come up, though.'

'Distract him, then,' Iris countered. 'Make sure you look amazing, so all he can think about is what he wants to do to you.'

Blushing, Hope checked to make sure none of the other Emporium staff were in hearing range. 'He's really interesting. I like hearing him talk.'

Iris shuddered. 'Do yourself a favour – never tell him that. In my experience, men don't need any encouragement to monopolize the conversation.'

She had a point, Hope thought wryly, but Ciaran wasn't like that. 'I don't know. I do want to see him but . . .'

She trailed off, unable to articulate the vague sense of reluctance she felt. Iris folded her arms. 'Listen, a good-looking Irish charmer in the hand is worth two in the bush.' Iris stopped, frowning. 'Okay, that needs work. Or maybe it doesn't. Anyway, what I mean is, some of us would love the opportunity to go on a date with a normal single man who doesn't spend all night staring at your chest.'

Hope couldn't help it – she laughed. 'When you put it like that . . . Fine, I'll message him to say yes.'

'You know it makes sense,' Iris said, looking satisfied. 'And Tuesday is the new Thursday, right? Especially when you have a bonus day off tomorrow.'

Ciaran would probably be too busy with end of year work to stay, Hope thought, but she didn't want to burst her friend's bubble. 'I'll let you know how it goes.'

Iris sighed. 'Please do. I need to know that good dates still happen.'

Hope expected Ciaran to suggest meeting in a bar but he surprised her by arranging to meet her in Tower Gardens, the small park that lay alongside Skeldersgate Bridge.

The heatwave of early June had passed but it was still a pleasant evening as Hope made her way past Clifford's Tower to the Gardens. She spotted him immediately, waiting beneath the tall oak tree in the middle of the grassy expanse.

As she got closer, she realized he was standing beside an out-spread picnic blanket.

'I thought we could make the most of the summer,' he said, waving at a wicker hamper resting on the grass. I've got bread, cheese, champagne and Maltesers.'

'All the main food groups,' Hope said, smiling. 'Thank you, this is amazing.'

'Something a bit different,' he shrugged, and stepped forwards to kiss her. 'You look gorgeous, by the way. A vision of loveliness.'

The compliments, together with the feel of his mouth on hers, gave Hope a warm glow and she was glad she'd agreed to see him. 'So, how have you been?' she asked, as they settled onto the blanket. 'I guess work has kept you busy.'

He ran a hand through his dark hair and Hope noticed a strand or two of silver glistening in the sun. 'It has,' he said apologetically. 'Sorry to go quiet on you – I kept meaning to drop you a message and then something would come up and . . .' He offered a smile. 'Well, you know how it is. We're here now.'

'We are,' she agreed. 'Tell me what you've been up to.'

'Oh, it's the usual boring stuff – undergraduates who somehow forgot they had deadlines, and exams. Marking.' He lifted the lid of the picnic hamper and pulled out a bottle of Veuve Clicquot. 'But it's almost the end of the year, which deserves some kind of celebration, and I'm here with the most beautiful woman in the city so I decided to push the boat out a little.'

The flattery was as outrageous as ever. She ought to be used to it by now, Hope thought, but it still made her head spin like a shot of the smoothest whiskey. She watched as he popped the cork and expertly filled two plastic flutes. 'What shall we drink to?' she asked, when he passed one of the glasses to her.

'World peace?' he suggested. 'Or how about three blessed months of no one telling me the dog ate their assignment?'

'Both,' Hope said with a grin. 'Cheers.'

He asked what she'd been up to and seemed genuinely impressed when she'd described the popularity of the window display. 'I'll have to walk past, take a look.' Reaching across, he wound one of her stray coppery curls around his fingers. 'Sounds like you've been busy as well. Too busy to miss me, at any rate.'

Hope thought guiltily of Elenor's journal. 'I have missed you,' she said hastily. 'But I knew you must be snowed under and thought you'd be in touch when things calmed down.'

'You were right,' Ciaran said, giving her another admiring glance. 'Brains, beauty and independence. You're a triple threat, Hope Henderson.'

He held her gaze and leaned closer to kiss her. But a polite cough from somewhere behind Hope made him pause and draw back. Hope twisted around to see a blonde-haired little girl staring at them in silence, with a tall, brown-haired man standing awkwardly behind her.

'Brodie!' Hope exclaimed in surprise. 'How lovely to see you. And you, Will.'

'Hello,' Will said, with a smile that didn't come close to hiding his embarrassment. 'I hope we're not intruding.'

'Not at all,' Hope said, with a smile of her own. 'We're just enjoying the sunshine. I imagine you are too – have you been playing, Brodie?'

The girl didn't smile. Instead, she transferred her gaze to Ciaran. Hope caught her meaning. 'This is Ciaran. He's a friend of mine – in fact, he's helping me to find out all about the lady who owned the ring you found in the puzzle box.'

Brodie's eyes widened as she studied Ciaran and she gave Hope another questioning look. 'He works at the university, teaching people about old things. Why don't you explain, Ciaran?'

'That's right,' he said, not missing a beat. 'I know a lot about Ancient Egypt and the Pyramids. Did you know that the ring probably came from Egypt?'

For a moment, Hope thought Brodie wouldn't react but then she gave the merest nod of her head. Glancing up at Will, she saw he was watching too and they shared a smile. 'Ciaran, this is Will. He's Brodie's guardian.'

Ciaran got to his feet and the two men shook hands. 'Good to meet you,' Ciaran said.

'And you,' Will said politely. He paused. 'Hope mentioned she'd taken the ring to you but I didn't realize you were still involved.'

'Sure,' Ciaran said, and fired a lingering look Hope's way. 'Yes, you could call it that, I suppose. We're pretty involved all right.'

The obvious double meaning made Hope suddenly hot with embarrassment. She scrambled to her feet, hardly able to meet Will's gaze. 'We're making good progress, actually. I should stop by the shop one afternoon, give you an update.'

Will nodded. 'I'd like that. You would too, wouldn't you, Brodie?'

This time, the girl's nod was emphatic.

Pushing her discomfort aside, Hope smiled at her. 'Excellent. Maybe we can play with your dolls together.'

And now Brodie smiled, giving Hope an altogether different warm glow. 'Drop in anytime,' Will said. 'I'll lock up the guard goose.'

'Thank you,' Hope replied gravely. 'The laser too, if you don't mind.'

Ciaran was looking back and forth between them, nonplussed. 'You keep a goose in your shop?'

Will grinned. 'Long story. Look, we've got to be getting home. Nice to meet you, Ciaran. And we'll see you soon, Hope.'

Nodding, Hope reached out to squeeze Brodie's hand. 'See you very soon.'

'Cute kid,' Ciaran said, once Will and Brodie had gone and they'd sat down again. 'But she doesn't say much, does she?'

'Nothing at all,' Hope said with a sigh and explained

about the terrible loss of both the little girl's parents earlier in the year.

When she'd finished, Ciaran shook his head in sympathy. 'God love her, that's an awful thing for anyone to go through, let alone a child. And Will has adopted her, has he?'

'There was no other close family,' Hope said. 'It's been hard for him too, losing his brother and sister-in-law. But I'm glad he and Brodie have each other.'

'Of course.' Ciaran eyed her thoughtfully. 'You can't have known him long. Unless you were friends before you moved back to York?'

Something in his tone made Hope frown, a hint of something she couldn't quite get a hold on. 'No, we didn't know each other before. But we've got a lot in common, what with—'

She broke off, remembering just in time that she hadn't told him about Rob, hadn't wanted to scare him off with the W word too early on. And now didn't feel like the right time or place to lay the story of her dead husband on the table – on the picnic blanket, in fact. It wasn't the kind of thing to be blurted out – she needed to build up to it carefully, both to do justice to Rob's memory and make it clear she was ready to meet someone new. '—with the ring and everything,' she finished, hoping the words didn't sound as lame to him as they did to her.

'I can see that,' Ciaran said, and took a long sip of champagne. 'Well, it's good that you're making friends, putting down roots in York. It means you'll still be here when I come back in September.'

She wanted to point out that her whole family lived in York but the observation was eclipsed by the clear indication that she wouldn't see him over the summer. 'We don't have to wait until September,' she said, carefully picking her way through the minefield of appearing too keen. 'I could always come over to Scarborough.'

He shook his head, looking regretful. 'I doubt I'll be there much. I've got a dig lined up in Sussex – a Roman villa. Not my thing but they're short of staff so I agreed to help out.'

'Oh,' Hope said, as leaden disappointment settled in her stomach. 'I see.'

'Believe me, I'd like nothing better than to spend the summer with you. But we've got a week or two until I go,' he said. 'Plenty of time to get to know each other better.'

The look he gave her chased away Hope's disappointment and replaced it with a delicious shiver. He reached out and took the champagne flute from her fingers and rested it on the grass. 'And on that note, I believe I was just about to kiss you,' he murmured.

Before she could reply, he pulled her close and kissed her in a way that sent the breath whooshing from her lungs. When he'd finished, he let her go and smiled. 'How about finishing this bottle of champagne in bed?'

Lips tingling, Hope had to stop herself from instantly agreeing. When exactly had she become the kind of woman who shamelessly snogged in parks and considered skipping the traditional drinks/dinner dating ritual to get to what came next faster? It wasn't even seven o'clock – maybe she should play a little harder to get. But then she remembered that evenings like this were going to be impossible once Ciaran had left for Sussex, and she threw caution to the wind.

'Sounds like an excellent plan,' she said. 'Let's go.'

It wasn't until much later in the evening that Ciaran discovered Elenor's diary.

The champagne had been finished and Hope was serving up a takeaway in the kitchen. She came through to the living room, plates in hand, to find him studying her jumbled notes, scrawled across a rainbow of Post-its and stuck to the pages of a notebook that lay open on the coffee table.

'What's this?' he asked.

Hope gave herself a mental kick; why hadn't she thought to clear the notes away? The journal itself was safely in its box but she'd been working on a timeline of events, complete with tell-tale initials and locations, details Ciaran would recognize instantly.

'I've been thinking about Elenor's part in the excavations,' she said slowly, trying to find the right words. 'I thought if we could establish when she was there, we might be able to cross-reference the Carter journal entries.'

It wasn't a lie – that was exactly what she had done – but Ciaran frowned. 'How did you know where she was, and when?' He tapped a Post-it. 'This one has the exact date she returned to England in nineteen twenty two.

Did you take a guess, based on when the winter season finished?'

And now Hope had a choice. She could say yes, which was a lie but might also be enough to prevent Ciaran from finding out about the box that sat on the shelf underneath the coffee table, or she could come clean and admit she had an amazing new source of information. The trouble was that a lie now would mean she couldn't share the journal with him at a later date – he would know she hadn't been honest with him and there might come a time when she did want his input. So, really, there was no choice. She had to tell him the truth.

'I had a bit of insider knowledge,' she admitted, laying the plates on the small dining table. 'I'll show you after we've eaten.'

Clearly intrigued, Ciaran tried to draw more information from her as they ate but Hope refused to say more until the table was cleared. Then she handed him the box and the white cotton gloves. 'I haven't finished reading yet but I think you're going to find it fascinating.'

She left him on the sofa and went to make coffee. When she returned, he was so engrossed in the journal that she wasn't even sure he'd noticed her come back. Wryly, Hope took a seat; she didn't mind that Ciaran's head had been turned by another woman, but she definitely felt an irrational flicker of something that it was Elenor – *her* Elenor. From the very first line, Hope had connected with the story unfolding inside the pages of the journal. It wasn't simply a mystery that she was curious about unravelling, as it had been when she'd first seen the ring and read the letter breaking off the engagement. Now she felt as though she had come to know Elenor and wanted to understand what had driven her to that final act of despair on the cliffs at Whitby. And she longed to discover what had happened to Khalid too, although she suspected his fate might be beyond her reach. Almost without Hope realizing it, the events of almost a century ago had crept into her heart, causing her to feel oddly protective. Which was crazy, because it was quite likely Ciaran would be able to help piece things together . . .

Ten minutes later, Ciaran raised his head to stare at Hope. 'This is incredible,' he said. 'I know people who'd give up a kidney for a first-hand account like this. Where on earth did you find it?'

'From Isobel,' Hope replied. 'She dropped it off at the shop. But it's only a loan – I don't think she'd be interested in swapping it for a kidney, or any other major organ.'

Ciaran laughed. 'No, I don't suppose she would. Good on her for sharing it with you, though. I've only skimmed the surface but I can tell it's an amazing piece of work.'

Hope leaned forwards. 'Isn't it? It's kept me up late a few evenings, turning the pages.'

'I can imagine,' he said, shaking his head. 'The maps are much better than any I've seen before and the descriptions of the tombs are meticulously detailed – in fact, there are artefacts mentioned here that I've never seen listed in the Tutankhamun excavation reports, or anywhere else. I wonder what happened to them.'

Of course he would see the diary from a field journal perspective, Hope thought. He was an archaeologist, after all. 'I found the descriptions started to blur after a while – there are only so many times I can picture a gold statue, no matter how well it's described.'

'That's because you're not an Egyptologist,' he said and raised a self-deprecating eyebrow. 'We're all secretly obsessed with gold. Haven't you seen *The Mummy*?'

Hope laughed. 'I didn't realize it was a documentary. But isn't that the one where they accidentally unleash the spirit of an evil priest?'

'That is a constant danger,' Ciaran replied gravely. 'And some people still believe there was a curse on Tutankhamun's tomb. Lord Carnarvon died a few months after entering and there were rumours of other sudden deaths.'

Hope's gaze travelled to the open journal resting in his white-gloved hands and she fought the urge to shiver. 'Things certainly went badly for Elenor and Khalid.'

He nodded. 'But most of the people associated with the excavations went on to have long lives. I can't claim to know if they were always happy but I don't think we can blame the mummies' curse for the tragedy of Elenor Lovelace.'

'No,' Hope said. 'We can lay the blame for that squarely at the feet of the living.'

'Exactly,' Ciaran agreed. 'People can be unimaginably cruel, especially in the name of love.'

Hope wasn't sure who he meant – Elenor and her behaviour towards Khalid, or the way her family had behaved towards them both – but his attention had been drawn back to the journal. He turned a few more pages, poring over them with an intense concentration that once again made Hope feel invisible. And then he sat back and stretched, checking the time as he did so. 'Damn it, I have to go,' he said, with genuine regret. 'I've a ton of work to do.'

'I understand,' Hope said, suddenly wishing he could stay, that they could explore the dusty tomb of Tutankhamun together.

He smiled. 'It's been good to see you, though. Really good.'

'You too,' Hope said. 'Thanks for suggesting it, and for the picnic too.'

Ciaran tilted his head. 'The plan was to spend a romantic evening there, watching the stars come out over the river before making our way back here for a night of passion. But you were just too irresistibly sexy, with the sun turning your hair to burnished gold. I couldn't wait.'

It was exactly the kind of comment that earned him his reputation as a charmer, Hope thought, but she couldn't deny the flutter of pleasure the compliment gave her. 'It's probably a good thing,' she said, raising her eyebrows. 'At least this way you'll get some work done too.'

'That's true,' he said. 'Although I'd obviously rather stay with you.'

The look that accompanied the words left Hope in no doubt that he meant it. 'Next time,' she promised.

He glanced at the journal and placed it back into its box. 'I don't suppose there's any chance you'd let me take this, is there? Just overnight, so I can cross-reference with some artefact reports, confirm my suspicions that a few things went astray.'

The question wasn't a surprise but Hope still felt her stomach sink. 'I don't think so,' she said carefully. 'I haven't finished reading it myself and I'd have to check with Isobel first.'

Ciaran nodded, as though he'd been expecting as much. 'I totally appreciate that. But maybe when you have finished – I could pop back, whisk you out for dinner and have a sneaky read myself.'

'It's hardly popping back if you're coming from Sussex,' Hope pointed out.

He winked. 'There's always the chance they might give me some time off, for good behaviour. But I don't want to put you in an awkward position.'

Hope bit her lip, wondering if she was being ridiculous. This was Ciaran – a well-respected specialist in the field of Egyptology, not some disreputable thief who'd make off with Elenor's journal. And hadn't she always intended to share it with him? 'Okay,' she said. 'Let me finish reading it and I'll see what Isobel says.'

'You're a doll,' he said, with a dazzling smile. Leaving the box open on the table, he got to his feet, looking around. 'Now, where's my phone?'

She frowned. 'Not in your jacket?'

His coat was strewn across the back of the sofa. He checked the pockets. 'No. I think I last had it in the bedroom.'

'I'll go and look,' Hope said, standing up and heading to the hall. But there was no sign of the missing phone there – not on the bedside table and not on the floor. She lifted the rumpled sheets and checked underneath the bed but eventually had to concede defeat.

When she walked back into the living room, Ciaran had removed the cotton gloves and was holding the missing phone in his hands. 'Down the side of the sofa,' he explained. 'I'd lose my head if it wasn't screwed on.'

He kissed her goodbye at the front door, promising another date soon. She wasn't sure whether it was the knowledge that they only had a few weeks left or the impact of his charm but Hope suddenly felt the desire to move things forwards. 'It's my parents' anniversary in a couple of weeks,' she said impulsively. 'They're having a party. Would you like to come?'

If he was surprised, it didn't show. 'When is it?' he asked, a thoughtful frown crinkling the corners of his eyes.

Hope made a conscious effort to sound casual. 'Saturday, third of July.'

His gaze narrowed, as though he was mentally flipping through dates. 'Dammit. I'll be in Sussex then.'

No mention of popping back for that, Hope noted, but shrugged the observation away. 'Never mind,' she said, forcing herself to smile. 'It was just an idea.'

He kissed her again, a swift apologetic peck. 'Sorry. But I'll make it up to you, I promise.'

'Really, don't worry. Good luck with the work tonight.'

'Thanks,' he said and took a step back. 'See you soon.'

She nodded and did her best to ignore the flat disappointment in her stomach. 'Sure, Ciaran. See you soon.'

Chapter Fourteen

The first message from Joe gave Hope a moment's panic, before she saw his follow up text and realized her younger brother was just being his usual melodramatic self:

> SOS. HELP!
>> What do you get the parents who have everything?
>> Asking for a sibling.

Smiling, she tapped out a reply:

> Of course they have everything – they have us! Are you
> stuck for an anniversary present? Because I'm sure seeing
> you will be more than enough X

Nineteen-year-old Joe was just finishing his first year at Edinburgh University and should have been back at home by the date of their parents' anniversary. But he'd concocted an excuse about needing to stay on for another few weeks so that he could surprise them at the party, although Charlotte had firmly vetoed his idea to jump out of an enormous cake.

Obviously but I want to get them something. Any ideas?

Hope mulled it over all morning as she worked at the Emporium. Joe didn't have much to spend and she knew he hated having to ask for help. But out of his three siblings, Joe had always been closest to Hope and if he was going to come to any of them, it was most likely to be her. She might have suggested he buy their parents a nice bottle of wine, to go with the exquisite decanter set she'd found, if Harry hadn't got in there first and bought six bottles of eye-wateringly expensive Burgundy from the year of their parents' marriage – 1981 had been a good year for grapes as well as weddings, it seemed.

The Emporium had nothing to offer, either – at least, nothing within Joe's price range. Then her eye was caught by a Victorian silver photo frame – still far too expensive, even with her staff discount, but it triggered an idea.

Have you still got the photo of Mum and Dad you took at Harry's birthday last year? she typed.

Joe's response was puzzled: Yeah???

Send it over. Hope typed, smiling to herself. I've got an idea.

It was just after closing time by the time she reached Will's shop near The Shambles, breathing a little heavily from walking fast. He unlocked the door when she tapped gently on the glass, smiling when he saw it was her. 'Hello. Come on in.'

'Thank you for doing this,' she said, once she was inside the brightly lit, glittering shop. 'It shouldn't take long.'

'No problem,' he replied. 'I've picked out a few frames that might work. Did you have any trouble with the photo?'

It had taken Hope four attempts to successfully transfer the photo on her phone to the self-service printing machine at Happy Snaps on Davygate, and even longer to get the size and resolution right. It wasn't that she lacked the technical skills, more that the machine seemed to have a mind of its own and clearly thought it knew what Hope wanted better than she did. But she had persevered and, with a bit of help from the only-slightly condescending shop assistant, she'd managed to get the job done.

She held up the jute carrier bag that held a cardboard A4 folder. 'We got there eventually,' she said. 'I used the meas-urements you suggested so fingers crossed.'

A number of silver photo frames were spread along one end of the long, glass-topped counter. Hope was just about to take a closer look when the door behind the counter inched open and she spotted a flash of movement in the room beyond.

'She's been like a cat on hot bricks ever since I men-tioned you were popping in,' Will murmured to Hope, then paused to glance at the door. 'Do you want to come and say hello, Brodie?'

There was a faint rustling, followed by the sound of small feet thudding across the floor. A second later, the door was pushed back and Brodie was there. The largest of the red and gold Matryoshka dolls Hope had given her was clutched firmly in one hand.

'Hello,' Hope said, with a little wave. 'Would you like to help me choose a frame for my photograph?'

Nodding, Brodie stepped forwards. Hope laid the jute bag on the counter and slid the cardboard folder out. 'This is a picture of my parents – it's their ruby wedding anniversary next week.'

Brodie gave Will a questioning look.

'That means they've been married for forty years,' he explained and glanced at Hope. 'But together for longer, I imagine.'

'Forty-two,' Hope said. 'They met at a Roxy Music gig in 1979. Dad always jokes that he owes Bryan Ferry a drink – "Love is the Drug" started just as Dad's eyes met Mum's and that was it.'

Will smiled. 'That's what you should have engraved on the frame – *Love is the Drug*.'

It was perfect, Hope realized, and even more so when she remembered the framed picture was actually a gift from Joe; he'd inherited their parents' love of music and played guitar in a band. 'Excellent idea,' she said, beaming at Will. 'Do you think there'll be space?'

'Depends on the frame,' he replied and gathered up the silver rectangles to lay them out in front of her. 'Why don't you see which one you like best?'

Hope's gaze slid to the little girl on the other side of the counter. 'What do you think, Brodie? Which one goes best with the photo?'

But Brodie's gaze was fixed on the picture. It was a black and white image, taken in the garden at Harry's birthday party the previous August; Hope's mother was seated and her dad stood behind the chair, bending to loop his arms around her. Joe had caught them mid-laugh – their father's eyes were crinkled with merriment and their mother's face was half-turned towards him, glancing up with her mouth curved in a wide grin. To Hope, it was the definition of joy and it made her smile every time she saw it.

'Do you like it?' she asked Brodie.

A flurry of emotions seemed to dance across the girl's face. Without warning, she dipped her head towards the doll she held. Hope saw her lips move but there was no sound.

'As you can see, Brodie loves the dolls you gave her,' Will said. 'This one is Titania, named after we watched *A Midsummer Night's Dream* on CBeebies.'

'That's a beautiful name,' Hope said, and thought back to the afternoon she'd given the set of Russian nesting dolls to Brodie. The little girl had immediately discovered the progressively smaller dolls inside, each decorated more delicately than the last, and had listened wide-eyed as Hope told her she could trust them with any secret she wanted to share. Judging from the wordless whisper Brodie had bestowed upon Titania's head, the little girl had taken Hope's story to heart.

'The other dolls have names too,' Will said. 'They often have breakfast with us.'

Hope hid a smile as an image of him serving up Rice Krispies to Brodie and her six wooden friends popped into her head. Not for the first time, it struck Hope how much Will's life must have changed since the accident that robbed him and Brodie of their family. But he seemed to be relishing his new role, both as a surrogate parent and in his unexpected side gig as chef to a family of Matryoshka. 'Wow,' she said. 'Do they leave toast crumbs in the butter?'

Brodie shook her head hard, causing Will to smile. 'No, but there was an issue with the Nutella. We had to set some rules.'

'I can imagine,' Hope said gravely. 'Is there anything worse than crumbs in the Nutella jar?'

His lips quirked. 'No Nutella at all? But we should probably work out which frame you'd like. Then I can get the engraving done in plenty of time.'

Hope studied the frames, most of which were considerably more modern than the selection she'd found at the Emporium. They were also a fraction of the price, despite being sterling silver, and she was sure she'd be able to find one that Joe would like. But before then, there was someone else whose opinion mattered. 'Which frame do you think suits the picture, Brodie?'

Shyly, and after a silent consultation with Titania, the girl tapped at a sleek plain oblong that had plenty of room for engraving around thick banded edging. Hope nodded in agreement. 'Great choice. I'm sure my brother, Joe, would choose the same one if he was here.'

'You'll need to tell me what you'd like written,' Will said. 'Then I can make sure it's all going to fit.'

Hope pursed her lips. 'I like the music quote idea. So perhaps that along the top. And the date of their wedding along the bottom, with their names. What do you think?'

'Shouldn't be a problem,' he said as he reached below the counter and pulled out a sheet of A4 paper covered in different fonts. 'All you need to do now is decide on a style.'

After some deliberation, she selected an elegant but unfussy font that she thought suited the frame, the photo and her parents' taste.

'Good choice,' Will said. 'I'll get the engraving done and fit the photo over the next few days. Is that okay?'

Hope smiled. 'That's great. My little brother will be thrilled.'

Will raised his eyebrows. 'I bet he will. He's going to get all the credit while you did all the work.'

'Not all the work,' she countered. 'You're doing the hard bit. So, on behalf of Joe and me, thank you. You're a lifesaver.'

Brodie had been waiting patiently but now she seemed to have decided there'd been enough talking. She tugged on Hope's sleeve and glanced towards the door that led to the workroom beyond.

'I'm not sure we have time,' Hope said in answer to the

unspoken question. Her eyes sought Will's. 'Do you mind if I say hello to the other dolls?'

'Not at all,' he answered. 'I've got a few things to tidy up anyway. Mind out for the goose, obviously.'

The workroom was exactly as Hope remembered it. Will's scarred oak workbench dominated in the centre of the room, dotted with the tools of his trade; she could imagine him sitting there, head bowed, hard at work under the spotlights while Brodie played on the rug or drew at the white wooden desk in the corner of the room. Her desk was covered in colourful hand-drawn pictures that spilled onto the floor and mingled with escaped felt-tip pens. She was clearly an artist.

The other Matryoshka dolls were laid out in a semi-circle on the rug. Brodie sat, cross-legged, in front of them and looked expectantly at Hope. 'That's very kind,' she said solemnly. 'I'd love to join you.'

Sitting beside Brodie, she allowed the girl to show her each doll. 'I can see you're taking very good care of them,' she said, once each doll had been introduced and returned to her place in the semi-circle. 'Mr Young will be pleased.'

Brodie nodded, then shuffled across the white wooden desk. She rummaged among the papers, sending more cascading to the floor, then seemed to find what she was searching for. She presented it to Hope, who immediately recognized the tall yellow building. 'Oh, it's the Ever After Emporium,' she exclaimed, examining the picture with delight. 'Are those the flamingos in the windows?'

She was rewarded with a smile and another drawing. This

one also showed the Emporium, with the stick figure of a woman beside it. She had a mass of curly orange hair and a smile so wide it surpassed her face. 'Is this me?' she asked, wanted to be sure. When Brodie nodded, she went on. 'What a lovely picture – you're very good at drawing.'

Apparently satisfied by the praise, Brodie turned her attention to the dolls and began to rearrange them. Hope twisted round and gathered up the sheets of paper that were scattered on the rug. There were several pictures of the Matryoshka, bright and colourful, and others that were clearly Will and Brodie; his hair was bigger than his head. But the image that caused Hope's smile to fade, the scene appeared over and over, was the one that contained two tall figures and one small one. Sometimes they were linked hand in hand, the little one always in the centre, but more often the adults were far away, leaving the child on her own. The only colour in those pictures was the yellow hair of Brodie and her mother, and the blue tears dripping down the little girl's face.

Hope's own eyes swam and she raised a hurried hand to dab at them. It wasn't a surprise that Brodie would express her grief through art – she was sure Will encouraged her to do so – but she wasn't prepared for her own reaction to the pain and loneliness that ached from the page. It brought back all the desolation of the early days after Rob's death, when she'd been breathless with loss and wracked by the unfairness of it all. But she had been an adult, and she'd known the day was coming. She couldn't begin to imagine how hard it had been for Brodie.

Hope only realized the girl was beside her when she took

the picture from her hands. It wasn't a snatch, just a gentle assertion of ownership. Hope blinked back the frosting of tears along her lashes. 'You must miss them very much.'

Brodie didn't look up from her picture but Hope thought her head inclined just the tiniest fraction. 'It's okay to feel that way. I lost someone too. It was a long time ago now but I still miss him every day.'

Her throat closed over the last word and she had to press her lips together to keep the sudden rush of emotion in check. Grief still caught her out sometimes and she supposed it always would. But she didn't know how to convey that to a four-year-old, not in a way that would be comforting, so she stayed quiet. Brodie was silent too but, after a second or two, her hand crept into Hope's. They stayed that way for a moment, then a gentle cough broke the spell.

'Time to head home, Brodie,' Will said as they both turned instinctively. 'Gather up Titania and the others.'

In an instant, Brodie was slotting one doll inside another. Hope got to her feet. 'I should be going too. I left Elenor on the brink of another date with Khalid last night and I have a feeling he might be about to pop the question.'

Will smiled. 'I'm amazed you were able to put the journal down.'

She gave a little huff that was partly embarrassed but mostly self-deprecating. 'I didn't. I woke up at three o'clock with the diary still open on my lap and a serious crick in my neck.' His obvious amusement made her laugh. 'I know. I need to get out more.'

'I'm in no position to judge – my evening routine consists of the CBeebies bedtime story and falling asleep on the sofa.' He gazed meditatively at the ceiling. 'I can't actually remember the last time I went out.'

With no family to help, it must be tough, Hope reflected. 'Can't you get a babysitter?'

He glanced at Brodie and lowered his voice. 'She doesn't like to be separated from me and isn't great with strangers, so it's been tricky to have people over. The therapist thinks it will pass, in time, but in the meantime . . .'

He trailed off, finishing with an accepting shrug. Hope flashed him a sympathetic look, which made him shake his head. 'It's fine, really. Anyway, my point was that I'd be swept up in Elenor's story too – from everything you've said, it sounds incredible and it's even better knowing it all really happened.'

'That's how I feel too,' Hope admitted. 'Although it's a bittersweet pleasure, knowing there's no sequel – no second season to binge on the moment it drops.'

'But also no disappointment when the writers get it wrong and ruin everything,' he joked, then hesitated. 'Would you like to come over for dinner on Saturday? It won't be anything fancy but we'd have more time to chat. Unless you already have plans with Iris or Ciaran, of course.'

Hope mentally reviewed her schedule for the weekend; she was going to the cinema with Iris on Friday night and had her regular family lunch date on Sunday. But Saturday night was free – Ciaran had already made it clear he wasn't around. She'd made tentative arrangements to try and catch up with friends in London but there was something in Will's tone, combined with her sudden suspicion that he was finding the change in his lifestyle harder than he'd admitted, that made her reconsider. 'I don't have plans,' she said, then bit her lip. 'As long as Brodie won't mind . . .'

'Mind?' he echoed, smiling. 'You're top of her VIP list. Although I have to warn you, she'll insist on giving you a detailed tour of the house.'

Hope grinned. 'I'll consider myself warned. Ten quid says we're asleep on the sofa by seven-thirty.'

'Oh, a late night?' Will said. 'The smart money is on seven o'clock. The CBeebies goodnight song is better than Nytol.'

'I think we can do better than that,' she replied, laughing. 'I'll bring coffee instead of wine.'

Will nodded. 'Good idea. And if all else fails, we can break out the matchsticks.'

Chapter Fifteen

The Minster bells were chiming six o'clock on Saturday evening when Hope arrived at the address Will had given her. The house was one of a cluster of terraced and detached properties tucked away down a narrow, cobbled lane off Marygate. As always in the city centre, space was at a premium and there were no expansive gardens attached to the houses. Will's home had a small courtyard out the front, surrounded by a low wall, and a well-tended apple tree was in full leaf at its heart.

She made her way up the short driveway and rang the bell, admiring the sage green paintwork on the door and windows while she waited.

'Perfect timing,' Will said, when he opened the door to greet her. 'We're just having hot chocolate.'

The interior of the house was all clean lines and sleek curves that cleverly made use of the compact space. A rounded staircase curled upwards from the hallway and two beechwood and glass folding doors led into a glossy modern kitchen. The effect of the minimalist white units was only slightly disrupted by a number of Brodie's drawings stuck haphazardly on the doors. At the far end of the kitchen, a set of folding doors opened onto what looked like a walled garden. Hope glanced inquisitively to the right and saw an inviting open plan living room with an L-shaped sofa and geometric patterned rug facing a wide flat-screened TV. Here too there were signs of a juvenile takeover; the rug was dotted with toys, and Charlie and Lola were dancing across the television screen, although the sound was off. Hope thought of the chaos that ruled both Harry and Charlotte's houses and wondered if Will had yet accepted he was fighting a losing battle.

Brodie was seated at the kitchen island, on a tall, velvet bar seat that Hope knew would be a magnet for sticky fingers. She smiled as Hope approached.

Will pulled a jug of steaming milk from the microwave and fired an enquiring look Hope's way. 'Want to join us? Or would you prefer a glass of wine?'

'Hot chocolate would be lovely,' Hope said and offered him the bottle of Sancerre she'd brought. 'Although maybe this can go in the fridge for later.'

He grinned. 'Good choice. But I thought you were bringing coffee.'

Hope lifted the jute bag from her shoulder. 'I did. And I found a little something Brodie might like – if that's okay?'

Brodie's eyes lit up as Will put the bottle in an undercounter fridge. 'You're spoiling her,' he said but without the slightest trace of reproach.

'It's educational too, if that helps,' Hope reached into the bag and drew out the brightly coloured picture book she'd spotted in the window of the Little Apple Bookshop as she made her way along High Petergate. 'It's a story about the Matryoshka dolls – where they come from and how they're made.'

Brodie sat up straight, holding out both hands. Hope gave her the book, savouring the look of delight on the little girl's face as she gazed at the cover and eagerly turned to the first page.

'What do you say, Brodie?' Will reminded her, his tone gently reprimanding.

She looked up fast and touched flat fingers to her chin, then pulled her hand away and down. Hope blinked in surprise. 'You're welcome. I didn't realize you know sign language.'

'Just a few easy signs,' Will explained. 'We saw them on a TV show and I thought it might help Brodie to communicate, at least in the short term.'

'Great idea,' Hope said admiringly, as Brodie turned her attention back to the book.

Will nodded in acknowledgement. 'Now, I've got whipped cream, marshmallows and chocolate syrup. Do you want to go all in?'

'It would be rude not to,' Hope said, and smiled. 'You've really got the hang of this.'

He seemed to understand that she didn't only mean the hot chocolate. 'Thanks. I'm trying. Although we discovered the hard way that there's a time and a place for chocolate syrup, and bedtime isn't it.'

The image of a bouncing Brodie, her bedsheets sticky with chocolate sauce, made Hope laugh. 'Oh dear. They do say parenthood is a steep learning curve.'

He shuddered as he placed two marshmallow-topped mugs on the black marble counter. 'That's a lesson I learned fast. Maybe put the book away while you drink this, Brodie.'

Once they'd finished the hot chocolate, Brodie was keen to show Hope the rest of the house. The ground floor mostly consisted of the hallway, stairs and open kitchen/ living room, with a bathroom tucked away under the stairs. The garden was a neat square of well-tended grass, enclosed on the remaining three sides by high, red-bricked walls. A smaller square of paving stones sat in the middle, with a patio table and chairs, and Hope could imagine Will sitting outside in the warm evenings, reading or doing whatever it was he did to relax. Upstairs, there were three bedrooms and it was very clear which one belonged to Brodie; there were toys and books everywhere. The Matryoshka dolls had their own shelf, in pride of place beside the bed. A multi-coloured marble run towered in the middle of the room and a vast box of Lego spilled out from one corner, making Hope wince as she recalled her siblings' stories of the agony inflicted by one of the plastic bricks under their feet in the dark. Seizing her hand, Brodie pulled her into the room and pointed to her favourite toys, while Hope exclaimed in delight. Eventually, Will took pity on her. 'That's enough now, Brodie. Poor Hope looks exhausted and it's almost time for bed.'

The little girl pouted but didn't fold her arms or stamp her feet in argument. Instead, she led Hope back downstairs and settled on the sofa, clearly determined that they would all watch *In The Night Garden* together.

'Sorry,' Will mouthed, pulling a face over Brodie's head.

Hope shook the apology away. 'Don't worry.'

It wasn't long before Brodie's eyes were drooping. By the time the final lullaby was playing onscreen, her head was starting to nod. Will stood up and scooped her into his arms. 'Say goodnight, Brodie.'

She yawned and raised a hand to wave sleepily. Will nodded to Hope. 'I shouldn't be long. Make yourself at home and help yourself to wine – there's a corkscrew in one of the drawers. Glasses are in the cupboard over the sink.'

'Thanks,' Hope said. 'Goodnight, Brodie.'

She watched as Will detoured to collect the picture book she'd brought, then disappeared up the curved stairs. The television screen announced that programmes were over for the day, so she found the remote control and switched it off. An empty plastic crate seemed to be there for toys; she gathered up everything scattered on the rug, then went to the kitchen and loaded the mugs from their hot chocolate into the dishwasher. For a moment, she was tempted to open the white doors and peep inside – you could tell a lot about a person by the contents of their kitchen cupboards – but she resisted and by the time Will came back downstairs, she was sitting in one of the patio chairs, flicking through a copy of *Yorkshire Life* she'd spotted on a coffee table.

'You didn't need to clear up,' he said as he sank into the chair opposite her.

Hope handed him the other glass of wine. 'I know. But it only took a minute.'

'Thank you,' he said. 'And thank you very much for the book. Brodie loved it – I can tell what I'm going to be reading every night for weeks.'

The thought gave Hope a little glow of pleasure and she was glad all over again that she'd stopped at the Little Apple Bookshop. 'You're welcome,' she said and tipped her glass towards his. 'Cheers.'

He smiled. 'Cheers.'

They sat in companionable silence for a moment, absorbing the balmy evening sunshine and sound of birdsong mingling with the hum of the city, then Will sighed and stretched. 'I hope you like risotto. I thought I'd keep it simple, rather than go all out to impress you and cock everything up.'

His candidness made her laugh. 'I love risotto. But I think you're being too modest – you seem to know your way around a kitchen.'

He grimaced. 'Heating milk for hot chocolate and adding squirty cream isn't exactly *haute cuisine*. Brodie mostly eats chicken nuggets or fish fingers so there's not much demand for my culinary skills and I'm usually too knackered to cook once she's in bed.'

He did look tired, Hope thought, studying him discreetly. There were smudges under his eyes and fine lines at the edges that gave him an air of weariness. 'Why don't I cook, then? I can manage risotto too – it's mostly just stirring – and you can put your feet up.'

'Absolutely not,' he said, sitting up straight. 'You've already tidied up, and what kind of host leaves the cooking to his guest?'

'An exhausted one,' she replied. 'Okay, how about you cook and I'll clear up afterwards?'

Will shook his head. 'That's not happening either but let's just pretend I agreed and we'll argue about it later. Deal?'

She couldn't imagine arguing with him about anything but she gave in gracefully. 'Deal.'

They sat for a few more minutes, chatting about their respective days, and then Will stood. 'I'd better get started or we'll still be sitting here at midnight.'

Hope checked the time. 'Hey, it's seven-forty and we're both still awake!'

Catching her gaze, Will smiled. 'Must be the company.'

The warmth in his expression chased away the tiredness and she was reminded how much she liked his smile. 'Must be,' she replied, feeling her own mouth quirk upwards.

Back in the kitchen, he asked how much further she'd got with Elenor's journal.

'Oh, I'm almost finished – Elenor is back in England and desperately unhappy at being separated from her love.' Hope paused and shook her head wryly as she watched him chop the onions. 'I don't know what I'm going to do with myself when I reach the end – I'm totally hooked.'

'Start all over again?' he suggested, and Hope nodded.

'Probably. And I'm sure I'll enjoy it even more second time around.' She sighed. 'That's the difference between Ciaran and me – he's all about the academic side of things, which I suppose isn't a massive surprise, given he's a Professor of Egyptology. And I love the descriptions of the excavations and all the amazing artefacts Elenor describes but that isn't what keeps me going back for more. It's the emotional journey she's on, the love between her and Khalid, the humanity of it all.'

Will nodded thoughtfully. 'I know what you mean. I think I'd be the same – I'm much more interested in people over things. It's one of the nice things about being a jeweller, actually – there's a story behind every customer and sometimes I get a glimpse of them. Like with Elenor's ring.'

'Exactly,' Hope said, snapping her fingers. 'You know, there's an article about Whitby in your copy of *Yorkshire Life* and I'm half-tempted to visit – to follow in Elenor's footsteps and try to understand why she took that awful last journey.'

He tipped the onion into a heavy-based saucepan and tilted his head. 'It's worth a visit regardless of that. I go quite often for work – I sell a lot of Whitby Jet jewellery through the tourist shops there. But there's no denying it's an odd place. There's a real sense of brooding about the town almost a kind of melancholy. A dark heart, if you like.'

He let out a self-conscious laugh but Hope thought she

understood what he meant. She hadn't been since she was a child, and had a confused jumble of memories that included the hulking silhouette of the ruined abbey and a vague feeling of menace. Harry had terrified her on the way home with a story that Dracula came for anyone whose name started with H and she'd been so afraid that it hadn't occurred to her that *his* name started with H too.

'I really think I want to go,' she said slowly. 'Is that completely mad?'

'Not at all,' Will said, and looked up from the saucepan. 'We could go together, if you like. I need to go and drop off some new stock to my vendors – we could make a day of it. Brodie and I can go and do our thing, you can do yours and then we can meet on the beach for fish and chips or ice cream. Probably both, knowing Brodie.'

Hope's first inclination was to say no. She had no idea what she wanted to do in Whitby, other than some half-formed notion of walking along the cliffs and feeling the sea breeze on her cheeks. But at the same time, the desire to go, to walk the same path that Elenor had taken and stand where she had stood – it was a need that burned in a corner of Hope's soul and she knew she would have to go at some point. Why not go with Will and Brodie, if they were going anyway?

'That sounds like a lovely idea,' she said. 'But I'm working three days this week – when were you planning to go?'

Will shrugged. 'I can arrange extra cover at the shop for whichever day suits you. When aren't you working?'

Hope considered her options. Monday was too soon – she

might not have finished the journal by then and she wanted some time to gather her thoughts, to make the most of being in Whitby. But she'd planned to keep Friday free in case Ciaran suggested getting together; the trouble with that was there was no guarantee he'd have time and then she'd be kicking herself for not having taken Will up on his offer.

'I can do Friday,' she said, after a few more seconds had ticked by. 'Is that okay with you?'

'Friday is perfect,' Will said, looking pleased. 'Why don't we pick you up around midday?'

The thought of a whole afternoon with Will and Brodie pleased Hope too. 'That would be great,' she said, with a smile. 'Thanks, this is really good of you.'

'It's no trouble,' he replied. 'And it will be nice to have someone to chat with – Brodie never complains but I'm sure she must get sick of me wittering on at her.'

Hope recalled the rare occasions she'd been in the same car as her nephews, who squabbled incessantly and were very rarely silent. 'I can be DJ, at least.'

'You can,' Will agreed. 'As long as you play all the Disney classics, we should have a smooth journey.' He turned to grab the kettle, and when he looked at Hope again, he wore a plaintive expression. 'I used to listen to Bowie. Now I catch myself humming along to "Let It Go".'

She couldn't help laughing. 'The perils of parenthood. Those Disney songs are serious earworms.'

The conversation moved on to favourite movies and Hope was pleased to find they had a shared passion for science fiction. They agreed that *Alien* was equally as good as *Aliens*, and that *Star Wars* rightly deserved its cult status, although they disagreed on the best film in the franchise.

'I can't believe you think *The Force Awakens* is better than *A New Hope*,' she said, topping up their glasses. 'Don't get me wrong, it's a great film. But there's just something about that first movie—'

'Which was actually the fourth part of the story,' he reminded her as he stirred the risotto.

'Oh, the first three don't count,' she said dismissively. 'Rob used to say that the only good thing about those films was Natalie Portman and even she couldn't stop them from stinking.'

She stopped, surprised at herself for bringing Rob into the conversation; the wine must be making her more relaxed than she'd thought. But if Will had noticed anything amiss, he didn't show it.

'Sounds like a wise man,' he said with a nod, then peered down at the saucepan bubbling on the hob. 'You know, I think this is ready.'

'Great!' Hope said, and instantly cringed at her overly enthusiastic tone. 'I'm starving and it smells delicious.'

He opened a cupboard and took out a pair of dinner plates. 'I really hope it tastes okay. We can always send out for pizza if it doesn't.'

It took one mouthful of the creamy rice for Hope to reassure him. 'It's amazing,' she said, digging her fork in for another taste. 'So good.'

Will grinned in relief. 'Thank god. I realized earlier on when I said that I couldn't cock risotto up that I was tempting fate.'

'Not at all,' Hope said. 'I'm starting to suspect you're hustling me here. The next thing I know you'll be challenging me to a cook off and then I'll discover you've been on *MasterChef*.'

Now he laughed. 'I think I can safely say that's never going to happen. But thank you.' He paused while scooping some rice onto his fork. 'So, the Rob you mentioned earlier – is he your ex?'

She forced herself to continue chewing, letting the action buy her some time. It wasn't that Rob was a secret among her new friends in York – she'd told Iris about him ages ago – more that she hadn't anticipated talking about him tonight. But she could hardly blame Will for asking – not when she'd dangled a big Rob-shaped carrot in front of him.

'In a way,' she said carefully. 'He was my husband. He died two years ago.'

Will was quiet for a few seconds. 'I'm sorry.'

'No need to apologize,' she said, managing a smile. 'You weren't to know.'

'But I should have guessed,' he said with a sigh. 'I overheard you talking to Brodie yesterday, at the shop. You told her you'd lost someone too. I should have put two and two together.'

He looked so wretched that Hope was tempted to reach across and squeeze his hand. She took a sip of wine instead.

'Really, it doesn't matter. It's not a secret or anything – I'm sure I'd have mentioned him at some point anyway. And it's been long enough that I can talk about it without falling apart.'

'Okay,' he said quietly. 'But I'm still sorry. You know, for your loss.'

'Thank you.' She hesitated. 'It's like I said before – you never really get over losing someone you love but it does get easier to bear. In time.'

They ate in silence for a moment, during which Hope guessed he was remembering his own loss, and that of Brodie. It was so much newer than hers, the pain must still be raw and crippling at times. 'So now you know, if you ever want to talk – with someone who has an idea how you might feel – then I'm here.'

His smile was a much sadder version than Hope was used to. 'Thanks.' He cleared his throat. 'So obviously you're dating again. How's that been going?'

Hope grimaced and gave him a brief overview of her experience of dating as a widow. Will listened sympathetically. 'And how did Ciaran react?'

The question caused Hope to shift uncomfortably. 'I – er – haven't actually told him yet. We've only had a few dates and now he's heading off for the summer, it doesn't feel like the right time.'

He nodded. 'It's a big thing, sharing something so personal. I think you have to really trust someone to be vulnerable in that way.'

She stared at him, surprised by his perceptiveness. The vulnerability of sharing her loss, and the way the men she'd dated had reacted, had taught her to be wary about who she trusted. And she had suspected Ciaran would be scared off if she told him about Rob, even after they'd spent the night together. They were dots she hadn't totally connected until now. 'You're right.'

'I don't tell people about Scott and Lucy,' Will admitted. 'It's easier to let them think Brodie is mine. And I have no idea what I would do in a dating scenario – that feels like a long way off right now.'

He looked down at his plate and sympathy welled up inside Hope. One of the things that had caught her by surprise was the loneliness that came with grief – not necessarily the physical solitude, because she was often surrounded by people, at least in the early days – but the deeper ache that came from feeling she was somehow removed from the world around her, an emotional distance that hadn't been there before. It was as though she experienced life from behind a window and even though the pain of grief had lessened, that faint sense of isolation had stayed. She recognized the same sense in Will now; not only was he mourning his loved ones, he was also grieving for the life he'd led before, and although she was sure he would brush the latter aside as unimportant, there was also no denying his loneliness was almost tangible. And she was glad all over again that she'd agreed to go to Whitby.

'Anyway,' Will went on, squaring his shoulders and

meeting her eyes. 'I guess what I'm trying to say is that I'm learning there's no right or wrong way to handle grief – you do whatever works for you.'

'That's a good way to look at it,' she said softly. 'Sometimes getting by is enough.'

Will summoned up a half-smile. 'Yes. It's okay to not be okay.'

'That too,' she agreed, and paused. 'It's nice to talk to someone who understands.'

'It's nice to talk to someone,' he replied dryly. 'Thanks for coming over, and for being so kind to Brodie.'

Hope almost brushed his appreciation away – he'd cooked a delicious meal for her and the conversation had flowed naturally all evening, even across the fractures of their sorrow. She'd enjoyed herself immensely. And surely only a monster could fail to be kind to Brodie. But then she remembered how important it had been to thank her own friends and family for their many kindnesses when she'd been adjusting to life after Rob, and instead she smiled. 'Any time, Will.'

Chapter Sixteen

17th April 1923, Whitby

*It is with a monstrously heavy heart that I write these words,
in what will be the final entry of this journal. My situation
becomes more intolerable with each passing day and my mind
grows ever darker. Soon I shall lose what little freedom I
have and it will be too late to free myself from this suffocating
prison. I must act now or die a thousand times more.*

*I pray that those who love me will understand — I am
sorry to visit more misery and scandal upon them but find
I cannot bear to contemplate a life without the man I love.
Indeed, without him, I have no life at all and so there can be
only one desperate course left to plot.*

*I do not fear what comes next and yet I am more afraid
than I have ever been. Even so, I place my faith in the moon
and the stars and trust that they will guide me home.*

Farewell.
Elenor Beatrice Lovelace

Hope read the last page of Elenor's diary three times before it truly sank in that she'd reached the end. The final entry was every bit as devastating as she'd known it would be; pain and desperation bled from every word and she could easily believe that Elenor had thrown herself off a cliff immediately after writing it. And it didn't matter that Hope had been expecting it – confirmation of Elenor's anguished state of mind still made for an unbearably sad end to what had been a brilliant life.

She replaced the journal in its box and slumped back against the pillows. It was late – well past midnight – and she had work in the morning. She ought to at least try to sleep, although she suspected a restful night might be out of the question now. Instead, she reached for her phone and tapped out a message to Ciaran:

> Finished the journal. Poor, poor Elenor – they really made her life impossible xx

She didn't expect an immediate reply but the double ticks turned blue almost instantly and the words Ciaran is typing … appeared on the screen. A few seconds later, his response arrived:

> Amazing. Dinner on Friday to discuss? xx

Hope let out a muted groan of frustration. Hadn't she known he'd do this? But as much as she wanted to see him, she had no intention of cancelling her trip to Whitby, nor did she want to be watching the clock while she was there.

> Busy then. Saturday? xx

Moments ticked by as she waited for his reply:

> Ah, you're a hard woman to pin down. Let me see what I
> can do. Sleep well xx

She had a sudden mental image of him then, his dark hair tousled and his grey eyes dancing, and found herself hoping he managed to shuffle things around to see her on Saturday. Placing her phone on the bedside table, she closed the box on the journal and moved it to the top shelf of the wardrobe, where she'd taken to keeping it. She might have finished reading the entries but there was still plenty of work to do before she returned it to Isobel Lovelace. She hoped her trip to Whitby might help pull together some of the loose threads; at the very least it would give her an insight into Elenor's last hours. And then perhaps she might have something to offer Isobel, in exchange for the privilege of reading the journal, as well as more to share with Ciaran.

But before any of that could happen, she needed to get some rest. Climbing into bed, Hope turned off the light and lay back in the darkness. As she'd expected, sleep took a long time to claim her.

*

It was almost four o'clock when Hope met Will and Brodie on Battery Parade. Across the bay to their right, the hulking ruins of the Abbey dominated the East Cliff and in front of them, the North Sea crashed against the harbour wall, gunmetal grey against the sullen and atmospheric sky. Will had said the town was brooding and melancholy, Hope recalled. After today's visit, she could only agree.

'So, how did you get on?' he asked, eyeing her with undisguised curiosity. 'Did you find what you were looking for?'

It was a good question and one Hope wasn't entirely sure she could answer. She'd done her best to follow in Elenor's footsteps, starting at the hotel she had described arriving at in the penultimate entry of her journal and tracing her path through the town and upwards to the East Cliff. She'd paused to admire the Abbey, shivering slightly as she noted the dark walls and long shadows, like fingers crawling across the land, and moved on to Saltwick Bay, where newspaper reports of the tragedy claimed Elenor had last been seen. There was now a well-worn walking trail but Hope had climbed over the wire fence to stand as close to the edge of the cliffs as safety allowed and tried to imagine summoning up the courage to throw herself off. And she must have looked at least a little convincing, because a white-haired couple stopped to shout at her to come back and the man began to climb the fence to retrieve her. Hope had waved her phone apologetically and said she was taking a photograph of the vicious rocks below, which earned her a disbelieving look and a muttered comment about 'Bloody daft-as-a-brush tourists.'

She'd sat on a nearby bench after that and contemplated the sombre grey clouds and roiling waves as gulls soared overhead. And after a while, a sense of acceptance had crept over her. It sounded mad, even to Hope; Elenor was nothing more than a character in a story to her – what was there to accept? But it felt like the last piece of the puzzle had finally slotted into place, after hours of turning it round and round, trying to make it fit. It felt as though the story was complete. Elenor's story, at least.

Dragging her thoughts back to Will, Hope tipped her head. 'I think so, yes. How was your afternoon?'

He glanced down at Brodie. 'We had a great time. After the deliveries were done, we had an ice cream on the beach and spent a small fortune in the amusements.' He ruffled her hair affectionately. 'Brodie had her eye on a plastic yo-yo and it only cost me five pounds to win it.'

On cue, the little girl opened her hand to display a neon-green toy that probably would have cost fifty pence to buy. Hope grinned. 'Sounds like a bargain.' She took a breath, taking in the salty air and the unmistakeable aroma of fried food. 'Did you work up an appetite? I'm pretty sure someone mentioned eating chips on the seafront.'

Will nodded. 'I did – everyone knows they taste better on the beach. Come on, there's a decent chippy around the corner.'

They took their paper-wrapped packages and sat at one of the benches along the harbour wall, burning their fingers on the too-hot chips and savouring the tang of the salt and vinegar. Hope described her walk, making Will tut and shake his head when she told him she'd gone beyond the fence.

'Those cliffs are unstable,' he said. 'No wonder the locals thought you were crazy.'

'I wasn't really in any danger,' Hope insisted mildly. 'But it did bring home to me how terrifying it must have been for Elenor. How bad must her situation have been for her to take that final step? And how could her family have driven her to believing it was the only way out?'

Will glanced uneasily at Brodie. 'It was a different time. Families had more control back then, especially the aristocratic ones and especially over women. They could easily have made her life a misery. In fact, it sounds a lot like they already had.'

That was certainly true, Hope thought. 'Elenor often mentions how scandalized they were by her relationship with Khalid,' she said. 'But how much of a scandal would it have been? It was the Roaring Twenties – attitudes were changing and Khalid was a well-respected scholar. Surely it's possible he might have been accepted into society, with the backing of Elenor's family.'

'I don't know,' Will said honestly. 'Ciaran is the man to ask about that, I suppose. But it does seem like the family's reaction was extreme. Maybe Khalid was already married.'

Immediately, Hope shook her head. 'That would have broken Elenor's heart but her family would have been thrilled, because any further relationship would've been impossible.'

'True,' Will conceded. 'I suppose they could have just been massive control freaks. Unless . . .'

He stopped, gazing thoughtfully out to see. 'Unless?' Hope echoed.

'Unless there was an added complication – something she didn't put in her journal.'

Frowning, she studied him. 'What kind of complication?'

Will pursed his lips. 'Didn't you say she came back to England because of an illness?'

'An infected mosquito bite,' Hope said. 'The same thing that killed Lord Carnarvon, actually.'

'So, what if it wasn't an illness?' he replied and gave Hope a sober look. 'What if it was a pregnancy?'

Hope nearly dropped her parcel of chips. 'No,' she exclaimed, as goosebumps nettled her skin. The thought was almost too much to contemplate. 'Elenor would never have – she'd never have done what she did if there'd been a baby. *Khalid's* baby.'

He inclined his head. 'I'm just putting it out there. A mixed-race baby, born out of wedlock, in nineteen twenties England. That's the kind of scandal no amount of family support could paper over.'

Hope's mind raced as she considered the awful possibility that Will was right. Reading between the lines, she was fairly sure Elenor and Khalid had spent the night together on more than one occasion so there was certainly a chance of an accidental pregnancy. And it might go a long way to explaining the extreme actions of Elenor's family, as well as her belief that things were only going to get worse. But she couldn't accept that the woman she had come to know through the pages of the journal would take the life of her unborn baby along with her own. It simply didn't fit with who Elenor Lovelace had been.

'No, I don't believe it,' she said decisively. 'And if Elenor was pregnant, she would have mentioned it in her diary, or at least alluded to it somehow. She can't have been.'

Will raised a conciliatory hand. 'Okay, you've read it and I haven't. It was just an idea.'

Brodie was tugging at his sleeve and he turned to her, pointing out the colourful boats in the harbour and the two lighthouses at the end of the twin piers. Picking listlessly at her chips, Hope mulled over the grenade he'd lobbed her way and dismissed it all over again. Elenor wore her heart on her sleeve. If she'd known she was pregnant, it would have been there on the page. And it hadn't been. Hope was sure of that, at least.

After a few minutes, Will cleared his throat. 'Brodie bought you a gift.'

The words brought Hope back from her musings. Mentally regrouping, she smiled at the little girl. 'That's very kind of you. But you really didn't have to.'

Brodie's gaze didn't waver and Will stepped in to translate. 'I think it's because you've given her a couple of presents now – she decided it was our turn to treat you. And she spotted this in one of the gift shops and thought you might like it.'

He dug into his coat pocket and pulled out a small paper bag sealed with a tiny sticker. Brodie held out a hand to take it, studied it for a moment, then presented it to Hope.

'Thank you,' Hope said, as she took the bag and peeled back the sticker. 'This is very exciting.'

She felt Brodie's scrutiny as she opened the bag and slid the contents onto the palm of her hand. A silver keyring in the shape of a mermaid lay against her skin, tail curling into a joyful smile, with a jade-green gem cupped between her outstretched fingers.

'It's sea glass,' Will said. 'Not quite an emerald but Brodie was quite insistent we bought a green one, like Elenor's ring.'

Hope held the keyring up, allowing the light to catch on the glass. 'It's beautiful. Thank you.'

Without warning, Brodie reached up to touch a coppery curl of hair that had escaped from Hope's ponytail. Hope laughed. 'Are you suggesting my hair is as wild as a mermaid's?'

The girl nodded shyly and Hope raised a hand to pull the scrunchie out, letting her hair cascade down her back and dance in the breeze. Brodie gasped in delight and held her fingers up so the strands tickled her skin. 'Of course, mermaids have magical hair that never tangles,' Hope said as the girl giggled. 'I wish I did.'

'It might not be magical but it is beautiful,' Will said, and Hope glanced across to see him watching her.

'Give it five minutes in this wind and you won't be saying that,' Hope replied, grimacing. 'My mother says the knots used to drive her to drink and she's very glad it's not her problem anymore.'

He fired a rueful look at Brodie's fine blonde hair. 'Now that I can identify with.'

It was another reminder of the steep learning curve he'd been on, Hope thought – even the everyday things must have been a challenge at first. Gently, she disentangled Brodie's fingers and snared her own unruly curls safely with the scrunchie. 'Thank you very much for my keyring,' she said again. 'I'm going to remember this trip every time I look at it.'

The little girl's answering beam was like the sun coming out. 'You're welcome,' Will said, as he gathered up their discarded chip wrappers. 'But sadly, we'd better think about heading home now otherwise Brodie will fall asleep in the car and will be wide awake at bedtime.'

Hope tucked the keyring into her handbag and stood up. 'Surely there's time for a race along the beach first?' She swung the bag onto her shoulder and set off at a run for the stone steps that led to the golden sand. 'Last one down is It!'

Inevitably, Brodie's eyelids fluttered closed almost before they'd left Whitby. It wasn't much after five-thirty but, as Will pointed out, she'd spent most of the afternoon wandering up and down the hilly streets of the town, not to mention twenty minutes playing on the beach before Will had finally called time on their game of It. She had to be exhausted.

'I could do with a nap myself,' Hope said, trying

unsuccessfully to hide a yawn. 'There's something about the sea air that wears you out, isn't there?'

Will nodded. 'That's why I suggested we pick up the coffees. I might regret it at bedtime but for now I'd rather be wired than weary.'

Hope took a sip of her latte and reached for the radio controls. 'Good shout. I'll see if I can find us some tunes to listen to.'

They chatted as the miles passed, occasionally disagreeing about a song or band, but Hope was pleasantly surprised to find there was plenty of overlap in their musical tastes. Will seemed relaxed enough for most of the journey but, as they neared York, she noticed he grew less talkative. His hands tightened on the wheel from time to time, and his eyes strayed to the rear-view mirror more often, checking on the sleeping Brodie. Hope thought she knew the reason for his change of mood but she didn't know how to respond; should she continue to talk, try to distract him? Or lapse into silence and allow him to concentrate?

In the end, she decided on the direct approach. 'It happened on the A64, didn't it?' she said quietly, after he'd been grimly silent for several long minutes. 'The accident that killed Scott and Lucy.'

He glanced across at her, surprised. 'Yes. How did you know?'

She sighed. 'Iris told me. But I would have known anyway. It's written all over you.'

He grunted and checked the mirror again. 'It's just up

ahead. Brodie doesn't know it was this road.' His jaw tightened but his tone stayed even. 'I don't want her to be scared every time we go in or out of York.'

'That's understandable,' Hope said, then paused. 'You're doing an amazing job of looking after her. I know you've had to learn on the job, as it were, and it hasn't been easy, but anyone can see she's in good hands.'

The ghost of a smile pulled at his lips. 'Thank you. It helps that she's such a good kid. But I worry that it's just me and her so much of the time – she doesn't spend much time with children her own age. Even when we go to the park, she doesn't stray far from my side.'

Hope frowned. 'She must be due to start school soon?'

'In September,' he said, nodding. 'I tried starting her at a new nursery, when she first came to live with me, but she screamed the place down whenever it was time for me to leave. In the end, her therapist and I decided it would be better to get her settled into life with me over the summer.'

Once again, Hope's heart ached. 'It sounds like the best decision for both of you.'

'Yeah, I think it was,' he said, with another sideways glance. 'I'm not sure how it's going to go at school, to be honest. It's going to be tough on her and kids can be cruel – they might pick on her for not speaking.'

Admittedly, Hope's knowledge of small children was mostly limited to her niece and nephews, and the children of friends, but in her experience they were far more accepting than adults. 'I imagine they'll be curious, at least at first,' she said. 'But they'll probably just take it at face value and move on.'

'I hope so,' Will said, studying Brodie's reflection. 'Maybe I should try and make friends with some other parents, to ease her into things. Although I'm not sure where I'd even begin.'

An idea occurred to Hope. 'Come to my parents' party,' she suggested spontaneously. 'My nephews will be there, they're around Brodie's age, and some of the guests are bringing children so there'll be plenty of kids for her to hang out with.'

Will shook his head. 'That's very kind but I couldn't possibly. I've never even met your parents – I can't just crash their ruby anniversary.'

'You'd be my guest,' Hope said. 'And Iris is coming – you'll know her.'

He threw her a suspicious look. 'Isn't she doing the flowers?'

'Yes,' she admitted, 'but she'd be coming anyway, as my friend. You and Brodie are my friends too.'

'I don't know ...' he said, slowing the car as they approached a roundabout, and almost did a double take as he recognized their location. 'Hey, we're here.'

Hope blinked in confusion. 'Here?'

'At the Hopwood roundabout,' he said, then paused. 'Past the place of the accident. We were talking so much I must have missed it.'

'Ah,' Hope said cautiously, trying to gauge his feelings. 'Sorry.'

Will eased the car back into the traffic. 'Don't be. I'd much rather be engrossed in conversation than be reminded of what happened.' He looked at her and smiled. 'I've had a really good time today. Thank you.'

Once again, Hope felt she ought to be thanking him. From her quiet reflections on the cliffs to the breathless laughter of chasing him and Brodie across the sand, she couldn't remember an afternoon she'd enjoyed more. 'Honestly, it was my pleasure,' she said warmly, then paused to fix him with a meaningful stare. 'And I'll tell you another great time just waiting to happen – my parents' party.'

He laughed. 'Do you ever take no for an answer?'

'Sometimes,' Hope said, grinning. 'And if you really don't think it's a good idea then I won't mention it again. But I'd like it if you came.'

He glanced across at her, still amused. 'How about I'll think about it?'

Hope sat back in her seat, satisfied. 'Good enough for now.'

Chapter Seventeen

'Your parents,' Iris said, nudging Hope with a deep sigh of admiration. 'They are just the cutest.'

It was just after eight o'clock in the evening and the party had been in full swing for over an hour. Hope wasn't sure what had tipped her mother into her first eruption of joyful but effusive sobs – the sight of so many of her friends and relatives unexpectedly gathered in one place, the fabulous ruby-themed flowers and decorations that festooned the marquee in such breath-taking fashion, or the bonus appearance of her youngest child with a bouquet that had been painstakingly made by Iris to replicate the one she'd carried at her wedding forty years earlier. It had taken a lot of champagne and many tearful hugs to calm her down and even now, Hope could see her fluttering as she moved from group to group – more tears seemed inevitable. Thankfully, Hope's father had reacted in a much more relaxed way and seemed to be exerting a calming influence on his wife, which, Hope reflected, was what had happened for their entire marriage.

'Yeah, they're not bad,' she said to Iris, leaning back in her chair and taking a sip of her own champagne.

Her friend raised a jet-black eyebrow. 'Not bad? They're relationship goals. I'd like to be half as happy with someone as they seem together.' She glanced around. 'In fact, your whole family is adorable, including your little brother. I can't believe you all have the same hair – you're basically the Weasleys, but better looking.'

Hope glanced over at Joe, who was hovering by the buffet, and caught him staring at Iris with undisguised interest. 'Hmmm. Well, watch out for my little brother. He can be quite the charmer and I think he's got his eye on you.'

'If only he was ten years older,' Iris replied with a sigh. 'Speaking of charmers, how's Professor Sex God? Did you see him before he vanished back to darkest Scarborough?'

Hope thought back to the previous Saturday, when she and Ciaran had spent the whole night alternating between talking and kissing and sleeping. Sunday morning had been devoted to discussion of Elenor's journal; Hope had been relieved when he'd agreed that it was unlikely there'd been a pregnancy. 'There's certainly never been even a hint of that in anything I've read about her,' he'd said, frowning. 'I think it's a red herring.'

He'd finally left around midday, giving Hope just time to throw herself into the shower and slap on some make up to prevent Charlotte from giving her the third degree over lunch. 'I saw him,' she told Iris carefully. 'He was still very interested in Elenor's journal.'

Iris nodded. 'Ordinarily I'd suggest boys only say that when they want to get you into bed but with him, I don't think it's true.'

Hope laughed. 'No. But I won't see him again until September at the earliest. He'll probably have forgotten about me and the journal by then.'

'Oh yes, that's likely,' Iris said, rolling her eyes in mock-annoyance. 'But I do think you should be—'

Whatever Iris had been about to say was lost as an insistent tinkling sound floated across the marquee. Hope looked up to see Harry tapping a glass with a fork and looking round expectantly. 'Ladies and gentlemen,' he said, lowering the glass and taking the microphone that someone was holding out. 'If you'd all like to gather round, my parents would like to say a few words.'

Applause broke out and people began to drift in from outside. Hope's parents waited for them to arrive, and for the clapping to die down, then her father took the microphone and began to speak.

'Dear friends and loved ones,' he said, with an encompassing glance that seemed to take in the whole room. 'Firstly, thank you so much for coming here to celebrate our fortieth wedding anniversary. I can't tell you how wonderful it is to see you all here.

'Many of you know the story of how Angela and I met – if you don't, catch me at the bar later and I'll bore you with the details – and some of you might even know that our son, Harry, was almost called Bryan. Very few of you know that Charlotte's middle name is Roxy but she doesn't like us to talk about that much so I'll leave it there.'

There was a smattering of laughter and Hope didn't need to look at Charlotte to know she was trying to hide a furious scowl.

Their father raised the microphone again. 'What I really wanted to say is that over the last forty-something years, not a day has passed that I haven't thanked my lucky stars for sending me to that gig.' He turned to his wife and took her hand. 'I couldn't have hoped for a better woman to share my life with. Here's to the next forty, my love.'

Now the applause was rapturous, so loud and long that Hope wondered whether the wedding guests from the other part of the venue had gate-crashed. But eventually it died down and Hope saw that her mother was holding the microphone. Hope exchanged a nervous glance with Charlotte, because their mother was clearly a little the worse for champagne, but there was nothing to be done.

'Friends,' she began, with only the faintest hint of a hiccup at the end. 'Thank you for making this special anniversary even more special. I'm sure it can't have been forty years since we said "I do" – inside, I still feel like the giggling teenager who saw the most beautiful man of her life at a concert and was lucky enough to marry him. But it's been a pleasure to grow older with him – I won't say old, because we all know sixty is the new forty – and I can't wait to see what the next decade brings us.'

She paused and Hope could see tears sparkling in her eyes as she looked around. 'We agreed not to buy each other a gift – it's enough that we still have each other – but, as some of you know, I've never been one for sticking to the rules. So, here's my gift to you, Gerry. I hope it makes you think of every minute we've had together, as well as all the time still to come.'

To Hope's astonishment, it was Will who stepped forward to pass her mother a small white box. Iris seemed equally nonplussed and the two of them exchanged puzzled looks as Hope's mother presented the box to Hope's dad. A whisper of curiosity ran around the room as he opened it and then it was his eyes that glistened. He pulled out a silvery watch and suddenly Hope understood.

'It's my grandfather's watch,' she murmured to Iris. 'Dad used to wear it all the time but it broke years ago and he never found anyone who could fix it.'

Iris caught on. 'Obviously, he never found Wonder Will.'

'Obviously not,' Hope agreed. 'Luckily for Dad, my mother did.'

'Thank you.' Hope's father spoke into the microphone again, his voice husky with emotion. 'And it's funny you got me a gift, even though you weren't supposed to, because I've never been very good at doing as I'm told either. So, I got you a present too.'

And now Hope stared in disbelief as Will came forward again, this time handing a box to Hope's father. 'You have got to be kidding me,' she said to Iris, who simply grinned in reply.

This box contained a pair of ruby and diamond earrings that flashed and gleamed in the lights. Murmurs of admiration and approval filled the air as Hope's mother gazed at them, then she threw her arms around her husband and the room exploded into whoops and cheers. A moment later, she let go and turned to throw her arms around Will. Beside Hope, Iris let out a delighted laugh and Hope couldn't help joining her.

'And now let's celebrate!' Hope's father called, which only increased the noise levels. 'See you at the bar!'

'Didn't I tell you?' Iris said, still beaming with evident satisfaction. 'They are the cutest.'

But Hope had caught Will's eye. She raised her hands in an obvious WHAT? gesture and he shrugged, pointing to the door that led out into the gardens. 'Back in a minute,' Hope told Iris. 'Don't forget, beware of Joe.'

It wasn't until Hope was outside in the cooling summer air, under the ghost of the rising full moon, that she realized Will was alone. 'Where's Brodie?' she asked the moment she was close enough.

'Over there,' he said. 'She's playing Giant Jenga with those two boys, who are very clearly related to you in some way.'

Hope followed his gaze and saw that Brodie was playing with her nephews, apparently oblivious that Will was not immediately beside her. 'Wow,' she said, smiling. 'Didn't I tell you this would be good for her?'

'You did,' he allowed. 'And you were right. Thanks for inviting us.'

She batted him playfully on the arm. 'Not that you needed the invitation – my mother has clearly decided you're part of the family now. Why didn't you tell me my parents had roped you into their gifts to each other?'

'I didn't know,' he said. 'Not at first, anyway. You mother came in with the watch last week but I didn't connect the dots until I framed your photograph of the two of them.'

'Of course,' Hope said. 'And Dad?'

Will spread his hands. 'He came in to buy some earrings. I recognized him too, as well as his name, and told him we were friends. I offered to bring the earrings with me to pre-vent the risk of your mother finding them before the party.'

Hope had to concede it had been a sensible suggestion. Her mother was infamous for rooting out gifts before the buyer could give or even wrap them. 'Of all the jewellers in all of York, they both happened to walk into yours,' she said, with an incredulous shake of her head. 'Amazing.'

'I know,' he said with a lopsided smile. 'I thought about telling you, but I didn't want to spoil the surprise.'

She wasn't sure whether he meant the gifts themselves or his involvement in them but she supposed it didn't really matter. His presence had made a wonderful moment even better. Sighing happily, Hope gazed around at the guests chatting in the fading sunshine, and the children playing on the immaculate lawn. She shivered as the evening breeze tickled her skin. 'I need a drink. Want one?'

He shook his head. 'No, I'm fine, thanks.'

'You're driving?'

'Parenting,' he corrected. 'And we'll probably be heading off soon. I don't want Brodie to get over-stimulated.'

Hope could understand that but surely drink one wouldn't hurt? He'd put away a few glasses of wine when she'd gone over for dinner, after all.

'Honestly, I'm fine,' he said, when she suggested one for the road. 'I had some champagne earlier and it's been a long day. Brodie is tired.'

Hope glanced over to where the little girl was bouncing around, apparently full of energy. She frowned. There was something stiff about Will's expression, a weird tension that seemed to have come out of nowhere. 'Is everything okay? You're being a bit ... off.'

His gaze skittered away. 'No, everything is fine.'

Less than convinced, she stepped nearer. 'You're sure? Did one of the kids say something to Brodie? Or was it my mother? I'm sorry about the over-familiarity, she gets like that after a few drinks.'

'No, it's nothing like that,' Will said, waving the apology away. He gave her a long look before sighing. 'It's not important.'

'Right, that's it.' She folded her arms. 'Something's definitely going on. Out with it.'

'It's nothing,' he insisted. 'Let's not do this here. Not tonight.'

'Do what?' Hope thought she might explode with frustration. 'What shouldn't we do? And why not tonight?'

'Because ...' He took a deep breath, as though he was

about to argue, and then deflated. 'It's just . . . have you seen Ciaran recently?'

Hope gaped. Whatever she'd been expecting him to say, it wasn't this. 'Not since last Saturday and he's on a dig in Sussex now. Why?'

Will shifted uncomfortably. 'Right. Have you heard from him much? Seen any photos from the dig?'

Now Hope stared at him outright, wondering if he'd put away more champagne than he was admitting. 'The odd message but no photos. Why, do you have a sudden burning urge to look at Roman pottery sherds?'

This drew a reluctant half-smile which faded faster than it had appeared. 'No.' He ran a hand through his hair and avoided her gaze. 'Look, I don't know how to tell you this, or even whether I should but . . . has Ciaran ever suggested he's – that he might be—'

'Just spit it out,' Hope said, as patiently as she could manage. 'Has Ciaran ever suggested that he's what?'

The seconds ticked by, during which Will grew more and more miserable. 'Married,' he said eventually. 'Has he ever told you that he's married?'

'No!' Hope said, and laughed incredulously. 'Why would he?'

He stared at her mutely, then transferred his gaze to the ground.

She laughed again, a gurgle of amusement that caught a little in her throat. 'I don't know where you got that idea from but Ciaran isn't married. He lives on campus five days a week and eats Pot Noodles for dinner.'

Again, Will stayed silent and Hope felt a bubble of bewilderment and anger start to grow inside her. 'Why would you say such a thing?'

He started to reply then stopped.

'Oh, for god's sake, speak!' She heard her voice getting shrill, just as she saw Will shrinking into his suit, but she couldn't seem to calm down. 'Seriously, what the hell would make you say such a thing?'

Will straightened up. 'Because he came into the shop yesterday,' he said, suddenly matter of fact. 'To buy an eternity ring for the woman he was holding hands with, to celebrate the fact that they'd been married for ten years. He looked a bit puzzled as we talked, like he was trying to place me, and I thought I recognized him but I didn't know where from until he handed over his credit card. So, then I looked him up online to make sure I wasn't wrong and ... it was definitely him.'

The blood rushed in Hope's ears as she stared at him. There must be some mistake, she told herself numbly as her heart thudded against her ribs. It couldn't be true. Ciaran had been in Sussex all week, he couldn't have been in Will's shop yesterday. There must be some mistake. 'You're lying.'

'I'm sorry, Hope,' Will said, with gut-wrenching apology. 'I didn't want to tell you, or at least not tonight, but I thought you should know.'

'You're lying,' she repeated, and now her voice sounded reedy and broken. 'Why are you saying this? Why would you—'

She stopped as the truth crashed through her flimsy denial. Will had no reason to lie and she knew him well enough to accept that he'd have made triple-sure he was not mistaken. Tears stung her eyes, rushing over her lashes like a bubbling geyser. Of course it was true. Letting out a half-sob, she turned away, running blindly to where she hoped the door to the marquee was. Behind her, she heard Will shout her name but she didn't stop until she crashed into someone coming the other way.

'Hope?' a voice said, ringing with concern. 'What is it? What's wrong?'

Shaking, Hope swiped at her eyes until her vision cleared. 'Oh!' she wailed, and threw herself into her sister's arms. 'Oh, Charlotte!'

PART THREE

Broken Promises

Chapter Eighteen

'Cheer up, love, it might never happen.'

The words were called from a white van that was trundling along Low Petergate, stuck in the slow-moving traffic that occasionally clogged York's narrow city streets, and the driver offered Hope a jaunty thumbs up as he crawled alongside. He meant well, she supposed with a grunt, but right at that moment she was tempted to tell him exactly where he could shove his thumb. It wasn't worth the ensuing argument, of course, but the thought was enough to raise the ghost of a smile, which only seemed to encourage the driver because he added a jolly blast of the horn. It didn't help with the headache that had lingered behind her temple for the last two weeks, nor did it cheer Hope up. She had good reason to be unhappy and it was going to take a lot more than an instruction from a random stranger to make her feel better.

Thankfully, the traffic began to move and the van, with its irritating driver, was swept along with it. Hope fixed her gaze on the pavement once more and continued on her way towards High Petergate. There were a few things with the power to make her forget her bruised heart; her family and friends were one, and her job at the Ever After Emporium was another. Being surrounded by so many antiques and vintage items – each with its own fascinating story – was a source of endless distraction and allowed her to keep reality at bay. It was only when she was alone, with nothing to distract her, that she found herself dwelling on the source of her misery: Ciaran McCormack and the hole he'd left in her life. And it didn't matter how many times her sister told her he'd behaved appallingly and that she was better off without him. Logically, Hope knew both of those things but when was the heart ever logical? She hadn't even been in love with Ciaran, it had been far too early for that, but she had lowered her guard which, in turn, had opened the door to tentative feelings, something she hadn't allowed since losing Rob some two years ago. It had hurt when she'd discovered Ciaran was married, and left her feeling foolish. She'd been taken in by his charm and flattered by his interest, it hadn't occurred to her that he might not be everything he claimed to be. But then, she hadn't been totally honest with him; she hadn't revealed she was a widow, suspecting he'd be scared off by her past. Perhaps she'd have saved herself some heartache if she had told him about Rob at the outset.

Her mood lifted the moment she stepped inside the Emporium, however. There were still twenty-five minutes before nine o'clock and the shop was almost silent, apart from the fading jangle of the bell above the door and the deep ticking of the grandfather clock that was out of sight along the aisle. Hope paused in the doorway, straining her ears for the faint, delicate tick of the cuckoo clock beyond the grandfather clock. She smiled when she heard it. All was well in the Emporium.

Her colleague, Frances, emerged from further along the aisle. 'Morning,' she called cheerily. 'I thought it must be you. How are you today?'

'I'm fine, thanks,' Hope replied, heading towards the old-fashioned, dark wood counter that was her usual Tuesday morning post. 'No Mr Young today?'

'Auction in Harrogate,' Frances said. 'I've been drafted in to fill the gap. But I thought we could hatch a plan for that third window, if things are quiet.'

Hope nodded. The window displays hadn't originally been part of her role when she'd first started at the Emporium, some four months earlier, but she'd been inspired by some of the stock in the storeroom upstairs and had made an idle suggestion about how the items might go together. Mr Young had been enthusiastic and suggested she work with Frances, whose job did include dressing the windows. The resulting Afternoon Tea at the Emporium display had proved popular with passers-by, which seemed to have led to an upturn in sales that had delighted the Emporium's owner. Frances had been pleased too; she'd confessed privately to Hope that she was running out of ideas herself and welcomed a fresh eye and imagination. And now they were planning their third window together, one themed around York's proud involvement in the chocolate industry; just thinking about it made Hope crave a KitKat.

She glanced out at High Petergate, where the summer tourists were already filling the street, and shook her head. 'I don't think we're going to be quiet – not if yesterday was anything to go by. But we can make a start, at least, and see how far we get.'

Just as Hope had predicted, there was a steady stream of customers across the morning, building to a rush in the afternoon. Some were clearly just browsing and Hope couldn't blame them – the Emporium had a way of drawing people in and leading them on through the aisles, like a Victorian lady showing a scandalous flash of ankle that promised so much more. Others were tempted to buy and both Hope and Frances were kept busy wrapping the smaller items and arranging delivery for the larger goods. And, of course, Hope felt a pang each time one of her favourites found a new owner, even as she was glad it would be loved and appreciated anew. Thankfully, her favourite antique of all – the magnificent walnut grandfather clock – was safely marked with a red, not-for-sale sticker. It was largely thanks to that clock that she'd got the job at the Emporium in the first place and she couldn't imagine how empty the shop would feel without its sonorous chimes and reassuring tick.

As closing time drew near, the flow of customers began to ebb, allowing Frances and Hope to relax a little. Hope was just about to turn the sign on the door to 'Closed' when she saw Iris making her way across the road from her flower shop, Blooming Dales.

'Hello,' she said, pulling back the door to allow the florist inside. 'I meant to pop over to see you at lunchtime but we've been working flat-out all day.'

Iris pulled a face. 'It's been non-stop for me too – did we miss the Shop-'Til-You-Drop memo or something?' She paused. 'Don't get me wrong, I'm not complaining. I'd just have bought more roses at the flower market if I'd known.'

'Whereas I would have brought something for lunch,' Hope replied ruefully. 'I'd planned to grab something on my break but I didn't actually get one. I'm starving!'

Her friend raised both eyebrows. 'In that case, I have an invitation that will probably make you drool,' she said and reached into the pouch of her apron. 'I delivered the usual displays to Isobel Lovelace today and she asked me to pass this on to you.'

She held out a square white card. Hope took it, frowning as she deciphered the looping handwriting. 'She wants me to come for afternoon tea?'

'I know,' Iris said, her eyes dancing. 'Isn't it so deliciously Jane Austen? But I bet she'll put on a good spread – or at least her housekeeper will.'

'It's for Friday afternoon,' Hope observed. 'I wonder what brought this on.'

'Maybe she wants to thank you for returning Elenor's diary,' Iris said.

That was a good call, Hope thought as she turned the

card over in her hands. She'd first met Isobel Lovelace after discovering a beautiful Art Deco ring and a letter breaking off an engagement inside an old wooden puzzle box at the Emporium. In fact, it had been Hope's efforts to uncover who the ring and the letter belonged to that had led her to Ciaran at the University of York. As a Professor of Egyptology, he'd been intrigued by the scarab beetle design of the ring and the letter's references to excavations in 1920s Egypt, and had quickly worked out that the letter had been written by local archaeologist, Elenor Lovelace. Eventually, they had found Isobel, Elenor's great niece, who had been reluctant to help at first but had relented, leaving her great aunt's diary at the Emporium for Hope's eyes only. The unexpected gift had sent Hope spiralling back in time, headlong into the astonishing discovery of Tutankhamun's tomb and a tragic story of doomed love. She'd reluctantly returned the journal a week ago and was still suffering from a book hangover of epic proportions. It really wasn't helping with the whole 'getting over Ciaran' thing.

'I guess she might want to thank me,' Hope said to Iris, with another thoughtful glance at the invitation. 'Although she really doesn't need to. In fact, I should be the one thanking her, for lending me Elenor's journal in the first place.'

Her friend sighed. 'I've got a horrible suspicion she might be lonely. I know she comes across as totally self-sufficient but I sometimes wonder if it's a bit of an act.'

It wasn't the first time Iris had suggested something along those lines, Hope thought, and it was entirely possible she was right. 'I'll go, see what she wants. A little company is the least I can do.'

'Speaking of company,' Iris said, fixing her with a meaningful look. 'Have you spoken to Will recently?'

Hope studied the ground. 'A bit.'

'I'm sure I don't have to remind you not to shoot the messenger,' Iris said. 'He didn't want to be the one to tell you about Ciaran's wife but he did it anyway, because he's a good friend.'

'I know,' Hope said, and sighed. 'It's just a bit awkward, that's all. I'm not *not* speaking to him.'

'But you aren't speaking to him, either,' Iris replied. 'Not like you were before.'

The observation sounded exactly like the kind of thing Hope's older sister, Charlotte, would say and it stung a little. 'It's not just me. He hasn't messaged much.'

'Because he feels awkward too.' Iris folded her arms. 'Do I need to knock your heads together or something?'

And now she definitely sounded like Charlotte. 'No, Iris,' she said meekly.

'Good,' the florist said, apparently mollified. 'Message him tonight. I'm sure he'll be glad to hear from you.'

'Yes, Iris.'

'And since I seem to have turned into your mum, eat some food.'

Hope couldn't help smiling then, because curvy, gorgeous thirty-something Iris was about as far away from her mother as it was possible to get. 'Okay, I will. And thanks for delivering Isobel's invitation. I'll let you know how it goes.'

'Please do,' Iris said. 'I'll trade you for details of my date on Friday night, although my expectations are low and I seriously doubt there will be any French Fancies involved.'

Hope's smile widened into a grin, because Iris's forays into online dating were always entertaining. 'You've got yourself a deal,' she said.

It took Hope six attempts to draft a message to Will. The first was too chatty, too effusive – she could imagine him reading it with raised eyebrows and a faintly puzzled expression. The second felt cold and abrupt; she could picture his frown, two thin creases between his hazel eyes and a bewildered twist around his mouth. Efforts three, four and five were better but still didn't capture the breeziness she felt was needed. Finally, she gave up trying to write something clever and opted for the truth.

Hello. I've missed you. How are things?

She hit send before she could second-guess herself any further and put her phone down on the coffee table. After a moment's thought, she put a magazine on top and, after a few more seconds had ticked by, got up to prowl through to the kitchen. The fridge was stacked with tempting snacks; Charlotte had reverted to full-on clucky Mother Hen mode as soon as the truth about Ciaran had broken and had insisted Hope must eat well.

'You don't need to fuss,' Hope had told her, as her sister loaded the fridge with falafel and humous and cheese. 'I'm fine.'

Charlotte's glance was sceptical. 'You didn't seem fine when you were sobbing in my arms. It's okay to admit you're hurting, Hope – we're here for you.'

And that was part of the problem, Hope had thought – it felt like she was lurching from one disaster to another and all her family ever did was pick her up after she'd fallen. 'I admit finding out about Ciaran was a nasty surprise,' she replied. 'But let's be honest, it's not in the same league as losing Rob. I really don't need looking after.'

Now Charlotte's expression softened. 'I know you don't and of course it's not like Rob. But I also know you trusted Ciaran and he let you down. That kind of betrayal hurts.'

Hope had opened her mouth to deny it, then sighed. 'I'll get over it.'

'You will,' her sister agreed firmly, and waved a wax-covered round of cheese. 'With time, TLC and this excellent chilli Red Leicester.'

The cheese was long gone now, replaced by other treats designed to encourage Hope to indulge herself. And while she felt her family's well-meaning interference was unwarranted, she had to admit it had helped. Right now, she was using her sister's shopping skills to distract her from wondering whether Will had replied, or whether he would reply at all. Loading a plate with food, she poured a glass of chilled Sauvignon Blanc and carried both through to the balcony that overlooked the wharf. By the time the plate was clean and the glass was empty, she felt robust enough to risk a glance at her phone.

Will had replied 43 minutes earlier, less than five minutes after she'd sent her message. Hope's finger hovered over the message for a few seconds, trying to dispel her uneasiness, and then the realization that she was being ridiculous crashed over her. She stabbed the screen and Will's words blossomed into view.

> Hey, great to hear from you. We're good, apart from a
> seriously out of control Paw Patrol habit – how are you?

The thought of him locked in a TV battle of wills with his niece, Brodie, made Hope smile. He'd only been her sole guardian for six months, with no experience of raising a child prior to that, and he freely admitted he was often out of his depth but Hope also knew he would do anything to make the little girl happy. Even if that meant numbing his brain with endless kids' TV.

> Oh dear, she tapped out in reply. Sounds like you
> need a new book to read!

Instantly, Will is typing … appeared at the top of the screen.

> Are you kidding? It's your Matryoshka doll book all the
> way. She sleeps with it. But don't think you're getting
> away with dodging my question. How are you?

Hope's fingers moved automatically to write the words *I'm fine* but then she hesitated. On the surface she *was* fine – hadn't she spent the past few weeks trying to convince her family that was true? But she knew Will understood about grief and loss and somehow that made her reluctant to gloss over the fallout from Ciaran's betrayal. And perhaps that was why she'd avoided contacting Will since finding out; subconsciously, she'd known her guard might come down. That and remembering the extreme reluctance with which he'd told her that Ciaran was married. It had been much easier *not* to contact him.

> I've been better, she typed. But also much worse, so I
> guess that's something. I'm sorry to go all silent on you. I
> suppose I didn't know what to say.

It was a shock when her phone vibrated in her hand and she saw Will's number on the screen. She stared at the arrows zooming upwards, then hit the answer button and lifted the handset to her ear.

'Is this okay?' Will asked, before she could even form the word hello. 'I thought it would be better to talk without actually stopping to think about whether you could. Say if it's inconvenient.'

'No, it's fine,' Hope said, as the sound of his voice caused a smile to tug at the corners of her mouth. 'Hello, Will.'

'Hello, Hope,' he replied and she thought it sounded as though he might be smiling too. 'Thanks for messaging.'

She shook her head. 'It should be me thanking you, for saving me from a horrible mistake.'

There was a brief silence. 'You definitely don't need to thank me, Hope. No one wants to hear news like that and believe me, I didn't want to be the one to tell you.'

His voice held the same strain she remembered from the party, when she'd forced him to reveal the wretched truth, and Hope could imagine his expression now. 'It wasn't a great moment,' she allowed. 'But I appreciate you telling me and I'm genuinely sorry I haven't said that until now.'

'It's okay,' he said, and she heard him draw breath. 'So, what have you been up to? The Emporium has looked busy every time Brodie and I have passed by.'

Hope felt a stab of guilt, because she knew how much the little girl loved the shop. Had Will been hurrying Brodie past to avoid an awkward encounter with her? She gave herself a brisk mental shake – of course he hadn't. There were any number of reasons why he might pass by instead of coming in, she told herself, and they had nothing to do with her.

'It's been really busy,' she said. 'Mr Young has been away at a few auctions recently so I've put in some overtime but I don't mind. It's been a good distraction.'

'I can imagine,' he replied sympathetically. 'My shop has been mobbed too – poor Brodie has had to entertain herself more than I'd like but she's a good kid, luckily for me.'

Hope pictured the girl sitting on the rug in Will's jewellery workshop, playing with her dolls. 'I suppose there's no chance of a nanny or a childminder, is there?'

'Zero.' Will's tone was emphatic. 'She still doesn't trust strangers.'

'That's going to be a problem in September,' Hope observed. 'What does your therapist say?'

'That it will be a slow process but we agree that starting school will be a huge positive in the long run. We've got a short getting to know you visit coming up this Thursday, actually, so I'll have a better idea then.'

He sounded weary but optimistic, Hope thought, and once again her heart ached for the two of them, but most especially for the child who'd lost both her parents and everything she'd known. Will was doing a great job and Brodie had adjusted as well as could be expected but it had to be impossibly hard. 'Let me know if I can do anything to help,' she said. 'I'm always here if you need me.'

'Thank you,' Will said and Hope felt the warmth behind the words. 'Let's grab a coffee or something soon. Brodie has missed you and so have I.'

'I'd love to,' Hope said. 'How does Friday morning sound? Charlotte was telling me about a new pop-up coffee van in Rowntree Park, near the playground. They sell out-of-this-world pastries, apparently.'

'Sounds like my kind of place,' Will said. 'Around eleven?'

'Perfect,' Hope said, smiling. 'That gives me plenty of time to find a new book for Brodie.'

'You really don't have to,' Will protested. 'I can do that myself.'

'I know I don't have to,' Hope replied. 'But I want to. Is that okay?'

'It's very okay,' he said. 'But only if you have time.'

She would make time, Hope decided, not that she needed much encouragement to browse the delightful Little Apple Bookshop a few doors down from the Emporium, but the look of delight on Brodie's face when she was presented with a new story from Hope would be an even greater pleasure. 'So, I'll see you on Friday,' she said aloud. 'By the playground.'

'Last one to arrive buys the pastries,' Will agreed. 'See you there.'

It wasn't until she'd ended the call and returned her phone to the coffee table that Hope realized she was still smiling. She'd approached the last few weekends with a sense of dull dread, knowing she had no work to distract her but, between Isobel's invitation and spending some time with Will and Brodie, she was looking forward to the next one. All of a sudden, Friday couldn't come fast enough.

Chapter Nineteen

Hope was relieved to wake up on Friday to bright July sunshine streaming through the skylight above her bed. The previous two days had been grey and wet, and she'd wondered whether she should suggest to Will that they reschedule their coffee date, or at least switch venue – a rainy park wasn't ideal, although Hope knew her brother, Harry, took his boys out in all weathers.

'Believe me, they are better outdoors than cooped up inside,' he'd said with a shudder on more than one occasion.

Will hadn't seemed fazed by the rain, either, but nevertheless, Hope was glad to see the sun. Everything felt better when the sun shone.

She arrived five minutes early, with the bag containing Brodie's new book tucked under her arm, and made straight for the children's playground. The pop-up coffee shop beside it was exactly as Charlotte had described – a yellow VW campervan bedecked with brightly coloured bunting, with an enticing menu chalked onto a blackboard to one side. There was a queue of people snaking away from the serving hatch and the sound of children's voices filled the air; it was such a charming scene that Hope couldn't help but smile. And then she saw Will and Brodie, a little way from the coffee shop, and her smile widened as she raised her arm to wave.

Brodie's face was as solemn as ever as Hope greeted them but she saw the little girl's eyes flicker to the Little Apple Shop bag. Will noticed too and gave an almost imperceptible shake of the head, which Hope took to mean the gift should wait.

'Thanks for sorting out the sunshine,' he said easily. 'I had visions of standing here in the rain.'

Hope grinned. 'I can't take the credit, I'm afraid. I thought it was you.'

Will returned her grin. 'Nope, not us. I suppose we should just be thankful.'

Brodie was tugging at his hand, casting longing glances at the slide, and he nodded at her. 'Go on, then. Don't go too high on the climbing frame.'

Surprised, Hope watched her beetle towards the play area. 'She seems more confident.'

Will tipped his head. 'She can be, if it's a familiar environment and she knows what to expect. I think playing with your nephews at your parents' anniversary party was a big help, to be honest – she learned I didn't vanish if she let go of my hand.'

His tone was matter of fact but Hope knew it was a significant step forward. And it was entirely understandable that Brodie would cling to him, given the tragedy that had already dogged her young life, but it was a promising sign that perhaps she was at least feeling more settled. 'That's great,' Hope replied. 'I'm so pleased. And how did the visit to school go?'

He hesitated. 'It wasn't as smooth as I'd hoped but we got through it. And the teacher was lovely – she made a real effort to include Brodie, even when she clung to my leg and refused to open her eyes.'

'Did she let go at all?' Hope asked.

'Towards the end,' he said. 'And then only long enough to grab a biscuit from the plate the teacher was holding. She wouldn't sit on the carpet for a story.'

'Perhaps it wasn't the right story,' Hope said, and patted the bag under her arm. 'I'm hoping she's going to love this one.'

Will nodded. 'I'm sure she will, since it's a gift from you.' He glanced towards the campervan café, where the queue was dwindling. 'I could murder a coffee. And I know I said the last one to arrive should buy the pastries but I'm pretty sure it's my treat so what can I get you?'

'A pecan and maple Danish,' Hope said promptly. 'Charlotte says they're incredible.'

They joined the briskly moving queue but Hope saw that he kept his eyes on Brodie, even as he chatted to Hope. The obvious bond between them warmed Hope's heart and she was glad they had each other. In the weeks and months after

Rob's death, she'd sometimes wished they'd had a baby, a living reminder of their love that she could focus on and cherish, someone to live for. But she'd also known it would have been harder in so many ways and it felt intolerably selfish to wish for a child to love, knowing they would grow up without a father.

A bench had become available by the time Hope and Will had their coffees and pastries. They sat in companionable silence, eating and watching the children play. Hope saw Brodie glancing over, checking on their location, and she gave her a reassuring wave.

'That was an excellent apple turnover,' Will said as he brushed stray flakes of pastry from his shorts. 'How was yours?'

'Blissful,' Hope said, once she'd swallowed the last mouthful of maple and pecan deliciousness. 'Thank you.'

'You're welcome.' He shifted round to study her. 'So how are things with you? What have you been up to?'

'Work, mostly,' Hope admitted. 'And family stuff. Mum and Dad are still away on their second honeymoon so we haven't had the usual Sunday lunches at home but I've seen a lot of Charlotte.'

Will gave her a sideways glance. 'Has that been helpful?'

She raised her eyebrows wryly. 'She means well. And sometimes I've needed the company so I can't complain.'

'I didn't mean to suggest you would,' he said, sounding a little embarrassed. 'But I know your family can be a bit overwhelming.'

'They really can,' Hope said, smiling. 'But I'm so glad I have them.'

Will nodded. 'Of course.' His gaze came to rest on Brodie once more. 'Have you heard from Ciaran?'

Instinctively, Hope's fingers twitched towards the phone on her pocket, as though drawn by invisible threads. 'Not since I told him not to contact me again. He's given me that, at least.'

Will grunted in derision. 'Yeah, what a guy.' Then he blinked, as though realizing he'd spoken aloud instead of in his head, and his cheeks reddened. 'Sorry. I just think he's an idiot. An utter tool, in fact.'

Now it was Hope's turn to blink. There was a vehemence behind the words that surprised her; Ciaran's behaviour was something both Charlotte and Iris held strong views about but Will was usually so mild-mannered and affable that it felt out of character to hear the condemnation in his voice. And Hope suddenly realized she didn't know much about his life before Brodie had come into it – perhaps someone had cheated on Will in the past. That would certainly explain his outburst, she thought. 'I can't argue with that,' she said ruefully. 'I just wish I didn't feel like such an idiot myself for not seeing it from the start.'

'This isn't on you,' Will replied firmly, without hesitation. 'You took Ciaran at face value, trusted him and he betrayed that trust. You couldn't have known, Hope.'

She knew it was true and yet there was still some part of her that was convinced she'd missed something, a clue or red flag that could have saved her so much heartache. But it didn't really matter now; what was done was done. All she could do was learn from the experience and be more guarded in the future. 'It's all water under the bridge now, anyway,' she said, straightening her shoulders. 'History. And speaking of history, guess who I'm going to see tomorrow afternoon . . .'

Will listened as Hope told him about Isobel's invitation. 'Do you think she wants something from you?' he asked once she'd finished.

'Like what?' she asked. 'Iris thinks she might be lonely.'

'It could be that,' Will agreed. 'I guess you'll find out soon enough.'

'I'll let you know how it goes,' Hope said.

He nodded. 'Please do.' There was a brief pause as his eyes sought Brodie among the melee of children. 'You could come over for dinner again if you like – maybe one evening next week? Brodie would love it and you could fill me in on what Isobel wants.'

Hope mentally reviewed her diary; apart from her belly dance class with Iris on Monday, she had no plans for the following week. 'Yes please,' she said. 'But I can't ask you to cook for me again. Let me bring something.'

'Honestly, don't worry,' he said, smiling. 'It's nice to have someone to cook for. Someone who doesn't demand chicken nuggets and exactly thirty-two peas, I mean.'

Hope grinned. 'Of course. I won't accept anything less than forty-nine.'

Will laughed. 'Noted. Let me know which day works for

you.' He turned his face to the sunshine for a moment, then sighed. 'And now I suppose I should think about getting back to work. Shall I call Brodie over so you can give her the book?'

'That would be great,' Hope said, patting the bag on the bench beside her. 'It's a counting rhyming picture book called *Snug as a Bug*. I thought it might help with the school prep.'

'I'm sure it will,' he said, and reached out to press her hand. 'Thank you again.'

His fingers were warm even in the heat of the morning. They rested there for a moment and then they were gone, leaving just the whisper of a tingle on her sun-kissed skin. Hope cleared her throat and picked up the bag. 'My pleasure,' she said.

Brodie was every bit as delighted as Will had predicted, and insisted Hope read the book to her as they sat together on the bench. When the story was over, the little girl immediately turned to the front and demanded Will read it.

'Told you she'd love it,' he said to Hope, smiling over Brodie's head.

It felt to Hope as though the smile lingered on her lips all the way home. If her afternoon with Isobel was even half as enjoyable as her morning, she'd be winning at Friday.

Isobel's apartment was almost exactly as Hope remembered it – impractically white, cool despite the July heat and as serene a space as she'd ever seen. The air was scented with flowers; last time, it had been lilies in tall vases in both the

253

hallway and the living room, and this time it was heady white roses, which Hope knew had been delivered by Iris just a few days before. The carpet was as pristine as ever – Hope had planned ahead and brought a spare pair of ballet flats to slip on as she waited at the front door. She had no intention of leaving even the slightest mark on the luxuriously thick carpets.

Isobel gave off the same intimidating aura that Hope remembered too, although she also knew the older woman could be gracious; she'd allowed Hope to read Elenor's diary, after all, and invited her round for tea. But there was still a stiffness to her greeting, which put Hope on a little on edge as she took a seat on the sofa opposite.

'Would you like some tea?' Isobel enquired as her house-keeper waited silently. 'Or perhaps a cold drink?'

'Some water would be lovely,' Hope said. 'Thank you.'

Isobel inclined her head towards the housekeeper. 'I'll have the same, Susan. With ice and lemon, please.'

As the other woman withdrew, Isobel fixed Hope with a knowing look. 'Well, Miss Henderson, I imagine you're wondering why I've invited you here.'

It was a typically blunt opening but Hope saw no reason to lie. 'A bit. It's very kind of you, nonetheless, and gives me the opportunity to thank you in person for the wonderful gift of Elenor's journal.' She summoned up what she hoped was a disarming smile. 'And please, call me Hope.'

Isobel brushed both the thanks and the request aside. 'I knew you could be trusted. There aren't many people I feel that way about.'

'Then I'm even more honoured,' Hope said and steeled herself. 'Especially since you chose me over Professor McCormack.'

'Seen his type before,' Isobel replied briskly. 'Too charming for his own good. And besides, Elenor rarely had a good word to say about the male professors during her university days, apart from Flinders Petrie, of course. No, it was always the women who inspired her – Margaret Murray was a particular favourite.'

Hope felt her curiosity stir. Of course, she'd known Elenor must have attended university – her detailed knowledge and understanding of her work shone from every page of her journal – but she hadn't been able to establish which one. She'd assumed Cambridge but the names Isobel had just mentioned were tugging at her memory. Maybe they'd come up in her early research, when she'd been trying to work out just who the mystery letter writer might be.

'Which university did Elenor go to?' she asked.

'University College London,' Isobel replied. 'Some of the finest archaeologists of the time taught or studied there. And it was a dream come true for Elenor, although her family couldn't have known how much it would change her life. They would never have let her go if they had.'

Life-changing was an understatement, Hope thought; ultimately, Elenor's career had led to her death. But it was easy to imagine her embracing university life – her love of learning had been evident from her journal entries.

Susan reappeared, bearing a tray that held two tall glasses

of iced water and a glass jug that was beaded with condensation. She offered one of the glasses to Hope, then placed the tray on the side table beside Isobel and silently withdrew.

'Tea will be ready presently,' Isobel said, as Hope sipped her water. 'But before then, I have something that might interest you.'

She rose and went to an elegant bureau along one wall. A fizzle of breathless anticipation ran through Hope as she sat up a little straighter. This had to be the reason for the invitation, and while she knew there couldn't be a sequel to the journal – the one she'd read had ended with Elenor's death – perhaps there were photographs or something that might add to what little she knew of Elenor's fiancé, Khalid.

'I thought long and hard about letting you see these,' Isobel said, turning back to Hope with a bundle of yellowed papers in her hands. 'But without wanting to sound mawkish, I'm getting older, with no family of my own left. There comes a time when stories should be passed from one person to the next, even when it means letting some secrets into the light.'

There wasn't a trace of self-pity in her voice, Hope observed. If anything, Isobel spoke with more dispassion than normal. But even so, there was an undercurrent of something beneath the words – a definite sense of something being left unsaid. Perhaps it was as Iris had suggested – the older woman was lonely and this was her way of reaching out. Whatever the motivation, Hope certainly couldn't deny that Isobel had her attention. She opened her mouth to speak but Isobel waved her into silence.

'That's why I'm sharing these with you now,' she went on. 'I don't want Elenor's story to be lost. I want someone to bear witness to her life, and you seem to be a trustworthy person for the job.'

So it was more of Elenor's story. Hope felt a flutter of excitement stirring inside even as she weighed Isobel's words. 'I'm pleased you feel that way. It's such a privilege to learn about Elenor's life and work and I really appreciate you sharing it with me. I—' She paused as she sought the right response. 'I feel like I've got to know her, at least a little. Almost like a friend.'

Now Isobel nodded, as though Hope had confirmed something she'd suspected. 'She was extraordinary. Which is another reason for me to make sure there's someone else to remember her after I'm gone.'

The final three words caused something inside Hope to go still. She didn't know how old Isobel was and would rather poke rose thorns under her fingernails than ask but surely she couldn't be more than in her early seventies. Hope tried to look casual as she appraised the other woman – tall and elegant, with ramrod straight posture, she certainly looked like the picture of health. Perhaps it was simply that Isobel was more aware of the passing years and had one eye on her own mortality, Hope thought uneasily. But it felt like there was more.

It was none of her business but she asked anyway. 'Is everything okay, Isobel?'

For a nanosecond, the older woman appeared to hesitate

but then she offered a brisk smile that banished any suggestion of indecision. 'Quite all right, thank you.' She glanced
towards the door that led to the hallway, where Susan
had just materialized. 'It appears tea is served. I do hope
you're hungry.'

It was well after five o'clock by the time Hope got home.
She lowered her bag to the end of the sofa and carefully
took the tissue-wrapped package of letters from inside,
placing it on the coffee table with reverential hands. Tea
first, she decided, even though she'd drunk several cups
of it while at Isobel's. That had been Earl Grey; what she
needed now was the robust strength of Yorkshire Tea. And
her cheerful Cornishware mug might not as sophisticated
as the matching bone china tea set they'd sipped from that
afternoon but it held significantly more tea. If her experience with Elenor's diary was anything to go by, once she
opened the letters, she'd be unwilling to interrupt her
reading for anything. A decent supply of tea could only be
a good thing.

Having produced the letters and offered them to Hope,
Isobel had seemed at pains to steer the conversation away
from Elenor and hadn't offered much more information on
what Hope might find in Khalid's words. Instead, Isobel had
been curious about Hope and especially interested in her
lifelong fascination with the Emporium. Inevitably, that had
led Hope into explaining the reason for her return to York
and she thought she'd detected a further softening of Isobel's

coolness when she'd mentioned Rob, although she saw the usual tinge of pity in her eyes too. As Hope had been leaving, the older woman had pressed the letters into her hands and smiled with genuine warmth. 'I know Elenor would approve of me entrusting these to you. I'm glad you were the one to find her ring.'

The first letter had been written while both Elenor and Khalid were still in Egypt, before their relationship had gone much beyond professional courtesy, but it was clear that he admired her already. Hope knew from Elenor's journal that she'd been equally swept off her feet. It would have been interesting to compare the letters she wrote back with the feelings she expressed in her diary – Hope could imagine Elenor composing her replies, striving for the required air of propriety that masked her emotions, while also hoping Khalid might read between the lines and understand that she admired him too.

Beside the unspoken attraction that lay behind every sentence, Hope also found herself entranced by the sense of history unfolding on the page. The heat of Egypt and the heady excitement of the search for the tomb of Tutankhamun was tangible; Hope could almost feel the brush of hot sand and see the sun set over the desert as Khalid asked questions and offered answers. Gradually, his feelings blossomed on the page too, until his letters were undisguised expressions of love. Part of Hope wished she still had Elenor's journal, so that she could cross-reference the entries corresponding to each letter and see Elenor's feelings bloom too, but it was enough of an honour to be able to slot these new pieces of the puzzle into place.

The last letter from Khalid was dated 1st April 1923, just before Elenor had written to end their engagement. That letter had never been sent, the breath-taking emerald engagement ring had never been returned, and Elenor had taken her own life not long afterwards. It was clear from Khalid's words that he was aware of her family's disapproval, even as he implored Elenor to come back to Egypt.

Love is a force that scorches all opposition, my dearest Elenor — if it demands that I give up my position, my work and my life then I shall. For without you beside me, I have nothing at all.

The quiet desperation brought tears to Hope's eyes, especially when she considered the tragedy that had followed. She sat back on the sofa, unable to prevent herself from wondering how Khalid had taken the news of Elenor's death. She had no doubt that he must have discovered the awful truth sooner or later; as the days stretched into weeks without contact, he would have reached out to his academic friends and acquaintances — and Elenor's death had made the newspapers, although it had been described as a terrible accident. Perhaps he'd only found out once he'd recovered from the beating he'd taken from thugs hired by Elenor's family. Hope sighed and wiped her tears away, feeling the ache of loss for both of them. Almost a century had passed and the story was still heartbreaking. But it also helped to put her own feelings into perspective – Ciaran might have treated her badly but at least she'd escaped with her heart intact. It was definitely time to dust herself off and look to the future. Her involvement with Ciaran McCormack belonged in the past.

Chapter Twenty

Got a bit of a problem. Don't suppose you can
come over?

The message from Will appeared on Hope's phone just after 6pm on Saturday evening. Frowning, she tapped out a reply:

Of course. Is everything OK?

She stared at the screen, waiting for him to read the message and reassure her there was nothing serious wrong. Minutes ticked by and she considered calling him. Just how serious was this problem? But then she saw the status change and, to her relief, he began typing.

Nothing major. How soon can you get here?

Hope reached for the TV remote and clicked the off button.

On my way, she typed, and reached for her shoes.

Will's house was across the River Foss, up towards York Minster and the University, and not a million miles away from Isobel's penthouse apartment. As always, the city streets were busy – the July sunshine had brought everyone outside but Hope was too preoccupied with coming to Will's aid to enjoy the summer evening. She dodged the tourists as best she could and heaved a sigh of relief when she turned into the side street that led to Will's house.

It felt as though it took an age for him to answer the door, although she knew it was less than a minute. When he did appear, she saw that he was holding a very unwilling Brodie by the hand. The little girl's face was red and furious and Hope also saw signs of stress in Will's expression.

'Hello,' she said, looking cautiously from one to the other. 'Everything okay?'

Will puffed out his cheeks and tried to smile. 'Yes. Hello. Come in.' He stepped back to allow room for Hope to enter and glanced at Brodie. 'Aren't you going to say hello?'

She shook her head mutinously.

'Brodie,' Will warned, a stern note in his voice. 'Say hello to our visitor.'

Anxious to avoid making an obviously tricky situation any worse, Hope ducked down to Brodie's level and waited until the little girl met her gaze. 'Hello,' she said, smiling.

'I've come to visit your dolls. Do you think they'd like to play with me today?'

Brodie hesitated, clearly tempted by Hope's approach. Her eyes flickered to the stairs, then up at Will, who sighed. 'I think the dolls are going to have to wait. We've got a bit of a situation.'

'Oh?' Hope said, trying not to frown. 'What kind of situation?'

'It's probably best if you see for yourself,' he replied, then turned his attention to Brodie. 'Now remember, we have to be quiet. No sudden noises or jumping around.'

Intrigued, Hope straightened up and stepped into the hallway. 'I'll try to remember that,' she said gravely.

To Hope's surprise, he led the way up the modern curved staircase, still holding Brodie's hand as though she might run away at any second. Hope slipped out of her shoes and followed. Will paused at the top of the stairs, in front of a slightly ajar door that Hope knew led to his bedroom. 'In here,' he said, gesturing awkwardly. 'Don't go in, just peer through the gap towards the bed.'

By now thoroughly mystified, Hope did as he asked. The bed was covered in a patterned Orla Kiely bedspread with matching cushions and it took Hope several seconds to identify what she suspected might be the problem. 'I didn't know you had a cat,' she said, glancing back at Will.

'That's just it,' he replied. 'We don't.'

Hope stared at him. 'You don't have a cat?' she echoed. 'Then why is there one on your bed?'

'That's a very good question,' he answered. 'I assume she

came in through one of the open windows. Can you see what she's doing?'

Hope peered through the gap again. The small white and grey cat appeared to be lying in the middle of the rumpled duvet, almost shielded from the world around her. She wasn't curled up or sleeping, the way cats usually were when they found a comfortable spot – this cat was lying prone on her side. 'Licking herself?' she hazarded.

Will shook his head. 'Not herself – if it was that easy, I'd have taken my life into my hands and moved her on already.'

Another thought occurred to Hope. 'Is she hurt?'

'Hard to say for sure,' he said. 'I can't get close enough to look. But I don't think that's the problem.'

Hope was about to give up when she saw the grey and white head turned to nudge something tiny and black. Her eyes narrowed as she suddenly understood. 'Kittens! She's got kittens.'

'Two of them. Apparently, my bed is the perfect nest,' Will said wryly. 'Who knew?'

Brodie was wriggling beside Will, trying to pull her hand from his to enter the bedroom, but Will held firm. 'I've told you already, you can't go in there,' he said. 'The mummy cat is looking after her babies and you'll scare her if you get too close.'

'So, let me get this straight,' Hope said with a frown. 'The cat on your bed doesn't belong to you, and nor do the kittens?'

'Correct,' Will said, as Brodie continued to grow more and more frustrated.

'And you don't know who the cat's owner is?'

He nodded. 'Right again. It's possible she's microchipped but I won't know until I can get her to a vet. There's no collar that I can see but I can't really get close enough, what with one thing and another.'

He meant Brodie, Hope thought as she caught his meaningful glance towards the little girl. Her perfectly natural excitement and enthusiasm was quite likely to disturb the cat and kittens on the bed and Hope didn't want to imagine what might happen if Brodie went bounding into the room.

'How long have they been there?'

Will shrugged. 'No idea. We came back from the shop this evening and found them. I thought I'd closed all the windows before we left this morning but we were in a hurry and I suppose I missed one.'

Hope's eyes travelled back to the scene on the bed. Obviously, the little family needed a new home. 'Have you got a box and a blanket you're not too attached to?'

'I think so, yes.'

'Then how about Brodie takes me to see her dolls while you encourage Mamma Cat to move house?'

Again, Brodie looked as though she was torn. But after a brief inward tussle, she let go of Will's hand and turned to walk along the landing towards her own room. Hope grimaced at Will. 'Good luck!'

Twenty minutes later, Will appeared in the doorway of Brodie's bedroom looking hot and flustered, with one hand wrapped in a damp flannel. Hope lowered the book she'd been reading to Brodie and surveyed him. 'Mission accomplished?'

'Mission accomplished,' he replied. 'And it only cost me three fingers and the skin on one hand.'

She winced in sympathy. 'So now what?'

'Now I call the vet and hope we can reunite the family.'

He went downstairs and Hope heard the low rumble of conversation as he talked on the phone. Once she'd finished reading the story, she smiled at Brodie. 'I don't know about you but I'd really love a hot chocolate.'

The little girl nodded eagerly and got to her feet. Her gaze slid towards Will's bedroom door as they passed it but she kept walking. In the kitchen, Will was jotting something down on the back of an envelope, his mobile tucked under one ear.

'Ok, that's great,' he said into the handset. 'See you then.'

Hope watched as he ended the call. 'Good news?'

'Sort of,' he said, pulling a face. 'The nurse doesn't recommend bringing the mother into the surgery – apparently, it could be quite distressing for her and she might reject the kittens. They recommend leaving some food and water close to the box and allowing the kittens to settle overnight. And they can't offer a home visit either but they did recommend a local charity who might be able to help.'

Hope raised her eyebrows. 'That's something at least.'

Will ran a hand through his brown curls. 'Yeah. I think the nurse felt sorry for me. She sounded very disapproving when she told me I shouldn't have moved them in the first place but what was I supposed to do – sleep on the floor?'

'Of course not,' Hope said soothingly. 'I'm sure you've done the right thing. Where did you put the box?'

'In the wardrobe, which was apparently the right thing at least.' He opened the fridge and studied the shelves. 'I think I've got some roast chicken here. If you were a cat who'd recently had kittens, how would you feel about that?'

'Like I was being well looked after,' Hope said with a smile. 'You're a good cat dad, Will.'

That coaxed an answering smile from him and she saw the frown that had creased his forehead since she'd arrived melt away. 'Maybe I'm getting the hang of this parenting thing after all.'

They ordered a pizza, to distract Brodie as much as anything, and settled down for several noisy games of Hungry Hippos. By the time they'd eaten, Brodie seemed to have forgotten about their unexpected houseguests. She snuggled on the sofa between Hope and Will, her head resting against his chest as they watched the CBeebies bedtime story wind its gentle way to the end.

'Time to brush your teeth, Brodie,' Will said, as the Goodnight message appeared. He glanced at Hope. 'You're welcome to stay, if you'd like. But you've seen us twice in two days so I'll totally understand if you have other things to do.'

Hope thought of Khalid's letters – she'd planned to spend her evening making notes and seeing what else she could find out about him. 'I did have something planned.'

He smiled. 'No problem. Thanks for coming over – I couldn't have done this without you.'

'Yes, you could,' she said. 'I hope you get some sleep. Let me know how your lodgers are in the morning.'

'I will,' he said, and ruffled Brodie's hair. 'Say goodbye to Hope.'

To Hope's surprise, the little girl turned and threw her arms around her middle in a hug. Will seemed equally surprised; his eyes widened as they met Hope's. 'Thank you, Brodie,' she said, gently hugging her back. 'I hope you sleep well too.'

Will and Brodie stood in the doorway to wave Hope off. She paused at the end of the driveway to close the gate and glanced back to see them framed by the roses climbing around the sage green woodwork. It was a sight that warmed her heart and she was suddenly glad all over again that she'd taken Iris's advice to get in touch with Will. Raising her hand, she gave a final wave and set off for home.

Iris had a sparkle in her eye during Monday evening's belly dance class but it wasn't until they'd finished dancing that Hope found out why.

'I met someone interesting,' she said, as they made their way along the street towards their favourite cocktail bar.

Hope grinned in delight. 'Your date on Friday night?'

Iris shook her head. 'Absolutely not – I got hatfished.'

'Hatfished?' Hope repeated, with an incredulous laugh. 'What is that?'

Her friend sighed. 'It's when someone wears some great hats in their profile photos and you meet them in real life and they take off the hat and . . . they're balder than your grandad.'

'Oh,' Hope said, and bit her lip to stifle another giggle.

'I don't have anything against bald guys,' Iris went on. 'I mean, just look at The Rock or Jason Statham – super sexy and hot. But that's because they own it and it's part of their vibe. This guy just felt like he was trying to hide it, or was hoping I wouldn't notice.'

Hope pushed open the door to the bar and led the way to their usual table. 'So, who did you meet? Was it through a dating app?'

Settling into the seat, Iris picked up the menu. 'Let's get a drink and I'll tell you everything.'

Hope could barely contain her curiosity. 'Well?' she asked, once their drinks had arrived. 'Who is he?'

'Someone I've known for a while,' Iris said. 'He designs exhibition stands for things like wedding fayres – the big fancy ones that the super wealthy exhibitors have. You know the kind I mean.'

Hope did. When she and Rob had been planning their wedding, they'd been to several wedding fayres, including one at the Olympia exhibition halls in London that had been so overwhelming it had left them both fantasizing about running away to get married in a registry office.

'And there's a three-day fayre coming up next month, here in York,' Iris went on. 'I usually have a small stand – nothing fancy, just a modest space to bring in new wedding clients. But I decided to splash out a bit, get something fresh and eye-catching, and I asked Martin to design it.'

Hope eyed her friend closely. Was it her imagination

or was Iris actually blushing at the mere mention of his name? 'And?'

Iris smiled. 'And something was different this time. He came up with some really clever ideas, made me laugh . . . I don't actually know what it was. We just clicked.'

Hope raised her eyebrows. 'Does he look like The Rock?'

Now Iris laughed. 'No! He's nothing like my usual type. He's quiet, maybe even a bit shy, which is probably why I've never thought of him in a romantic way.'

'So, what's different this time?'

'I genuinely have no idea,' Iris admitted. 'It might have been the way he took the time to explain things – there's something deeply sexy about a man who is passionate and knowledgeable about his work, isn't there?'

Hope couldn't help thinking of Ciaran then; his passion for Ancient Egypt had definitely been part of what had made him irresistible. But she kept her mouth shut and waited for her friend to continue.

Iris tapped the side of her glass thoughtfully. 'Or maybe I'm just tired of wasting my time on flashy men who seem perfect on the screen but never live up to their profiles. Maybe it's time I tried a different approach.' She stopped and shook her head. 'Maybe I want someone real and dependable and honest, instead of guys who promise everything and vanish after the second or third date.'

There was a sincerity behind the words, a yearning that Hope wasn't sure Iris was even aware of. 'Sounds like he's made quite an impression. Do you know whether he's single?'

Iris grinned. 'I bloody hope he is – he's taking me out for a drink on Thursday night.'

She looked so happy that Hope grinned too. 'Fingers crossed he's everything you want,' she said.

'I'd settle for a date that doesn't make me want to give up and adopt a cat,' Iris said and took a long sip of her cocktail. 'Now, tell me what you've been up to. Any hot dating action you've been hiding from me?'

Hope let out a snort of derision. 'No. I'm definitely considering becoming a mad cat lady. Which reminds me, actually – you won't believe what happened to Will at the weekend . . .'

When she'd finished, Iris shook her head. 'I wonder if someone's missing their pet. It's a shame the charity couldn't find a microchip.'

'I'd be beside myself with worry if I'd lost my cat,' Hope agreed. 'Will printed off a load of posters and we've stuck them up all around town. And the charity has an excellent local network, so they took some photos to share on their social media accounts.'

'That's something, at least. What if no one comes to claim her?' Iris asked.

It was a good question, Hope thought, and she knew Will had wondered about that too. The trouble was that Brodie had fallen head over heels in love with their visitors and spent hours sitting silently on the floor in Will's bedroom, watching the cat from a distance as she cared for her kittens. There were going to be serious tears when it came to rehoming them.

'I don't know,' she told Iris. 'I think Will might have spoken to the charity about next steps but it's still early days. He doesn't want to stress the mother cat or the kittens by moving them out before they're ready.'

The florist pulled a disbelieving face. 'I think we both know how this is going to end. Will is too soppy for his own good.'

It was more likely that he'd want to keep Brodie happy, Hope thought, but three cats was a big jump from zero cats. And surely Will had enough on his plate without the added responsibilities that came with pet ownership. 'I'm sure he'll do what's best for them all,' she said.

'Oh, he means well, without a doubt,' Iris said. 'But I'd be wary if I were you.'

Hope gave her friend a puzzled look. 'Me? Why?'

Iris tapped her nose. 'Beware of jewellers bearing kittens,' she said. 'Just say no, Hope.'

Both her friends and her family had suggested she got a pet after Rob had died – something to focus on, they'd said – but Hope had never been especially tempted. 'No chance,' she said firmly. 'I might be thinking about becoming a cat lady in the future but I'm not ready to go there just yet.'

All the same, it wouldn't do any harm to make sure Will knew she wasn't in the market for a kitten, Hope decided as she walked briskly home. As cute as they would undoubtedly become, it was better to nip that idea in the bud before it could bloom.

Chapter Twenty-One

Hope was in the first-floor stockroom, searching for a Victorian silver locket Mr Young was keen to take to an auction, when Frances interrupted her.

'There's a customer asking for you downstairs, Hope,' she called from the doorway.

'For me?' Hope repeated, pausing with an open jewellery box in her hand. She cast her mind back over her dealings with the public over the past few weeks, trying to recall if there was anyone to whom she'd promised information or a favour. 'Any idea what it's about?'

'Sorry, I didn't think to ask,' Frances said. 'But he's quite attractive, if that helps.'

Hope eyed her, frowning. It wasn't like her colleague to get flustered over a customer. 'Not really. But give me a minute and I'll be down.'

The last person she expected to see standing beside the grandfather clock was Ciaran. The sight of him was like a blow; her stomach contracted and she let out a stifled gasp. Thankfully, he was facing away from the stairs that led down from the first floor which won Hope a few seconds to compose herself at least. What she really wanted to do was turn around and hide in the stockroom until he went away.

His smile when he saw her was like another blow, although this one had more to do with her body's treacherous leap of greeting than shock. What the hell was he doing in York, she wondered. Wasn't he supposed to be digging in Sussex all summer? Or had that been another lie? And beneath those jumbled thoughts was the question of how – how could he stand there smiling, as though he hadn't trampled her heart through the dust?

Straightening her shoulders, she tightened her shaking hands around the box that held the locket and reluctantly closed the distance between them. It was hard to look at him; his dark hair flopped lazily onto his forehead exactly the way she remembered, his skin was a little more golden and he still exuded the irresistible air of an off-duty rock star that had knocked the breath from her lungs the first time she'd seen him. 'Ciaran,' she said when she reached him, and she fought to keep her expression blank.

His grey eyes travelled over her and his smile deepened as he took a step forward. 'Ah, Hope. It's good to see you. You're looking radiant.'

His voice was just as she remembered too; warm and lilting, with just a hint of a rasp. There had been times when

275

that voice had turned her insides to liquid. Digging her nails into the palm of one hand, she pushed the memories away. 'Is there something I can help you with?'

If he was surprised by the coolness in her tone, he didn't show it. 'You're angry and you've got every right to be. But at least give me an opportunity to explain.' He paused and ran a hand through his hair. 'I know I messed up, Hope. But really, it's not what you think.'

She almost laughed at his sheer audacity but she was very aware that they were in the Emporium; one or two customers were already firing inquisitive sideways glances their way. And Hope was certain Frances wouldn't be too far away, trying to work out who Ciaran was.

'I'm working,' she said as evenly as she could. 'I can't do this now.'

He nodded. 'No, I know. But you told me not to message you, and I needed to speak to you so . . .' He ran a hand through his hair and Hope thought she caught a hint of genuine discomfort. 'Please just give me a chance. Thirty minutes of your time. That's all.'

As much as Hope wanted to tell him where to stick his thirty minutes, she knew she wouldn't. But was there any point in letting him explain? The fact that he was married was undeniable – anything else was just window dressing. And yet there was something in his eyes, a vulnerability she'd never seen before. Nothing he could tell her would erase the way he'd behaved so was there any danger in hearing what he had to say? It might even help her to close the door on the whole sorry affair. 'I'll think about it,' she said, after several long seconds had ticked by. 'But don't get your expectations up.'

'Thank you,' he said. 'So, you'll message me?'

Hope shook her head. 'I don't have your number any more. I'll email you, at your university address.'

Again, Ciaran nodded. 'Okay. There's no rush but I'm only here until Sunday. If you do decide you want to talk.'

'Noted,' Hope said, as coolly as she could. 'I need to get back to work now.'

'Of course,' he said, and glanced round in admiration. 'This is quite the place, isn't it? I haven't been inside for years but I can see why you love it.'

Hope shifted uncomfortably. Standing here with him was harder than she would have thought possible. The memories of being close to him were resurfacing; her fingers longed to reach up and brush the hair from his forehead and her lips tingled with the ghosts of kisses past. She cleared her throat. 'Yes. It's a shame Mr Young isn't here – I'm sure he would have like to say hello.'

'Maybe another time,' Ciaran said easily. 'I'll get out of your hair, anyway. It's really good to see you.'

It took all of her strength not to respond with, 'You too.' Instead, she met his gaze with what she hoped was tranquil indifference. 'Okay. Take care, Ciaran.'

She didn't wait for him to leave. Instead, she turned to walk along the aisle, away from the desk where she knew Frances would be doing her best not to stare. Her feet brought her into the restful silence of the book room, which was blissfully empty of customers. Hope leaned carefully back against the glass that covered the nearest floor-to-ceiling bookshelf and allowed the scent of old paper and ink to soothe her. She always found this room comforting, as though being surrounded by so many stories tucked away inside their leather and hardback covers could ease her troubles away. In this room, happy ever afters awaited the reader on every bookshelf; the path wasn't easy but true love often conquered all and sometimes even death could be cheated. When the Emporium was quiet, Hope sometimes imagined she could feel the words vibrating, the pages gently rustling as they waited to be released. It was the perfect place to gather her thoughts and recover from the shock of seeing Ciaran, even though she knew it was going to take more than a few minutes of deep breathing to calm her tumultuous emotions. And once her jangling nerves had settled down, she would have to decide whether she wanted to hear him out. Her head was adamant; he had no right to explain anything. But her heart – her treacherous heart – was already whispering that listening wasn't such a bad idea.

As she stood there among the books, Hope realized she had no idea which voice she wanted to win. None at all.

'Are you out of your mind?'

Charlotte's expression was incredulous as she stared across the table of the café they'd chosen for lunch. 'Seriously, Hope, why would even consider saying yes?'

It was just after midday on Saturday and the café's outside courtyard was busy. 'Keep your voice down, please,' Hope said, as her cheeks started to burn. 'I don't need everyone here to know I'm an idiot.'

Immediately, her sister looked contrite. 'Okay, I'm sorry,' she said, lowering her voice. 'And I didn't mean to make you feel crappy. I know how much you liked Ciaran and I wish I could tell you he's worth listening to. But leopards don't change their spots and nor do adulterers.'

The final word made Hope's cheeks flame even more. 'Yeah, I know,' she mumbled.

Charlotte eyed her steadily. 'Besides, I think you know it's not just thirty minutes of your time he's after. He's trying to wriggle his way back into your life.' She paused. 'Or into your bed, more accurately.'

'Charlotte!' Hope protested as a woman at the neighbouring table glanced sideways. 'Can you just not?'

'Someone has to say it,' Charlotte replied in a stout tone. 'Or maybe they already have – what does Iris think?'

Hope fixed her eyes on her plate. 'I haven't mentioned it to her yet. She's finally met someone she likes and I don't want to crash her mood with my romantic woes.'

'And you also know she won't approve,' Charlotte said. 'Look, I know it's tempting. I've been in your shoes. But please take the advice of your older and much wiser sister – it's never a good idea to give men like Ciaran a second chance.'

It was hardly a second chance, Hope wanted to point out,

but she knew from experience that there was little point in arguing with Charlotte when she was in full flow. And there was an element of truth in what she was saying; there was no getting away from the fact that Ciaran was a married man. What possible justification could he have for the way he had behaved?

'I'm not going to give him a second chance,' she told Charlotte. 'It's more like . . . closure.'

Her sister gave her a long look. 'Do you really need it? I'm all for squaring things off but when someone treats you this badly, that's probably all the closure you need. Are you sure this isn't just an excuse to see him again?'

Hope knew it was true the moment she said it. Shifting uncomfortably on her seat, she forced herself to meet Charlotte's gaze. 'Possibly.'

'I do get it,' she said, leaning forward with a sympathetic expression. 'Really I do – sexual chemistry is so hard to ignore. But you're worth more than the occasional night of passion, Hope. You deserve someone who can give you everything and, deep down, you know Ciaran has nothing to offer.'

Hope studied the remains of her Caesar salad. 'You're right, of course,' she said quietly then glanced up at her sister. 'When did you get so wise?'

Charlotte winked. 'I always have been. It's just taken you all this time to appreciate it.'

'I do appreciate you,' Hope said, with a reluctant smile. 'Thanks for always being there.'

'You're welcome,' Charlotte replied, and reached out to squeeze her hand. 'What are sisters for?'

As one week flowed into the next, Hope gradually found Ciaran slipping to the back of her mind once more. It helped that the Emporium was busier than ever; Mr Young had asked her to work an extra day each week to assist him with the auction side of the business, preparing lots to go under the hammer and sourcing antiques for clients. In the evenings, she lost herself in Khalid's letters to Elenor, although she occasionally wondered what Ciaran would make of them. He hadn't tried to contact her again and she assumed he had taken her silence as evidence she didn't want to talk. It really was all for the best, she decided, grateful too that he wasn't in York. She didn't need to worry about bumping into him, at least.

She'd visited Will and Brodie a few times too and had marvelled at how fast the kittens were growing. Their eyes had opened now and both of them showed signs of starting to crawl, which delighted Brodie and terrified Will.

'Brodie knows she'd not allowed to touch them but I still have visions of her forgetting they're not teddies,' he confided in Hope as they sat on the sofa on Friday evening. 'I don't think any of us could cope if there were any accidents.'

Hope thought about the careful way Brodie kept her distance from the nest, even when it was obvious she was fascinated. 'I'm sure you don't need to worry.'

He sighed. 'I feel awful for even thinking it but I'm still watching her like a hawk. Better to be safe and all that.'

'Any news from the charity about the owner of the cat?' she asked.

'Not yet. We don't even have any idea how far she travelled – cats are so independent that she could be a long way from home.'

Hope gave him a sideways glance. 'Have you thought any more about what you'll do if the owner doesn't come forward?'

'Not really,' Will admitted, rubbing his eyes. 'I guess the charity will be able to help but right now I'm just taking things one day at a time.' He shook his head. 'Listen to me – you'd think something awful had happened. None of this is a huge problem, in the scheme of things.'

'Pets are a big responsibility,' Hope said. 'Especially when you didn't choose to get them.'

Will smiled. 'It's safe to say I wasn't thinking of adding to my family responsibilities. But even so, I should stop complaining. Tell me about your day.'

'Not much to tell,' Hope said. 'I spent most of it in the stockroom, getting things ready for tomorrow's auction. I did manage to catch up with Iris at lunch, though.'

Will took a sip of wine and settled back against the cushions. 'How is she? Any update on the new man?'

Hope thought back to the sparkle in the florist's eyes and the enthusiasm in her voice when she'd described her date with Martin – plain and simple drinks in an unfussy bar that had given them plenty of opportunity to talk. Her obvious happiness had given Hope a momentary stab of jealousy but she'd quickly pushed that away: if anyone deserved to find the man of her dreams, it was Iris. 'I think she's smitten,' Hope told Will. 'Or at the very least optimistic about a second date.'

He laughed. 'He must be a keeper if she's considering another date. Hardly anyone makes it through her screening criteria.'

'You make her sound ferocious when really she's just practical,' Hope objected. 'What's the point in going on a second date when you know there's no chemistry?'

'I'd settle for going on any dates at all,' Will grumbled. 'But you're right, Iris has her head screwed on. I'm glad this new guy seems to be ticking a few boxes.'

'Me too,' Hope said, and hesitated. 'I suppose dating is impossible for you at the moment.'

He rolled the wine glass between his fingers. 'Pretty much.'

Hope sipped her own wine. He sounded matter of fact, almost resigned, and she suddenly found herself wondering what type of women he'd dated in the past. Hadn't Iris once told her he'd been single when the accident had turned his and Brodie's lives upside down? Perhaps he'd been playing the field, which must have made him feel even more isolated when he couldn't go on dates. 'That must be tough,' she observed. Not to mention lonely, she thought silently.

'At least I don't have to deal with the inevitable drama,' Will said, shrugging. 'Between work, Brodie and unexpected kittens, I don't think I've got the energy for a relationship.'

Hope started to form a reply but Will suddenly looked at

her. 'How about you? Have you thought about dipping your toe back into the dating waters?'

'No, not really,' she said, fixing her gaze on her glass. After her conversation with Charlotte, she'd decided not to tell either Will or Iris about her encounter with Ciaran. Apart from anything else, she'd wanted to move on and couldn't face rehashing the conversation twice more. But it did present her with an uncomfortable dilemma now: should she continue to pretend it hadn't happened or mention she'd seen him but play everything else down?

Will watched her in silence for a moment. 'I suppose that's understandable. But we're not all like Ciaran. Some of us are nice guys.'

His words were mild but she sensed something behind them and, once again, she found herself contemplating his relationship history. Had someone hurt him the way Ciaran had hurt her? 'I know,' she said, summoning up what she hoped was a reassuring smile. 'You're great, Will. Any woman would be lucky to be with you.'

He studied her, a slight frown creasing his forehead. 'Do you really think that?'

'Of course! You're successful, good-looking, independent and smart,' she said, ticking each item off on her fingers. 'And look how amazing you are with Brodie – you're doing a brilliant job with her. Trust me, when you're ready, women will be falling over themselves to date you.'

His cheeks turned pink, which caused Hope to wonder if she'd overdone the compliments. But his expression seemed pleased and everything she'd said was true. 'I'm not sure they will. Thank you, though. You're very kind.'

'I'm not being kind,' Hope said firmly. 'It's the truth.'

A glance at the clock told her it was after eight o'clock. 'I should be making a move,' she said, draining the remainder of her wine. 'I'm babysitting for Charlotte tomorrow morning so need an early night to make sure I'm on top auntie form.'

Will smiled. 'If the way you are with Brodie is anything to go by, I'm sure you'll do a sterling job.'

Hope grimaced as she got to her feet. 'Brodie is no trouble. The last time I babysat for Charlotte, I turned my back for a second and Amber had a mouthful of the dog's food. She's exhausting.'

'But very cute,' Will observed. 'Good luck, anyway.'

The evening air had cooled while Hope had been inside the house; she paused at the front door to pull on her jacket and glanced at Will. 'I hope your housemates let you sleep.'

'Me too,' he said, pulling a face. 'Thanks for coming over.'

'Any time,' Hope said.

As she was about to cross the doorstep, Will placed a hand on her arm. She turned to look at him and realized he'd taken a step towards her. 'Hope, I —'

He stopped, as though weighing something up, and then moved forward impulsively. Before Hope could speak, he leaned in to plant a soft kiss on her lips.

For a second, she was so surprised that she didn't react. The warmth of his mouth on hers was unexpectedly sweet and comforting and her eyes instinctively drifted shut even as she reeled in surprise. She felt her body start to respond, then sharply remembered who it was she was kissing and her eyes snapped open. She stepped hurriedly back.

'Will,' she said, feeling embarrassment crawl over her. 'That's not – I don't … I think there's been a misunderstanding.'

She watched realization dawn on his face. He flushed a deep rosy red and moved backwards so that he was standing in the hallway again. 'Sorry. I'm such an idiot. I thought –' He stopped and ran a distracted hand through his hair. 'Never mind what I thought. I'm sorry.'

Hope sucked in a deep breath. 'It's okay,' she said, with conviction she didn't feel. 'It's just a misunderstanding, that's all – no harm done.'

Will looked as though he wanted the ground to open up and swallow him. 'Shit.'

Hope didn't know what to say – every part of her wanted to run away and an awkward silence grew. She cleared her throat. 'Why don't we pretend that never happened?'

He stared mulishly at the ground, then let out a soft bark of laughter. 'Sure. Let's do that.'

She stared at him for a moment, feeling his mortification adding to her own. 'I'm going to go now. But let's talk tomorrow, okay?'

He didn't meet her gaze. 'Just let me know you've got home safely.'

'Of course,' Hope promised. When it became clear he

wasn't going to say anything more, she turned around and crunched her way to the gate. She didn't dare look back, in case he was watching; instead, she allowed herself to briefly shut her eyes and let out a long shuddering silent groan before she made for the safety of home.

Chapter Twenty-Two

Iris gaped at Hope, her expression utterly bemused. 'He did *what*?'

They were sitting on the sofa in Iris's living room, in her flat above Blooming Dales, where Hope had stumbled after Will had kissed her. 'I know,' she said. 'I can't get my head around it either.'

'Clearly,' Iris said, and pushed a steaming mug of tea towards her. 'Here, drink this. It'll help with the shock.'

Hope picked it up gratefully and took a sip. 'Thank you.'

Iris shook her head. 'And you had no idea he was going to do it? None at all?'

'None,' Hope echoed. 'I mean, we'd been talking about dating and I'd told him I thought he was a catch.'

'A catch?' Iris repeated, and raised her eyebrows. 'Were those your exact words?'

It hadn't been the phrase she'd used but Hope wasn't sure she remembered what she had said. 'No. He was down about not being able to date so I told him he'd have no trouble finding someone when he was ready.'

'Uh-huh,' Iris said, pursing her lips. 'And how did he react to that?'

'He seemed pleased. Maybe a bit embarrassed.' Hope frowned as more of the conversation came back to her. 'I said he's good-looking and smart. And I might have rounded things off by saying any woman would be lucky to have him.'

Now Iris raised her eyebrows. 'Wow. That's high praise.'

'Maybe,' Hope conceded. 'But it is all true. He's a great guy.'

'Hey, you'll get no arguments from me,' Iris said, holding up her hands. 'I think he's a catch too.'

'Right?' Hope exclaimed. 'He is.'

'But look at it from Will's perspective. Do you think there's a chance he heard what you said and got the wrong end of the stick?'

Hope considered the conversation again, her frown deepening. She'd intended to be a supportive friend and bolster his spirits, the way she would with Iris or any of her other friends. 'I don't see how he could.'

Iris eyed her with some pity. 'Will is a man, Hope, and we both know men often hear what they want to hear. If a beautiful woman is paying them compliments and telling them they're great – well, it's easy to see how Will might have thought you were trying to tell him something.'

A tendril of unease burrowed into Hope's certainty. 'Are you saying I led him on?'

'Not deliberately,' Iris said. 'But I can see how the misunderstanding happened. Can't you?'

Now that her friend had pointed it out, Hope could see it all too clearly. A hot shudder of embarrassment ran through her. 'I only meant to boost his confidence.'

'It sounds like you succeeded,' Iris said. 'Perhaps all the compliments went to his head.'

Hope wanted to bury her head in her hands. 'So, what do we do? Pretend it didn't happen? That's how we left it but I don't want things to be awkward.'

'That all depends,' Iris said, shrugging.

'On what?'

Iris gave her a mischievous look. 'On how good the kiss was.'

'Iris!' Hope said, almost spluttering her tea all over the coffee table.

Her friend spread her hands innocently. 'I'm just saying. The best way to get over someone is to—'

'Stop,' Hope cut in, before Iris could complete the sentence. 'This is Will we're talking about.'

'I know,' Iris said, her eyes dancing. 'Good-looking, sexy, lovely Will, who you said any woman would be lucky to have. What's stopping you from kissing each other?'

Hope opened her mouth to say there were about a hundred reasons why she shouldn't kiss Will; she valued him as a friend, for a start, and nothing more. Which wasn't to say she couldn't see his appeal – obviously, she could, that was the whole reason she was in this mess. But there was more to her reluctance than that: Hope knew from her own tentative experiences that dating came with risks and anyone who dated Will would eventually come face to face with the fact that Brodie was part of the deal. And while Hope had come to care for the little girl very much, the added pressure around starting something that might not end happily loomed large, and it felt like more responsibility than Hope could handle. Brodie had been hurt enough with the loss of her parents, there was no way Hope wanted to risk anything that might cause her any further pain or upheaval.

'I just don't see Will like that,' she told Iris, injecting as much conviction into her voice as she could. 'He is great and I meant everything I said about him but we're better as friends.'

Iris sniffed, as though she didn't believe a word of it. 'You know your own mind, I suppose.' She paused and eyed Hope inquisitively. 'Was he a good kisser, though?'

Hope couldn't help smiling at her determination. 'Yes, Iris, he was a good kisser. Now can we please talk about something – *anything* – else?'

Iris sat back, apparently satisfied. 'I thought he would be. The quiet ones usually are.'

It had been completely different to the way Ciaran kissed her, Hope reflected. Will's kiss had been a question, soft and tentative, whereas Ciaran's had been a statement, full of assurance and certainty. She wasn't about to tell Iris that, however – there'd been quite enough focus on the subject already. But it wasn't until she was making her way home – much later than she'd planned – that Hope realized kissing Will had somehow made her miss Ciaran more fiercely. It wasn't the tight, physical ache of the early days after the break up – this was a more considered longing, a wistful desire to hear his voice and watch him laugh. Perhaps she'd been too hasty to dismiss his request to talk, she thought as she crossed the bridge over the River Foss – the bridge where he'd first kissed her. Maybe she should have listened to what he had to say, despite the voice in her head that said he didn't deserve it. And maybe it wasn't too late.

There was no getting away from it: Hope was nervous.

It had taken her over a week of back-and-forth arguments with herself, a seesaw of emotions before she gave in and emailed Ciaran. And then she'd faced an anxious wait for his response, which had taken a few days, plus several more days until he was going to be back in York. All in all, it had taken two tense weeks to reach the point of actually meeting. On top of that, things with Will had felt unsettled and difficult too – she'd tried to keep her messages upbeat and normal and Will appeared to have done the same but there had been no requests for her to visit and she hated the inevitable undercurrent of awkwardness she sensed. She hoped it would pass with time, in the same way that she hoped the feeling of nausea that had settled in her stomach from the moment she'd woken up that day would pass too.

Glancing around the living room, she straightened the cushions on the sofa for the umpteenth time and checked her phone. Ciaran was due to arrive in five minutes, at 6.30pm, and she wasn't sure how she'd cope if he was late; her nerves were already stretched to breaking point. She wasn't even sure that arranging to meet him at the apartment had been a good idea – on one hand, she'd wanted the privacy and space to talk without worrying whether others might overhear, but on the other, she knew how charming he could be. It was going to be undeniably more difficult to be alone with him but it was too late to suggest meeting anywhere else now. She planned to suggest they sit at the dining table and hoped it, and her determination to keep things platonic, would be enough.

The knock on her door at exactly 6.30 made her jump – she'd been expecting to have to buzz him in. But a quick look through the spyhole in her front door told her it was him. Someone must have let him downstairs. Taking a deep breath, she smoothed her sweaty palms on her jeans and opened the door.

He looked even better than he had the last time she'd seen him – working outdoors evidently suited him. His eyes lit up at the sight of her, as though he hadn't quite believed she'd be there. 'Hello.'

Hope's own reaction was the same as it always was, a sharp explosion of attraction that set her nerve endings tingling. She folded her arms and managed a tight smile. 'Hello. Come in.'

He stepped inside and suddenly the hallway felt small and claustrophobic. Hope hurried into the living room. 'Would you like a cup of tea?'

Following her, he held out the bottle she hadn't registered he was carrying. 'I thought we might need something stronger but tea would be grand if that's what you're making.'

He placed the bottle on the table and Hope saw it was an expensive-looking Chablis. Just for a moment, her determination wavered and then rallied. 'I think we'll stick with tea,' she said stiffly. 'How do you take it?'

It was a cheap shot, because she'd made him plenty of tea in the mornings after the nights before, but he didn't rise to the bait, which caused her to wonder if he'd even noticed. 'Milk, no sugar,' he said easily. 'Thanks.'

Once the tea was made, she carried both mugs to the table and place them opposite each other. Ciaran's mouth quirked when he saw her take a seat on one side of the table but he didn't question it, merely settled into the chair across from her. 'So,' he said. 'Here we are.'

Hope steeled herself. 'Here we are.'

'I must admit I was surprised to get your message,' he said. 'I thought you'd decided you never wanted to see me again.'

'I almost did,' Hope replied, frankly. 'But I think we need to clear the air and it's impossible to do that via email.'

Ciaran tipped his head and sighed. 'That's true. Too much potential for misunderstandings. I'm glad we see things the same way.' He paused and shook his head, smiling. 'God, it's good to see you. Have you been keeping well?'

Once again, Hope felt the need to fold her arms. Having him there in her home was proving more difficult than she'd anticipated and she wasn't sure she could do small talk. 'I'm fine,' she said, fighting to keep her tone neutral. 'Keeping busy.'

'I'm sure,' he said, and his gaze roved around the living room. 'Are you still working your way through Elenor Lovelace's old journal?'

She might have expected he'd ask about that, Hope thought. He might not look like an academic but archaeology was still his passion and he had been fascinated with Elenor's story. 'No, I returned it to Isobel.' She fixed him with a direct look. 'As nice as it is to catch up, I have plans later this evening so we should cut to the chase. What is it you wanted to explain?'

If Ciaran suspected she was lying, he didn't show it. 'Of course. It's Saturday night and you're a busy lady.' He took a long sip of tea and cleared his throat. 'So obviously the first thing I have to say is sorry. I've got no excuse for the way I treated you – I did a truly terrible thing and I can't tell you how much I regret it.'

Hope pressed her lips together and said nothing. The memory that had made her contact him – her recollection of their first kiss on the bridge – had faded but the urge to clear the air remained as strong as ever. If they were going to do that, she had to let him speak first.

He leaned forwards. 'But I don't want you to think I regret what happened between us. You were like precious water to a dying flower, Hope – you opened my eyes to what living really is and made me see I'd been letting myself wither away.'

From anyone else, it would have sounded ridiculous but somehow Ciaran's lilting accent made the words sound like poetry. Even so, Hope knew him well enough to resist the pitch-perfect delivery and read between the lines. 'Are you about to tell me your wife doesn't understand you?'

He winced. 'Ouch. I suppose I deserve that. But the answer is no – on the contrary, Lily understands me very well. That's why she's divorcing me.'

It was the last thing she'd expected to hear. 'Sorry?'

Ciaran gave a self-deprecating half-smile. 'I know. How could she divorce a charmer like me, right? It's a long, sad story – one I won't bore you with now – but the truth is we haven't been happy for years. We tried to make it work, until one day I guess we both gave up.'

Hope frowned in bewilderment. 'But you bought her an eternity ring. You went to Will's shop in the Shambles – that's how I found out you were married.'

'She wanted the ring as part of the divorce,' he said simply. 'In fact, she said ten years of being married to me felt like an eternity and deserved some kind of reward.'

Ignoring the feeble attempt at humour, Hope gave him a disbelieving look. 'Will said you were holding hands.'

Ciaran shrugged. 'Maybe we were. Lily has a strange sense of humour – she'd have found it funny to act all loved-up when nothing could be further from the truth. But I promise you, there's nothing between us. Yes, we're still married but only until the divorce is finalized. After that, I'm a free man.'

Hope stared at him, trying to take everything in. Could

she believe him or was this just another cruel attempt to fool her? 'Why didn't you tell me any of this?'

He laughed. 'Ah sure, what a chat up line that would have been. But I didn't plan for this to happen – I thought you were way out of my league.' He shook his head. 'I mean, you're practically a goddess – why on earth would you look twice at me? And the more time we spent together, the more I fell under your spell. By the time I realized I was in trouble, it was way too late to drop the whole tragic marriage tale on you.'

'So you lied to me instead,' she said, blinking in confusion.

'No,' he said instantly. 'I never lied. Perhaps I was a bit sparing with the truth here and there, glossed over a few things, but you're not going to sit there and tell me you didn't do the same?'

And now Hope started to feel uncomfortably hot because she had been economical with the truth when it suited her. She hadn't told him about Rob, for a start. 'I'm not married, though.'

For a moment, she thought he was going to launch into another blustering defence but then he seemed to deflate. 'No. It was unforgivable of me not to tell you about Lily. I'm the worst kind of idiot.'

She stared out of the window, watching the clouds scud across the pale blue sky without really seeing them. Could she believe him? It all sounded very convenient – she could almost hear Charlotte snorting in derision – but it could easily be the truth. Marriages faded away all the time and people took years to face the truth and divorce each other. And it was certainly true that Ciaran didn't spend a lot of time at home with his wife – he lived on campus in York during term-time, while Lily presumably lived in Scarborough.

'I don't know what to think,' she said, running a shaky hand across her eyes.

Ciaran watched her, his expression remorseful. 'There hasn't been a day gone by that I haven't kicked myself for putting you through this,' he said. 'And I don't expect anything to change – you had every right to hate me after what happened and I wouldn't blame you for still hating me now. But I'm glad you gave me the chance to explain at least.'

The words rang with sincerity, Hope thought, but charm and persuasion had always seemed as easy as breathing to him. And none of it changed the fact that he'd misled and hurt her. It could have all been so different if he'd been honest from the start. 'I'm not sure I—'

She broke off as a loud knock reverberated through the hallway.

'Expecting someone?' Ciaran asked, as Hope frowned.

'No.' She got to her feet and headed towards the front door. 'And people tend to press the buzzer – they're not supposed to be able to walk right in.'

Once again, she found herself peering through the spyhole to the long hallway beyond. But this time, her heart sank to her toes when she saw who it was. Standing on the other side of the door was Will.

Biting her lip, Hope glanced over her shoulder towards

the living room and Ciaran; it was the worst possible timing. Could she pretend not to be home? Tell Ciaran it was a cold caller? She looked through the spyhole again and saw Will wasn't alone. Brodie was with him – of course she was. Frantically, Hope racked her brain in case they'd made plans she'd forgotten about but she had no recollection of anything. She'd been distracted in the weeks since she'd contacted Ciaran but surely she'd remember inviting Will and Brodie over to her flat.

But whether they were invited or not, she couldn't leave them standing outside. Squaring her shoulders, Hope opened the door.

'Hello,' Will said, with a smile that was just a fraction too bright. 'We thought we'd surprise you with a picnic, to say thanks for all your cat-related help over the last few weeks.'

There was a wicker basket at his feet. Brodie was clutching her Matryoshka doll and beaming at Hope in a way that caused her heart to ache. 'Oh, that's – uh – a lovely idea. I wish you'd told me, though.'

Will mock-rolled his eyes. 'Then it wouldn't have been a surprise, would it?'

'No,' Hope said weakly, and resisted the urge to look backwards over her shoulder. 'The thing is—'

Understanding dawned across Will's face. 'You've got plans.'

'Sort of,' Hope said, and now she did glance towards the living room. 'But I'll be free soon.'

Will flashed another smile that was too cheery and she

felt the weight of the awkwardness that had dogged their messages press down on her again. 'Don't worry – it was just an idea. We can go and have our own picnic in the park.'

The expression on Brodie's face as she looked back and forth between them was so disappointed that Hope wanted to cry. 'No, it's fine. Just give me ten minutes and I'll come and join you. I just need to—'

At that moment, her luck ran out; Ciaran loomed in the doorway to the living room. 'Who is it?' he called. 'Have they got the wrong door?'

Will froze at the sound of his voice and turned an incredulous look Hope's way. 'Seriously?'

Hope shook her head. 'It's not what you think.'

But Ciaran had crossed the hallway to stand behind her. 'Ah, it's the jeweller man and his little girl.' He placed a hand on Hope's shoulder, as though claiming possession. 'Birdie, isn't it?'

'Brodie,' Will corrected tightly. 'But I can see you're busy, Hope. Sorry to intrude.'

Again, Hope shook her head. 'Honestly, Will, give me a few minutes—'

But Will was already reaching for the basket. 'Like I said, don't worry.' His voice vibrated with suppressed emotion. 'Come on, Brodie, we'll see Hope another time.'

It was almost more than Hope could bear to watch the little girl's face crumple with incomprehension. 'Will, please . . .' she began as he turned away.

If he heard her, he didn't show it. 'Let's go.'

'I'm sorry,' Hope called in desperation as Will trudged away. 'I'll see you soon, Brodie.'

Behind her, Ciaran let out a long puff of breath. 'Someone's got a bee in their bonnet. What was all that about?'

Suddenly overcome with weariness, Hope closed the door. 'They wanted to surprise me with a picnic.'

He raised his eyebrows. 'Didn't he know you already had plans this evening?'

It took her a second to remember her white lie from earlier. 'Obviously not.' She rubbed her face and sighed. 'But it's probably a good idea for you to go. I – I need to get ready.'

He studied her briefly, then nodded. 'Of course. Will you think about what I've told you?'

She couldn't help the quiet snort that escaped her. 'It's going to be impossible not to.'

'Yes, I suppose so,' he acknowledged and took a step towards her, taking both her hands in his. 'Just as long as you know I'm truly sorry I hurt you, Hope. You're amazing – I've never met anyone like you.'

Hope's head started to whirl. Together with Will's unexpected appearance, it was all too much to take in and now Ciaran was going to kiss her and she wasn't sure she wanted to stop him.

'I can't tell you how much I want to kiss you right now,' Ciaran murmured. He let go of her hands with a regretful sigh. 'But it wouldn't be right. The next time I kiss you, it will be because you've asked me to.'

It was another jolt to Hope's reeling senses. Blinking, she

watched as he opened the front door and stepped briskly through it. 'I'll leave you in peace now,' he said. 'Thanks again for listening.'

Dipping his head, he pressed a fleeting kiss on her cheek and strode off down the hall. A moment later, he was gone, leaving her staring down the empty corridor. She stood frozen for a second or two, then gasped and dashed back into the living room to grab her phone. She pulled up Will's number and waited for it to connect.

'Come on, come on,' she muttered, watching the arrows scroll up the screen. 'Pick up, Will.'

But the phone simply rang and rang, then played a disappointed melody to tell her the call had failed and the screen cleared. Either Will was choosing not to pick up or he was somewhere without signal, and Hope had a horrible suspicion she knew which it was.

'Shit,' she whispered, staring at the floor with numb frustration. 'Shit shit shit shit.'

Chapter Twenty-Three

The week that followed was wretched. Hope's messages to Will went unread, her calls went unanswered and she drew the line at going to the shop, where she knew he'd be with Brodie. It somehow felt more invasive to trap him at work.

'He's hurt and disappointed,' Iris had said, when Hope asked for advice. 'The best thing you can do is leave him alone – he'll come round.'

'Have you spoken to him at all?' Hope pressed, seeking some reassurance that they didn't both hate her. 'How's Brodie?'

Iris nodded. 'I took some sunflowers over for Brodie on Monday. They're both fine, don't fret. And so are the kittens.'

Charlotte had been altogether less sympathetic. 'I can't believe you gave that toerag Ciaran the time of day, Hope. After everything we talked about!'

Hope had felt compelled to defend herself. 'Nothing happened. We just talked.'

Her sister had snorted. 'And have you been in touch since?'

'No,' Hope said, glad she was able to meet her gaze with a clear conscience. 'I do have some self-respect, despite what you think.'

'Good,' Charlotte said. 'I don't care how much he claims to be available, he still kept the truth from you. And if he wasn't honest about something that important, what else is he going to hide from you?'

It was a thought that had kept Hope awake at night when she'd lain in the dark, turning things over and over in her mind. 'I know.'

Charlotte had been silent for a moment, then she'd sighed. 'Just because I'm permanently exhausted and have forgotten what sex even is doesn't mean I don't get the whole grand passion thing. I know Ciaran was dynamite in bed and made you feel things you haven't felt since – well, since Rob – but relationships like that aren't meant to go the distance. Believe me, the slow and steady man is the one you want. Kindness beats hotness every time, Hope.' She glanced over at Amber, who was banging two stickle bricks together. 'I learned that the hard way and I'm grateful every day that I did.'

There was no escaping her meaning. Hope shook her head stubbornly. 'Will is just a friend. Although he's not even that right now.'

'He'll get over it,' Charlotte predicted. 'And the strongest relationships can be built on friendship. You have to take a risk sometimes.'

That was half the trouble, Hope thought – look how many

misunderstandings and problems there had been so far. No, she decided, there was too much at stake if things didn't work out, but that wasn't what her sister wanted to hear. 'Maybe I'll think about it,' she offered.

'Good girl,' Charlotte said. 'And delete Ciaran McCormack from your brain as well as your phone. He's definitely not a keeper.'

And it hadn't been a lie – in the days that followed, Will crept into Hope's thoughts more and more often, if not in quite the way Charlotte had wanted. She missed talking to him, missed Brodie too, and she even missed the kittens. His absence left a hole in her life, one that she couldn't seem to fill with her work at the Emporium or drinks with Iris or dance classes. After ten days of silence, Hope's resolve finally cracked and she found herself standing in the lane that led to Will's house. It was after eight o'clock on a Thursday evening, when she'd calculated Brodie would be safely tucked up in bed and Will would either be tidying up after the day or fast asleep on the sofa. She was hoping it wasn't the latter or it was going to be even harder to do what she was about to do. But standing in the road wasn't going to get her anywhere either . . . Screwing up her courage she walked up the driveway and rang the bell.

It felt like an age before Will opened the door and even longer before he spoke. 'Hope.'

His tone was flat and unwelcoming. She took a breath and let it out before she replied. 'Hello, Will. How are you?'

He folded his arms. 'I've been better. What can I do for you?'

She studied him, taking in the bags beneath his eyes, the two-day stubble on his chin and the weary set of his shoulders. He looked miserable and she hated the thought that she might have contributed to his unhappiness, even inadvertently. 'I think we need to talk, don't you?' she said gently.

Several long seconds ticked by, during which she fully expected him to shut the door in her face, but eventually he gave a reluctant nod and stepped aside to allow her in. 'Brodie's asleep,' he said, unnecessarily.

Hope nodded as she followed him into the pristine white kitchen, noting the glorious yellow sunflowers that stood proud on the counter. 'How has she been?'

'Up and down,' he admitted and glanced briefly at Hope. 'She misses you.'

Unexpected tears flooded Hope's eyes. 'I've missed her too.' She hesitated. 'Both of you, actually.'

Will's lips pressed into a hard line and Hope couldn't tell if he was angry or disbelieving. Then he shook his head and she saw some of the tension leach out of him. 'I've got wine or hot chocolate. Don't expect marshmallows – Brodie secretly scoffed them while I was cleaning the cats' litter tray.'

The image made Hope smile in spite of the prickle behind her eyes. 'Oh dear.'

'She said they gave her a sore tummy, which was an important lesson in why crime doesn't pay,' he went on. 'But crime also affects the wider community, which is why I don't have any marshmallows for your hot chocolate.'

'A glass of water would be perfect,' she said. 'I don't want to cause you any trouble.'

He grunted and Hope noticed he didn't tell her it was no trouble. She waited until he'd placed the glass on the counter before speaking again. 'You've been ignoring my messages.'

'Yeah,' he said and had the grace to look embarrassed. 'Sorry. Things have been a bit full on.'

'I'm sure they have,' she said evenly and took a steadying breath, 'but that isn't why you're ignoring me. You're angry with me.'

He looked at her then, his eyes flashing. 'Yes, I'm angry with you. I couldn't believe it when I saw you with Ciaran – he's a married man and he treated you terribly. How on earth could you go back to him? I thought you were better than that, Hope.'

The accusation stung her. 'I haven't gone back to him. He came round to talk.'

Will's expression was sceptical. 'Is that what he told you? Men like him never settle for just talking.'

Hope felt her temper flare and folded her arms. She had planned to tell him exactly what Ciaran had said but his attitude was infuriating. 'It doesn't actually matter what he wanted – the fact of the matter is that it's none of your business.'

'And that's what you came round to say, is it?' Will demanded. 'That your life is nothing to do with me?'

'No,' Hope snapped. 'I came round to apologize for disappointing you and Brodie, and to try and make it up to you.

But clearly you're too pig-headed to listen. I shouldn't have bothered.'

The mention of Brodie seemed to puncture Will's anger. He placed both hands flat on the worksurface and let out a long slow breath. 'You're right. I'm sorry.'

Unclenching the fists she hadn't even realized she'd made, Hope allowed her own anger to melt away too. 'I don't want to argue, Will. I meant it when I said I miss you – I miss having you as my friend. I miss asking your advice about which shoes to wear and stupid things that really don't matter. I miss saying good morning to you.'

He stared at the kitchen counter. 'Yeah, I know. I miss those things too. Well, maybe not the shoes but everything else.'

'And I'm gutted I missed the picnic,' she continued. 'I bet you had those dinky little sausages and cucumber sticks and Percy Pigs, didn't you?'

'Maybe.'

There was the faintest hint of a smile around his eyes when he looked at her, which gave her the confidence to reluctantly raise the last thing she knew they needed to deal with. 'While we're in the awkward zone, do you think we should talk about the thing we agreed not to discuss?'

Will's cheeks turned pink and he groaned. 'When I made a complete tit of myself, you mean?'

'When we got our wires crossed,' she corrected kindly. 'And I think I'm at least fifty per cent to blame for that.'

'I don't know what I was thinking,' Will said, picking at

a microscopic dot of something on the countertop. 'You'd been so lovely and complimentary and it's been so long since someone said such nice things and – well, I think it made me see things that weren't there. Sorry.'

Hope felt her own cheeks start to grow warm. 'I didn't think, either. But I meant everything I said – most women would fall over themselves to be with you.'

She thought he winced slightly at the 'most women' but he didn't pick her up on it. 'Thank you. I'll try to remember that if and when I'm ready to start dating again.'

'You won't need to remember,' Hope said, smiling. 'I'll be on the side-lines, cheering you on.'

He laughed. 'With actual pompoms?'

'Maybe not with pompoms,' she said, grinning. 'That would be too weird. But I'm afraid you're stuck with me as a friend, the kind who tells you how great you are.'

'I think I can live with that,' he said warmly, after a momentary silence. 'Brodie is going to be very happy too.'

He held her gaze and Hope thought he looked a little less weary than he had when she'd arrived. She felt light too; she was glad she'd followed her instincts and come to see him. 'How are your housemates? Still keeping you up at night?'

'Very much so,' he said, rubbing his stubbly chin. 'But they're super cute so I forgive them. Want to come and see?'

Hope straightened up in anticipation. 'I thought you'd never ask.'

Once upstairs, she realized that Will had very much undersold the kittens' cuteness. They were both grey and white like their mother, but one had grey ear tips and a tail that looked as though it had been dipped in a paint pot, and the other was dappled with tiny spots that looked like a sprinkling of freckles. They miaowed in greeting as Will bent down to stroke them and the mother cat began to purr.

'Wow, they absolutely love you,' Hope observed, her tone warm with admiration. 'And they're so much bigger.'

'They love me because I feed them,' Will said wryly. 'Which has something to do with your second comment too.'

Hope knelt down and reached out a hand to touch the downy soft fur of the nearest kitten. 'How old are they now?'

'Five weeks,' Will said. 'The charity says they'll be ready for rehoming at eight weeks.'

The kitten patted at Hope's hand with a tiny paw and she felt her heart melt. 'And how are you feeling about that?'

He sighed and rubbed his chin again. 'Worried. Brodie has obviously become very attached to them. I think it's going to break her heart to give them away to strangers.'

Of course she was, Hope thought with a shudder. It didn't bear thinking about. 'No news about the owner?'

Will tickled the mother cat behind her ears and the purring intensified. 'A couple of enquiries but they were both cases of mistaken identity. I don't know what's going to happen if we don't find her owner.'

All three cats would need to be rehomed, Hope thought uneasily; the kittens would be no problem – people were always looking for them – but a mature cat might be more difficult to find a forever home for. 'It's not going to be easy,' she observed soberly.

'No,' Will agreed and hesitated. 'I did wonder if—'

Here it comes, Hope thought as she twirled the kitten's tail, recalling her conversation with Iris weeks earlier. 'Yes?'

Will watched her. 'We can't keep all three cats and I think Brodie might find it easier to say goodbye if she knew where the kittens had gone. So, I wondered whether you might be in the market for a furry flatmate.'

The other kitten chose that moment to tumble across the carpet and pounce on its sibling. They rolled over and over, play fighting and batting each other with their tiny pink paws and Hope couldn't help smiling at their antics. 'They are very sweet.'

He gave her an optimistic glance. 'Is that a yes?'

Hope shook her head as she realized he'd known she wouldn't be able to resist once she'd seen how cute the kittens were. 'It's not a no.'

'Sold to the lady with excellent taste in kittens,' Will said promptly. 'That's a legally binding verbal contract, by the way. Ironclad.'

The kitten with the grey ears mewed loudly and raced away from its sibling. 'Oh, don't worry about that,' Hope said absently, her eyes fixed on the adorable fluffy bundles. 'I think they had me at miaow.'

Chapter Twenty-Four

August saw footfall at the Emporium reach its height. Hope had forgotten just how crazy the peak of the tourist season was; the city's streets and shops were thronging with visitors and she found herself working even longer hours to keep on top of her responsibilities. As part of her training, Mr Young had invited her to join him at several auctions and although she'd loved getting a glimpse of the excitement and glamour of a real auction house, it had also meant less time for keeping on top of the window displays and stock-taking. She'd taken to heading to the Emporium on Monday mornings, when things tended to be quieter, and working her way through the stock checks after the buying frenzy of the weekend. Which was where Frances found her again on a Monday in mid-August.

'There's someone asking for you downstairs,' she said.

Hope turned around to stare at her. Surely it couldn't be Ciaran *again*? They'd exchanged a few casual messages but between her increased workload and the impending new term at the university, neither had pushed to meet up. But one look at Frances's face told her it wasn't Ciaran. She looked worried.

'Who is it?'

Frances bit her lip. 'I don't know but she's got a scowl that could freeze the sun. Older lady, white hair. Sounds posh.'

Hope frowned. That sounded a lot like Isobel but she had no idea why she might have come to the Emporium – the last time they'd met had been the previous week, when Hope had returned Khalid's letters. 'I'll come down,' she said, saving the spreadsheet she'd been working on.

Her suspicions were correct – Isobel was standing beside the dark wood counter near the entrance to the Emporium. Hope hurried forward to greet her but her smile faltered when she saw the icy expression on the older woman's face. 'Isobel,' she said as soon as she was close enough. 'Is something wrong?'

Isobel's eyes narrowed as she drew herself up to her full height. 'Miss Henderson,' she said in a loud crisp tone that carried across the entirety of the Emporium. 'When I entrusted you with my great-aunt's journal, did I not expressly request that you treat the contents with the utmost confidentiality?'

Hope stared at her in consternation. 'Of course. I respected that completely.'

'Did you?' Isobel arched an eyebrow. 'If that's the case, then how do you explain this?'

She pulled a white envelope from her handbag and slapped it onto the wooden counter. From the corner of her eye, Hope saw several customers edging nearer. She cleared her throat. 'There's an office upstairs. Would you prefer to discuss this in private?'

'I would not,' Isobel snapped, with such ferocity that Hope saw Frances flinch. 'Whatever is said here needs witnesses.'

Heart in mouth, Hope reached for the envelope and opened it. Inside, there was a folded sheet of A4: a letter on headed paper from something called the Abyssinian Institute. Frowning, Hope glanced up at Isobel. 'What is this?'

'Read it,' Isobel instructed. 'Although I'm sure you must already know.'

Hope did as she was told. The letter began with an introduction – the Abyssinian Institute was the name of a collection of Egyptian artefacts and ephemera based in Oxford. They had heard that Isobel had a journal belonging to the esteemed archaeologist Elenor Lovelace and wanted to know if it was available for sale. The letter went on to explain that they had seen photographs of the journal and, after verification, would prepared to pay a considerable amount of money to add the diary to their permanent collection.

'I don't understand,' Hope said. 'Who are these people? How do they know about the journal?'

'That is precisely what I want to know,' Isobel said. 'And I'm afraid there is only one possible explanation.'

A cold claw of foreboding clutched at Hope's stomach. 'You don't think I had anything to do with this?'

Isobel's expression grew even chillier. 'It must be you, Miss Henderson. No one else has had access to the journal. I've kept it to myself all these years, no one knew it even existed.' She paused and took the letter from Hope's unresisting hands. 'Photographs. They have photographs! You of all people know how incredibly personal Elenor's journal is – some of those entries could bring scandal on my family name.'

'But how could they have photographs?' Hope said, her head buzzing. 'The journal stayed in my apartment the whole time I was reading it. No one knew I had it, apart from Mr Young and –'

The realization was like a deluge of glacial water. Someone else had seen the journal – she'd put it in his hands herself. And he'd even asked about it when he'd come to see her. Ciaran.

'How much did they pay you?' Isobel demanded in a furiously haughty voice. 'Whatever the fee I hope it was worth the shame and dishonour you've brought upon yourself and this establishment. Or perhaps this is how you and your employer conduct your business – fooling old women into trusting you so you can exploit them.'

'Absolutely not, and it certainly has nothing to with Mr Young,' Hope protested as a feeling of utter nausea grew inside her. How had Ciaran got photographs? She hadn't left him alone with the journal. And then she remembered: he'd been looking for his phone – she had gone to the bedroom to search there and when she'd returned, the phone had been in his hand. Was it possible he'd lied about losing it to get her out of the room? Could he really have been that underhanded?

She met Isobel's gaze and saw to her shock that there were tears in the older woman's eyes. 'I trusted you,' she said, and now her voice shook with emotion. 'All those lies about feeling as though Elenor was a friend. I trusted you with my family's secrets and this is how you repay me – by selling them to the highest bidder.'

'I can assure you that I didn't,' Hope insisted. 'It was my honour to read Elenor's journal, I would never have dreamt of selling anything to anyone. But it's possible I know who did.'

Isobel glowered at her, one hand gripping the wooden counter so tightly that Hope could see her knuckles whitening. 'I don't believe you.'

Hope puffed out a long breath. 'I know. And I can't say I blame you. But apart from Mr Young, the only person who saw the journal was Professor McCormack.' She hesitated, wondering whether she should point the finger at him and then realizing she had no choice. 'I'm very much afraid the blame lies with him.'

'Perhaps you're working together,' Isobel said, and Hope saw her other hand lift to touch her chest as she took a breath. 'Perhaps you're nothing but a pair of confidence tricksters.'

She was pale, Hope observed, even paler than usual and there was a sheen of sweat on her forehead. 'Are you okay, Isobel?' she asked, concerned.

'I'm fine,' she snapped, although Hope thought she looked anything but fine. 'Don't try that game with me—'

She let out a sudden gasp and clutched the counter sharply. Hope saw her eyelids flutter and darted forwards, reaching her just in time to catch her as she fell.

'What's wrong?' Frances cried, as Hope did her best to gently lower the older woman to the floor of the Emporium.

'Call an ambulance,' she cried urgently, feeling for a pulse. 'Now!'

PART FOUR

Christmas Wishes

Chapter Twenty-Five

It was a scene that played out in Hope Henderson's nightmares for weeks after the event: Isobel Lovelace collapsing onto the floor of the Ever After Emporium. Sometimes, the flashing lights of the ambulance appeared immediately and the bad dream got better as Hope watched the paramedics whisk the older woman to hospital. On other nights, they took forever to arrive and Hope was forced to do what she'd done in real life – place Isobel in the recovery position and hold her until the terrifying seizure had passed, praying that help would arrive in time. And, once, they didn't come at all, causing Hope to run outside into York's streets to beg for assistance, but no one would stop. She woke up drenched in sweat after that dream, her heart thudding and her face wet with tears, and found it impossible to get back to sleep.

In reality, the reassuringly calm paramedic team had taken excellent care of the unconscious Isobel. Hope had hesitated over whether to accompany her in the ambulance – Isobel had been furious with her and might not appreciate waking up to find Hope at her side, but there was no family for Hope to call and she couldn't let Isobel go alone. The hours spent in A and E, waiting for news, were horribly tense and Hope only began to breathe easily when she heard Isobel had regained consciousness and was undergoing tests.

'Why don't you go home?' a kindly nurse had advised Hope as midnight came and went. 'She's resting now, and we'll know more in the morning.'

There had been guarded good news when Hope rang the next day; Isobel continued to respond well to treatment and seemed to have suffered no lasting effects from the seizure. She spent several days in hospital before being discharged into the care of a private nurse and was now back in her penthouse apartment, recovering, although Hope hadn't been to see her. Their last meeting had been angry and full of accusation. Hope was convinced it had helped to trigger the seizure. She wasn't sure how much Isobel remembered, or whether she knew that Hope had accompanied her in the ambulance, but she wasn't keen to upset her again.

'You'll have to speak to her eventually,' Iris pointed out over drinks as two weeks stretched into three. 'She needs to understand it wasn't you who sold her family secrets.'

Hope sighed. 'I did tell her. But I don't know if she remembers.'

Iris narrowed her gaze. 'On that subject, has that cock-womble archaeologist admitted responsibility yet?'

She meant Ciaran McCormack, Professor of Egyptology

at the University of York, and the insult was only improved by Iris's no-nonsense Yorkshire accent. It raised a reluctant smile from Hope, who had received a message only that morning. 'No, not yet. He wants to meet up to convince me of his innocence.'

'Of course he does,' Iris said with a level look. 'But he's about as innocent as Dick Turpin.'

Again, Hope couldn't help smiling. The infamous high-wayman had been imprisoned and eventually executed in York, for horse theft. She knew he had a reputation as a roguish charmer, although the truth was his crimes had often been fairly brutal when viewed with an unromantic eye. There could be no doubt of his guilt, however, and that was the point Iris was making. 'There isn't anyone else who could have taken the photographs,' she conceded. 'It had to be Ciaran.'

The source of Isobel's anger had been a letter from the mysterious sounding Abyssinian Institute, a historical society claiming to have seen pictures of an old journal belonging to her great-aunt, Elenor Lovelace, and offering to buy the diary for its collection. The only person Isobel had shared the journal with was Hope. She had misguidedly shown it to Ciaran and, since the writings made reference to a shameful family scandal, Isobel was understandably furious to receive a letter that suggested the journal's contents had been leaked. Hope knew it must have been Ciaran who'd been responsible. There was no other explanation.

'Cockwomble,' Iris repeated, with increased disgust. 'As if

it wasn't bad enough that he started seeing you when he was still married. You should report him to the university – if nothing else, it's extremely unprofessional behaviour.'

Hope couldn't argue with that but she had no proof that Ciaran was behind the leaked journal, other than opportunity, and a married man having an affair was hardly unusual. 'I'm half-tempted to meet him,' she admitted to Iris. 'I think he might come clean, face to face.'

Iris snorted. 'I doubt it. He's lied to you before, remember – what's to stop him doing it again now?'

'He didn't exactly lie,' Hope said, hating the defensive note in her voice. 'He just didn't tell me everything.'

'That's right,' Iris said, nodding with infinite patience. 'Because he is a duplicitous weasel who is not worthy of you. And the fact that he used your relationship to acquire and sell Isobel's family secrets is all the proof you need. Don't give him the opportunity to try and snake round you again, Hope. That's exactly what he wants.'

Taking a long sip of her Cosmopolitan, Hope pictured Ciaran, all floppy dark hair and chiselled chin and sparkling grey eyes. Everything about him suggested he'd just returned from seeking the Lost Ark of the Covenant and it was partly his good looks that had drawn her in so completely. That, and his easy charm and gorgeously lilting Irish accent that made even the most mundane observation sound poetic. And because of that undeniable attractiveness, Hope knew she had to be even more on her guard because, in spite of the way he'd treated her, deep down she suspected there was part of her that wasn't quite over Ciaran McCormack.

'What does Will think?' Iris asked.

And now Hope's mind flipped to their mutual friend, whose opinion of Ciaran had never been high to start with. 'About what you'd expect,' she told Iris. 'But I think he's trying to keep most of his thoughts to himself.'

Iris nodded. 'Unsurprising, given you fell out for weeks the last time he gave his opinion.'

Hope shifted in her seat, remembering how miserable she'd been when she and Will hadn't been talking. 'Yeah, it's safe to say we haven't really discussed it. He was concerned about Isobel's wellbeing, obviously, but once we knew she was going to be okay, we let the subject go.' She paused and shook her head. 'But enough about me – how are things with you? How's Martin?'

An uncharacteristically bashful smile crossed her friend's face. 'He's good. Great, in fact.'

For as long as Hope had known Iris, she'd been struggling with the frustrations and disappointments of online dating and even though they'd often laughed about the disastrous dates Iris had sat through, she knew the florist craved the elation and security of a relationship with someone who complemented her instead of trying to compete. From what she'd said, Martin was nothing like the men she'd dated previously but perhaps that was the reason things seemed to be working out. Whatever the difference, Hope was pleased Iris had finally met someone who made her happy. 'I'm glad,' she said simply.

'I think you'll like him,' Iris went on. 'Will too. I'd love for you both to meet him sometime.'

That might prove tricky, Hope thought. Will was guardian to his niece, Brodie, who had an aversion to strangers, which meant Will was unable to go out in the evenings, since babysitters were out of the question. The loss of both her parents in a car accident had left Brodie silent and suffering from separation anxiety, and although the little girl had come to accept Hope's presence in Will's house, it had taken time and perseverance to form a bond Brodie was comfortable with. All of which meant Will's social life was severely limited and Hope couldn't see the situation changing any time soon. But that didn't mean she couldn't meet Martin and give him the best friend seal of approval. 'I'd like that too,' she told Iris. 'He sounds great.'

'He is,' Iris said and gave Hope a sidelong look. 'Want me to see if he has a single friend I can match you up with?'

'No thanks,' Hope said, holding up her hands to ward off the well-meaning suggestion. Between the hurt Ciaran had inflicted and the disastrous misunderstanding that had led Will to try to kiss her, romance was the last thing she needed right now. 'I'm taking a break from men.'

Iris gave her a sympathetic look. 'I don't blame you. But don't give up completely – the right guy for you is out there somewhere. You just haven't found him yet.'

Except she already had, Hope thought wistfully, and cancer had stolen him away far too young. But it wasn't that no one could live up to the memory of Rob – she was under no illusion that he'd been perfect – more that she'd yet to meet anyone who fitted her like he had, someone who was like a warm coat on a cold day, someone who felt like home. Ciaran had been the first man she'd allowed close since Rob's death and she'd been hopeful her attraction to him might blossom into love, but the revelation of the wife he'd failed to mention had caused those hopes to wither. It felt easier to avoid romantic entanglements all together.

'Maybe you're right,' she said to Iris with a sigh. 'But I'm too tired to go searching.'

Her friend reached across to squeeze her hand. 'You won't have to look far. I have a funny feeling he's just around the corner.'

The following morning, Hope woke up from another dream about Isobel with Iris's comment revolving around her head – *You'll have to speak to her eventually.* It wasn't that she didn't want to contact Isobel – the truth was she was desperate to hear how the older woman was doing – but she was wary of upsetting her. No one wanted a repeat of the seizure that had landed her in hospital.

But at last Hope's curiosity and need to explain outweighed her reservations and she landed on the idea of writing a letter. Her relationship with Isobel had begun with a letter and it seemed somehow fitting to reconnect with her now via the same medium. And it was a real pleasure to place the nib of the fountain pen she'd bought especially for the task onto the thick, expensive writing paper. She paused after *Dear Isobel* and composed her thoughts, then wrote without interruption, allowing the words to flow. When she was finished, she read the letter over once and sealed it in a matching envelope. The plan was that Iris would deliver it, along with a bouquet of summer blooms. Surely it couldn't make the situation any worse.

The letter she received in reply, almost a week later, was stiff and formal in tone but Hope was relieved to see that Isobel was prepared to accept her explanation, although she took an extremely dim view of Ciaran's alleged involvement. The style of writing was typically Isobel but the handwriting itself caused to Hope to frown – spidery and loose, it was a long way from the older woman's usual impeccable presentation. A deep uneasiness wormed through Hope; just how badly had the seizure affected Isobel? Iris had said that, on the surface, she appeared to be almost back to her normal imperious self but the handwriting told a different story.

'Why don't you go and see her if you're worried?' Will suggested, when Hope dropped round on Friday evening. 'Iris delivers to her apartment, doesn't she? I'm sure she'd let you tag along the next time she calls in.'

'Maybe,' Hope said doubtfully, wondering how Isobel would view an uninvited appearance. 'I don't want her to feel ambushed, though. I'm trying to rebuild her trust and it might put Iris in an awkward position too.'

'Good point. Maybe a neutral location would be better,' Will said and cleared his throat. 'Speaking of trust, I wanted to sound you out about something.'

The suddenly peculiar expression he wore piqued Hope's curiosity. 'Oh?'

'It's more of a favour, really,' he went on, shifting on the sofa. 'An old friend is visiting York next week and wants to go out for dinner one evening.'

There was a brief pause, during which Hope thought she knew what was coming – the torn look on Will's face told her everything. But she didn't want to pre-empt him, so she waited.

'Normally, I'd say no but . . .' he trailed off, then threw a resolute look Hope's way. 'Well, I need to stop depending on you for my entire social life. So, I wondered whether you might babysit Brodie for a few hours. We'd go somewhere local, obviously – I could be back in minutes if she needed me—'

'I'd love to,' Hope said, gently interrupting. She studied him, taking in the faint circles beneath his hazel eyes, the weary set of his shoulders. 'You're entitled to some time for yourself, Will – it's been a rough year for you too.'

The tension seemed to whoosh out of him then, as though he'd been expecting her to say no. 'Really? You don't mind?'

'Are you kidding?' Hope said, with undisguised enthusiasm. 'It'll be my pleasure. We'll have a proper girls' night – pizza, popcorn and *Peppa Pig*.'

His eyes crinkled as he smiled with obvious gratitude. 'She'd love that. Thank you.'

A warm glow washed over Hope; was it her imagination or did he look a tiny bit less exhausted already? 'Just tell me when.'

'Maybe Thursday?' he said. 'But we can work around you.'

Hope mentally reviewed her diary. 'Thursday is fine. I have dinner with the belly dancing ladies on Friday evening and I usually go to see my parents on Wednesdays but I'm sure Dad won't mind if I miss a week.'

Will shook his head. 'No, I won't make you change your plans. Why don't we pencil in Thursday, then, and I'll confirm once I've spoken to Alex. Thanks again, Hope, I really appreciate this.'

His beaming smile was all the thanks Hope needed. 'I'm looking forward to it already,' she said, and meant every word.

Chapter Twenty-Six

'Bedtime is no later than seven-thirty and make sure you tuck Mr Mopsy in too,' Will told Hope for the third time as he dithered by the front door, trying to project an attitude of casual confidence that was undermined by the tension in his voice. 'Brodie, be a good girl for Hope. Make sure you brush your teeth and go to sleep when she tells you to.'

Brodie gave him a solemn faced nod that made her seem older than her four years. Will checked his phone. 'I'll only be round the corner, at La Luna – it's less than ten minutes away. Call if you need anything.'

'I know,' Hope said, with a reassuring smile. 'I've eaten there. But we won't need to call you – we're going to have a great time, aren't we, Brodie?'

Instead of nodding again, the little girl slipped her hand into Hope's. Will glanced at his niece, then at Hope, and she saw the tightness around his mouth relax a little. 'Go,' she said gently. 'Have a wonderful time. I'll see you in a few hours.'

With another look at his phone, Will seemed to reach some kind of decision. 'Okay,' he said. 'Bed at seven-thirty and don't forget—'

'Mr Mopsy,' Hope finished in mock exasperation. 'I know, Will. Stop fussing, we'll be fine. If you don't leave soon, you'll be late.'

Crouching down, he took Brodie's free hand in his. 'Sleep well, Dee-dee. I'll come in for a goodnight kiss when I get home.'

The little girl nodded, her eyes fixed on his and Hope felt something inside her turn liquid at the love between them. For a moment, the three of them were linked by their joined hands. Then Will gave Brodie's hand a final squeeze, stood up and squared his shoulders. 'Thank you for doing this. I won't be late back.'

Hope smiled. 'Would you just go already? Brodie and I have a hot date with Tom Hardy on the *Bedtime Story* and we're going to need snacks before then.'

Will laughed and held up his hands. 'Fine, I'm going. See you later.'

She half-expected him to dither some more but he smoothed down his fitted white shirt and turned to crunch down the drive. At the gate, he turned to wave and they watched him turn left and vanish from sight along the narrow road that led past the university gardens to York's twisty snickelways. Hope glanced down at Brodie on the doorstep, wondering how the little girl would react to his absence; it was the first time they'd been apart since she had come to live with him over six months earlier. And sure enough, there was a faint wobble around Brodie's lips and the hint of tearfulness in her eyes.

'I don't know about you, but I'd love a hot chocolate,' Hope said, without closing the door. 'I brought some raspberry syrup and unicorn sprinkles.'

Brodie's gaze turned sharply upwards as she considered her options. After a moment's thought, she stepped backwards and started to lead Hope towards the gleaming white kitchen. Easing the front door shut, Hope allowed herself to be led. No doubt the incoming sugar rush would scupper Will's instructions for a seven-thirty bedtime but Hope was more concerned with getting through the evening without having to bother him and the best way to manage that was by distraction. Which was why she'd stopped at the supermarket on the way to Will's house earlier in the evening; she and Brodie had already polished off the pepperoni pizza she'd brought, and watched several episodes of *Peppa Pig* with a large bowl of popcorn while Will ironed his shirt and got ready. Now it was time for Phase Three – hot chocolate on the sofa, followed by as many bedtime stories as Brodie needed to fall asleep.

In the event, they were true to their promises and Brodie was safely tucked up in bed, with Mr Mopsy beside her, at seven-thirty. Her eyelids were drooping by the end of the first picture book, although Hope knew she was fighting sleep with everything she had. Five minutes later and she was gone, her long eyelashes dark against her creamy pale skin and Mr Mopsy clutched under one arm. Hope watched her slumber for several minutes, aware of a gradual soothing sense of peace easing through her, and then crept noiselessly out and pulled the door shut. She was about to go downstairs when she heard a muffled thump coming from Will's bedroom, where the kittens he'd unwittingly fostered still lived with their mother, whom they'd nicknamed Missy. Surely Will wouldn't begrudge her a quick peek at the feline family? It was practically her job as babysitter, after all . . .

The thud had been a book falling off the bed, dislodged by the two kittens tumbling across the duvet cover, engaged in a ferociously cute play-fight while Missy watched from her seat on a nearby chair. They were so cute together – it was going to be a wrench to separate them when the time came for Hope to take one of them home with her but she could always bring her new flatmate back for kitten play dates. Smiling at the thought, Hope retrieved the paperback from the floor and studied the cover. It was a battered, well-thumbed copy of *The Lord of the Rings* – clearly a favourite – and Hope had a sudden image of Will propped up against the dove-grey pillows, absorbed in the soaring battle to save Middle Earth. Although knowing how tired he usually was, she could easily imagine his eyes drooping and the book dipping towards the duvet. It was a curiously intimate scene, especially when Hope realized Will was bare chested, and she felt warmth suffuse her cheeks. Hurriedly, she placed the book on the bedside table and, after risking shredded fingers in a quick ruffle of each kittens' fur, she retreated to the landing and headed downstairs.

Finding the novel in Will's bedroom had sparked Hope's curiosity about the bookshelf that stood tucked away in the corner of the living room. Making herself a cup of tea, she lingered beside the shelves, running her fingers along the glorious variety of spines. The lower shelves obviously belonged to Brodie – Julia Donaldson's *Room on the Broom* jostled with Abie Longstaff's *Fairytale Hairdresser* and Michael Rosen's *We're Going on a Bear Hunt*. There were non-fiction titles too – animal facts and world geography. Hope was pleased to spot a copy of *Fantastically Great Women Who Changed the World* by Kate Pankhurst and wondered whether it had been Will who had bought it for Brodie or her parents. Will rarely talked about Scott and Lucy so Hope had no sense of the kind of people they'd been but, judging from the wonderful daughter they'd created, she thought they must have been excellent parents.

Will's taste in books was varied and there was no particular order to their position on the shelf. Hope saw a smattering of science fiction – Philip K. Dick and Iain M. Banks – and several Hilary Mantel novels. *Dracula* cosied up to *Birdsong* and *The Handmaid's Tale*, and Bernardine Evaristo's *Girl, Woman, Other* sat next to *1984*. There was a complete set of Ben Aaronovitch's *Rivers of London* novels, which Rob had loved, and plenty of other titles that were unfamiliar to Hope. Once again, she was struck by a vision of Will reading, this time on the sofa, and it made her smile. Exploring his taste in books only made her happier they'd become friends.

She was engrossed in her own book – a biography of Howard Carter that dwelt in depth on his discovery of the tomb of Tutankhamun – when she heard the front door opening. A quick glance at her watch told her it was ten-forty and she blinked in surprise – where had the time gone? It only felt like five minutes since Will's last text checking in but that had been just after eight o'clock.

'Hello,' she said, as Will appeared in the door of the hall-way. 'Did you have a nice evening?'

She could see from his carefree expression that he had, even before his enthusiastic nod. 'Brilliant, thanks. How has Brodie been? Any problems?'

'None at all,' she replied, getting up from the sofa. 'She was an absolute poppet and as I said in my text, I haven't heard a peep from her since she went to sleep. How was dinner?'

Will ran a hand through his hair, a gesture that Hope knew well, and she saw him relax. 'It was great. Really nice.' He hesitated, as though debating whether to say what was on his mind. 'Good to be out on my own, actually. I can't remember the last time that happened.'

Hope threw him a shrewd look. 'You shouldn't feel guilty when you say that,' she observed, and recalled something Charlotte had once said. 'Being a parent isn't the be all and end all – you're entitled to a life too.'

'I know,' he said quickly. 'It's just been such a roller-coaster, the past six or seven months. I haven't really had time to think of anything that didn't involve Brodie or work or keeping things running here. And suddenly, I was in a restaurant on my own and the biggest decision I had to make was whether to have the steak or the chicken.' He shook his head and let out a soft huff of laughter. 'I spent the first hour feeling as though I'd left my right arm at home.'

Hope smiled. 'That's normal. But everything was fine – you had a good time and so did Brodie. Next time it will feel more natural.'

Will puffed out a long breath and gave her a grateful look. 'I know. Thank you.'

'Don't mention it,' Hope said, and reached for her book. 'I'm glad you had a good time with your friend – Alex, wasn't it?'

He nodded. 'Yeah. It's been a long time since we talked. I was worried things might be awkward, but it was great to catch up.'

There was a hint of something unsaid that made Hope wonder if there'd been a falling out but Will looked so light-hearted that she didn't want to raise unhappy memories. 'Excellent,' she said instead. 'And now I'd better make a move. I'm filling in for Frances at the Emporium tomorrow and there's the belly dance dinner in the evening. I'm going to need plenty of energy to keep up with those ladies.'

'Of course,' Will said, grinning. 'Have fun. And thanks again.'

Hope laughed. 'Stop thanking me! I told you, I'm happy to help. It's what friends do.'

He tipped his head, accepting her gentle admonishment. 'In that case, I might ask you to do this again. It's such a weight off my mind, knowing Brodie is with you – means I can actually relax a bit.'

She studied him more closely then, noticing how less weary he seemed, how much happier. He looked younger somehow, with a merry light that danced in his eyes, and she could almost picture who he'd been before the terrible accident that had changed his and Brodie's lives forever. If this was what a night off from responsibility could do, Hope was absolutely prepared to help out more. 'Any time,' she said.

Will suddenly raised a hand to his mouth, covering a yawn. 'Looks like it's past my bedtime too,' he said wryly.

She smiled as she crossed to the kitchen island and collected her bag from the velvet stool. 'It does. Don't stay up too late reading, will you?'

The Greek restaurant was packed and noisy with the buzz of happy diners. Cutlery and glasses clinked, voices were raised to be heard and above it all lay catchy melodies that begged Hope to get up and dance. She had no intention of answering their siren call; dancing was still something she only did in the safety of her Monday night belly dance classes with Iris and the other women sat around the long rectangular table, but she did allow herself to sway a little to the beat as she listened to the conversations unfolding among her friends.

The women surrounding Hope were as diverse a group as she could possibly imagine. When she'd first begun belly dancing, not long after moving back to York, she'd expected the studio to be filled with impossibly beautiful bodies, clad in gauzy chiffon and sequins and undulating in perfect time to the evocative music that was the hallmark of the dance. But while the sequins and sparkle had been very much in evidence, she'd quickly discovered that belly dancing was not only reserved for those blessed with a dancer's figure. Only their teacher, Fleur, had that and, as Iris had pointed out on several occasions, she was basically a goddess. The other bellies on display ranged from gently rounded to outrageously curvy, from mid-twenties to almost seventy, and belonged to women from a variety of cultures. Dancing with them was a celebration of the female body, a joyous hour of surrendering to the shimmy among friends, and Hope had soon learned to leave her inhibitions at the door. She'd grown in confidence too, as the weeks and months passed, although she knew she'd never possess the grace and sensuality of Fleur or even Iris. Belly dance classes were one of the things she loved most about her return to York and she would be forever grateful to her new best friend for introducing her to this group of extraordinary women.

Iris turned away from her conversation with Celia and Traci to survey Hope. 'You didn't tell me – how did the babysitting go last night?'

Taking a sip of wine, Hope inclined her head. 'Really well. I think it did Will good to get out on his own – he seemed revitalized when he came back.'

Iris grinned. 'I'm not surprised. That's his first date in months, he's bound to have enjoyed it.'

Hope stared at her, wondering if she'd misheard. 'It wasn't a date. He met up with an old friend – someone called Alex.'

The grin faded a little as Iris puffed out a breath. 'Well, I suppose you could call her an old friend. They dated for two years.'

And now Hope felt her food-laden stomach contract, sending needles of unease spiking along her nerves. 'What?'

Iris raised both eyebrows. 'Didn't Will tell you? They broke up last year – he wanted to settle down, she wasn't ready and they hit a bit of an impasse. Things came to a head when he suggested they moved in together – she ended up leaving York after the break up and got a job in Edinburgh. I didn't know she'd come back until Will said he was having dinner with her.'

Hope was silent for a moment. The new information shouldn't make any difference – Will was under no obligation to explain who he'd been out with and up until now Hope had been happy that he'd enjoyed himself. But she couldn't deny that knowing he'd been on a date made her feel . . . what? Uncomfortable? Disconcerted? She wasn't sure exactly, but her nerves were tight and she was aware she was frowning. 'Oh,' she mumbled, unable to think of anything else to say. 'No, he didn't mention any of that.'

Her friend was eyeing her closely. 'I could be wrong. From what I remember, he was pretty cut up at the time but it happened over eighteen months ago. Maybe they've decided to be friends now the dust has settled.'

But her earlier words echoed in Hope's head – *his first date in months*. Iris clearly didn't believe Will and Alex were just catching up. Taking another sip of wine, Hope summoned up a brisk smile. 'It's none of my business anyway,' she said. 'Whatever the occasion, I'm just glad he had a good time.'

Iris narrowed her gaze in typically knowing fashion, clearly about to say something blunt, when the tinkling of metal against glass cut through the hubbub around the table. Conversations trailed off as everyone looked at Fleur, who was standing up with a spoon in one hand and a glass in the other. 'I'm sorry to interrupt,' she said, with a dazzling smile. 'But now that we've all finished eating, I thought this might be a good moment to make an announcement.'

Looks were exchanged and Hope saw Traci whisper something to her friend, Nic, who then passed whatever the secret was onto Fiona. Iris widened her eyes at Hope but said nothing.

'As most of you know, I encourage you to see dancing as something you do for yourselves – a way to nourish and love your bodies when society often tries to shame us into hiding them,' Fleur went on. 'But, as with any artistic endeavour, its value is only increased when it connects with an audience. And you all dance so beautifully that it would be a terrible waste to deny you the opportunity to create that connection. So, I have booked the stage at the York Theatre Royal for one performance only in November and I very much hope you will dance with me there!'

Most of the women broke into applause at Fleur's final sentence. Beside Hope, Iris beamed, her eyes full of twinkling excitement but Hope felt her own spirits plummet even further. November was only three months away – how could she possibly be good enough to share a stage with Fleur by then? The truth was she would never be good enough – Fleur had a natural talent and years of training; Hope had no doubt she shone on stage. Whereas Hope was tall and uncoordinated, she still occasionally turned right when she should have turned left, and her brain struggled to retain even the simplest choreography.

Iris seemed to read all of this on Hope's face because she leaned in to whisper. 'Don't worry – we don't actually dance with Fleur. She teaches us a routine and we have weeks to work on it. Once we've all performed, that's when Fleur takes to the stage and shows everyone how it should be done.'

That still left plenty to worry about, Hope thought anxiously. The idea of having to dance in front of an audience, in York's famous theatre, was more than enough to make her feel sick. But again, Iris guessed what she was thinking. 'We'll work on it together,' she promised. 'By the time the performance rolls round, you'll be desperate to show off your moves.'

There wasn't the slightest chance that Hope would feel that way, not even if she had twelve months to practise, but Iris was bubbling over with enthusiastic anticipation and judging from the excited chatter around them, the rest of the class felt the same. The last thing Hope wanted was for her own lack of confidence to ruin the vibe for her friends, so she plastered on a smile and did her best to look encouraged. 'Thanks, Iris.'

Fiona, a dark-haired woman in her late forties, leaned

across the table towards Hope. 'I know it sounds scary – I was terrified the first time. But you know what, it was a lot of fun. And if I can let it all hang out after three kids and a lifelong love affair with chocolate, you can.'

Her enthusiasm was so contagious that this time Hope's smile was genuine, if a little reluctant. 'Okay.'

Apparently satisfied, Fiona turned back to Nic and began chatting again. Iris was discussing costumes with Celia, which left Hope temporarily alone with her dismay. It wasn't the first time Fleur had raised the idea of a performance but the last mention had been so long ago that Hope had persuaded herself it wasn't really going to happen. And, of course, no one was going to force her to dance if she didn't want to – she wasn't at school, for goodness' sake. But there was a niggling sense that she'd somehow be letting the others down if she didn't take part – that she'd be letting herself down and it wasn't a feeling she enjoyed. Maybe Iris was right – maybe with a lot of practice she might at least remember the choreography. And she could always stand at the back. Someone needed to, after all.

It wasn't until she was making her way home, buoyed up by several more glasses of wine, that Hope remembered what Iris had revealed about Will's dinner date. Once again, the thought caused her stomach to lurch. She wasn't sure why – as she'd pointed out, Will was free to see whomever he chose and it really was nobody else's business. But the knowledge that he had met up with his ex sat like a stone inside Hope and weighed her down all the way back to her wharf apartment on the other side of the River Foss. She dropped her keys onto the hall table and headed for the balcony, staring moodily out at the city's twinkling lights. It made no difference whether Will had been on a date or not, she told herself, leaning her too warm forehead on the cool glass of the balcony door. What mattered was that he'd had a brilliant time and had returned home happy.

Hope didn't begrudge him that happiness at all but was it so very wrong that she wished for a little of the same for herself? Her thoughts inevitably strayed to Ciaran, who'd messaged again that morning to suggest meeting up:

> Just a drink, nothing more. I'm so much better at explaining in person – please say yes. It might help smooth things over with you and Isobel X

And part of her had wanted to give in, but she'd held out:

> Are you ready to admit you're working for the Abyssinian Institute?

His reply hadn't surprised her:

> No. But I have heard of them. Maybe I can help – shall we talk? X

Hope hadn't bothered to reply but the temptation to message now was strong. His reply would be immediate, she was sure, and it might possibly soothe the loneliness she felt, at least temporarily. But she also knew no good would come of messaging Ciaran so late at night – it would only encourage him. With a swift movement, she turned her phone off. She'd just have to find some other way to stop wondering about Will's love life, she told herself sternly. One that didn't involve Ciaran McCormack.

Chapter Twenty-Seven

Hope arrived at the Ever After Emporium early on Sunday morning. Her role there had begun as a part-time position three days a week and although her work had expanded as she grew more experienced in the ways of the antiques business, she still rarely worked weekends. Today was an exception, however; she'd come in at six o'clock to work on a new window display before the shop could be overrun with late-summer tourists.

The sun was just stretching its rays over the spires of York Minster as she hurried through the silent streets to the Emporium. Yawning, she let herself in and switched off the alarm. Her colleague, Frances, had stayed late the night before to clear the existing window display and leave Hope with a blank canvas. All she had to do now was bring down her carefully curated items from the stockroom on the first floor and arrange them into something that might catch the eye of the public passing by outside. And, if Hope was lucky, it might draw in someone else too.

But before she began the first of her many trips up and down the stairs to the stockroom, Hope did what she always tried to do when she arrived at the Emporium each morning – she stood beside the heavy dark wood counter and took a moment to listen.

The most obvious sound was the ticking of the tall grandfather clock, closely followed by that of the much smaller cuckoo clock. But beneath both timepieces, in the silences that lay between the comforting tick and tock that was the heartbeat of the shop, that was when Hope fancied she could hear echoes of the other items that made up the Emporium. If she listened carefully, she could hear the clink of a cup on a saucer as the Wedgwood tea sets were used to serve up afternoon tea, or she might catch the faintest snippet of carefree laughter as a child rode on the magnificent rocking horse that stood at the far end of the shop. Often, she heard a snatch of faraway music from the gramophone player and sometimes it was so quiet that she thought she could hear the dust motes sighing as they drifted through the still air. That was the magic of the Emporium, she thought, as she stood and strained her ears for new sounds. It always had something to offer if you kept an open mind.

Hope was expecting Iris around eight o'clock but the florist's jaunty tap on the window still made her jump. She spun around, flustered, to see Iris standing on the pavement with two small palm trees in containers on a low trolley.

The florist raised one hand in a thumbs up gesture and Hope waved her towards the shop entrance.

'You scared the life out of me,' Hope said, as she opened the door and helped Iris inside with the trolley.

'Sorry,' Iris said. 'I did try waving but you were in another world.'

She had been in 1920s Egypt, Hope thought, trying to channel the heat and history and breath-taking romance of the time so that she could recreate an echo of it in York a century later. 'I should be the one apologizing,' she said ruefully. 'I got you out of bed at the crack of dawn on a Sunday to supply me with palm trees.'

'It's a good thing I like you,' Iris replied, with a long-suffering sigh but she didn't sound in the least bit resentful. 'Oh, who am I trying to kid? I have to admit I can't wait to see what you're going to come up with this time.'

'Help me get these into the window and I'll tell you everything you want to know,' Hope said, tapping the stem of the nearest spindle palm tree.

Once the palms were in place, Hope unrolled two long canvasses. 'Want to help me attach these?' she asked Iris. 'I can do them myself but if you want to know what I'm planning, these will give you a big clue.'

Iris laughed. 'I think we both know there's only one answer to that question.'

The canvasses were designed to form the backdrop of the display. Hope and Iris hung them securely from the curtain hooks in the ceiling and Hope caught her friend squinting at the painted lines, trying to work out what they might be. 'Wait until you've got a bit of distance,' she told her. 'It will all become clear then.'

'Sounds likes good advice for life,' Iris observed, raising one eyebrow.

But the gasp she let out once they were in the street, gazing into the window, was gratifying. 'Oh, it looks exactly like we're standing beside the pyramids! Is it a tribute to Elenor Lovelace?'

Hope nodded, feeling a fizzle of excitement at the effect. She'd hoped the *trompe l'oeil* on the canvas would give passers-by the feeling they'd been transported to Egypt but she hadn't dreamed it would work as well as it did. 'An artist friend of my mother's painted it for me. Isn't it brilliant?'

'It is,' Iris agreed. 'But not as brilliant as you. This is going to stop traffic!'

'Elenor didn't excavate at the pyramids, of course, but she definitely spent time there – it was in her journal,' Hope said, trying not to show how ridiculously pleased she was with the praise. 'I've got a ton of sand from Fraisthorpe beach to lay and then I can add the finishing touches.'

'Can I help?' Iris asked. 'I know you don't need me to but I'm not going anywhere until I've seen the finished display so I might as well. I promise not to claim any creative credit!'

Hope grinned at her. 'Absolutely. I'd love some help.'

An hour later, they were standing on High Petergate once more, gazing critically into the window of the Emporium. The palm trees worked perfectly to add depth to the *trompe l'oeil*, as Hope anticipated they would. An old-fashioned camera stood on a tripod, pointed towards the pyramids with its black cloth trailing down towards the sand. To the left, there was a table laden with maps, an ancient pair of binoculars and a leather-bound journal. An archaeologist's trowel sat on the seat, with a ladies' hat dangling precariously from the back of the chair. And the emerald scarab beetle engagement ring sat in pride of place on an open map at the centre of the table, glinting under the golden filtered lights. A shiver ran down Hope's spine as she studied the scene. It was vibrant, alive with the searing heat and breathless drama of the setting. The only thing missing was Elenor herself and there was a definite feeling that she was somewhere nearby, perhaps excitedly discussing her latest discovery with her fiancé, Khalid.

'It's extraordinary,' Iris said, after a few moments of silent contemplation. 'Really amazing, Hope. You've outdone yourself.'

Most unexpectedly, tears pricked at the back of Hope's eyes; she blinked them away. 'Thank you. And thanks for all your help – you made it so much easier.'

Her friend waved the appreciation away. 'You didn't need me. Well, maybe for the palm trees. They look good, don't they?'

'They look brilliant,' Hope said. 'A hint of lushness in the desert.'

Iris smirked. 'I might steal that for my online dating profile,' she said with a wink. 'Not that I'm logging in much these days.'

Hope eyed her, taking in the sudden spots of rosiness that had appeared in her cheeks. 'It's still going well with Martin, then?'

'Seems to be,' Iris replied. 'Hey, you should come and visit me at the wedding fayre in September, say hello to him. He'll be on site in case anything goes wrong with any of the stands he's designed.'

Her happiness was so obvious that Hope found herself suddenly curious about the man who could make her friend glow like this. 'I'd like that,' she said. 'Tell me which day works best and I'll see you there.'

'That's if you can spare the time,' Iris said, transferring her gaze back to the window once more. 'You're going to be the toast of the town once people get a load of this. You might be too famous for your old friends.'

Hope laughed. 'Hardly. And there's only one person who I really want to see it.'

Iris squinted at her. 'Not Ciaran, surely.'

'No!' Hope spluttered, although now she couldn't help wondering what he would make of it. 'Try again.'

'Isobel,' Iris guessed, and this time Hope nodded. 'Relax. She's going to love it.'

'Fingers crossed,' Hope replied. She hadn't wanted to crowd Isobel by materializing unannounced on her doorstep; she suspected the older woman might be more comfortable if she felt the whole idea of reaching out had been her own. The window display was, in part, designed to encourage her to do that.

Iris reached out and squeezed Hope's hand. 'I know how much this means to you. Believe me, I've got everything crossed.'

Word soon spread about the window display at the Ever After Emporium and, as Iris had predicted, crowds gathered on High Petergate, causing occasional problems with irate drivers. The Bank Holiday weekend was particularly hectic; the city council erected safety barriers to manage the flow of visitors to the shop and they had their own policeman for the duration of the long weekend, ensuring the road was kept clear. Business inside the Emporium had never been brisker – the number of people browsing meant they had to operate a one-in-one-out system and the queue snaked all the way along the alley of Minster Gate.

Ciaran had clearly seen Hope's handiwork too, because his praise managed to be both effusive and typically self-serving:

Great window! How about meeting up to toast your brilliance in person? X

She'd shaken her head and planned to reply later, and then a customer had needed her help and Ciaran's message had slipped out of her mind. By the time September arrived, Hope was ready for things to calm down. But with Mr Young spending more time away from the Emporium, sourcing stock to replace the items that were flying out of the door now that their reputation was growing, she found herself working more. Mr Young had recruited another assistant for the shop floor, which freed Hope up to undertake more of the administrative duties he would normally cover, but there still seemed to be too much work and not enough time.

'Be careful what you wish for, eh, Hope?' Mr Young said ruefully, as they passed on the stairs one afternoon. 'We're victims of our own success.'

She hadn't had time to see Will and Brodie since babysitting, although she and Will had spoken on the phone and exchanged messages. She'd carefully avoided asking him any further questions about his date but the spectre loomed up again when he asked if she would look after Brodie again on Saturday night.

'She starts school on Monday and I want to make sure I'm home every night next week,' he explained down the phone. 'So this weekend is really the only possibility. Are you around? Would you mind?'

'I can do Saturday night,' Hope said slowly, aware of a sudden knot of reluctance in her chest. 'The same time as before?'

'Great,' he said, sounding pleased. 'And yes, around the same time as before would be perfect. But I might stay out a bit later, if that's okay. Live dangerously.'

Hope could hear the anticipation in his voice. 'Sure,' she said. Taking a deep breath, she aimed for casual interest. 'What are you up to? Anything fun?'

Was it her imagination or did he hesitate before

answering? 'Just meeting a friend for a drink and something to eat. Nothing fancy.'

'Anyone I know?' Hope said, although the truth was she hadn't met any of Will's friends, because he hadn't seen much of them himself since Brodie's arrival. But he'd talked about them and she knew most of them by reputation, at least.

This time there was a definite pause before he replied. 'No, I don't think so.'

Hope waited to see if he would elaborate but the silence stretched and no more information was offered. Forcing herself not to dwell on what that might mean, she did her best to sound normal. 'I'll see you on Saturday, then. Around five o'clock.'

'Thanks, Hope,' he said warmly. 'See you then.'

Saturday followed much the same pattern as the previous evening Hope had spent babysitting, although she thought Will had put a little more effort into his appearance this time. His shirt seemed crisper and he exuded a subtle woody scent with a hint of citrus that Hope hadn't known him to wear before. There was a faint nervous energy about him as he said goodbye, along with a spark of suppressed excitement. Whoever he was meeting, he was looking forward to it, she decided as she closed the door.

Pushing the thought from her head, Hope smiled down at Brodie. 'What shall we do first – watch *Peter Rabbit* or crack that jigsaw puzzle?'

Once the little girl was in bed, Hope spent a blissful fifteen minutes playing with the kittens, then went downstairs and flicked through the channels in search of something to keep her mind from imagining what Will was up to. One of the movie channels was showing the Indiana Jones trilogy. With a self-deprecating smile, she settled down to watch *Raiders of the Lost Ark*; the hero would remind her constantly of Ciaran but at least she wouldn't be thinking about Will.

She must have dozed off part way through the second movie because she woke up to the sound of Will's keys in the lock and the sight of Sean Connery looking like the ultimate silver fox on the screen.

'Oh god, you were asleep,' Will exclaimed when he caught sight of her yawning on the sofa. 'I'm sorry it's so late.'

Hope peered at her watch and saw it was after midnight. 'It's fine, don't worry. Did you have a nice evening?'

But she didn't need a reply to know the answer; it was written all over him. She could tell he'd had a few drinks – there was a relaxed set to his face that told her alcohol had temporarily removed some of his stress, but that wasn't what gave him away. Everything about him radiated happiness, from his posture to the sparkle in his eyes. He looked like a man who couldn't stop grinning at his own good fortune.

'I had a great time, thanks,' he said, his voice bubbling with cheeriness. 'Was Brodie well behaved?'

Hope nodded. 'She was an angel, as always.' Glancing at him, she steeled herself. 'So, when are you seeing Alex again?'

The faintest flicker of guilt crossed his face, followed by a frown. 'I'm not sure. Who told you about Alex?'

'Oh, Iris mentioned her last week,' she answered, striving for a couldn't-care-less tone. 'She said the two of you dated for a couple of years.'

Will stared at her for a moment, then came to sit on the sofa. 'Yeah, we were pretty serious for a while. Or I was, at least.' He grimaced. 'It turned out we weren't quite on the same page and she wasn't ready to settle down.'

'Ah,' Hope said carefully. 'That sounds tough.'

'It was, at the time,' he said, sighing. 'But if I'm honest, she did the right thing. I don't think I was ready either – moving in just felt like the next logical step in our relationship, rather than something I actually wanted. It took a few months after the break up for me to see that.' Pausing, he met Hope's gaze. 'And then Brodie arrived and I haven't had time to think since. I don't think I could have coped with looking after her and juggling a relationship at the same time. Something would have had to give.'

Not to mention the grief that came with losing his brother and sister-in-law, Hope thought but didn't say. 'But things are different now,' she said, and it was more of a statement than a question.

'I think so,' Will said thoughtfully. 'Brodie and I are a lot more settled, although starting school next week will be a big test. But I think we've adjusted to the situation now and I feel as though I've got some spare bandwidth for a social life.' He smiled at Hope. 'And, of course, we've got you. I know I speak for Brodie when I say we're both really happy we sheltered from the rain in the Emporium that morning and found you there.'

'Me too,' Hope said. She tried to return his smile but her mouth wouldn't make the right shape and she wasn't sure why, because she was really happy they'd come into the Emporium too. 'Do you think . . . are you and Alex back on, then? How does she feel about Brodie?'

He puffed out a long breath. 'I don't know, to be honest. It's early days. But obviously we're not the same people we were when we split up – Alex understands about Brodie and says there's no rush to get back to where we were.' He shook his head, as though in wonder. 'It's funny how things turn out, isn't it? I never expected to see her again, much less start dating her. But here we are.'

'Here we are,' Hope echoed and this time she forced her mouth into a smile. 'I'm happy for you. Fingers crossed it works out this time.'

'I'm taking it one day at a time,' he said. 'But I've enjoyed spending time with Alex and I guess I have you to thank for that as well. You were the one who encouraged me to start dating again, after all.'

He leaned back against the sofa and, once again, Hope was struck by how much more relaxed he seemed, how contented he was. She was pleased for him, of course – he'd been through so much that he deserved this happiness – but at the same time, there was a cold hard lump in the pit of her stomach that had been there since Iris had first revealed who Alex was. Except now Hope knew what it was: jealousy. Which didn't make any sense because she didn't fancy Will. She hadn't enjoyed it when he'd kissed her – in fact, it had felt all wrong, because he was her friend, nothing more. So this jealousy of Alex was even more irrational. But that didn't mean it wasn't real.

'I'm glad you're happy,' she told Will, hoping the sentiment didn't sound as wooden as she felt. And the words of Mr Young came floating back to her – *be careful what you wish for, eh?*

Chapter Twenty-Eight

In the weeks and months following Rob's death, Hope had lost count of the number of times she'd heard that staying busy was the key to learning to live with grief. At first, it had felt almost impossible to leave their flat – everything she saw seemed to remind her that Rob was gone. Even a visit to the local supermarket was difficult; she'd broken down in the milk aisle, because they'd run out of the gold top he'd always preferred. But slowly, the business of living got easier and she found herself able to function better. And in time, she discovered that keeping occupied did help. She never forgot Rob was dead but there were moments when the knowledge no longer dominated her thoughts. And although her jealousy over Will's blossoming love life was nothing like the loss of Rob, she did find it looming large in her mind and decided once more that the best thing she could do was to stay busy.

Thankfully, the Emporium came to her rescue. While it wasn't as crazily full on as the end of August had been, the second week of September was more than demanding enough to keep Hope's attention focused on work. She kept contact with Will to a minimum, only getting in touch to ask how Brodie's first day at school had been, and politely answering his questions about how she was doing. If he noticed the reserved tone to her replies, he didn't raise it and Hope assumed he was too wrapped up in messaging Alex to observe any distance in his other friendships. If she was honest, his preoccupation suited her – it meant she didn't have to examine the reasons behind her reluctance to stay in touch and that helped her to pretend everything was fine.

On Friday afternoon, she took herself across York to the racecourse, where Iris's wedding fayre was being held. The bewildering array of stands and displays inside the exhibition space reminded Hope of the weekends she and Rob had spent wandering around similar fayres when they'd first got engaged. If the York wedding fayre was anything to go by, the industry seemed to have grown since then and Hope was soon helplessly lost among the maze of stalls. Pulling out her phone, she messaged Iris.

> I can see a cake seller called Chocwaves and cocktail stand called Tipsy's. Can you guide me in? X

A few minutes ticked by before Iris read the message. Her reply made Hope sigh with relief.

> Wait right there, I'm coming to get you! X

'Thank goodness,' Hope said, as Iris wove her way through the crowds to reach her. 'I was beginning to see cupcakes everywhere I looked.'

Her friend nodded. 'It does get a bit like that. But you weren't far away – I'm just around the corner.'

Hope didn't know what she'd been expecting but she gasped when she saw the Blooming Dales stand. It wasn't the biggest by any means but what it lacked in size, it more than made up for in wow factor. Spot-lit in soft pastels, it boasted a three-dimensional flower arch that spanned the entrance, and the inside walls were covered from floor to ceiling in delicate silk blooms. An exquisite, oversized glass vase held the most amazing arrangement Hope had ever seen: creamy roses nestled beside proud lilies and extravagant sprays of gypsophila. In amongst the flowers, tall ivory feathers reached for the ceiling and competed with shimmering crystals for the eye of the beholder. The overall effect should have been showy and overdone but somehow it wasn't. It almost made Hope wish for a wedding of her own to plan, just so she could incorporate Iris's genius.

'This is incredible!' she told her friend, standing back to absorb the full effect all over again. 'I bet you've been run off your feet.'

'Pretty much,' Iris admitted. 'I think I'm booked solid until February.'

'Wow,' Hope said, marvelling at her friend's cool demeanour. 'February next year – that's fantastic.'

Iris grinned. 'February the year after,' she corrected. 'I'm fully booked for the next eighteen months, at least. And some of the couples here are planning weddings a couple of years away, so I think there'll be plenty more bookings.'

Hope shook her head in wonder. 'That's insane.' She gave Iris a sidelong look. 'You're going to need a bigger shop.'

But Iris folded her arms. 'No way. I'm never leaving High Petergate – I love looking across at the Emporium every day and seeing York Minster peeking over the top. But I might have to source a workshop somewhere nearby, and maybe take on another florist.'

Hope looked at the stand again, which had a steady stream of customers winding in and out beneath the flower arch. Three young women were waiting inside, each wearing pink Blooming Dales t-shirts, and helping with enquiries, while a fourth was standing in the aisle, handing out branded postcards. 'This is a slick operation, Iris,' she said with undisguised admiration. 'I'm really impressed.'

'Most of it is pretty standard,' she replied modestly. 'The girls are just temps, although they've had some basic training so they can answer simple floristry questions. They take names and contact details, check the diary if a couple wants to take the plunge and book right away, and I only get involved if something comes up that they can't answer.'

'It's brilliant,' Hope said. 'And your stand is hands down the best I've seen – that extra investment has really paid off.'

'In more ways than one,' Iris said happily. 'Speaking of which, do you want to meet the man himself?'

Hope grinned. 'What kind of question is that? Of course I do.'

Iris waved a hand at the crowds filing past them. 'Believe it or not, this is the afternoon lull. Let me tell one of the girls I'm taking a quick break and we can head over to the champagne bar. I'll tell Martin to meet us there.'

The Moët and Chandon bar was in the centre of the wedding fayre and had been fashioned in a horseshoe shape that sparkled under the bright lights. Hope and Iris snagged a couple of stools at the chic ivory and gold bar and ordered a glass of champagne each. 'Martin won't have one while he's working,' Iris said. 'It's unlikely he'll have to do any major restructuring mid-fayre but alcohol and power tools really don't mix.'

Two flutes of bubbling champagne materialized in front of them. Iris raised her glass to Hope's and smiled. 'To us,' she said, with evident satisfaction. 'Both absolutely smashing it at work.'

Hope laughed. 'To us,' she agreed. 'Cheers.'

The champagne was crisp and perfectly chilled on her tongue. She savoured the first mouthful, enjoying the buttery undertones beneath the sharper surface, and gazed around. Everywhere she looked, she saw happiness. But perhaps that wasn't a surprise; weddings usually brought out the best in people, although she knew that wasn't an absolute rule, especially since the expense could be ruinous and the stress unbearable. Even so, wedding fayres were all about promise – the possibility of what a couple's big day might be, whether big or small – and surely it was hard to be downhearted in a place that offered such joy.

She was pulled from her musing by Iris tugging on her sleeve. 'There he is – coming towards us, twelve o'clock.'

Hope saw a tall man in a navy-blue polo shirt heading their way. He had black curly hair and a short, well-trimmed beard; as he got nearer, Hope could see strands of grey catching in the light, giving him a distinguished air, and he had nice eyes – bright blue and thick lashed. But for all that, if someone had asked Hope to choose a man to date stylish, glamorous Iris, she didn't think she would have picked Martin out of the crowd. Then again, hadn't Iris herself said he was different to the kind of man she normally dated?

Iris slipped from her seat and kissed him. 'Martin, this is my friend, Hope. She works at the Ever After Emporium.'

Smiling shyly, Martin raised his hand in a little wave. 'Hello. Nice to meet you.'

'And you,' Hope said, returning his smile. 'I've just come from seeing the amazing stand you created for Blooming Dales. I'm in awe.'

Two spots of pink coloured Martin's cheeks at the compliment. 'Thank you. Although from what Iris tells me, you're pretty good at visual design yourself.'

Puzzled, Hope looked at Iris. 'He means the windows at the Emporium,' her friend explained. 'I showed him my photos of the Egypt display.'

'Oh, I see!' Hope exclaimed, suddenly embarrassed. 'But that's nothing compared to what you've done here. Not even close.'

Martin opened his mouth to respond but at that moment, Hope's mobile began to ring. She flashed him an apologetic look and pulled it out of her pocket, frowning when she saw Will's number.

'Hello?' she said into the handset. 'Everything okay, Will?'

'Thank god you answered,' Will said, and Hope heard panic in his voice. 'I need a massive favour. Where are you?'

Hope's frown deepened as she glanced at Iris, who had caught Will's tone, if not the exact words. 'I'm at the racecourse with Iris. It's the wedding fayre today. Why, what's wrong?'

There was a loud crackle of static then Will's flustered voice was in Hope's ear again. 'I'm on my way back from Whitby and there's been some kind of accident on the A64.' She heard the tension in his tone and winced, knowing that was the road on which Brodie's parents had been killed. 'Nothing's moving and the police aren't telling us anything. I don't know if I'll be back in time to collect Brodie from school and I don't want her to be upset, thinking I'm not coming or – or anything.'

His voice caught and she knew he must be thinking of Scott and Lucy again, of the way Brodie had waited for them to collect her on the day of the accident. 'I can pick her up,' Hope said instantly. 'Ring the school and let them know – I'm down as an emergency contact anyway so it will all be fine. And then you can collect her from me once you're through the traffic.'

'Thanks, Hope, you're a lifesaver.' His relief was obvious.

There was a brief silence, during which Hope could hear him murmuring, as though talking to someone else, and then he was back. 'I'll call the school now and let you know my ETA once things start moving here.'

'Don't worry,' she said, trying not to wonder who he'd been speaking to. 'Drive safely.'

He thanked her again before ringing off. Hope reached for her champagne and took a long sip before placing the flute regretfully back on the bar. 'Duty calls, I'm afraid,' she said and relayed what had happened.

'That road,' Martin said, shaking his head. 'I can't tell you how many times I've been caught up in jams there.'

Hope exchanged a look with Iris. 'I'd better go,' she said, checking her watch. 'I should have plenty of time to get to Brodie's school but I don't want to risk being late. It's going to be unsettling enough that it's me collecting her when she's expecting Will.'

'But she absolutely loves you,' Iris pointed out. 'She's going to think Christmas has come early.'

Hope smiled an apology at Martin. 'Sorry to dash off when we've only just met. With a bit of luck we'll have more time to chat next time.'

Once again, he flashed her a reticent smile. 'Absolutely. I hope you make it to the school on time, and Will gets through the traffic soon.'

She pulled her bag onto her shoulder and reached across to hug Iris goodbye. 'Me too.'

*

Brodie had clearly been told about the change of plan before Hope arrived because she came skipping across the playground at the end of the school day and enveloped Hope in a thigh high cuddle. Over her head, Hope met the eyes of her class teacher and gave her a wave, before taking the little girl's hand and leading her out through the St Wilfrid's school gates.

'Did your teacher explain that Will is caught up in traffic?' she asked Brodie as they made their way along Monkgate.

The little girl nodded her blonde head, neat ponytail bobbing, and Hope saw that as Iris had predicted, she wasn't the least upset.

'We're going back to my flat for hot chocolate and Will is going to collect you later,' she went on. 'Does that sound okay?'

Again, Brodie's head bobbed as she skipped along, her hand in Hope's. They turned left onto Jewbury, making their way towards the River Foss, and before long they were crossing the bridge and climbing the stairs to Hope's apartment. Once through the front door, Brodie stopped and looked curiously around, taking everything in, and Hope recalled it was the first time she'd been inside.

'One hot chocolate, coming right up,' she said, dropping Brodie's school bag on the sofa and switching on the television. 'I'm afraid I don't have any marshmallows but I do have chocolate sprinkles.'

Leaving Brodie watching CBeebies, Hope headed to the kitchen and made two mugs of hot chocolate. When she came back into the living room, Brodie wasn't on the sofa and the television was playing to an empty room. Frowning, Hope put the mugs down on the coffee table and went to find the missing child.

She eventually discovered her in the spare bedroom. Iris had insisted Hope borrow several belly dance costumes, even though they didn't quite fit, so she could get a feel for moving in the full skirts and beaded bras. They were draped across the bed, a jumble of chiffon, satin and sparkles that glistened in the afternoon sunshine streaming through the window. Brodie was sitting beside the pile, apparently mesmerized by the vibrant greens, blues and pinks. As Hope watched, she plunged her hand into the heap and let the gauzy fabrics cascade through her fingers onto the bed, a smile of pure delight on her small face. The light caught on the sequins, which only made her happier, and she repeated the action again and again.

'Do you like the colours?' Hope asked gently from the doorway.

Brodie looked up, her eyes shining, and nodded fiercely.

'These are costumes for me to dance in,' Hope went on. 'I'm going to wear one of them on stage, for everyone to see. Which colour do you like best?'

Immediately, Brodie's gaze dropped to the material and she frowned as her fingers ran across each one in turn. Hope waited patiently, in no hurry, until at last Brodie seemed to reach a decision. She pointed at the emerald-green skirt and met Hope's eyes with firm resolution.

'That's my favourite too,' Hope said, smiling. 'Would you like to see what it looks like?'

The little girl nodded and Hope stepped forward, teasing the skirt and matching accessories out from the other costumes. 'Okay, just give a minute to put it on. Why don't you wait in the living room?'

As always, Hope felt faintly ridiculous in the beautifully embellished costume. It wasn't terribly big on her but somehow she couldn't shake the notion that she was still a child dressing up in her mother's clothes. Fastening the sequined belt around her waist, she adjusted the beaded bra and reluctantly eyed herself in the full-length mirror. The colour suited her, at least, contrasting with her pale skin and tumbling red curls. Self-consciously, she attempted a sequence of hip lifts, followed by a three-step turn and finishing by bending into a flourish of Aladdin arms. The image in the mirror showed a woman Hope didn't really recognize; she was smiling when Hope was certain she must be grimacing, and the costume glimmered and shone as she spun. And then a movement from the doorway caught Hope's eyes, followed by the faintest whisper of sound, and she realized Brodie was watching her, transfixed.

The little girl stared at her, wide-eyed, and Hope saw her lips move. She froze, ears pricked for the whisper she wasn't sure had escaped from Brodie's mouth. For a heartbeat, she didn't dare speak. Then she smiled at Brodie. 'Did you say something? I couldn't quite hear.'

Brodie continued to stare. Seconds ticked by. After what

felt like an age to Hope, the girl parted her lips again and spoke on a breath that was barely more than a sigh. 'Pretty.'

It was the first word she'd spoken since the death of her parents. Not wanting to break the spell, scarcely daring to breathe, Hope performed another three-step turn. The emerald-green skirts swished around her and the light danced on the sequins and beads. 'It is pretty, isn't it?'

Brodie nodded and a beaming smile lit up her face.

'Would you like to learn some dance moves?' Hope asked, wondering how she could encourage her to speak again. 'We could do them together.'

Once more, Brodie nodded but Hope put a hand to her ear. 'Sorry, I didn't hear you that time. Would you like to dance with me?'

And this time, Hope heard a single whispered but ever so clear word, one that brought tears to her eyes and was worth a thousand from any other child. 'Yes.'

Chapter Twenty-Nine

Will looked grey and haggard when Hope opened the door to him, just after five o'clock.

'I'm so sorry,' he croaked, as Hope stepped back to allow him into the hallway. 'How is she?'

Hope hadn't wanted to disturb him while he was driving so had kept her messages to the bare minimum. She smiled and tried to suppress her own excitement, wondering how he was going to take the news she was about to give him. 'She's absolutely fine. In fact, something rather amazing happened. She—'

At that moment, Brodie appeared in the hallway. She ran forward to greet Will in exactly the same way she'd met Hope in the school playground. 'Hello, you,' Will said, ruffling her loose blonde hair. He looked over at Hope. 'I'm sure this was tied up when I dropped her off to school.'

'It was,' Hope agreed. 'In a tidy ponytail that impressed me no end, I might add. But we've been dancing and I'm sure you understand that swishy hair is very important for that.'

Will grinned and raised a hand to his own head. 'It's not something I've enjoyed myself but I'll take your word for it.' He glanced down at Brodie again. 'Have you been good for Hope?'

'She's been wonderful,' Hope said, as Brodie nodded. 'Why don't I make you a cup of tea and we can tell you all about our afternoon.'

Will sat with Brodie while Hope was busy in the kitchen – she could hear the low rumble of his voice as he asked about her day. Now that he was here, she wasn't sure how to tell him Brodie had spoken, or even whether she should tell him. Was it kinder, more satisfying to let him to find out in his own time, when Brodie was ready to speak again? The last thing Hope wanted was to put pressure on the little girl, and that was a very real potential side-effect of making a big deal out of her first words after so long. No, Hope decided as she slid the milk back into the fridge and gathered up the tray holding the tea and biscuits, it was better to wait until later and mention it in private, once Brodie had gone to bed.

She'd just reached the living room when she became aware of the silence. *Peppa Pig* was frozen on the television screen and the remote control was in Will's left hand. But his eyes were fixed on Brodie and his expression was one of profound astonishment. And suddenly Hope knew what had happened.

He turned to stare at her as she placed the tray on the table and offered Brodie a biscuit. 'I know she shouldn't have one so close to tea time,' Hope said into the silence, 'but it's been a bit of an unusual day. Do you mind?'

Will opened and closed his mouth, as though he didn't know what to say, so Hope held the plate towards Brodie. 'Would you like a biscuit?'

The little girl began to bob her head but Hope caught her eye and she stopped. 'Yes.'

Will's mouth fell open but no sound came out. Brodie took a biscuit as though nothing had happened and Hope placed the plate back on the tray. She lifted a mug of tea and gave it to Will. 'Drink this,' she said sympathetically. 'It'll help with the shock.'

The hot drink in his hand seemed to shake Will out of his stupor. 'I thought I'd imagined it,' he said hoarsely, taking his eyes off Brodie to look at Hope. 'But I didn't. And you already knew.'

Hope took a sip of too-hot tea. 'Yes. It happened earlier, while we were dancing. But I wasn't sure whether to mention it now or later.' She smiled. 'Luckily, Brodie has taken care of that dilemma for me.'

But Brodie was now gazing pointedly at the television screen, so Will clicked the volume button and the flow of animated conversation resumed between the characters.

'Do you know how long it's been since she spoke?' Will asked quietly, once he was sure Brodie's attention was fixed on the screen. 'Almost seven months. Her therapist thought it might be years before she felt able to talk again.'

He had the air of a man who'd woken from a dream, Hope

thought. 'I know. Maybe it's being at school, where the other children probably chatter all day.'

'Maybe,' he replied doubtfully. 'We thought that might make her more introverted, though, at least initially. Looks like it had the opposite effect.'

Hope glanced at the silent little girl, watching the cartoon pigs jumping in muddy puddles. 'I wouldn't say that exactly. But it's a start.'

Will smiled. 'True. What did she say to you? When she first spoke, I mean.'

Hope hesitated, embarrassed to tell him that Brodie had called her pretty. But she could always suggest it had been the costume that had earned the compliment, rather than her. 'I was showing her my belly dance outfits,' she said lightly. 'And she liked the green one so I put it on and did a few spins for her. She thought it looked pretty and said so.'

'Really?' Will said, blinking in surprise. 'A full sentence?'

'No,' Hope said, shaking her head. 'She just said "pretty". And I think she struggled with it that first time, as though she'd forgotten how to make the shapes and form the letters.'

Will gave Brodie a thoughtful look. 'That's a good point. It might be worth looking into speech therapy if she really has found her voice. What else did she say?'

Hope shrugged. She hadn't wanted to make too much of things and thanked Brodie before wrapping a belly dance coin belt around her shoulders so that it jingled when they spun around together. She'd much preferred to allow the little girl to choose when she spoke, although she'd encouraged her to say yes rather than nod when there was something she wanted. 'Not much. I didn't want to push it. We mostly danced and had fun, to be honest.'

He was quiet for a moment. 'That was probably the best thing you could have done. I need to take a leaf out of your book and not want too much, too soon. I've always hoped she would talk when she had something to say and I guess that's exactly what happened.'

'Maybe,' Hope replied. 'But you should give yourself credit, Will. The home you've provided for her is what's really made the difference. She's so obviously happy and settled with you – that's what brought this about.'

He blushed but Hope thought he was pleased too. 'I can't believe I missed it. I feel like one of those dads who works all the time and suddenly realizes his kids have grown up and left home.'

And now Hope laughed. 'Hardly. And I'm going to remind you of this at some unspecified time in the future, when she's such a chatterbox that you're wondering if she'll ever shut up.'

'Never,' Will said fervently, glancing at the little girl with such fierce affection that it made Hope's heart ache a little. 'I never want her to be silent again.'

It wasn't until Will and Brodie were leaving, with a promise from Hope to pick the little girl up from school again soon, that Will fired a curious look Hope's way. 'So, this belly dance costume,' he said. 'Am I allowed to see it sometime or is it a girls-only thing?'

The question was so unexpected that it took Hope a moment to gather her thoughts. She could tell him it was only for practising, of course, but the trouble with that was that she'd told Brodie about the upcoming performance and she had a sneaking suspicion the little girl wasn't going to forget about it. So Will would almost certainly find out, one way or another – if Brodie didn't tell him then Iris probably would. Taking a deep breath, Hope tried to sound casual. 'No, it's not a girls-only thing. We're planning a performance at the Theatre Royal in November. You'll be able to see it then.'

'Ah,' Will said, his eyes widening. He turned his gaze towards the little girl by his side. 'That sounds like fun, doesn't it, Brodie?'

She looked up at him, smiling. 'Yes,' she said.

The weather broke in the third week of September, bringing rain and a chill to the city streets. It meant fewer people passing by the Emporium, which in turn brought some welcome relief to Hope, who had begun to wonder if she'd ever get on top of her backlog of work. Unfortunately, it also gave her more time to think about the things that were worrying her: Ciaran's continued campaign to persuade Hope to meet for a drink, while simultaneously refusing to admit responsibility for leaking Elenor's journal or the ensuing rift with Isobel, the belly dance performance that was approaching far more quickly than she'd like, and Will's relationship with Alex, which also seemed to be speeding along. But as Hope's older sister, Charlotte, pointed out, not all of the things she was worried about were inside her control.

'Change the things you can change, let go of the things you can't,' she'd told Hope, with sympathetic but unwavering pragmatism. She had considered the advice for a moment, then added, 'And always buy the dress. You'll only regret it later if you don't.'

So Hope had increased the amount of time she spent working through the belly dance routine she'd have to perform with the rest of her class, and practised spinning so that she could handle the turns without wobbling. There wasn't much she could do about Ciaran – she had no intention of meeting him – but she did her best to be happy for Will, continuing to babysit when he asked and marvelling at Brodie's speech, which was coming along well. And she resolved to contact Isobel to clear the air between them. But before she could make the trip to Isobel's penthouse apartment, the older woman surprised her by coming to the Emporium.

It was the first dry day for over a week, with the kind of crisp autumnal air that made the season one of Hope's favourites. The bell over the door to the Emporium chimed in its usual overzealous manner, ushering in a cool breeze that caused Hope to look up from behind the dark wood counter and see Isobel walking slowly towards her. She held an ebony cane in her right hand and leaned on it with each step but that was the only change in her outward appearance. She still kept the same impeccable posture, still drew the eye with her imperious manner and still demanded attention when she spoke.

'Miss Henderson,' she said, with some satisfaction when she reached the counter.

Hope noted the formal use of her name and decided to disregard it. 'Hello, Isobel. It's lovely to see you.'

The other woman looked around, as though remembering the circumstances of her last visit, and then back at Hope. 'I thought perhaps I should thank you for your letter in person. I trust you received my reply?'

'I did,' Hope said. 'Thank you. And I wanted to come and see you but I wasn't sure how well you felt after – after . . .'

She trailed off awkwardly, uncertain how to describe what had happened almost exactly where she was standing right now. 'After my seizure,' Isobel supplied. She glared at her cane with a look of ill-concealed disgust. 'As you can see, I am almost as well as I was.'

Hope frowned as she untangled the sentence. Was Isobel trying to tell her she was fully recovered? Or simply that she'd got over the seizure, albeit with the addition of a walking cane. It was hard to tell.

'Are you working alone today?' Isobel went on, with another sweeping glance that took in the length of the Emporium.

'Frances is here,' Hope said, wondering why Isobel wanted to know. 'She's upstairs in the stockroom but should be back down any moment.'

The older woman tipped her head graciously. 'Very well. I

thought you might accompany me on a walk around Dean's Park. My doctor says fresh air every day will do me good but I'm not supposed to go alone and my nurse is an absolute ninny.'

It was a statement rather than an invitation but Hope wasn't sure Isobel knew how to act in any other way. 'I'd love to,' she said honestly, because she very much wanted to ensure there was no more bad feeling between them. 'Let me tell Frances I'm popping out.'

Dean's Park was one of Hope's favourite places to eat her lunch, although it was often hard to find a seat in the height of summer. The chill in the air seemed to have deterred most people that day, however, even though the ground was dry and the sun was trying to break through the overcast sky. But Isobel wasn't interested in finding a seat; she was intent on moving, and slowly but steadily they made their way around the Minster. Hope was surprised to see the western end of the park seemed to be in the process of being fenced off and mentioned it to Isobel, who sniffed. 'Some kind of dreadful Festive Fair,' she said dismissively. 'Opening in November with an ice rink and all manner of tawdry fairground stalls. I don't know what the Archbishop was thinking by allowing it to go ahead.'

Probably the considerable income it would raise, Hope thought irreverently but she didn't say so. The whole idea sounded wonderfully Christmassy to her; she could imagine the Minster surrounded by twinkling fairy lights, with skaters twirling in the shelter of its benevolent shadow. But she also knew that it wouldn't be Isobel's thing at all, so she kept her opinion to herself.

'How have you been?' she asked Isobel as they passed the ruined remains of the city walls. 'Iris has kept me up to date with your recovery – but she hasn't been able to give me much detail.'

Isobel gave her an impatient look. 'Why would she? I can assure you I am quite well.'

Hope gave her a sideways look, certain now there was something the older woman wasn't saying. '*Quite* well isn't the same as very well, though. And you can tell me to mind my own business if you like but I know you don't have any family to talk to so . . .' She trailed off, not daring to look at Isobel's expression, and then summoned up the courage to finish the sentiment. 'You once told me you trusted me with your family secrets. I hope you know you can also trust me with yours.'

They walked in silence for several long moments. More than once, Hope was tempted to speak, to dispel the awkwardness she felt building up around them, but she sensed Isobel was trying to decide what to say next. Sure enough, after almost a minute of silence, Isobel let out a short-tempered huff of irritation. 'It's a brain tumour.'

Hope stopped walking, staring at her in horrified disbelief.

'I've known for months,' Isobel went on, continuing to walk as though they were discussing an ingrowing toenail rather than a life-threatening growth on her brain. 'They tell me it's inoperable – something to do with the position inside the skull – and treatment options are limited at my age. Not that I'd willingly submit to the indignity of losing my hair anyway. But they say I have a year left. Maybe two if I am lucky.'

Hope was still aghast at the news but in another part of her head, things were dropping into place. 'So that's what caused the seizure. It was a side-effect of the tumour,' she said slowly, while hurrying to catch up with Isobel. 'And that's why you shared Elenor's journal and Khalid's letters with me – you were worried they might be forgotten otherwise.'

'Yes,' Isobel said simply. 'And then that letter from the Abyssinian Institute arrived and I thought I'd made a terrible mistake in trusting you.'

Hope hung her head. 'I am sorry that happened. Even though it had nothing to do with me, it was still someone I knew who shared the photographs and put you in an uncomfortable position. So, for what it's worth, I'm sorry.'

Isobel gave her a measured look. 'As I said in my reply to your letter, I don't blame you at all. But I would like assurances that you will exercise more caution in the future, should I choose to share any more of Elenor's secrets with you.'

The idea of uncovering more of Elenor Lovelace's story sent shivers racing along Hope's spine. 'I can honestly promise you it will never happen again.'

'I should hope not,' Isobel replied sternly, then paused. 'I saw the window you created in Elenor's honour. That particular species of palm isn't found in Egypt and the binoculars were of a brand not commonly in use until the 1930s but overall, I thought it was very well done.'

'Thank you,' Hope said, gratified by the praise even as she inwardly grimaced at the criticisms. She'd created the display hoping to catch Isobel's eye and it seemed the plan had worked. But her mind soon circled back to Isobel's bald statement about her failing health. 'You will let me know if there's anything I can do to help, won't you? If you need anyone to take you to appointments or – or – '

She trailed off because Isobel was looking at her with icy scorn. 'I'm not that helpless yet, Miss Henderson.'

'No, but—' Hope began but the look on Isobel's face once again made words fail her. 'Won't you call me Hope? Miss Henderson is unbearably formal and surely we're more than just acquaintances now.'

The older woman was silent again, walking on several steps before she stopped and turned to glance backwards. 'I find I am suddenly tired. Do you think you could walk me to my front door, Hope?'

'Of course,' Hope said, and resisted the temptation to reach out and squeeze Isobel's arm – she didn't want to discover just how much damage that ebony cane could do. 'Anything I can do for you is fine by me.'

Chapter Thirty

Hope read the message from Will three times before she believed it was true.

Alley Cats have found Missy's owner!

It had been well over two months since Missy had snuck into Will's house and given birth on his bed. All efforts to find the cat's owner had failed and Hope knew Will was planning to adopt both Missy and one of her kittens if the situation didn't turn around. The other kitten would go home with Hope and she couldn't wait for the day her new flatmate moved in. Her soft furnishings were definitely going to suffer but the cuteness was going to be off the charts, and what could be better than a winter's day spent reading with a cat curled up on her lap?

She messaged Will back immediately.

Really? What does that mean?

Will is typing … appeared at the top of Hope's
screen. A minute later, she read his reply.

It means she gets to go home. But the kittens stay here.

Hope thought for a moment.

How is Brodie taking it?

This reply took a little longer to arrive and Hope could
imagine why; Brodie had become very attached to Missy
since her arrival – understanding that the cat needed to
return to her rightful owners was going to be difficult.

She's sad about Missy going away but happy she gets to
keep a kitten.

Another message arrived hot on the heels of the last.

When are you going to take Topsy home?

Gnawing at her lip, Hope considered her reply.

Whenever Brodie is ready. Maybe she'd like to come with
me when I do, see him settled in his new home?

Will's reply was instant.

She'd LOVE that. Thank you! How about this weekend?

Shortly after she'd agreed, Will had rung Hope to delicately ask whether she might like to look after Brodie overnight. 'Only if you're comfortable with the idea,' he said, managing to sound embarrassed and hopeful at the same time. 'I just thought it might be nice, since she'll be at your place anyway, settling the kitten in. Say if you're not happy.'

It didn't take a genius to work out what was going on, Hope thought – Will wanted Alex to stay the night. But since he hadn't introduced her to Brodie yet, overnight stays were out of the question. Or maybe Will was planning to stay with Alex – Hope didn't want to know. All she needed to do was say yes to having Brodie for a sleepover. She pushed everything else firmly out of her head.

Her suspicions were confirmed when she took Brodie home the following Sunday. There was no sign of Alex – Will was far too good a parent to foist her onto an unsuspecting Brodie – but Hope detected the hint of an unfamiliar perfume in the living room and saw two unwashed wine glasses by the kitchen sink. There were several long blonde hairs in the bathroom sink upstairs and somehow the house felt different. But it was none of her business, Hope reminded herself as a now familiar knot settled in the pit of her stomach. This was Will's home and he could invite whoever he wanted to stay. All the same, she made her excuses and left as soon as she could. It was one thing knowing that Will and Alex had spent the night together, and quite another to be presented with the evidence.

If it hadn't been for Topsy awaiting her at home, Hope might have taken refuge in the Ever After Emporium. The temptation to stay late was strong but the thought of the kitten all alone in her flat, missing his sister and mother, was enough to send Hope hurrying home at the end of the day. Even so, Mr Young seemed to realize that she was in need of distraction, because he asked if she would like to accompany him to an auction in Harrogate.

'It's about time you experienced how it all works,' he said jovially. 'And you've got a good eye – you might spot a gem.'

He explained that they didn't have anything to sell on this occasion, but he often took some of the more valuable items to an auction if he considered they'd get a better price there. This visit was more of a reconnaissance trip. 'To check out the competition,' Mr Young said, with a twinkle in his eye. 'And there are usually a few items I'm looking for – sometimes a client will ask me to source a piece for their collection.'

Hope hadn't known he did that, although it made perfect sense – he was a well-respected expert, after all. 'Thank you for inviting me today,' she said, as they drove the twenty or so miles to Harrogate. 'I know I've still got a lot to learn about how the Emporium works and I can't wait to see an auction first-hand.'

Mr Young smiled. 'You've earned the opportunity. I knew from the moment you walked into the Emporium that you were a perfect fit and you've proved me right a hundred times over.'

The praise made Hope's cheeks burn, especially when she recalled how afraid she'd been that he would laugh her out of the door for her lack of experience. She might have made more than her fair share of mistakes since moving back to York but at least Mr Young appreciated her.

The whirl of the auction certainly kept Hope on her toes. There was so much to take in, from the variety of lots up for sale to the characters she saw everywhere she looked. Most of the people strolling around were perfectly normal but others were more eccentric, whether in the clothes they wore or the larger-than-life personalities they displayed. But it wasn't until the bidding began that Hope's head really began to spin. Some bidders almost stood up and waved to get the auctioneer's attention, while others barely seemed to move and yet somehow their bid was noted. Mr Young favoured a subtle tip of his head but it took a winning lot for Hope to even notice he'd been in the race; it was only when he raised his paddle at the end that she understood he'd been bidding. And the prices on some lots reached dizzying heights; she was astonished to see Mr Young join the bidding for an exquisite Edwardian vase that eventually sold for £32,000. He was typically good-natured about losing out, however.

'More than my client wanted to pay,' he told Hope, as the auctioneer introduced the next lot. 'It's easy to get caught up in the thrill of the chase but half the skill is knowing when to bow out.'

He seemed satisfied enough as they made their way back to the Emporium's van, having acquired a watch, two paintings and a pair of Georgian chairs that he assured Hope had been a steal. There was also a crate of Victorian glassware that he'd bought unseen, having studied the list of items inside. 'One for you to unpack over the next few days,' he said, smiling at Hope.

It wasn't until they were well on their way along the A59 that Hope realized her employer was eyeing her in a speculative manner. She shifted uncomfortably, wondering if she'd somehow breached auction etiquette and was about to get a dressing down, but Mr Young surprised her.

'You'll have noticed that we err on the side of informality at the Emporium,' he said out of nowhere, as they passed the A1 junction. 'We don't have a probationary period or performance appraisals or the like.'

Hope nodded, because she had observed the difference between her last job and her current one. But she hadn't minded in the least – it had felt like a breath of fresh air not to have to worry about hitting targets or KPIs or any of the other constraints she'd worked under before and her job satisfaction was considerably higher at the Emporium.

'That doesn't mean I don't keep an eye on you all,' Mr Young went on, his eyes fixed on the road. 'As you know, the Emporium is something of an unusual workplace and I often think the shop picks up on the positive or negative vibes of the staff – I'd go so far as to say she even has her favourites.'

From anyone else, it would have sounded ridiculous. How could a building feel anything for the people who worked inside? But this was Mr Young and he was referring to the

Emporium, somewhere that had cast a spell over Hope since childhood. There was something soothing about being inside, a magic she'd never encountered anywhere else. It wasn't a leap to believe that it had a personality and preferences of its own.

'I'm happy to say that you're one of those favourites,' Mr Young said, with a sideways glance. 'You fit in so well that I'm not sure how we coped without you. The window displays you've created with Frances have been nothing short of miraculous. So, with that in mind, I'd like to offer you a full-time role.'

Hope gaped at him. 'Really?'

He chuckled. 'Yes, really. And there's no need to look so surprised – you're practically doing the hours already. This is just recognition of that, with a commensurate pay rise and a new job title, although Assistant Purveyor of Treasure lacks a certain something so we'll work on that. But, essentially, you'll be doing everything you're already doing, plus taking a little more responsibility here and there. And we can talk about your training – there are qualifications you can work towards which will widen your horizons and keep things interesting.'

She didn't know what to say. When she'd first taken the job at the Emporium it had been on a whim, because she'd known she needed to do something after moving back to York but hadn't known what. And it had turned out to be the best thing she could have done, because she'd found more than just a job there. She'd found friends and new talents and a passion for her work in a place she felt she belonged. But she'd never sought additional recognition or a pay rise for her efforts; it had never been about the money. She'd felt lucky just to be allowed to work there and now Mr Young was offering her the chance to spend more time doing the job she adored.

'I'd love to accept,' she said at last, as his words started to sink in. 'Yes to all of it. But you don't need to pay more—'

'I'm sure that I do,' Mr Young cut in, his tone amused. 'The Emporium wants you to stay and I always do what she wants. So there'll be a pay rise, and training and the freedom to decide your own role. Just as long as you promise to stay for as long as you enjoy the work.'

Hope smiled. 'That will be for ever, then.'

He inclined his head. 'Well, maybe not quite for ever. But long enough to take care of the Emporium when I'm no longer able to, perhaps.'

She threw him a sharp look, suddenly fearful he was going to reveal some terrible news, as Isobel had done during their walk in the park. But he gave her a reassuring smile. 'Oh, I'm as fit as a fiddle, don't you worry. But make no mistake, Hope, I am looking for a successor – someone to take over ownership when I can't manage the Emporium's needs. And I've never met anyone better suited to it than you.'

And now Hope's head really did whirl. Surely, he couldn't mean what she thought he meant. 'But ... don't you have family? Someone else to leave it to?'

Mr Young shook his head. 'No. No family and no descendants. I never married, you see, and children were out of the question.'

She saw his hand stray to the pocket watch he always kept in his waistcoat jacket and wondered yet again who had given it to him. She knew it had been a much-loved gift from the way he treasured it and had always assumed there had been a Mrs Young. Clearly, she'd been wrong.

'But that's not to say I've never loved,' he said, his voice low and warm. 'Just that it burned a little too brightly to last. I have the memories, at least. And what memories they are.'

There wasn't a trace of sadness or regret behind the words, just an expression on his face that spoke of choices made and a life lived accordingly. Hope would never dream of prying into Mr Young's past but his reminiscences reminded her of the way the Emporium sometimes felt: full of stories half-told and remembrances of lives gone by. It was the thing she loved most about the shop, those echoes of the past that were so real they were almost tangible.

'I don't know if I'm the right person to follow in your footsteps at the Emporium,' Hope said, after a few minutes of silence. 'But I'd be honoured to help in any way I can.'

A smiled creased her employer's face. 'That's all I can ask. Welcome to the family, Hope.'

'He said what?'

Charlotte had stopped pushing the buggy containing her daughter, Amber, and was staring at Hope in amazement.

'That I might be the one to take over the Emporium,' Hope repeated, incredulity washing over her again. 'I know. I still can't believe it either.'

Blinking, her sister began to walk once more. 'That's one bloody enormous promotion, Hope. How do you feel about it?'

It was Sunday afternoon and the October air was crisp beneath the cloudless blue sky as they ambled around Upper Poppleton, stomachs groaning after the usual family lunch at their parents. Hope hadn't told anyone about her conversation with Mr Young – she had wondered for a few days whether she'd dreamt it – but now, almost a week later, it was starting to sink in. 'I don't know,' she admitted, pulling her coat closer around herself. 'I mean, obviously, I love working there and never want to leave. But owning it one day? That's a huge responsibility.'

Charlotte nodded. 'I'll say. But it's not something you have to agree to now, is it? He's not about to pop his clogs tomorrow, is he?'

'No,' Hope said quickly. 'He says he's in perfect health. I think he just wanted to sound me out, give me a reason to stay.'

'He obviously rates you, though,' Charlotte said thoughtfully. 'And being able to decide your own role is great.'

Hope bit her lip. 'I don't really know what I want it to be yet. I'm pretty happy with things as they are now.'

'Yes, but this is a promotion, right? So, you need a good title to go with it – Head of Customer Engagement, maybe,' Charlotte suggested, then pulled a face. 'No, far too corporate – you want something grander and more romantic. How about Empress of Hidden Treasures?'

That made Hope laugh. 'Absolutely not.' She shook her

head. 'I don't think I need a title, actually – I think my role is going to evolve into whatever the Emporium needs me to be.'

'It's not how most job progression schemes work but okay,' Charlotte said, shrugging. 'Congratulations, anyway.'

Hope smiled. She knew her family hadn't necessarily understood her desire to work part-time at the Emporium, although her dad hadn't been in the least surprised. But they'd supported her, in the same way they had throughout her life, and she was glad she could offer this evidence that she was doing well. 'Thanks, Charlotte.'

Her sister glanced over her shoulder, as if checking to see who was within earshot. 'So, what else is new? Please tell me you're not still pining over Professor McBackstabber.'

A snort of amusement escaped Hope at the name Charlotte had given Ciaran. 'He's been in touch.'

Charlotte's inquisitive gaze bore into her as they passed beneath the russet and gold trees that lined the path around the village green. 'And?'

Hesitating, Hope wondered how much to reveal. 'He's still keen to meet.'

'I hope you said no,' Charlotte said. 'The audacity to even ask after everything he's put you through. What does Iris think?'

Hope let out a sigh and kicked at a cluster of fallen leaves. 'She's in love – everything smells like roses to her.'

'That might be true, but I refuse to believe she thinks meeting that weasel is a good idea,' Charlotte replied with certainty. 'Who's the lucky man?'

Hope recalled Martin's shy smile and quiet demeanour; lucky was exactly the right word. 'Someone she met through work – a designer. You'd never put them together but she seems utterly smitten.'

Her sister glanced across at her. 'Sometimes it's the quiet ones who offer the most. And if he makes her happy, who are we to judge?'

That was the thing, Hope thought with a hot burst of what felt a lot like envy, Iris *was* happy. Blissfully, relentlessly, wonderfully happy. It was obvious every time Hope saw her. And she'd seen how Martin had looked at Iris, that expression of stunned adoration which told the whole world that he knew *exactly* how lucky he was. It wasn't that Hope begrudged her friend for being so happy, it was more that she envied her for finding someone who made her feel that way. It was the way Hope wanted to feel. It had been so long since she'd felt loved.

'And what does Will think?' Charlotte asked.

Hope frowned at her. 'Of Martin?'

There was a long-suffering sigh. 'No, about Ciaran. I'm sure he has views.'

And now Hope endured another burst of acid in her stomach, because jealousy had made itself at home in her relationship with Will too. 'I haven't told him,' she said shortly and took a deep breath. 'He's dating too.'

Charlotte said nothing and Hope had the distinct impression she was biting her tongue. 'Good for him,' she announced eventually, then paused. 'So that's both of your closest friends loved up. Must be tough on you.'

'Not really,' Hope said stoutly. 'I'm over the moon for them.'

'I wouldn't be,' Charlotte sniffed. 'I'd be simultaneously jealous and wondering what the hell was wrong with me. But I wouldn't let those feelings drive me towards someone I knew was trouble.'

Hope's cheeks grew warm. 'Relax, Charlotte. I'm not going to fall into that trap.'

But her sister knew her too well to be fooled. 'You say that now but there'll be a time when you're tempted – an evening when you're on your own and maybe had a glass or two of wine to really heighten the self-pity, and it will feel like the most natural thing in the world to message him. Just a quick "Hey, how are you doing?" to see how he responds. And before you know it, it'll be the morning after and he'll still be a cheating arsehole who has nothing to offer you but more lies.' She stopped to draw breath and gave Hope a meaningful look. 'Just say no. You'll find someone better than him, I promise.'

Hope did her best not to blush, because she'd very nearly messaged Ciaran on more than one occasion. Besides, hadn't Iris said something very similar a few weeks ago? 'I know. But thank you.'

'You're welcome,' Charlotte said. 'And if you won't delete his number, at least change his name to Professor McBackstabber. If that doesn't remind you of why he's no good for you, nothing will.'

Chapter Thirty-One

November rolled around faster than Hope could have believed possible, bringing with it darker evenings and more than a hint of frost on the cobbles. Hope's breath steamed on the air as she made her way to and from the Emporium, walking fast in hat and gloves. In less than eight weeks, it would be Christmas and the city was showing clear signs of embracing the festive period; twinkling lights had been strung above the streets and snickelways, although they had yet to be switched on, Christmas gifts had begun to appear in shop windows and the ice rink and fair Isobel had grumbled about were complete and ready to welcome their first guests.

The Emporium was preparing too; Hope had already begun work on a Victorian Christmas window display. This time, she'd employed the skills of Martin to create an old-fashioned mahogany mantelpiece and hearth, which cleverly disguised a tablet showing the flames of a leaping log fire. Four long, stripy stockings hung from hooks beneath the mantelpiece shelf and she'd placed a large ornate carriage clock above them. To the right-hand side, Hope had positioned a bushy fir tree in a red-ribboned pot – sourced by Iris, of course – and decorated it with home-made paper chains and sweets in shiny wrappers that glistened beneath the subtle, flickering spotlights. And on the left, she'd placed a writing desk and tall-backed chair, set aside as though the occupant had just got up, with a feather plume and ink pot on the desk.

'The Spirit of Christmas Past,' Mr Young exclaimed, surveying her handiwork with obvious delight. 'You've outdone yourself, Hope.'

But the arrival of November also meant time had run out for Hope to perfect her grasp of the choreography for the belly dance performance. Every Monday night for weeks, Fleur had put her students through their paces, gently offering tips and advice to help them perfect an array of shimmies, spins and shoulder rolls, while also building their confidence and encouraging them to enjoy their performance. It wasn't enough, Hope thought with some queasiness as she packed her bag and set off for the theatre. It would never be enough.

The show was a matinee, due to start at two o'clock. It would begin with the Level 1 Beginners group, which was the group Hope attended, but Iris was also dancing with the Level 2 Improvers immediately afterwards. Then the Level 3 and 4 groups would perform and the afternoon would culminate in a drum solo dance from Fleur herself. Even as she felt sick with nerves, Hope had to admit she was looking forward to watching her teacher dance. It was going to be a show-stopping performance.

The atmosphere in the dressing room was heady with excitement as the women got ready to take the stage. Hope had decided on the green costume Brodie had loved; it had been the one she'd practised in at home and she trusted it would bring her luck, or at the very least be familiar enough to prevent her tripping over her own feet as she danced. But now she wasn't sure – her skin looked too pale under the dressing room lights and she would only look paler under the bright stage lights. Perhaps she should have chosen the pastel pink, which at least would have created less of a contrast.

Iris paused in the act of applying another layer of powder to her face and smiled into the mirror. 'You look beautiful. Seriously, that green with your colouring and curls – dynamite.'

Some of Hope's anxiety slipped away. 'You look gorgeous too,' she said. 'Red is definitely your colour.'

It was true – a cascade of dark waves tumbled down her friend's back and her brown eyes were almost black amid the exaggerated kohl eyeliner that surrounded them. Somehow, Iris's creamy skin only made her scarlet costume more vibrant. She looked every inch a belly dancer and it was hard for Hope to see her and not feel like an imposter.

Iris appeared to read her mind. 'You can do this,' she said, reaching over to squeeze Hope's hand. 'Trust your body to remember the moves and try to forget there's anyone watching.'

But that was easier said than done when all Hope's family, friends and colleagues were in the audience. Even so, she did her best to shake away the nerves. 'I'll try.'

'You can't see their faces from the stage anyway,' Iris said encouragingly. 'Once the music starts, you'll be fine.'

Hope had jolted awake from several anxiety dreams over the past few weeks that had seen her on stage only half-dressed, with the music about to begin, or fully dressed but all alone, and she wasn't entirely convinced Iris was right. But again, she attempted to channel her friend's positive vibes. 'Okay.'

Her phone vibrated on the table and she glanced at it to see a message from Will.

We're here. Break a leg! X

There were several other messages too – one from her parents, and all three of her siblings. Her youngest brother, Joe, had been particularly unhelpful, advising her not to fall off the stage, but since she knew he'd mostly come along because he fancied Iris she had plenty of ammunition to fire back at him.

Iris glanced over at her phone. 'Is that from Will?'

Hope nodded. 'They're here.'

Her friend turned back to the mirror and began touching up her pillar box red lipstick, although Hope noticed she continued to watch her. 'Did he tell you Alex is coming too?'

'Yes,' Hope said, trying to sound casual. She'd finally

met Alex the week before, when Will had brought her home after a night out and Hope had been babysitting. One look at the petite, blonde woman at Will's side had been enough to tell Hope that Alex was everything she wasn't, and she wished Will hadn't invited her to the performance.

Iris studied her for a moment longer, then pulled her make up bag towards her. 'Sit down,' she ordered a startled Hope. 'I think we need to make you a tiny bit more fabulous before you go on stage.'

It was an odd feeling, having her make up done by Iris. She knew she could never pull off the winged eyeliner and lush lipstick that were the florist's trademarks and she really hoped Iris wasn't going overboard. It was true that stage make up needed to be heavier and more exaggerated than its everyday counterpart but she didn't want to look like she'd fallen face first into a glitter factory.

'Close your eyes,' Iris demanded as she applied more eye-shadow. 'Now look up.'

And then the speaker overhead crackled. 'Beginners on stage. That's beginners on stage, please.'

'There,' Iris said, sitting back to admire her handiwork. 'Perfect timing. What do you think?'

Almost reluctantly, Hope glanced in the mirror and gasped. She hardly recognized herself. Iris had accentuated her green eyes with black eyeliner and shades of gold so that they seemed impossibly large, and highlighted her cheek-bones to give her a noticeable but delicate peach flush. Her lips gleamed with a rusted orange gloss. She looked like a different woman.

'Wow,' she said, unable to tear her gaze away from her reflection. 'You've worked a miracle.'

Beside her, Iris grinned and held up her phone. 'How amazing do we look? I think this calls for a photo, don't you?'

She put one arm around Hope and drew her head nearer as she snapped the picture. Then she pressed a few buttons and flashed a wicked smile Hope's way. 'I sent it to Will.'

Hope blushed. 'You didn't!'

'I did,' Iris said, unrepentant. 'No harm in reminding him there's more to you than brilliant babysitting.'

She got to her feet and swished from the dressing room, leaving Hope to stare after her in consternation. Then she remembered she needed to get to the stage too and hurried after Iris.

Fleur was waiting for them on stage, an angel in her exquisite silver and white costume. Hope exchanged nervous smiles with Traci and Nic, accepted a hug from Celia and bumped fists with Fiona. They all looked incredible in their outfits and Hope felt a tiny bit better. Surely no one was going to notice her among this multi-coloured explosion on the senses . . .

'I know some of you must be scared right now,' Fleur said, addressing them all. 'Don't be. Remember that this audience is made up of people who love you – just seeing you on the stage will make them smile. And the more you enjoy yourself, the more enjoyment they'll feel too.' She paused to gaze at each of them in turn. 'Listen to your bodies, feel the music flow through you and, above all, trust yourself. You are all beautiful dancers – let's show our loved ones what we can do!'

It was impossible not to feel empowered after a speech like that, Hope thought, as Fleur moved around the group, hugging each of the fourteen women. When she reached Hope, she clasped her hands and murmured, 'Let go of your fear. It's time to step into the light and shine.'

Then she was gone, vanishing into the darkness at the side of the stage, and the whisper of 'Places!' made its way around the group. Hope headed for the back, although she knew she couldn't stay there for the whole dance, Fleur had made sure of that. But for the moment, she was protected by the other women and it gave her enough strength to force down the rising tide of panic. Iris appeared and pulled her into a brief, powerful hug. 'Let's shimmy!'

Stepping back, she took her place beside Hope and raised arms into the opening pose. Sucking in a deep steadying breath, Hope did the same. And then the curtain was opening and the lights were blinding and the opening bars of the intoxicating melody Fleur had chosen were floating across the stage.

There was a heart stopping moment when Hope was sure she'd forgotten everything. Then her feet moved, apparently of their own accord, and her arms caressed the air, and it all came back to her. It seemed as though someone else danced and whirled and shimmied through the routine – a woman who looked a lot like Hope but had all the grace and elegance she usually lacked. She was aware of the blackness where the audience must be but couldn't see any faces and didn't really have the time to look. All her attention was focused on a sudden fierce need to dance, to twirl beneath the hot shimmering lights and hit every beat with a hip drop, chest lift or shoulder roll. And just as Fleur had predicted, her body responded perfectly, transferring her weight from one leg to the other without conscious thought, preparing her for the next move with the kind of ease that only came from dedicated practice and muscle memory. As the music reached its end, and the dancers struck their final pose, Hope knew she was smiling – not the fixed grin she'd learned to plaster on her face during rehearsals but a wild, genuine smile of pure joy. She'd done exactly as Fleur had commanded – she had stepped into the light and shone more brightly than she could have imagined.

The audience erupted into applause and cheers. As Fleur had taught them, the dancers spread their arms in gracious acceptance, stepped forwards and curtseyed. Hope looked out from the stage once more and this time, the dazzling lights had dimmed, allowing her to scan the crowd. Her eyes found Brodie, who was jumping up and down, clapping her hands over her head. Hope gave a special little wave, just for her, before she was swept along by the other women into the wings.

'Oh my god, that was amazing!' Celia squeaked beside her. 'I absolutely loved it, didn't you?'

'I did,' Hope admitted, scarcely believing what she was saying. 'I loved it too.'

Iris materialized beside her, grinning like a cat who'd got the cream. 'I hate to say I told you so . . .'

Hope laughed. 'You did. And I'm sorry I didn't believe you.'

'Just wait until you see the recording,' Iris said, her eyes gleaming. 'You won't recognize yourself.'

'There's a recording?' Hope said, some of her joy dipping.

Iris nodded. 'There is. But don't worry, you looked incredible. I was dancing next to you and I could barely take my eyes off you. Basically, you smashed it, Hope.'

'So did you,' Hope pointed out, feeling her cheeks grow warm with gratification.

'I did,' Iris replied with unabashed pride. 'Go us!'

Amid the silken rustling of costumes, Hope saw the Level 2 dancers taking to the stage. She pressed a hand to her friend's arm and whispered, 'Time to shine all over again. Break a leg!'

Now that her own part in the performance was over, Hope relaxed. She watched Iris from the wings, marvelling at the extra layer of complexity this routine commanded, and admired the way her friend twisted her way effortlessly through the moves. Except that it wasn't effortless, she reminded herself with a slight twist of her mouth. It took a lot of bloody effort, actually.

The crowd seemed to grow more and more effusive with each successive performance but they fell utterly silent when Fleur took to the stage. Hope watched from the side, surrounded by the rest of Fleur's students, and she thought they could have heard a feather drop from the gods it was so quiet. Then the rhythmic beat of the drum solo thundered out and Fleur began to mesmerize them all and Hope wasn't aware of anything else until the music crashed to its sudden triumphant crescendo.

The applause was instant and so loud that Hope had to wonder whether there were two thousand people in the stalls rather than two hundred. With a radiant smile, Fleur moved to the front of the stage and dropped into the kind of curtsey only a true dancer could achieve. Arms aloft, like a queen receiving the adoration of her subjects, she swept off the stage and into the excited praise of her students.

'One final bow, ladies,' she said. 'Everyone back on stage now!'

The crowd continued to cheer as they took several company bows and then the curtains closed. Adrenaline fizzed in Hope's veins as she turned to Iris. 'Now what?'

Her friend laughed. 'Now we go and meet our admiring public!'

Hope glanced down at her costume. 'Dressed like this?'

'Dressed like this,' Iris said firmly. 'Come on.'

The foyer of the theatre was crowded and it took Hope a moment to locate her family. Her mother swept her into a hug. 'Well done, darling, you were magnificent.'

Her father grinned over the top of her mother's head and she thought his eyes looked suspiciously damp. 'You looked wonderful up there.'

Her brother Harry squeezed her shoulder and congratulated her, while Charlotte couldn't stop shaking her head and telling her how incredible she was. Even Joe seemed at a loss for an insult and simply hugged her in silent approval. And then she saw Will, with Brodie hopping impatiently from one foot to another.

'Back in a minute,' Hope told her family and made her way through the crowd.

'Hello,' she said breathlessly to Will. 'Thanks for coming.'

His cheeks were pink as he shook his head. 'Wouldn't have missed it for anything. You were amazing.'

Hope felt her own cheeks grow hot and she turned her attention to Brodie, bending slightly to make eye contact. 'And what did you think?' she asked, as the little girl beamed at her.

'Pretty,' Brodie said clearly. 'Pretty like a princess.'

Hope's eyes widened in astonishment as she glanced briefly at Will to see if he'd heard. His proud smile told her he'd caught every beautifully uttered word. 'That's very kind of you,' she said, transferring her gaze back to Brodie. 'Thank you, I'm glad you enjoyed the show.'

As she straightened up, Hope realized what had been niggling at her. 'Is Alex in the ladies?' she asked.

With an uncomfortable grimace, Will shook his head. 'She – uh – couldn't make it.'

'Oh,' Hope said, processing both the news and the grimace that had accompanied it. 'Oh, that's a shame.'

She was about to invite him to join her family for

something to eat when she saw his face change again. This time his expression was wooden and fixed, and aimed over her shoulder, with a hint of suppressed anger around his eyes. Hope turned, wondering what on earth had made his mood shift so dramatically and then she understood only too well. Standing a few metres away was Ciaran.

'Hello, Hope,' he said, with a smile that still had the power to turn her insides to mush. 'That colour really suits you. Are you sure you don't have a grandmother from Tralee you've forgotten about?'

Chapter Thirty-Two

Hope closed the distance between them in three strides.

'What are you doing here?' she demanded in a hushed tone, all too aware that people were already firing curious glances their way.

'I came to see you,' he said mildly. 'You don't answer my messages any more so what else could I do? We need to talk.'

'That doesn't give you the right to just turn up, when all my friends and family here,' she said, feeling her temper rise. 'They're going to think I invited you!'

'So?' Ciaran asked, then sighed. 'Look, I'm not here to make things awkward – I know we can't talk now. Just give me a time and a place where we can get together to sort things out and I'll get out of your hair.' He paused as his gaze travelled to the loosely arranged curls dangling down her neck. 'Although actually what I want is to get into your hair. Quite badly, as it happens.'

'Stop it,' she hissed, furious at his audacity and the

treacherous dart of pleasure it caused inside her. 'Okay, fine. I'll meet you. Wednesday evening, six o'clock, at the Botanist on Stonegate. '

He nodded. 'Good choice. I'll look forward to it.'

For a moment, she thought he would say something more but he seemed to think better of it. Instead, he turned and headed for the exit. Taking a deep breath, Hope glanced around to see if anyone was watching and caught Charlotte staring daggers at the swinging theatre doors. None of Hope's family looked especially pleased and she knew with a sinking heart that her prediction had been proved right – they all thought she'd invited Ciaran herself. Which also meant—

Hope spun to face where Will and Brodie had been standing moments earlier. As she'd suspected, they were gone. She clenched her fists, hiding them in her skirt, and willed herself to breathe. It could all be straightened out – she'd simply explain that Ciaran had turned up out of the blue and she'd sent him away. She didn't have to tell them that she'd agreed to meet him. No one needed to know about that.

Plastering on a bright smile, Hope went to face her family again.

Ciaran was waiting when Hope arrived. He stood as she approached the table, his welcoming smile fading a little when she didn't return it. 'What can I get you to drink?'

'Just a water, thanks.'

He threw her a pained look. 'Hope, seriously. I can't talk about everything we need to if you're going to sit there glaring at me over a glass of water, like my great aunt Clodagh. Have a proper drink, please, or at least something that isn't free.'

Hope glanced at the spot-lit shelves behind the bar; the Botanist had a reputation for excellent cocktails and she was keen to try them but she didn't want Ciaran to get the idea that this was in any way a social occasion. And it wouldn't hurt to remind herself, she thought sternly, as her stomach flip-flopped in recognition at his nearness. 'I'll have a gin and tonic, then,' she said, striving to keep the regret from her voice as she ignored the cocktail menu on the table. 'A single.'

The bar wasn't especially busy and he was back quickly with a rounded Copa glass for her and a pint for himself. He placed them both on the table and sat down, before fixing her with a penitent stare.

'Let me start by assuring you I had nothing to do with that awful letter from the Abyssinian Society.'

Hope raised her eyebrows at the directness of his approach. She'd expected at least ten minutes of charm before he got to the point. 'I find that hard to believe,' she said coolly. 'You're the only person to have read Elenor's journal, besides me, and the letter mentioned photographs. I certainly didn't take any and I'm sure Isobel didn't. So, the only other possibility is you, Ciaran.'

He stared moodily at his pint for a moment, then puffed out his cheeks. 'Okay, I admit I took the photos. I know I shouldn't have but you need to understand, the journal was such an extraordinary find – a first-hand, reliable account of the discovery of Tutankhamun's tomb.'

'I know,' Hope said dryly. 'I've read it, remember?'

Ciaran nodded impatiently. 'Of course you have but – you'll forgive me for saying this – you're not an expert in Egyptology. I wanted to study the journal – compare it to other texts and see what light it might shine on what we already knew – but you were dead set against me taking it away. There didn't seem to be much harm in taking a few photos to look over later.'

His tone was so reasonable that she was almost persuaded. 'You could have asked me.'

'You'd have said no,' Ciaran replied without hesitation. 'So I made up a little white lie about losing my phone and took the pictures while you were searching for it. I'm not proud of myself.'

At least he'd admitted taking the photos, she thought, and he did seem to be genuinely remorseful about it. 'And then what happened? How did they end up in the hands of the Abyssinian Society?'

He spread his hands in sorrowful incomprehension. 'I haven't the first clue. I showed them to a colleague or two, but they were sworn to secrecy.'

Hope frowned. 'Colleagues at the university?'

'Colleagues at a university, yes,' Ciaran agreed evasively.

Hope read between the lines. 'So you sent them to people at other universities. As jpegs.'

'I might have done,' Ciaran said slowly. 'But they're all

respected academics – I can't see them passing them onto the Society either.'

'But one of them did,' Hope said, with a groan of disbelief at his idiocy. 'And the Society wrote to Isobel, and Isobel blamed me. Did you know that the resulting stress gave her a seizure?'

His face turned ashen. 'I had no idea. Is she okay?'

'She is now,' Hope said, slightly mollified by his obvious shock. 'But she's not especially well and doesn't need any more upsets. So, if you could find out whoever leaked the pictures and make sure they don't push the matter any further, that would be helpful.'

Ciaran waved a distracted hand. 'Of course. I'll do my best.' He took a swig of his pint and glanced pensively at Hope. 'I know Isobel won't want to part with the journal, in spite of its academic significance, but the university has expressed an interest in buying the emerald ring. Obviously, it's not a genuine Egyptian artefact but they're putting together an exhibition for the spring term, based on Elenor's life, and they've asked me to enquire whether Isobel might be prepared to sell it, or perhaps offer a permanent loan.'

At first, Hope thought she must have misunderstood. He couldn't seriously be asking to buy Elenor Lovelace's engagement ring from her only living descendent after he caused her such distress already. But then she looked into his eyes, his gorgeous grey eyes that had always made her melt inside, and she saw that she hadn't misunderstood at all. 'No, Ciaran, I don't think Isobel would be remotely interested in that. Sorry.'

'I thought you'd say that,' he said, sighing. 'Never mind, it was just an idea.'

He lapsed into silence, gloomily staring into his pint, and Hope realized she'd never seen him so downcast. He'd always been so full of charm and self-assurance that she'd come to believe he must be like that all the time. But this was a new Ciaran – a more human version – and she found herself feeling a little sorry for him. 'It could have all been so different.'

He raised his head to look at her then. 'Don't I know it. I've kicked myself a thousand times for not being honest with you about the situation with Lily. If I'd just explained at the start . . .'

Would it have made a difference? Hope wondered as he trailed off, and decided it probably would. She'd have understood, at least. But then he'd also lied about the pictures of the journal. In fact, he'd lied to get the pictures in the first place, sending her off on a wild goose chase to give him the time to snap the photos.

He let out another sigh. 'And then I ran away, to Sussex, when I should have stayed to fight for you.' When his gaze met hers, Hope saw that his expression was suddenly so earnest that he looked almost boyish. 'I wish we could run away together now – just you and me, away from all the mess and misunderstandings.'

'Ciaran—' she began, hoping to head him off but he ignored her and kept talking.

'I'd love to wake up with you every morning, with your glorious hair all tangled, and kiss the sleepiness away. I want to hear your views on everything, to watch the way your forehead creases when you're thinking and see your dimples deepen when you laugh. I want you to be my whole world, Hope.'

The words were so heartfelt that Hope felt the ground drop a little beneath her. Could he mean it this time? Was it possible that he truly felt this way – that he loved her after all?

'But it's up to you,' Ciaran went on. 'I told you once that I wouldn't kiss you again unless you asked me to. But –' he broke off to gaze deep into her eyes, 'I'd very much like you to ask, Hope.'

The foundations beneath Hope's determination shifted even more – in fact, they seemed to be built on quicksand. There had been so many times when she'd have given anything to hear him say words like these, for him to practically beg her to fall into his arms. And it would be so easy, she told herself now. All she had to do was lean forward the tiniest fraction, to ask him to kiss her and that would be all it took.

Then she remembered the tears she'd cried, the long nights when she'd wondered what was wrong with her, the times Charlotte and Iris and Will had spent worrying about her ... and she knew all the golden words in the world wouldn't be enough. She wouldn't ask Ciaran to kiss her.

'I'm sorry,' she said, leaning back in her chair. 'It's too late.'

The stricken look in his eyes as he registered her meaning would stay with Hope for a long time. But she didn't waver. Instead, she got to her feet, leaving her drink untouched on the table. 'Thank you for finally being honest with me,' she said, gathering her coat and bag and praying he didn't see her hands shaking. 'Take care, Ciaran.'

And before she could change her mind, she walked out of the bar.

A week after the belly dance performance, Hope visited Isobel at home for afternoon tea. It was a bitterly cold mid-November day, and Hope was glad to wrap her hands around her teacup as she listened to Isobel complain about the Christmas Fair beside York Minster.

'It's not the crowds I mind so much as the stench,' the old woman said, wrinkling her nose as though she could smell the offending aroma now. 'They've got one of those so-called authentic Bratwurst stalls and the whole park stinks of sausage.'

Hope, who had always found the smell of sizzling sausages to be mouth-watering, hid her smile. 'Oh dear.'

'Have you been?' Isobel demanded.

Shaking her head, Hope decided not to mention that a visit to the accompanying ice rink was on her Christmas wish-list. 'No. Apart from anything else, I haven't had time. Mr Young has me accompanying him to auctions now, so I can get a better grip on how they work, and the Emporium has been busy too.'

Isobel grunted. 'I'm glad he appreciates you. About time.'

'And . . .' Hope trailed off, wondering how to broach the subject of her meeting with Ciaran. 'I don't think you'll be receiving any more letters from the Abyssinian Society. I spoke to Professor McCormack and he admitted that he'd taken photographs of the journal and shared them with colleagues. I can only assume that's how they came to the attention of the society.'

'The man's a first-rate fool,' Isobel snapped. 'I got the measure of him from the moment I met him.'

'I wish I had,' Hope said with a sigh. 'He even asked if I thought you'd be interested in selling Elenor's ring to the university, for an exhibition. Can you believe it?'

'Of course I can,' Isobel sniffed. 'A man like that will ask anything if he thinks there is a chance the answer might be yes.' She gave Hope a long, measured look and her steely gaze softened somewhat. 'But at least you got the truth from him in the end.'

Hope took a long sip of tea, reflecting that she hadn't needed to do much persuading – Ciaran had made the admission willingly. Perhaps he had changed, at least in some ways. 'An exhibition in Elenor's honour at the university might be nice, though. She deserves some recognition for her work – I've always felt sad that her brilliance got so thoroughly overshadowed by her death.'

A closed look came over Isobel's face then. 'Well, quite,' she said, and reached for a miniature Battenburg cake. 'Absolutely.'

She ate in silence, watching Hope as though weighing something up. Finally, she swallowed and pursed her lips. 'What if I was to tell you Elenor didn't die?'

The words were so unexpected that Hope almost dropped

the teacup she was holding. Hastily, she lowered it to the saucer and moved her hands to her lap, out of harm's way. 'Sorry?'

The older woman studied her again for several long seconds. 'What if I told you that instead of throwing herself off the cliffs at Whitby, Elenor made her way back to Egypt where she married Khalid?'

Hope could scarcely believe what she was hearing. 'I'd be delighted if you told me that,' she said breathlessly. 'Is it true?'

Rather than answer, Isobel rang a small silver bell, summoning her housekeeper, Sarah. After Isobel murmured an instruction Hope couldn't quite hear, the other woman left the dining room. A moment or two later, she reappeared carrying a thick bundle of envelopes, which she handed to Isobel.

'These are letters Elenor wrote to her sister – my grandmother – after her dramatic escape,' Isobel said, as Sarah left once more. 'They cover a period of around twenty years, during which Elenor and Khalid fled to Abydos, where they inhabited a mudbrick house, and lived happily ever after.'

Hope stared at her in confusion. 'But I thought Elenor's family were against the marriage. Forgive me for saying this but why would she write to your grandmother after she'd got away, risking her secret?'

'Not all Elenor's family were against Khalid. Didn't you ever wonder how Elenor got to Whitby?'

The question was so random that it took Hope a moment to consider it. She shook her head. 'It didn't occur to me. I suppose I thought she drove herself.'

Isobel smiled. 'Her sister drove her, and then planted the seeds that made it so clear Elenor had taken her own life. It was a triumph of subterfuge – no one suspected a thing.' She brandished the bundle of letters. 'It's all here. Would you like to read them?'

Hope almost ran around the table to snatch them from Isobel's hands. 'Yes, I would,' she said, as politely as she could manage. 'I'd like that very much.'

Isobel inclined her silvery head. 'Then you can take them with you when you leave. Read them at your leisure.'

It was the kind of gift Hope had never expected – the ending to Elenor and Khalid's story that she'd given up on ever finding. 'Thank you,' she said quietly.

'You're welcome. I know I can rely on your discretion.' There was a long pause while Isobel stared at the letters in her hand. 'And one more thing. I would like to sell Elenor's ring, as it happens, to raise some money for charity. Elenor left it to my grandmother, and she passed it to me, although it was lost long before I came to inherit. Is a sale something you and Mr Young can arrange?'

'At auction?' Hope said, once again taken aback. 'Yes, we could arrange that. But are you sure?'

Isobel's gaze met hers. 'I'm certain. That ring brought Elenor so much misery, although I don't imagine she ever saw it that way. And if the university wants it for an exhibition, they can pay through the nose for it. At least this way we can raise some funds for a deserving cause, one Elenor might have chosen herself. Will you make the arrangements?'

'Of course,' Hope said, wondering whether she should let Ciaran know that the ring would be coming up for sale. And then she heard Charlotte's no-nonsense voice in her head, telling her it was just her treacherous heart, looking for a reason to contact him again. She smiled a little sadly and nodded at Isobel. 'I'll let you know once everything is in place.'

'Thank you,' Isobel said. 'The sooner that ring is gone for good, the happier I'll be.'

Hope stripped off her coat the moment she got home, dumping it unceremoniously on the floor in the hallway and shedding her hat and scarf in much the same way. Kicking off her heavy boots, she sank onto the sofa, clutching the precious bundle of letters as though it was made of spun glass. Topsy pounced on her immediately, purring his usual greeting and she tickled his ears absently before moving him onto the floor. Finally, she was going to discover what had happened to Khalid Al Nazari almost a century ago and, as a totally unexpected additional delight, she would learn the truth about the remarkable Elenor Lovelace too. It was so much more than she'd ever anticipated and she wasn't sure she'd ever be able to express her gratitude to Isobel for sharing the last of her precious family secrets with her.

Mewing in protest at her ignominious treatment of him, Topsy jumped back onto the sofa and settled beside Hope's feet. After another affectionate rub of his ears, she scrabbled in the drawer of the coffee table until she found a pair of white cotton gloves and tugged them over her impatient fingers. Pulling at the knotted string that held the bundle together, Hope let out a long slow breath as she slid the first letter out of its fragile envelope.

28th May 1923

My Dearest Judith,

I can hardly believe that I am writing this to you from Egypt. It worked! Our desperate plan worked. And I have you to thank for my freedom — you, my brave, resourceful sister. Without your help I would not be here with my beloved Khalid, who sends his very best regards and eternal thanks.

The crossing was terrible, as we knew it would be. The boat was so tiny and the waves so large. But the fisherman knew the way, at least, and at length we landed in Belgium. I fear I may never remove the scent of fish from my hair but it is a small price to pay and I am otherwise quite well.

The journey across Europe took longer than we hoped but concealment was my main concern and we took a circuitous route. But I am certain our secret remains intact. Can you offer the same assurance?

More soon, my dearest. I remain forever in your debt.

Yours always,
Elenor

Once she'd finished reading the letter, Hope turned the envelope over to study the address. As suspected, it wasn't that of the Lovelace family home but addressed to *Miss J Lovelace, C/O Briar Cottage, Whitby*. So either Elenor and Judith had an accomplice, or they'd had access to an address their family knew nothing about, Hope surmised. Perhaps Isobel knew the answer – Hope would have to remember to ask.

She read through each of the letters, smiling in delight as another piece of the puzzle dropped into place. But it wasn't until she opened a letter dated 30th October 1923 that she got the answer to a question that had been troubling her for months. Tucked in between the folds of paper was a photograph of Elenor and Khalid. And in Elenor's arms was a small bundle wrapped in white.

'So there *was* a baby!' Hope breathed, with a faint huff of happiness. That explained everything, she thought – why Elenor had been so desperate to escape her family, why she'd risked the terrible journey across the North Sea and why she'd returned to Egypt. If she'd remained in England to give birth to a mixed-race baby, the scandal would have been unbearable.

Gradually, the letters became less frequent. As the years passed, Elenor had joined Gertrude Caton-Thompson's all-female excavation team, travelling all over Africa under an assumed name, while Khalid stayed at home with their three children. Elenor never returned to England, as far as Hope could tell, and her sister didn't dare risk discovery by travelling to Africa to see her. But the bonds of sisterhood remained strong and their love shone from every letter.

When Hope had finished reading, she sat for a long moment, damp-eyed and smiling at nothing. Then she gathered all the letters up, returned them to their envelopes and put them back into date order. She'd read them all again soon but, for now, she just wanted to bask in secret knowledge of Elenor's hard-won happy ever after.

Chapter Thirty-Three

'Spoken to Will recently?'

Hope looked up from the Christmas wreath she was decorating. They were in Iris's workshop, putting the finishing touches to decorations for Hope's family. Christmas carols played quietly in the background and there was a glass of prosecco at their respective ends of the workbench, although Hope's had a lump of moss floating in it. She studied Iris with a frown. 'Not for a few days. Why?'

The florist reached for a bundle of cinnamon sticks and shrugged. 'No reason. I just realized you hadn't been round there to babysit for a few weeks and thought I'd better check the two of you hadn't fallen out again.'

'Oh,' Hope said and shook her head. 'No, we haven't fallen out. I guess Alex is comfortable enough staying over now so she and Will are having more nights in. Maybe he'll ask as we get nearer to Christmas and the party season kicks in.'

'Maybe,' Iris said. She hummed along to 'Good King

Wenceslas' for a moment. 'And you haven't seen Ciaran again, have you?'

Now Hope stared at her. 'No. I have no reason to see him. We're done.'

'Good,' Iris said, and she focused on threading a bauble through the greenery of the wreath. 'It's just ... well, you know you light up when you talk about him, don't you?'

Hope stopped work on her wreath, her forehead crinkling with confusion. 'Who, Ciaran?'

A small smile played around her friend's lips as she shook her head. 'No, not Ciaran. Will.'

'Right,' Hope said slowly and cast a suspicious glance at Iris's half-drunk prosecco. 'How many of those have you had?'

Iris grinned. 'Not enough. But here's the thing – you're one of my best friends, Hope, and I hate to see you unhappy. And whether you admit it or not, you are unhappy. Or at the very least, you're not happy.'

'I'm happy in lots of ways,' Hope objected. 'Do you want me to give you a list?'

Iris raised her mossy hands in mock-surrender. 'Okay, I know. But there's one big thing missing from your life right now and I know we're all supposed to be self-sufficient women these days and not need a man but I think you're lonely. And I can't stand it – not when I know the right man is practically standing in front of you.'

Hope shouldn't have been surprised – this was a subject Iris had been dancing around for months. 'Will isn't – I

424

don't – he isn't the right man for me, okay? And even if he was, I wouldn't say anything.'

'Why not?' Iris demanded. 'What have you got to lose?'

'Let's see,' Hope said, dropping her wreath to the tabletop. 'One, our friendship. Two, my relationship with Brodie, who doesn't deserve to have someone fade in and out of her life because the adults can't act like adults. Three . . .'

Iris cackled in triumph. 'You can't think of a three.'

'Three, it doesn't matter what I feel because he is dating someone else.' She stopped suddenly, because saying the words out loud for the first time had caused a hard lump to appear in her throat. 'So I'm never going to say anything because it's too late.'

Her friend's eyes were shrewd. 'You'll never know unless you tell him.'

'I can't,' Hope said miserably. 'He's with Alex now.'

'Only because he can't be with you.'

Hope shook her head. 'That's not true. He doesn't see me that way.'

'Believe me, he does,' Iris insisted. 'Why do you think he kissed you?'

'That was—' Hope started to remind her the kiss had been down to a misunderstanding, a situation she'd accidentally manufactured by telling Will she thought he was a catch, but she knew, even as the words died in her throat, that Iris didn't believe it. And who could blame her, when Hope no longer believed it herself? 'That was a long time ago,' she amended quietly. 'Things have changed.'

'If by that you mean that you have changed then I agree.' Iris sent a gentle smile her way. 'Will has been trying to tell you for ages that he's interested in being more than just your friend but you pushed him away. That's why he started seeing Alex, because he thought you didn't want him.' She paused to playfully nudge Hope. 'So, all you need to do now is tell him you do.'

But the time for that had long gone, Hope thought in dejection. 'It doesn't change anything,' she said in a flat tone. 'He's still with Alex. And Brodie is just getting used to having her around – I don't want to make things awkward or cause any problems.'

Her friend raised one eyebrow. 'Newsflash, Hope – it's already awkward. Anyone with half a brain could see how Will feels about you and Alex is a smart woman. She knows. Come to think about it, that's probably why Will hasn't asked you to babysit – Alex doesn't want you anywhere near him.'

Hope lifted her wreath to examine it, then laid it flat and reached for a gold ribbon. She hated the idea that Alex might feel threatened by her – it wasn't at all what she'd intended. 'All the more reason to never tell Will how I feel,' she said with as much finality as she could muster.

Iris took a long sip of prosecco and sighed. 'Okay, if you're sure. But I can't bear the thought of you being alone at Christmas. I'm sure Martin must have at least one single friend.'

Tying the ribbon in a big bow, Hope shook her head. 'No thanks, I'm happier on my own.' She held up the wreath for Iris to inspect. 'How does it look?'

'Lovely, but it needs a bit more attention,' Iris replied and offered her a lopsided smile. 'Just like you.'

Hope didn't think she'd ever seen the Harrogate auction house so packed. She wasn't sure if it was the effect of Christmas, or whether there were some especially good lots up for grabs but there seemed to be more buyers than ever wandering around. With a bit of luck it meant they might get a good price for Elenor's ring, which was the second lot of the afternoon.

The ring had been valued between eight and ten thousand pounds in the presale assessment and the auctioneer had been given permission to reveal all proceeds were going to a refuge in Whitby for victims of domestic violence that Isobel had picked out. Both Hope and Mr Young were optimistic they might get a good price but it all depended on who came to bid. As long as they met the reserve price, Hope told herself.

'Lot number two is a delightful Art Deco ring, dated from the nineteen twenties and styled in the Egyptian Revival manner,' the auctioneer said. 'Made from twenty-four carat gold, with platinum details, it features a large emerald in the shape of the sacred scarab beetle and is inscribed with hiero-glyphs underneath. All proceeds for this lot will be going to a local charity of the owner's choice and the auction house will waive its standard fee. What am I bid for this most unusual item – shall we start the bidding at two thousand pounds?'

Hope held her breath but almost immediately she saw a flicker of movement on the far side of the auction room. 'Two thousand. Do we have two thousand five hundred?'

Another twitch and the bidding went up again. 'That's interesting,' Mr Young murmured. 'We have a phone bidder.'

Who could that be, Hope wondered? She'd spent a few minutes scouring the room for Ciaran and concluded he wasn't among the crowd. But he could be bidding by phone, on behalf of the university. Just as long as the mystery bidder wasn't the Abyssinian Society. She wasn't sure Isobel would be happy about that, no matter how much money was raised.

'Four thousand, then,' the auctioneer said calmly. 'Do I have five thousand?'

He'd increased the bid by a thousand now, Hope observed, which was a good sign. It meant he thought there was enough interest to push the price up, which in turn meant more money for Isobel's charity. And then she thought of the ring itself, remembering the day it had fallen into her hand and glistened under the lights of the Emporium. It had been the start of Elenor's mystery, the thing that had piqued Hope's interest and sent her to Ciaran in her search for more information. Will had played his part too – cleaning it up and ascertaining that it hadn't been made in the UK. And while Hope could fully understand why Isobel considered it to have brought nothing but misery to her family, Hope wasn't so sure Elenor would see things that way. It had been a gift from her fiancé, after all – a token of his undying love. And yet she hadn't taken it with her when she'd left for Egypt, leaving it instead for the person who had helped her escape. Then again, maybe it had been too risky to take. Or perhaps she'd wanted her sister to keep it. They would never know.

When Hope roused herself from her musing, the bidding had reached £8000.

'It's with the telephone bidder,' Mr Young said. 'But there are two other bidders in the room.'

Whatever the price, they were going to be getting a unique prize, Hope thought, and she was suddenly sad that she would never see the ring again. Unless Ciaran won it for the university, she supposed, but she had no way of knowing whether he was even bidding.

'Ten thousand pounds,' the auctioneer announced. 'Eleven thousand . . . twelve thousand.'

A low murmur rustled across the room and Hope understood why: the ring was surpassing expectations.

'Thirteen thousand then,' the auctioneer's voice rang out. 'Are we all done at thirteen thousand pounds? Going once. Going twice.' He banged his gavel down. 'Sold.'

Hope allowed the tension to leach from her shoulders. 'That's a good price. I wonder who bought it?'

'Leave it with me,' Mr Young said with a wink. 'I'll see what I can find out.'

Moments later, he was back and Hope thought he looked pleased. 'It went to the University of York, for their new exhibition. It looks like Professor McCormack did the right thing at last.'

Hope's feelings were mixed as she digested the news but finally a smile won out as she imagined all the good uses the women's refuge might find for £13000. 'Yes,' she agreed with Mr Young. 'I think he actually did.'

The text from Will arrived on a frosty Saturday morning in mid-December and it caught Hope completely by surprise.

Fancy a trip to the ice rink? My treat.

She stared at her phone for several long seconds, questions circling in her head. Skating was definitely a romantic thing to do – why was he inviting her and not Alex? But she couldn't very well ask that, so she tapped out her second most pressing question instead:

Can you actually skate? I don't want to deal with any broken limbs.

And then she wondered if he was actually going with Alex, and had only invited Hope so she could look after Brodie, which would be fine. But his reply seemed to suggest that Alex wasn't part of the outing.

I can skate and so can Brodie. Can you?

Hope smiled.

I think so. What time?

They arranged to meet at the Bratwurst stall at midday. Hope grinned as she remembered Isobel's objections and wondered whether the sausages would smell as divine as she dreamed. Wrapped up warmly in a hat and matching gloves, Hope spotted Will first. Brodie was beside him, wearing a blue coat that Hope thought looked new; was it her imagination or had Brodie grown in the weeks since she'd last seen her? Will looked the same as ever, although his cheeks glowed pink beneath his curly brown hair and his hazel eyes danced when he saw Hope. 'Hello. You look nice and warm.'

She returned his gaze, noticing the layer of stubble across his cheeks. 'Hello. I am, thank you. Growing a beard?'

He shook his head, grinning. 'Nah. Just too lazy to shave. Brodie says it feels like billy goat whiskers.'

Hope laughed. 'I bet it does – all tickly and rough.'

Beside Will, Brodie laughed too. 'Hello, Hope,' she said shyly.

The breath caught in Hope's throat as she realized it was the first time the little girl had ever said her name. 'Hello to you too. Are you ready to skate?'

Brodie nodded and Hope held out her hand. 'Then what are we waiting for?'

They collected their skates from the collection point, swapping them for their boots. Hope watched Will fasten Brodie's laces and decided she liked his layer of stubble. Perhaps it was Alex's influence, she considered, and reflected that was something else she'd never ask.

The rink was pleasingly busy, with plenty of families with young children, and plenty of twinkling lights to satisfy

Hope's Christmassy yearnings. She soon realized that Will hadn't exaggerated either his own or Brodie's skating skills – they were both much better than her.

'Family holidays in France every year,' he explained, when she complimented him. 'We can ski too.'

'I've never even tried,' Hope said, and squeaked as she almost lost her balance. 'God, this is harder than I remember.'

'Look!' Brodie called as she whizzed by, looking every inch the ice princess.

'Beautiful!' Hope called and wobbled again.

'Here,' Will said, half-laughing, and caught her outstretched hand. 'Hold on to me.'

Instantly, Hope felt safer. 'Uh – thanks,' she said.

They skated together in silence for a few seconds. Hope tried to focus on her feet, rather than on how nice it felt to be holding Will's hand, but it was hard when his fingers were so warm in hers. She'd removed her gloves to tie her laces and forgotten to put them back on, and now she was glad. *Stop it,* she told herself firmly. *He's only holding your hand to stop you falling on your backside.*

'So,' she said, when she couldn't bear the silence any longer. 'Doesn't Alex skate?'

Will sent her a swift sideways glance. 'I don't know. There's – erm – something I need to tell you about that, actually. We're not dating any more.'

Hope stared at him in genuine dismay. 'Oh no. I'm really sorry, Will. What happened?'

He glanced at her again and she thought he looked oddly

cheerful for a man who had broken up with his girlfriend. 'It happened about a month ago. Just before your belly dancing show.' He paused to look behind them, locating Brodie and ascertaining she was safe, then carried on. 'It turns out she's allergic to cats.'

Hope's spare hand flew to her face. 'Oh! Bloody hell, that's unlucky.'

Will nodded. 'It is. But obviously there was no way I could get rid of Lyra – not when Brodie is so attached to her.'

'Well, no,' Hope said, frowning. 'But surely that's not enough of a reason to break up. Things were going so well!'

He waggled his head from side to side. 'I can see how it might have looked that way, from the outside. We still got on well and both wanted it to work but ...' A long sigh escaped him. 'Let's just say there were reasons for breaking up the first time and it became apparent those problems were still there. So, we agreed it wasn't going to work out and went our separate ways.'

What did that mean, Hope wondered – that Alex still wasn't ready to settle down? Or had she struggled with the extra commitment of Brodie? 'That sounds very grown up of you both,' Hope observed slowly as they rounded the bend. 'But I'm still sorry.'

He puffed out his cheeks. 'Don't be. I think we both real-ized we were going through the motions a bit, doing it for the wrong reasons.' He shot another sideways glance Hope's way. 'At least I was, anyway.'

Once again, she wasn't exactly sure what he meant but she didn't want to intrude. 'But you're okay? And Brodie too?'

Will smiled. 'We're both fine, don't worry.' Hope wobbled again, her free arm circling wildly, and he guided her towards the barrier. 'Let's stop here for a minute. There's something I want to give you.'

Much to Hope's disappointment, he let go of her hand. She clutched at the wall for support and eyed him quizzically as he reached into his coat. 'I hope you haven't got me a Christmas present. I've got something for Brodie but I didn't buy anything for you – I didn't know we were doing gifts.'

'We're not,' he said. 'Well, unless you want to. This is more of a thank you present, for everything you've done for me and Brodie over the last eight months.' He pulled out an emerald-green jewellery box and handed to her. 'Sort of a memento. I hope you like it.'

The gesture was so kind and generous, so typically Will, that she simply stared at him for a few seconds. And then, aware of her heart thudding in a way that had nothing to do with the exercise she'd been doing, Hope lifted the lid of the box. Nestled inside was an exquisite jade pendant shaped like a scarab beetle and encased in gold, with tiny diamonds dotted along the silver legs. It hung on a delicate gold chain and it was the most beautiful thing Hope had ever seen. 'Oh!' she gasped, as tears flooded her eyes. 'It's the same as Elenor's ring!'

'Not quite,' Will said, with a modest little laugh. 'I couldn't quite run to a gigantic emerald, obviously, so I replaced it with jade. But it's the same in all other aspects, including the hieroglyphs underneath.'

He reached out a careful finger to tilt the beetle, showing her the carving on the underside. 'Do you like it?'

'Like it?' Hope said, gazing down at it in wonder. 'Are you serious? I love it!'

'Good,' Will said. 'Because it took me forever to do. But Iris told me that Isobel sold the ring at auction and I wanted you to have something to remember it by.'

Hope ran her fingers across the shiny green gemstone and wondered what else Iris had told him. 'Thank you. It's absolutely perfect.' She looked up at him, drew in a deep breath, and borrowed some more of her friend's wisdom. 'A bit like you.'

He froze, staring back at her as though he wasn't quite sure what he'd heard. 'Do you – do you mean that?'

Her hand tightened on the barrier and she knew it wasn't solely to make sure she stayed upright; she needed its support in other ways too. 'Yes. But you've just come out of a relationship and maybe you need some time, or – or –' Hope felt her confidence deserting her. 'I'm happy just to be friends, is what I mean.'

'Friends,' Will repeated slowly. 'There it is again. What on earth makes you think I see you as just a friend? I don't kiss my friends, Hope. At least not like that.'

Hope felt heat swirl over her cheeks as she remembered the kiss they'd shared. There hadn't been anything platonic about it, she recalled now, but she'd told herself over and over that it had been a mistake, that she felt nothing more than friendship for him. And then, when she'd realized she felt so much more, her subconscious had come up with other reasons to stay silent – reasons that had seemed to make sense at the time. But now, standing here beside him, she knew them for what they were: excuses.

'I – I'm scared,' she said, in a voice so low that he had to lean in to hear her. 'I don't want to love you if I'm only going to lose you.'

It took a second or two for understanding to dawn in his eyes. 'I can't promise that won't happen,' he said gently, meeting her gaze. 'Nothing comes with a guarantee, least of all love. Everything has risks. But if there's one thing grief has taught me, it's to live every day. And what I've realized lately is that I want to live every day with you.'

She felt the sting of tears long before they spilled down her cheeks. 'But I'm still scared,' she whispered. 'And it's worse because now I know . . . I love you.'

The words hung in the air until Will lifted Hope's chin and softly wiped away her tears. 'I don't know if that fear will ever go away. I live with it each day and so does Brodie. But I love you too, Hope Henderson. And I couldn't go another hour without telling you.'

Hope stared at him, her vision blurred, willing herself to believe him. Of course he loved her – she'd known it for a long time, although she'd been frightened to admit it. But she couldn't spend the rest of her life being afraid – she had to play the odds sometime. And if she couldn't take a chance with a man like Will, a man who was kind and dependable and offered her everything she'd ever wanted, who could she take a chance on?

'Do you think,' she said, trying not to sniff, 'that you could kiss me again?'

He smiled the warm, welcoming smile she'd always loved and the skin at the corners of his eyes creased. 'Yes, I think I definitely could.'

Bending his head to close the last few centimetres between them, he pressed his lips to hers and it felt to Hope as though the kiss was familiar and brand new all at the same time. His mouth was warm and gentle and once again, she had the sense that she was kissing a friend. But somehow it didn't feel wrong this time – there was more depth now, a slow lazy heat that started low in her belly and radiated up and out until she thought she must be glowing. Reaching up, she brushed her hand against the soft stubble on his chin, moving on past to sink her fingers into his curls. And suddenly the slow burn caught fire and she wanted nothing more than to kiss him like this every day for the rest of their lives.

When they finally broke apart, gazing at each other as though seeing the other truly for the first time, it took Hope a moment to realize they had an audience. She dragged her gaze from Will and saw Brodie perfectly poised on the ice, watching them from a metre or so away. Seeing them both looking at her, she skated nearer and beamed at Hope.

'See? Billy goat whiskers!'

And Hope laughed and reached up to briefly kiss Will again. 'Yes,' she said. 'Definitely all tickly and rough!'

Acknowledgements

As always, huge thanks to Jo Williamson of Antony Harwood Ltd, my agent right from the start – I'm constantly grateful you said yes. A massive thank you to Clare Hey for her expert York input, and to lovely Molly Crawford for crafting Hope's story with skill, patience and humour – your margin comments are always very much appreciated. Thanks to absolutely everyone on the Books and the City team for ensuring this book is such a gorgeous package – special thanks to Pip Watkins for smashing it out of the design park AGAIN, and to SJ Virtue for constantly championing my stories. And, of course, I must thank my Twitter followers for all their York intel and recommendations – utterly invaluable to a locked-down writer!

There are always people who help supply those hard to research titbits of information – thanks to Tara Haworth for advising me how to handle unexpected kittens. Your advice was so very helpful, even if I did tweak some of it for the sake of drama.

I am so grateful to have the wonderful Miranda Dickinson as my go-to gal for Chris Evans gifs and general brainstorming — the scenes in Whitby were inspired by her brilliance. Enormous thanks to Charlotte Dennis, my medical consultant and running partner — twenty-six miles is nothing with you next to me. And as ever, huge thanks to Clare Watson for being everything a best friend should be. All my love to T and E, for ever. And last of all, thanks to my readers — as usual, I wrote this book for you. I hope you enjoy browsing in the Ever After Emporium. If you listen, I think you can still hear the faint tick and tock of the grandfather clock . . .

Coming Home to Brightwater Bay

Holly Hepburn

On paper, Merina Wilde has it all: a successful career
writing the kind of romantic novels that make even the
hardest hearts swoon, a perfect carousel of book launches
and parties to keep her social life buzzing, and a childhood
sweetheart who thinks she's a goddess. But Merry has a
secret: the magic has stopped flowing from her fingers. Try
as she might, she can't summon up the sparkle that makes her
stories shine. And as her deadline whooshes by, her personal
life falls apart too. Alex tells her he wants something other
than the future she'd always imagined for them and Merry
finds herself single for the first time since – well, ever.

Desperate to get her life back on track, Merry leaves London
and escapes to the windswept Orkney Islands, locking herself
away in a secluded clifftop cottage to try to heal her heart
and rediscover her passion for writing. But can the beauty of
the islands and the kindness of strangers help Merry to fool
herself into believing in love again, if only long enough to
finish her book? Or is it time for her to give up the career she's
always adored and find something new to set her soul alight?

'Joyous – a treat of a tale that whisks your heart
away to the beautiful shores of Orkney. Prepare
to fall in love with this fantastic series!'
Miranda Dickinson

AVAILABLE IN PAPERBACK AND EBOOK NOW

**SIMON &
SCHUSTER**